Critical acclaim for [illegible] *Robbins*

Scorched Earth

'A powerful story in which justice and the law conflict ... a memorable and moving story, beautifully told' Susanna Yager, *Sunday Telegraph*

'A fine and highly memorable novel' *Crime Time*

The End of War

'Robbins has created credible and unusually powerful physical scenes of war ... *The End of War* is a compelling tale of the final days of the most catastrophic event in all of recorded history'
Washington Post

'Some wonderfully poignant moments ... Robbins' deeply researched tome will give readers a breathtaking view of the war as it's strategically played out' *New York Post*

'A deeply felt antiwar suspense ... Robbins renders his real people superbly, making them vivid, even fresh – a notable accomplishment ... Brilliant storytelling by an author who continues to grow and impress' *Kirkus Reviews* (starred review)

David L. Robbins, author of four previous novels, lives in Richmond, Virginia. Visit his website at www.davidlrobbins.com.

By David L. Robbins

Souls to Keep
War of the Rats
The End of War
Scorched Earth
Last Citadel

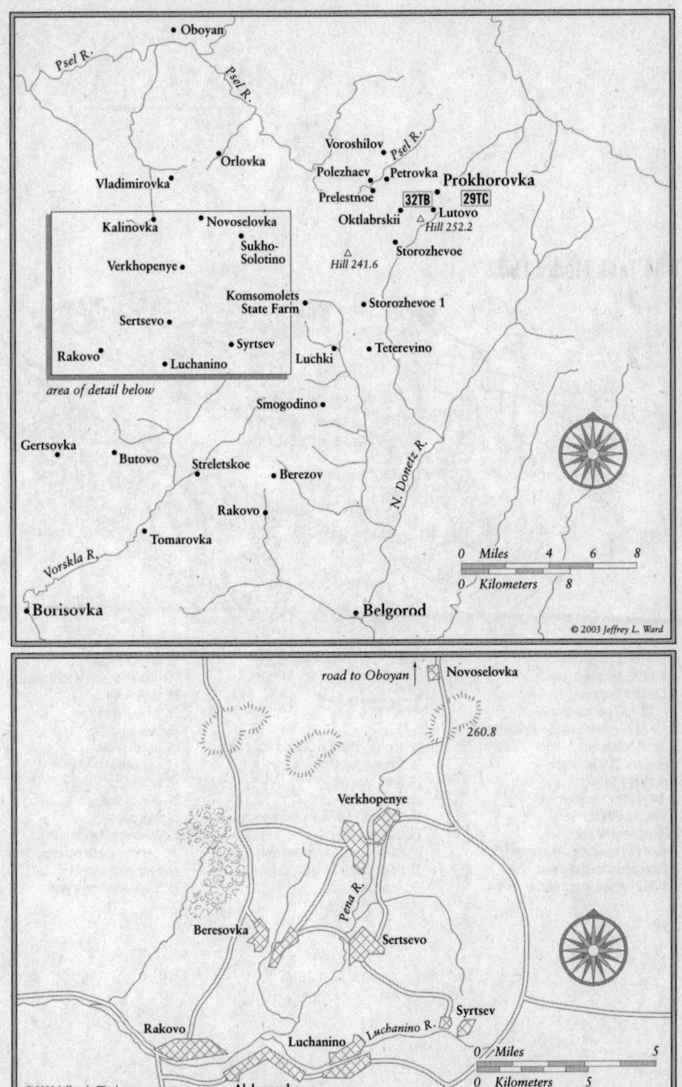

Oboyan
Psel R.
Psel R.
Orlovka
Vladimirovka
Voroshilov
Psel R.
Polezhaev
Petrovka
Prokhorovka
Prelestnoe
32TB
29TC
Oktlabrskii
Lutovo
Hill 252.2
Kalinovka
Novoselovka
Sukho-
Solotino
Verkhopenye
Storozhevoe
Hill 241.6
Komsomolets
State Farm
Storozhevoe 1
Sertsevo
Syrtsev
Rakovo
Luchanino
Luchki
Teterevino
area of detail below
Smogodino
Gertsovka
Butovo
Streletskoe
Berezov
N. Donetz R.
Rakovo
Tomarovka
Vorskla R.
0 Miles 4 6 8
0 Kilometers 8
Borisovka
Belgorod
© 2003 Jeffrey L. Ward
road to Oboyan
Novoselovka
260.8
Verkhopenye
Pena R.
Beresovka
Sertsevo
Syrtsev
Rakovo
Luchanino
Luchanino R.
0 Miles 5
0 Kilometers 5
Alekseyevka
© 2003 Jeffrey L. Ward

T-34 Tank Model 1942

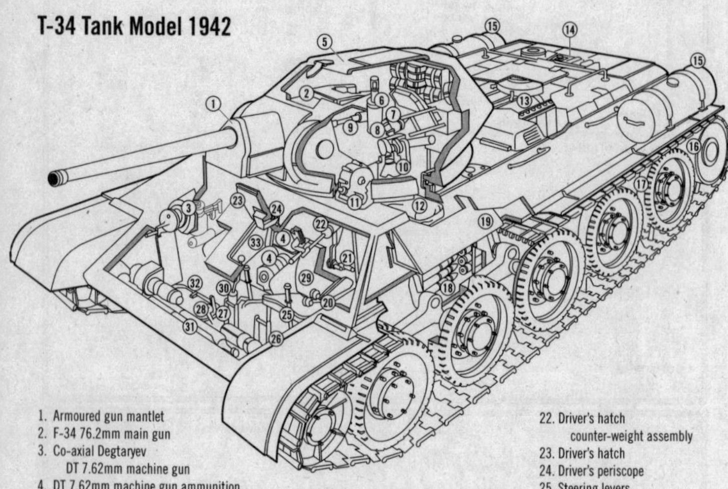

1. Armoured gun mantlet
2. F-34 76.2mm main gun
3. Co-axial Degtaryev DT 7.62mm machine gun
4. DT 7.62mm machine gun ammunition
5. Turret hatch
6. Gunner's PT-5 periscope
7. Periscope sight
8. Range scale elevation knob
9. Telescopic sight
10. Power traverse gearbox
11. Main gun elevating mechanism
12. Commander/Gunner's seat
13. V-2 12 cylinder diesel engine
14. Transmission and braking assemblies
15. External fuel tanks
16. Drive sprocket
17. Main road wheel
18. Left-hand side main gun ammunition
19. Internal fuel tank
20. Speedometer and rev counter
21. Firing pedals for main gun and machine gun
22. Driver's hatch counter-weight assembly
23. Driver's hatch
24. Driver's periscope
25. Steering levers
26. Clutch pedal
27. Foot brake
28. Accelerator
29. Driver's seat
30. Gear lever
31. Compressed air bottles for engine cold weather starting
32. Belly escape hatch
33. Machine gunner's seat

PzKpfw VI Tiger (SdKfz 181) Ausf E

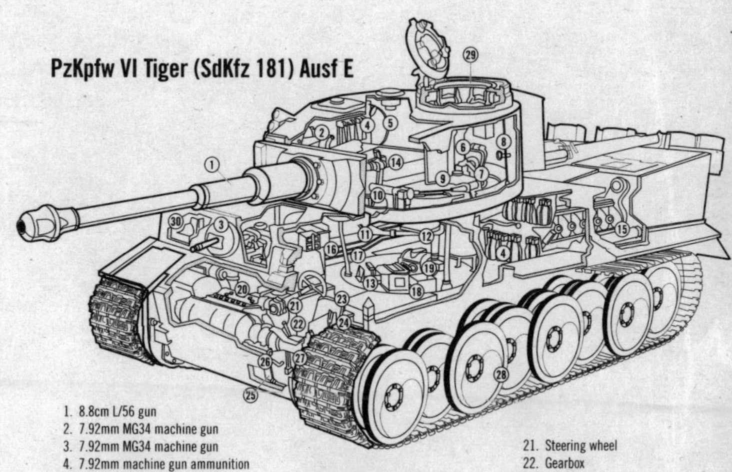

1. 8.8cm L/56 gun
2. 7.92mm MG34 machine gun
3. 7.92mm MG34 machine gun
4. 7.92mm machine gun ammunition
5. Escape hatch
6. Commander's seat
7. Commander's traverse handwheel
8. Revolver port
9. Traverse gearbox
10. Gunner's traverse handwheel
11. Gunner's elevating handwheel
12. Gunner's seat
13. Machine-gun firing pedal
14. Binocular Telescope
15. Maybach Engine
16. Radio Set
17. 88mm ammunition bins
18. Hydraulic traverse foot control
19. Hydraulic traverse unit
20. Steering unit
21. Steering wheel
22. Gearbox
23. Driver's seat
24. Handbreak
25. Accelerator
26. Foot break
27. Clutch
28. Overlapping bogie-wheels
29. Commander's cupola
30. Machine-gun ammunition storage

LAST CITADEL

DAVID L. ROBBINS

An Orion paperback

First published in Great Britain in 2003
by Orion
This paperback edition published in 2004
by Orion Books Ltd,
Orion House, 5 Upper St Martin's Lane,
London WC2H 9EA

A CIP catalogue record for this book is available from the British Library.

ISBN 0 75285 925 0

Printed and bound in Great Britain by
Clays Ltd, St Ives plc

www.orionbooks.co.uk

For Lindy

A SIGNAL TO THE WORLD

I have decided to conduct Citadel, the first offensive of the year, as soon as the weather permits.

This attack is of the utmost importance. It must be carried out quickly and shatteringly. It must give us the initiative for the spring and summer of this year. Therefore all preparations are to be carried through with the greatest care and energy. The best formations, the best armies, the best leaders, great stocks of ammunition are to be placed at the decisive points. Every officer and every man must be impressed with the decisive significance of this offensive. The victory of Kursk must be a signal to the world.

Adolf Hitler
Operations Order (No. 6)
April 15, 1943

RUSSIA
July 4, 1943
Lake Lagoda
Leningrad
Moscow
WESTERN FRONT
BRYANSK FRONT
ARMY GROUP CENTER
Orel
CENTRAL FRONT
Kursk
Voronezh
VORONEZH FRONT
STEPPE FRONT
Oboyan
Prokhorovka
ARMY GROUP SOUTH
Belgorod
ARMY GROUP KEMPF
Kiev
Dnieper R.
Vorskla R.
Khar kov
SOUTHERNWEST FRONT
Don R.
Volga R.
Stalingrad
Donetz R.
Don R.
0 Miles 100 200
0 Kilometers 200
Rostov
Odessa
Sea of Azov
CRIMEA
Krasnodar
Caucasus
Black Sea
© 2003 Jeffrey L. Ward

ONE

May 10, 1943
1440 hours
Reichs Chancellery
Berlin, Germany

The SS colonel eased shut the high, heavy door. The portal closed with a hiss and a soft tap. How many trees went into this, he wondered, lives sacrificed out of the forest to make one of Hitler's castle gates? The black eagle emblem of wartime hung at eye level against the carved wood. Colonel Abram Breit imagined this symbol of the Reich to be a spread-winged vulture. That's what he left behind in the briefing room – a death scene, a picking apart, sinew by vessel, of Germany.

Breit walked several steps into the hall, striding across the same black eagle laid in mosaic in the floor. Blood-red banners trickled down the walls. He buttressed his back against one of them and lit a cigarette.

He exhaled smoke and stared into it, tired and sad. He replayed the voices of the briefing room, Hitler with his generals and advisers. Citadel – the looming, titanic battle for Kursk on the Eastern Front – consumed the hours. Since morning Breit had watched the little wars between the generals, battling over Hitler as if the *Führer* were a spot of high ground; candor fell in combat with flattery, reason was mauled by pride. Around and above the grand table, more banners festooned the room, great ebony swastikas circled like the buzzards of Breit's imagination. Everywhere Hitler's minions had hung the images of Hitler's belief, to let no eye wander to another way of thinking, to any other allegiance, certainly to no thoughts of Germany's welfare, only the Nazis'.

Breit ground the last of the cigarette into the sole of his boot. He pocketed the white shred and lit another. In the smoke he recalled Hitler's eyes, gray and wavering. In the past month, Hitler had become obsessed with reading about Verdun, the meat-grinder battle of World War I France. Hitler had been a corporal on the Western Front. As a runner he was wounded and gassed. Breit saw in Hitler's eyes the memory of the trenches, and the parallels to be drawn between the butchery of Verdun and what awaited Aryan manhood in the trenches of the Kursk bulge.

This was Germany's third summer of campaigning in Russia. The Reds had yet to swoon the way these generals had promised Hitler before the invasion in '41. Now the army lacked the resources for another major offensive in the East. Instead, their available forces were to concentrate on one smashing blow against the Kursk salient, a segment of the front line that ballooned westward into the German midsection.

The plan called for two immense forces to blast across the Russian defenses – Field Marshal von Kluge from the north, Field Marshal von Manstein out of the south – and converge in the center at the city of Kursk, pinching off the Soviet bulge. The operation was designed to surround massive Soviet formations and, more important, shorten German lines to free up men and machines desperately needed elsewhere. The Americans were sure to come to Italy this summer, and *Il Duce,* Mussolini, was ill-prepared to go it alone.

Hitler was going to commit every available soldier, gun, tank, and airplane to the action. This would be the largest buildup of German armed power of the war. If Citadel succeeded, it would be a loss of blood that Hitler could scarcely afford. If Citadel failed, the ruin of men and matériel would be even greater; worse still, Germany would be exposed to a Russian counterstrike. That could be fatal, the beginning of the end. Citadel would be the last German offensive of the war in the East.

The stakes for Hitler were higher today than at any time in the war. He was being asked to gamble, to throw the dice once on Citadel with everything riding on the table. There would be no second go-round, no backup plan. This was do or die.

The chief problem was that Citadel was obvious. A quick glance at the map of the Eastern Front lines presented the most elementary scenario to any war college student. The Kursk bulge was clearly the best place for an attack, a pincer action was the plain solution. Germany knew this. Russia knew this. The coming fight was going to be without surprise; once begun, it would be brute strength against strength, two behemoths pressing chests.

The *Führer* fretted aloud in the briefing room. He stabbed his finger at the maps spread across his conference table, aerial photos of Soviet defenses in the Kursk region. Even from three miles in the air, the groundworks dug by the Russians looked incredible; the amount of armaments and men flowing into them was monumental. And these defense works would be arrayed directly in the path of the planned German offensive. How could this be, Hitler wanted to know.

The buzzards flew from their perches then.

Field Marshal von Kluge spoke first, flapping to the table and sweeping a hand in the air over the foreboding maps. We will crush these pitiful defenses, the Field Marshal vowed, speaking in bald propagandistic phrases, the kind Hitler loved to hear. German ground forces have always penetrated enemy defenses and will do so in this case. Besides, look at the technological advantages we have, *mein Führer*. Look at our new tanks. Our Panthers and Tigers. Our tanks will make the difference, without fail.

Colonel Abram Breit had been brought to Berlin and was in the room to speak to this question of what impact the superior German armor would have on Citadel. Breit was the intelligence officer for the 1st SS Panzergrenadier Division *Leibstandarte Adolf Hitler*. His division was to be in the vanguard of the Citadel assault. *Leibstandarte* would enter the fight with thirteen of the new Tiger tanks. It was his job to predict how the battle would go. After von Kluge spoke, Hitler glanced at Breit.

Field Marshal von Manstein, the man whose proposals gave birth to Citadel, replaced von Kluge at the map table. Hitler smiled over at Breit. This was when Breit saw deeply into Hitler's eyes, when Hitler with a look apologized for skipping over Breit. They were the eyes, he realized, of an ill man. Hitler's physician had been treating him for constipation, prescribing ever more powerful laxatives. Hitler's eyes were lusterless, their striking blue was clouded. The Field Marshal began his comments. He said we may have waited too long. The Reds are getting ready for us. We should have attacked them in April, just after the spring thaw, the Russian *rasputitsa*. Breit watched Hitler agree, the dull eyes growing duller in disappointment and pain. Hitler did not know what to do. He slumped beside the great table where Germany lay and watched his visions of conquest and empire be pecked at by his commanders, who could not agree. His puffy face nodded; his chin sagged to his chest.

Field Marshal Keitel spoke next. We have to attack in Russia this summer, he said. For military as well as political purposes. Our allies demand that Germany not be passive in the East. The Italians need to see our resolve, as do the Finns and the Turks. Japan is concerned that we have not made sufficient progress against Russia. The German people require this, as well. The bombings and the failure at Stalingrad have taken their toll on morale. We must fight and win, Germany must retake the momentum. Our troops insist on a victory. Hitler listened and nodded, swayed again by whatever voice held the floor.

Breit backed quietly out of the room while Keitel talked. He came out here alone into the bannered hall and smoked.

The great door to the conference room slid open. Another black uniform with silver gleams and black leather strapping, the garb of the SS, slipped out. From the pack in his hand, Breit shook out the nub of another cigarette and held it up.

'Captain Thoma.'

The young SS officer accepted the cigarette and a light. He sucked the first drag down like a man without fear of ever dying, smiling and posing in the soft light, his blond head tilted back.

'What do you think, Colonel?' Thoma asked. The captain had been invited to the conference to speak to the training progress of the SS tankers in their new Tiger Mark VIs. Thoma, too, had been ignored by the generals during the meeting, left to stand aside as some kind of statuary, an example for Hitler of how attractive Germany's soldiers were.

He spoke now with the smoke coming out of his nostrils like a young dragon.

Breit said, 'I think, Captain, they don't care a fig about what you and I have to say.'

'I suspect they should listen. You and I know more than all of them put together.'

'Do we?'

'Did you hear what Guderian asked? "Why should we attack in the East at all this year?" Of course we should attack.'

Yes, Abram Breit thought, I heard Guderian, the general in charge of rebuilding Germany's armored forces. And I heard Hitler's reply: 'Whenever I think of the attack my stomach turns over.'

'Tell me, then, Captain, why you believe we should attack Russia this summer. Even if we grind through those growing Russian defenses, will we be able to hold our gains? The Reds outman us two to one, they outgun us two to one. And after we surround the Soviets, can we keep the pocket sealed? Will we be able to clear the pocket with the forces we'll have left after fighting our way to Kursk north and south? In view of all this, tell me why Guderian is wrong, Captain.'

Thoma tossed his cigarette to the polished floor and ground it out, careless and again very young. 'We have the tanks, Colonel. The Tigers. I've been training with them for the last five months. My men and I are more than ready. The Tiger can beat any tank it meets on any battlefield. Sir.'

'But out of twenty-three hundred tanks, you've got only a hundred Tigers for the battle. The Soviets have over three thousand T-34s.'

'One Tiger is worth a hundred Red tanks.'

'Is this what you would have told the *Führer* if he'd asked?'

'Yes. Absolutely.'

Thoma had almost come to attention with his remarks. It seemed he was defending a maligned friend. Breit took in the tank commander's hard posture and erect Aryan beauty. How many, Breit thought, how many of these young men will be flung into the flames to forge Hitler's dreams?

'What about the new Panther tanks?'

Thoma grinned a little at this. Both men knew about the difficulties the Mark V had been having in development. The Panthers had not yet proven themselves reliable, yet Hitler's generals had insisted that Citadel be postponed for months in order that two hundred of the Panthers be built and shipped to Russia for the offensive. Thoma reveled a bit in the Panthers' failures, none of which had cropped up in his Tigers.

'They'll do their best, Colonel. But the Tiger will be the tank history remembers when Citadel is done.'

'The Americans are going to land on the Continent, Captain Thoma. We don't know when but it will be in Italy and it will be this summer. That would be a very bad thing if we don't have enough forces there to hold them off.'

Breit rattled out one more cigarette for himself. He would go back into the briefing after finishing it. He'd heard all he needed in the room, but did not want anyone to note his absence for too long. Breit did not want to be noticed at all.

He offered another cigarette to Thoma. The Captain shook his head.

'There will be a Citadel, Colonel. There has to be.'

'Why, Captain?'

'Because this is our time.'

'Yes, Captain. I quite agree. I think we should slip back into the room separately. It'll be quieter that way. You first, please.'

Thoma clicked his heels unnecessarily, there had been nothing formal about their chat out here in the hall. The sound was hard, the way Thoma made himself at Breit's doubting of the coming battle. Thoma is right, Breit thought, watching the young officer pull open the huge door and disappear behind it. There will be a Citadel. Yes, there must be. Because it is indeed Germany's time.

Time for Germany's doom.

May 11
1210 hours
Old National Gallery
Berlin

The Impressionists room was often crowded at lunchtime. The more beautiful the weather, the more Berliners strolled for their midday break. The Americans and the British did not bomb on perfect spring afternoons. The Yanks did their work only in the mornings, and the Brits raided at night. So far, they'd mainly contented themselves with wrecking the areas in north Berlin, the manufacturing districts. Downtown remained the nerve center for running the Nazi state, for parks and museums, and the myth of German survival.

Abram Breit carried his sack lunch, a sandwich and a French apple, here to the Old National Gallery beside the Spree River. He spotted an opening on a bench across from a Monet, a blue and violet study of the *Palazzo da Mala* in Venice. Monet had been so smitten with the dazzling light of Venice on his first trip there that he stayed for four months, painting the ancient facades and canal waters. Breit walked in front of the painting on flat soles, careful not to clout his polished boots against the wood floor.

He snuggled in on the bench. The buttocks of a heavyset woman rested against his hip, she stared at a Cézanne on another wall, a sketch pad in her lap. Breit dug his sandwich out of the paper bag and unwrapped it, making a game of how quietly he could handle the wax paper. He chewed and looked at the Monet. Breit had always wanted to view the world the way a painter did, to see behind form and color to the world's vibrations, to gaze not just at an object but at light itself. Abram Breit had tried as a child to make paintings, drawings, anything with a brush or pen, and failed; he lacked the gift of the painter, the sight. So he chose instead to exercise his love of art by becoming a student of it, then a teacher. When the war began, he was a thirty-eight-year-old professor of art history at Heidelberg University facing the reality of military service. He approached the SS, which quickly accepted him into its intelligence corps. Breit was an educated man, with the manners and bearing of the upper class. He was an exemplar of that legend of superiority the SS liked to concoct, especially in *Leibstandarte,* the first of the SS divisions, grown out of Hitler's personal bodyguards.

Breit began his work for the Reich by valuating art taken from dispossessed Jews. He made no judgments on where the art came from; few in Germany did that sort of thing once the deportations started. The plight of the Jews was not his concern. Breit busied himself arranging collections and shows, selecting which pieces would be put on public display and which would hang in the private galleries of Goebbels, Speer, Himmler, Göring, Hitler. For this service, the *Führer* had awarded him the War Merit Cross with swords that hung on the left breast of his tunic. Breit had chosen this Monet for this museum.

He finished his sandwich and began his apple. He was wary not to crunch through the skin and pulp. Breit made no noise.

He never did, and he knew this. As a child, he'd abandoned his wish to be an artist, letting it loose without a pin drop in his heart. As a student, he'd kept his nose in books while Germany rebuilt itself from the debacles of World War I. Again, as a young professor, he stuck to his classrooms and towers at Heidelberg, avoiding the street clashes between the roving brown shirts of the National Socialists and the red sashes of the Communists. When the war started, Abram Breit took up his duty in the dungeons of Jew basements, in echoing great galleries, peering through magnifying glasses at canvases and into tomes of art history. A few years and five million men marched past him, history fell out of the sky, horror rolled past in trucks and train cars, Germany tore itself to pieces across the globe, and Breit stood silent.

No more.

He chewed the apple thoughtfully, mulling the pulp on his tongue. He stood and walked around the bench to face the other direction, away from the vivid Monet. Sitting, he set his eyes to the Picasso and the Braque he'd chosen for display in this room.

The war had cost Breit his love of the Impressionists. Those painters had become bourgeois, coveted by the well-to-do, sold for large sums, even during their lifetimes. Their groundbreaking work – softening the image, the destruction of age-old realism – had fallen headlong into the mainstream. Monet, Manet, Renoir, Seurat – these weren't the names of painters any longer so much as they were investments, portfolios for the Jews and others to hedge their bets during the war, hide their money in something other than currency, no different than gems or gold bars. Breit cared only for one Impressionist now, the crazy Dutchman van Gogh, who never while alive sold one painting. Van Gogh, of all the Impressionist masters, was untouched, left alone with that madness that had become his vision. Breit preferred the Cubists, the artists who had moved away from the emotion and decorative symbolism of Impressionism. The Cubists – Picasso and Braque among them, who were put on their path first by the prophetic work of Cézanne – reconstructed the form on the canvas out of its base geometric elements, the spheres, cones, cylinders, and boxes of every object. These were egalitarian ideals, to break man's world into simple patterns, into every man's vision, mad or genius or gifted or not, even Abram Breit's.

The Impressionists looked at their world and made it pretty, captured like butterflies pinned to a mat. But not

Picasso. Not Braque. Not like the abstract Russian Kandinsky. These men shattered the world in their hands and gave it back made only of building blocks, with room for the individual and imagination; they invited the viewer onto the canvas and asked him to build a new world out of these raw parts. Abram Breit had fallen in love with the Cubists.

He remained a silent man. There was nothing he could do about his nature. But he could do with his life what the Cubists had done with the image, break his nature into its basic elements and take a clean look. So Breit did this, slowly, with the small brush strokes he never could muster with his hands, but could with his mind. In the mirror, in his tailored SS uniform, he began to see what he was made of. He shuddered to find so much reluctance and cowardice. Abram Breit faced the fact that he'd turned into a man he'd never wanted to become; he was not an artist, not a teacher anymore, not an individual at all. He wore SS black, the absence of all color. Abram Breit had become so silent a man that he was gone. His cowardice had erased him.

Breit was aroused for more truth. Yes, he'd been a coward. And what had been the canvas for his cowardice? He looked outside his window, into battered Berlin, across Europe, to the Balkans, into Russia. There he saw Germany's fear and vanity. Undisguised, plain as paint and framed in flame, Breit grasped Hitler's madness and genius – genius is madness, in a way – the driving forces behind the war, a global conflict made by Breit's country and people; but Hitler's madness was not like van Gogh's. The *Führer* had grown openly corrupted by power, by the saluting hordes and goose-stepping world risen around him. Hitler had men on all sides who were devious for their own gains. Germany was in the wrong hands. That, like a sphere, a cone, a circle, a square, was an elemental truth. No man was so silent he could turn away from this.

First, Breit requested a transfer from the art archives to military intelligence. Most of his cataloging work was concluded; the flow of confiscated art had slowed as Germany became *judenfrei. Leibstandarte* granted his request. In late 1942, Breit trained for three months in Munich. Then he was assigned back to Berlin, as divisional liaison to Hitler's staff. The *Führer* himself made the request, delighted with the artwork Colonel Abram Breit had selected for his chalets and castles.

Abram Breit became a spy.

This was not so hard to do. There were many ears in Germany listening for betrayal, some to punish the betrayers, some to welcome and encourage. Breit let slip a comment or two here and there, words that he could have easily explained away as too much *schnapps* or a simple misunderstanding. He traveled to East Prussia, around Germany, to conquered France, a loyal and efficient junior member of the general staff. It was in Switzerland he was approached.

All he knew was that he would be working for something called the Lucy network. These were German patriots, he was told, like him, men and women who were the real guardians of Germany's precious future. They would do everything they could to stop the Nazi war machine. Whatever secrets Breit could funnel into Lucy would be channeled to Hitler's most powerful enemy, Soviet Russia.

Breit was unfazed at the destination for his treasons. What he wanted most was what the Cubists demanded: a change, a new world, a new Germany, a renewed Breit. The Russians could give him all that.

He finished the apple. He slipped the core into the paper sack, making less rustle than the woman still sketching the blue Monet. Breit set the bag on the bench beside him. He cupped his chin in his hand and rested his eyes on the Picasso. The painting was one of the artist's early Cubist treatments, *Bread and Fruit Dish on a Table*. In this work, Picasso had brushed away all depth perception. The table and its bowl and loaves all seemed to be on a single plane; the backdrop of a curtain and a wall came forward, impinging on the objects they ought to exist behind and apart from. There is no difference, Picasso painted, between the object and its surroundings. Everything is one. Everything is connected. Art can change minds. And because it can, it must.

Breit stood. He left the paper sack on the bench, it was trash. He stepped toward the door to leave the museum.

A blue-suited security guard, an older gentleman with a handlebar moustache, swept in behind him. The guard gave Breit a *tut-tut* for leaving the rubbish of his lunch on the bench. The elder man scooped up the paper sack and took it away. Breit nodded his head in silent apology. The man inclined his own head and disappeared.

Breit walked out of the museum with a hundred others, lunchtime was done. He ambled along the banks of the Spree to the Monbijou Bridge. He crossed halfway over the river. Cars trundled behind him, Berliners strolled past returning to their work administering the Nazi regime. The river glistened under the sun. Breit tried to view the light on the green ripples the way Monet had seen the canals of Venice, and could not. All he caught was glare and motion, people on his left and right ignoring him and the river. This was unfair, Breit thought, to be excluded like this, to be as blind as everyone else.

But I am not blind, Breit thought. And I am not mute.

At that moment the old museum guard would have in his hands two folded sheets of paper pulled from the crumpled bag Breit left on the bench. The Old National Gallery was one of a half-dozen drop sites around Berlin the Lucy network had arranged for him. The two pages were filled front and back with coded script. They would reach Moscow tomorrow, after being routed through

Lucerne, the base for Lucy. The coded sheets gave an exacting report on Hitler's meeting yesterday with his generals, every detail Breit could recall about the coming battle for Kursk. Breit related the *Führer*'s desperation, the indecision of his generals, the immensity of the forces to be committed to Citadel, the fantastically high political stakes for Germany, the last throw of the dice. He described the deterioration of Hitler's physical condition, Hitler's obsessive fretting over an approaching American invasion of Italy and Mussolini's chronic weakness, even the training and morale of young Captain Thoma's Tiger tank crews, the number of tanks to be involved, the mechanical problems popping up with the Panthers, everything Breit could gush to the Russians to help them beat the Nazis out of Germany like dust out of a rug.

Abram Breit was a spy. He remained a quiet stroller through the war, but he was not a mote or a minion, not like these speechless souls shuffling across the river. Breit was a changed man whom Hitler would personally hang on a meat hook if even a whisper surfaced of who he was, and how much influence Abram Breit was finally having with what he could see, hear, and tell.

CHAPTER 2

June 28
1430 hours
Vladimiriovka, USSR

Dimitri Konstantinovich Berko laughed and could not hear himself. He bumped his head hard but his padded helmet softened the jolt. He straightened his goggles over his eyes and licked dusty sweat. The metal around him humped and bucked and because it was Dimitri making all this happen he laughed more and whooped.

He rammed his left boot down on the clutch and in the same instant mashed the brake with his right. The tank ground to a halt. Dimitri hauled the gearshift into reverse; the gears of the new tank fought him for only a grinding second, confused by the speed of his hands and feet, then meshed. He stepped on the gas and popped his foot off the clutch. The tank around him jumped and slammed down, the tracks spun fast and bit farther into the dirt. Dimitri hit the brake and clutch again, shifting to neutral.

Whorls of dust, the black spume of the steppe, spilled into the open driver's hatch, riding on the June sun. He let the tank idle, hoping to hear screams from the men beneath it; the engine growled out any sound but its own. This is the way of the tank, Dimitri thought. You hear nothing, see nothing, feel nothing, but the tank. You have to imagine the rest.

Oh well, he thought, I'll keep having fun even without

the screams. Looking out through the hatch, he saw the whole company had gathered to watch his antics, the way Dimitri could make a tank shudder and dance, spin, and even run in place to dig its way down into a trench. They should see me on a horse, Dimitri thought. Next to an old Cossack on a horse, this tank, this machine, is nothing.

He shifted into gear, hit the gas, and let the clutch fly again. The tank bolted, its treads scoured the ground. Dimitri nodded; this T-34 fresh from the factory had some fire in its belly. He felt the chassis drop again toward the men in the narrow trench while dust thickened the air inside the tank. He pulled his hands off the twin steering rods. Rearing his goggled head out of the hatch, he raised both arms in the air and shook his fists for the crowd. I am the best driver! I am the Cossack of the tanks! He did not hear the men's shouts but saw them raise their arms in reply, Yes, you are!

While he waved his fists in the air, several men broke ranks from the crowd and ran toward the tank. They dove through the dust cloud into the trench. Dimitri leaned over to see just how far he'd scraped down to the 6th Guards infantry trainees who'd hunkered under his bouncing T-34. Good, he thought. Almost all the way down to the undercarriage. That must have put some shit in a few britches under there, watching the bottom of a thirty-ton tank bore its way down on you. That was the point, wasn't it? This was an exercise to help these peasant boys get rid of their fear of tanks. A job well done, then, Dimitri told himself.

He lowered himself through the hatch back into his driver's seat. He gunned the engine and pulled the T-34 off the trench. The diesel engine spit black fumes onto the trainees in the trench and doused those do-gooders helping their quaking comrades. Dimitri yanked back on the left steering lever and shoved on the right, spinning the tank in a tight circle, gouging out one last billow of dust. He shut the tank down.

He climbed onto the glacis plate and slid to the ground. Six soldiers staggered out of the trench, three helping another three whose legs wobbled. Those who could muster angry stares shot them at Dimitri, but like the tank his armor was sufficient to repel them. With his soft helmet and goggles pulled from his head, he could now hear the cheers. Dimitri ran a hand through his gray, close-cropped hair. He waved, then bowed.

When he straightened, he saw a sergeant stomping furiously over to him.

'Private. What do you think you were doing?'

The commander of Dimitri's tank was neat and good-looking, wearing the Russian tankers' slate-gray coveralls like Dimitri, except his weren't so sweaty and smirched. He was built like Dimitri, a bit long for a tanker, not so squat and thick to fit inside these cans of war. He was no peasant.

'What I was ordered to do, Comrade Sergeant.'

Dimitri was calm. The man was much younger than him. All of the men were.

The crowd went quiet.

The sergeant worked his jaw, careful with Dimitri but resolute to show displeasure.

Dimitri spoke first.

'A lot of these men have never been in combat. You and I have, Sergeant. What did you want me to do, be nice to them?'

The sergeant's eyes cut away. Dimitri followed where he looked. A colonel stood in the crowd of men, hands on his hips, unhappy. The officer was obviously from 3rd Mechanized Brigade headquarters, come to watch the progress of the anti-tank training. The men were supposed to wait in the trench for Dimitri's tank to roll past, then jump out behind the T-34 and clap magnetic mines on the rear above the tank's engine and air-filtration systems. What the colonel had seen instead was a tank driver thwarting the training for some amusement and torment.

The sergeant brought his gaze back around to Dimitri. Bugs buzzed in the tall steppe grasses. Other tanks on other training areas growled in their own exercises. Dimitri lowered his voice below the insects and engines so only the sergeant could hear.

'Who is that?'

The sergeant kept his voice low, as well.

'It's Babadzhanian.'

Dimitri grimaced. Colonel Babadzhanian was the commander of their 16th Regiment.

Dimitri looked down to think, but also to look sorry.

'Slap me.'

The sergeant bristled at this.

'I will not.'

'I was insolent. Slap me now.'

'No. It's against regulations.'

'And if you don't, I'm headed for the stockade. Come on, boy, show some balls and save me a week behind bars. I hate their food.'

The sergeant held still. 'No.'

'Your mother was a whore.'

'I know.'

'You should have been drowned at birth.'

'I know.'

'Then slap me.'

Dimitri shuffled his heels in the torn-up earth. This was taking too long. Many more seconds and the colonel himself would stride forward to mete out regimental justice. Dimitri gritted his teeth.

'Alright, Valentin. What will it take?' he asked.

'Your promise.'

'What, to be good?'

'Yes.'

Dimitri hesitated.

'For how long?'

Both the sergeant and private saw the colonel take a step into the ring of quiet men.

'Alright,' Dimitri said.

Valentin's hand lashed across Dimitri's face, turning his head with the force of the blow. A good shot, Dimitri thought, over the burn in his cheek.

'Private!' the sergeant shouted. Dimitri sneaked a glimpse at the colonel. The officer was holding his ground.

The young tank commander laid it on. 'The men in that trench are your comrades, Private. The Red Army has no place in it for behavior like what you just displayed! You will apologize to these men and you will in future conduct yourself according to the rules set out in the training manual. Or I will personally see you to the stockade myself! Is this understood?'

Dimitri stiffened. 'Yes, Comrade Sergeant! Deeply understood!'

Everyone in the company who knew Dimitri knew this was more of his clowning, but they also knew no one had better laugh in front of the colonel, or Dimitri would not be so funny later.

Valentin stabbed a finger at the T-34. 'Now get back in your tank. You will do another shift and you will perform your duties without flaw. Or there will be consequences. Move, Private!'

Dimitri ran the several steps to the tank. The green-painted metal was warm under the summer sun, filthy with flung dirt. With practiced ease and agility beyond his fifty-five years, he lifted himself and swung his legs through the hatch, settling into his seat. With swift hands he flicked the ignition switch and hit the starter. The diesel engine coughed and fired. Dimitri pulled down his goggles and gripped the twin levers. This was the third tank he and Valya had been given. In the last year they'd had two shot out from under them, one in the pocket outside Stalingrad in the winter, one more in the lost battle for Khar'kov three months ago. With their tanks went two crews; twice, he and Valya had been the only ones to escape. Four dead, all the hull machine-gunners and loaders. And when you die inside a tank, you always die ugly. Dimitri looked around the compact room of the T-34, designed for battle, not comfort. Metal everywhere, and where there was not steel there were glass gauges. When the armor gets pierced by a shell, the compartment turns into a razor storm, a pit of flame, a gas chamber, any number of things that will kill you faster than a blink. Dimitri permitted himself a wistful second, recalling what he had seen inside these tanks. When will the luck run out for him? And Valya?

It'll happen, he thought, somewhere on the road ahead. It's always been there. So why worry? Dimitri laughed at this. He wanted a saber in his hand and a strong horse between his legs, to gallop off down that road ahead, to find what waited for him there and call it to a challenge. But he had no horse, he was a Cossack without a steed or a blade. Instead he gunned the engine of the tank the Red Army gave him to ride, he looked up at the long barrel of the gun this sergeant was given to fire, and for now these were good enough. Valentin's head appeared in his hatch.

'Private.'

'Yes, I know.'

Dimitri grinned.

'Valya,' Dimitri said.

'What?'

'Next time don't smack me so hard.'

Valentin drooped his eyes and shook his head. The boy is always amazed at me, thought Dimitri.

Dimitri sprang the catch on the driver's hatch and let it

fall shut with a clang. He charged the gearshift forward, let go the clutch, and the tank surged ahead. He couldn't see, but he knew his son had to leap clear fast.

June 28
1440 hours

Dimitri rumbled the tank away from the training field to a clearing. He was filthy with dust and perspiration. Valentin kept him going back and forth over the trenches until the new tank was almost out of gas. He eased above the trainees in the ditch, even braked for them to catch up to him and lay their wooden disks, the fake mines, over his ventilation system. Valentin stood always in his vision, signaling him to turn and do it again. In his gritty cabin, Dimitri cursed the boy.

The tank, one of the new T-34/76 1942s, responded well. The designers had added only a few improvements over the 1940 and 1941 models. The treads were slightly broader, reducing the ground pressure per square inch, letting the tank handle better. There was added armor on the turret face and sides. The hull gunner's position had a protected mount now. The turret overhang was reduced to keep from reflecting incoming rounds down onto the turret ring. The big difference was the longer-barreled main gun for a higher muzzle velocity. Shells fired from this tank would penetrate far better than anything the Red Army had ever mounted. But it still might not be enough. Dimitri heard talk of the new German super-tanks, Tigers and Panthers with massive guns and the thickest armor ever seen on the battlefield. When the fighting starts again, those new beasts will be arrayed across the steppe from him. Again, he laughed at his own worries, and once Valentin let him off duty, he parked his own new beast under a tree. In the shade, he rose from his seat, tossing helmet and goggles to the grass. He slid down the glacis plate and stood stretching his back and stiff neck. He looked out over this land the Germans and Russians decided would be the stage for their apocalypse. Eternal swaths of reeds and grasses rolled in ripples of green and wheat. This was beautiful cavalry country, classic campaign terrain, where giants could fit all their killing wares at once and surge at one another, to clash eye to eye.

Twenty miles south from here the Germans had gathered, with more land and air force than at any other time in the war, the reports said. A hundred miles north they'd done the same. Any time now, they'd attack from two directions toward the center, aimed at the city of Kursk, to pinch and surround the million and a half Russians defending it. In the south, there was just one road to Kursk. It cut through the town of Oboyan ten miles at his back. Dimitri, his son, and their 3rd Mechanized Corps straddled this road. Three major defense belts have been dug into the earth between Oboyan and the Germans. The Red Army had put everything it could muster in front of Oboyan, including Dimitri. If the Germans took this road, if Dimitri was alive to see them sweep north past him, he would be alive to see the battle lost.

Dimitri yawned. He turned away from the coming battleground and crawled between the tracks of the T-34. The gut of the tank was caked with soil and he kicked off dangling clogs to make room. The cooling aluminum engine *ping*-ed. Dimitri patted the tank's underbelly, then curled over on his shoulder and fell asleep.

Hours later, when he slid from beneath the tank, he was stiff, his body cranky.

'Alright, my lad,' he said, standing with a soft grunt. He'd taken a shard in his right calf six months ago outside Stalingrad and never had it removed. Over his half century of fighting and carousing and galloping, he'd fallen off fifty horses and been kicked by a hundred. He'd pulled plows when the mules were starved in the collectivization years in the Kuban. His knuckles were scarred and knobby from farm machines, swords, jaws, guns, and now tanks. Dimitri opened his hands, then worked them into fists. His forearms bulged no less than they did thirty years ago when he was a rider for the Tsar. His nails were stained now with grease and not the loam of the farm or the lather of a war charger. He opened one thick hand and laid it across the tank's fender. He walked all around the tank, touching it, reached up to the thick turret, cooler now for its time beneath the tree. He slid his fingers down the long green length of the main gun, at its open mouth remembering sugar cubes and carrots, knowing he must ride this beast toward death and having nothing in his pockets to give the machine to please it and bond it to him.

'Before we do anything else,' he said aloud, 'you need your name.'

Dimitri walked to another tank crew and from them got a brush and a canister of white paint. Walking back he read the titles given to others of the newly minted T-34s: *Motherland; Our Nation's Defense; Stalin The Father*. The commissars loved it when you dubbed your tank something like that. Dimitri would not sloganeer for the Communists. He was the driver. This tank was his to name. He returned to his clearing and climbed aboard. In minutes, on the port side of the turret, he scrawled in large letters the name of his previous two tanks, *General Platov*, the great Cossack warrior from the bloody war with Napoleon.

'Now, *General*,' he said in a soothing tone, 'let's see what you've got.'

From his other two T-34s and over a year of fighting, Dimitri had assembled a box of tools he kept strapped to the hulls. With every tank he abandoned, the box was the last thing he scrabbled for before running for cover. He opened it now and took out a wrench. At the rear of the tank, he unfastened the hatch. The first thing in the compartment was the transmission. The makers of the T-34 were clever fellows. They knew the transmission in their tank was garbage, so they put it right where you could get to it easily, chuck a bad one away and shove in another. This location in the back had one drawback for the driver: it made the tank's gears tough to shift because of the long drive train running through the floor. Dimitri and the other Russian tank drivers learned to keep a hammer under their seats for the more stubborn moments of the T-34's transmission.

The next item in the rear compartment was the twelve-cylinder engine. It, too, was easy to dispose of and replace. And spare parts were plentiful during action, a sad and smoking, sometimes burning, vista, but convenient for a buzzard mechanic like Dimitri. He had to hand this to Stalin: While the Germans littered the land with several makes of tank – and from the rumors were about to add two more, larger models – Stalin announced he would shoot any factory manager producing anything but his T-34. A thousand T-34s were pumped out every month in the Urals, to replace the thousand left charred on the steppe or snow or rubbled city streets. Stalin was also pursuing a new, heavier tank design, the KV-1, but these had not yet made any impression in battle, and as far as Dimitri knew there were none in the Kursk salient. The main battle tank for the Red Army remained the T-34, whether it was a good machine or not. This was the Russian way to fight a war, with numbers, massed waves of men and matériel. Lenin himself said it: Quantity is its own quality. The immediate problem facing the Russians was not with the amount of tanks available; every week there grew fewer and fewer trained men left to fight in them.

Dimitri dug his head into the engine compartment, looking over the heart of his new tank. And it was a good heart. The T-34's motor made it the fastest tank on the field, always, with a top speed of thirty miles per hour. The engine was diesel, efficient, giving a range of up to 260 miles. And unlike the Germans' gasoline-powered Mark III and IV tanks, the motor also lacked the troubling tendency to blow up in combat.

Dimitri poked around awhile with his wrenches, checking bolts and hose couplings, filters and fittings. He talked to the machine, gentling it, getting it accustomed to its new name, *General,* and the feel of his hands on its secrets. The designers had three elements to balance when devising this tank: speed, protection, and power. Too much armor slows down speed, too much speed sacrifices the weight needed to carry a big gun and ammo. The T-34 was as good a compromise as any Dimitri had seen on the battlefields. And even when these tanks were knocked out by the hundreds, more kept coming. The Russian way.

Satisfied, he pushed himself out of the engine compartment. He bolted the rear panel tight and laid his tools in the metal case above the fender.

'Another *General Platov.*' Dimitri did not turn to the voice. Instead, he finished his chore. 'Maybe this time the good *General* will have better luck. How many lives does a Cossack have, Private?'

Dimitri crouched to wipe his grimy hands on the grass. 'As many as he needs.'

Valentin stayed quiet for uncomfortable seconds. Then Valentin said, 'It's a bad thing when a son has to slap his father.'

Dimitri kept his eyes away from Valentin. The time mounted between them like something coming out of the ground. Valentin lifted himself onto the tank and into the commander's hatch. The T-34's large hatch cover hinged toward the front, forcing the commander to stand behind it. It was done this way to protect the commander during combat from ahead, but in the end it was simply cumbersome, difficult to see around, and the cause of many bloody noses during sudden stops. But Valentin looked good in the commander's spot, peering down at Dimitri kneeling in the grass. He had a Cossack nose, sharp and long like a sword, a square jaw, and the blue eyes of the Azov sky, the ancient canopy for the Kuban and Don horsemen. Dimitri had passed to his son his own wiry build and black hair. But the boy did not always keep his head up, and Dimitri lamented that he had given Valentin a Cossack's body but not his soul.

Dimitri rose and stepped back from the *General,* to let the boy have it to himself for a while, for it was new to him, too. Valentin's head disappeared into the tank, the hatch banged shut above him. In seconds the tank came alive. The periscope in the commander's hatch began to rotate. Then Valentin worked the manual crank to elevate the main gun. The long barrel lifted to its full height, thirty degrees, then drooped to its lowest elevation, minus three degrees. The turret's low profile made it a hard target, but the closeness of the gun mantlet to the chassis made it impossible to depress the main gun far. This restricted the gunner's ability to fire at close targets, or to level the barrel when the tank sat behind a protective berm with the hull tilted up. So many compromises, Dimitri thought. So much left undone in the making of a tank, a son.

Dimitri watched the tank, silent and motionless now, wrapped around his boy. Together he and Valya had fought and killed, escaped and spit smoke and blood. Dimitri did not know how many German tanks they'd faced in the war, hundreds certainly. He had no count of how many they'd beaten. Enough to still be standing here, whatever the number. Valentin in combat was an excellent gunner, his marksmanship with the 76 mm main gun was as good as any tanker. But as a commander, when the bold time came, that moment in every battle when you face life or death and leave it to God to decide, the boy could hesitate. He waited for instructions, held in check by the Communists, who fight sometimes as if they're afraid to go in alone, so instead they die in ten thousands. These times Dimitri took over, he turned the tank toward God and the Germans and told the boys over the intercom to keep shooting. The others in their crews, the ones dead now, believed he was insane. He wasn't, ever. He was a Cossack.

The commander's hatch lifted with a creak. I'll need to grease that, thought Dimitri. I'll need to groom the whole damn thing, and then some German will shoot it out from under me again. Valentin hoisted himself out of the hatch, dropping gracefully to the ground.

'Good,' he said.

'I think so,' Dimitri agreed.

Valentin stuck his tongue inside his lip. He looked at his boots. 'I'm sorry I'm such a disappointment to you.'

Dimitri glared at the top of his son's head, longing to yank Valya's eyes up from the earth.

'You're soft,' he told his son.

'I follow orders.'

'You follow Communists.'

'Stalin's winning the war.'

Dimitri held out one veined forearm. He pointed at the blue tracks marbling the muscle. 'You see this? *This* is what's winning the war. Russian blood. Not Stalin, not Lenin. Me. You. You know what the word 'Cossack' means. It's Turkish, from *kazak*. It means – '

'Freedom, Papa, it means freedom. We've had this discussion.'

'And I want to have it again.'

'I'm not going to fight with you.'

No, thought Dimitri, it seems you're not.

The son, born under the reign of Lenin, turned his back on his father, born under Tsar Alexander III. He took several steps with Dimitri glaring at his back.

'When will we get our new crew?' Dimitri called, his tone controlled, as if he were a private asking his sergeant.

Valya stopped. He did not turn or raise his head. Face me, thought Dimitri, get your fucking head up.

'In a few days, I'm told.'

'Well, if you've been told, I'm sure that's what will happen.'

The boy's jaw was set. Dimitri nodded at this, pleased.

'My mother was a saint.'

Svetlana. Dead. Starved by Stalin ten years ago in the Ukraine along with ten million others. There she was, in Valentin's lean Cossack face, just for an instant, defending herself on his lips. *Dima, Dima, you bastard!* she'd shouted at him a thousand times; *Dima, you fool,* she'd laughed a thousand more.

'Yes, she was,' Dimitri answered.

Over the battleground of the mother and wife, father and son stood equal for a few seconds. Then she was eclipsed by the boy's own spirit and Valya's eyes dropped again.

'Leave me alone,' Dimitri told him, 'and let me get this tank ready.'

Valentin walked away into the hip-high grass, following the tank tracks crushed there by his father.

June 28
2315 hours

Outside the tarpaulin, the sun refused to go down. It's late, thought Dimitri, go away, let a man sleep. Valentin, stretched on the grass opposite him beside the tank, snored. It was a young man's gift to sleep like that. The sun hung on with desperate last rays, waiting until the moon could take hold full in the sky.

Dimitri rolled from beneath the tarp and got to his feet. The world was more lit than he'd realized, ridiculous, he thought, so close to midnight. The moon seemed hot and urgent. Standing in the grass, in the moonshadow of a tree, Dimitri appeared to himself white and cadaverous. How can a man sleep under this son of a bitch of a moon? he wondered. Go away, all of you, everything, let a man rest.

He walked past the four tanks of his platoon, then down the line of the twelve T-34s in his company. He lit a cigarette, strolling, trailing gray haze. Hushed voices rose in the twilight. 'Dima, can't sleep?' 'Not nervous, are you, old man?' Dimitri waved the dot of his cigarette at the good-natured taunts from under the tarpaulins, he moved through the thicket of youthful snores in the macabre light. There were forty-five tanks in his battalion, all of them parked in four rows. He walked until the signal flare went off.

The streak was green, a brilliant, crackling dot trailing smoke high into the moon's reach. The ground shimmied under the flare's flicker. The lighting of the world went backward, from dead to sickly, but the action around him was immediate. Emerald shadows leaped from their sleep, tarps were torn down, men teemed to their tanks. Dimitri cast away his cigarette and ran back to his tank.

This is not an attack, he thought, careering between men and waking machines. The German assault hasn't begun yet. Even though the front line was well beyond the dim horizon, there would have been flashes of artillery fire on the rim. There would be air assaults, more flares around the 6th Army's position awakening other divisions, more confusion, some panic. To Dimitri, this smelled of drill, another round of war games.

When he reached the *General,* Valentin was already

standing in place behind his open hatch door. Dimitri was the last driver in their company to jump into his seat. Valentin said nothing while Dimitri cranked the engine. The tank shuddered and the diesel added its racket to the rumbling night.

Dimitri slipped on his padded cloth helmet and goggles. He plugged in the interphone cable and buckled the strap under his chin, adjusting the throat microphone in the strap over his Adam's apple. The earphones in his helmet buzzed. Valentin's voice said only, *'Test.'*

'Clear.'

Dimitri glanced at the empty chair beside him; the Degtaryev machine-gun's pistol grip had no hand on it. This better be another drill, he thought, we've got no hull gunner. And beside Valentin was another empty padded seat. We've got no loader.

Moments later, the tank in front of Dimitri pulled forward. He did not wait for Valentin's order to fall in, but shifted to first gear and rolled ahead, allowing ten meters to grow between the *General* and the next tank, the correct amount of distance when traveling in column formation. He had no idea where they were going. Their destination was Valentin's job, the commander's job. Dimitri looked over his shoulder and up, to see his son. The boy was folded into his seat, a map spread over his lap, a small light glowing over his head. Dust and smoke flew in the night air, mixed with pollen and torn grasses. The column moved with their running lights off, to avoid being spotted by prowling enemy night bombers. Dimitri couldn't see the tank in front of him, so he drove the *General* straight into the dirty cloud that was its wake.

The column turned south. They stayed west of the Belgorod-Oboyan road, tramping up and down the rolling plain. They'd come this way five days ago, to stop at a narrow branch of the Solotino outside the village of Novoselovka. The first T-34 to cross the river bridge had cracked through the pilings and crashed on its side in the shallow water in a magnificent splash. Its crew broke some bones and the march was halted. Engineers were called up to make the bridge secure, something that should have been done weeks ago but someone missed it. Tonight, the column of tanks roared across the little span without incident. Jolting over the new timbers, Dimitri wondered if that lead tank was still tilted beneath him in the water. Probably, he decided. But there are no kids playing on it during the daylight. The entire area along the bulge of the 250-mile-long front line had been evacuated and turned into a fortress. Every bridge was mined, a thousand of them. Every solid house of every village had a machine-gun in a window. Roaring out of Novoselovka, Dimitri could not see one light in any dwelling, not one cow or chicken along the road. Where there are no chickens, he realized, there are no Russians.

The column moved without break for two hours, coursing south over fields parallel to the Oboyan road. In that time, Valentin did not speak, but studied his maps in his command position. This was the son he had raised. A map reader, following the terrain on a sheet of paper instead of by the stars and landmarks. Dimitri's father, Konstantin, could not read a word, let alone decipher a military map. But the old man and his horse were never lost, not on weeklong hunting trips, not when he rode across these same steppe lands beside his own son, galloping under a raised saber and the white flag of Nicholas against the tightening rule of the Communists. Konstantin had taught Dimitri how to ride the earth like a horse, follow its movements, keep himself in its stirrups. Now Dimitri listened to the soft hum of nothing in his earpieces, from a silent son and commander. Dimitri had not taught the boy well. His old father would be angry.

Dimitri checked the gauges mounted just below his hatch opening. The new *General* was running well. One shade of paint coated everything in the cockpit, a sort of muted, snotty mint. Outside, the tank was a deep forest green. All the T-34s were this color. The Red Army way, equality, the nail that sticks out is hammered down. Dimitri longed to roar out of the line he'd been in for hours, his hands ached with following.

Within the hour the column stopped. Valentin laid the flat of his boot between Dimitri's shoulder blades, the unspoken signal to halt. Often during combat, when there was too much noise or the interphone was broken, Valentin rode with his feet on Dimitri's shoulders, guiding him with pressure to turn left or right; a boot to the neck meant forward, to the top of the head was speed up, two feet on the shoulders was reverse. The boot in Dimitri's back was gentle enough; when the blood was up in the fighting, there had been some kicks. Dimitri shifted to neutral and idled.

Valentin stood in his place. Dimitri saw nothing but the rear of the tank in front of him, close and stinking of diesel exhaust. An officer walked along the line of tanks shouting orders up to the commanders. Valentin gave Dimitri the order to shut down.

The tank shuddered to a hulking quiet. Dimitri rose out of his hatch, filling his lungs with his first clean breath in hours. He lifted the goggles from his eyes; sweat had caked with the dust against his skin. He stepped out of the tank and slid to the ground. His legs needed a second to firm.

The dozen commanders in his company clustered around a captain. Dimitri walked away from the settling fumes and heat of the tanks, a little ways into the surrounding field.

In the silvery light he made out dots on every hill, in all directions. Perhaps two hundred tanks had been shaken awake hours ago and force-marched in the night to this staging area. Dimitri's 3rd Mechanized Brigade was one of several units arrayed in an east-west line. The noise of tanks moving up on all sides sounded like the rattling of giant chains, there was a metallic moan to the treads eating into the earth, a whine from the engines, and Dimitri imagined this was the clamor of gathering titans.

One of the drivers walked beside Dimitri, offering a cigarette. The two men smoked while the commanders conferred and the tank engines cooled and knocked.

The driver was a dairy farmer from the Caucasus, an older fellow named Andrei. 'This is going to be one shit pile,' Andrei said. 'This is our battle right here.'

The man swept a hand across the rippling southern plain, gray as gravestones.

'That's where the river runs, east-west. It isn't much but the Germans have got to cross it. And that's where the road branches. They'll come right up from Tomarovka and Belgorod. And there,' he swung the hand left, to the east, 'is where the road splits off to Prokhorovka. We'll meet them here, on the way to Kursk. Right fucking here, above the river. They've got to go around or through us.'

'You and me, Andrushka,' Dimitri said, patting the man's back. 'We're the reason we'll win. Hitler's only brought his young pups.'

Andrei laughed, and he looked younger behind his cigarette. This is God's bargain during war, Dimitri thought. If you face Him, face death, you are rewarded with living – truly living – every second you have left.

Andrei glanced back toward the tanks. The commanders were still confabbing.

'How's it going with your pup?' he asked.

Now Dimitri laughed. 'I've finally got him pissing on the newspaper.'

'Well, there's hope, then!'

Andrei dropped his cigarette and stepped on it. 'Ride hard, Cossack.'

'You, too, goatherder.'

Andrei returned to his tank. Dimitri flicked away his cigarette. He put his hands on his hips and leaned his head back into the cascading moonlight. He knew how the rest of the night and morning would go. Andrei was right, this was going to be their main defense region. Their battalion, all fifty tanks, would dig ditches deep enough for them to roll the T-34s into, hull down, so only the turrets were exposed. They'd dig shelters for ammunition, later in the day the shells would be brought up and stacked. There would be practice in camouflage and target acquisition. They'd drive over the plain and mark march routes for wetlands and boggy patches, they'd ease past minefields and mark them, too. They'd identify lanes of retreat should the Germans push them back from this second defense line to the third and final belt in front of Novoselovka, the last stand before Oboyan and Kursk. The generals would let German spotter planes photograph them here, let them report to their own command how the Russians have occupied this fork on the Oboyan road. Then tomorrow night, after the T-34s had gone, engineers would build *maskirovka* tanks here out of barrels, hay, and poles.

Hitler's waiting. He should have come at us months ago, when we were still reeling from the Khar'kov loss. Now, with the spring and summer, we've packed so many men and guns around Kursk we're tripping over each other.

The Red Army generals definitely know where Hitler's going to attack, even if they're not sure when.

But Hitler knows something we don't. He's let the weeks go by without concern that the Red Army has dug in. The bastard's got something up his rotten little sleeve.

This is going to be a tank battle, that's certain.

That's it, of course. Hitler's not worried about our million and a half men, our three thousand tanks, or our uncountable anti-tank mines and guns. He figures he's got a weapon to turn the battle his way, no matter how ready we get. He's waiting for his new tanks. The Tigers. His super-tanks.

Dimitri had never faced a Tiger. The hulking things had only made fleeting appearances during the debacle at Khar'kov. But every report, every rumor, told that wherever the Tiger appeared, it dominated. T-34s by the dozens were left in wreckage by a handful of Mark VI Tigers.

Around him, for miles in every direction, more and more moonlit tanks pulled into position. The T-34 was quick, even nimble, with Dimitri at the reins. It had excellent armor, a strong main gun. He recalled Andrei's hand sweeping over this small southern portion of the battlefield inside the Kursk bulge, studded with Russian tanks. Can Hitler bring enough super-tanks here to kill all of us?

In the sky, between Dimitri and the moon, a shadow skittered, like a crone on a broomstick. Then came the faint clatter of engines. The sound headed south, toward the German lines. In a minute it was gone, and the night belonged again to the dark, idling tanks spread across the fields and hills.

Valentin appeared beside him. The boy, too, had his eyes raised to where the black flash had cut across the moon.

'Night Witches,' murmured Valentin.

'Yes,' Dimitri answered. 'I saw them.'

He scanned the sky farther to the south, away from the moon's aura, and caught what he was looking for. One star blinked in and out, then another winked in line, and he wondered if this was Katya.

CHAPTER 3

June 28
2320 hours
one thousand meters above Syrtsev
ten miles north of the front line
Voronezh Front

The flying was effortless. Katya pulled her hands from the stick, her feet from the rudder pedals, and the U-2 flew itself, straight and deliberate, heavy with four 200-pound bombs strapped under the low wing. The night let her pass unescorted except for what she brought with her, the *pop-pop-pop* of her little engine, the flap of wind in the percale of her wings, and the siffle of air slipping through the wire struts that held her bi-plane together.

Below, the earth slid by, the color of cobwebs and ghosts, soaked in the full moon. Plumes of dust rose from the vast grasslands, the thin stalks were smashed flat in straight lines, the unmistakable sign of tank columns. These are our tanks, she thought. Hundreds of them, on night maneuvers.

Katya put her hands and feet back on the controls. She shoved the stick hard to the left. Even laden with bombs, the plane snapped into a quick barrel roll. Blood rushed behind her eyes, bulging them, but she kept her stare on the dim horizon. When the world had twirled once, she returned the stick to center and leveled the U-2.

The voice of her navigator, Vera, seated in the cockpit

behind her, nibbled in her headphones.

'Saying hi to your papa?'

'Just in case he's looking.'

Katya scanned her dials and gauges. Air speed was sixty mph, at thirty-one hundred feet. The U-2 was made of plywood and fabric. A flight trainer before the war, it held no radio, almost no navigational equipment, no armor to protect a pilot and navigator who were without parachutes, and had a maximum speed of seventy-two miles per hour. But the bi-plane was steady in flight, easy to control, and capable of sustaining uncommon damage. It could be flown low and slow for accurate bombing runs and required very little room to land and take off. The U-2 was flown against the Germans, at night. It was piloted, navigated, armed, and maintained by squadrons of women.

'How far?' Katya asked.

She waited moments for Vera's answer. The navigator had to compute direction and distance by landmarks and maps, also by a stopwatch. The plane's compass would not work dependably in the skies over this region of the steppe because of the huge iron-ore deposits around Kursk. Katya marveled at the navigators' abilities; it was these women's job to get the bombers to the night's target, then guide them home, steering their pilots on the darkest eves by stars and ticking seconds, in fog banks and clouds by instinct. Tonight the moon made Vera's job easier while it made Katya's harder. The pale light and clear air also provided a splendid backdrop behind their little plane for the Germans to spot them.

'Hold at this speed and heading. Ten minutes, thirty seconds.'

About twelve miles, thought Katya. Good. If Papa and Valentin are below in that field, they might be able to see the explosions. The target tonight was an ammo dump.

Katya and Vera were the lead flight on this mission.

The planes behind her would zero in on the fires they started. The entire regiment would be in the air, one plane every three minutes, all night long.

Katya took a gulp of the warm night air rushing past her open cockpit. The U-2 engine *pop-pop*-ed and spit burps of blue flame from the exhaust ports. She mimicked the noise, popping her lips, bored with the straight flying and exhilarated by the thrill and danger of the mission, all at once. She released the stick and pulled her boots up into the seat. Katerina Dimitriyevna Berkovna stood, bending her knees to miss the upper wing and fuel tank, and stretched her arms wide.

Vera, with a duplicate set of controls in the rear cockpit, made sure the U-2 stayed even, not because she was worried about her pilot falling out, Katya knew, but because to deviate would disturb her calculations. Katya was trained from birth to stay in any saddle, on any horse, even a flying one. Now she sat down, feeling Vera's hands release the stick to her.

'One day,' Vera spoke into the intercom.

'One day for everything,' Katya answered. She reached one arm out of her cockpit and slapped the cloth fuselage to pretend she could make it go faster. In her earphones, Vera laughed.

The ground below did not alter its outward character – the earth rolled by in brackish swaths, villages clotted dark and abandoned – but the forces moving along it changed utterly. The Red Army's tanks gave way to densely packed outposts pocked into the earth, with clusters of anti-tank weapons inside trenches and behind sandbagged revetments and dirt berms. The defense works were miles in depth and as wide as Katya could see in the moonlight, but in minutes even these floated behind her. Then she was over no-man's-land, a three-mile-wide plain of minefields and barbed wire, tank obstacles and ditches. Below, ten thousand Soviet soldiers stared across a lethal grassland at their German counterparts. Katya felt herself flying into a chill, the way she always did entering the airspace above enemy territory. The plane bumped, as if the tension coursing back and forth beneath it created its own turbulence.

She put her hand hard on the stick and eased out the throttle. Vera said, 'Climb,' and Katya pulled back on the stick. This was to gain altitude over the approaching target, as well as get distance from the first small-arms fire from the ground, soldiers aiming up into the gloom hoping for a lucky shot, recognizing the sound of the approaching U-2s, the popping engines, the slow and low flight of the woman bomber pilots they'd come to call Night Witches.

Katya took the U-2 up to four thousand feet and leveled. She waited for Vera's voice, they were over the German lines now. The engine thrummed and the slipstream whistled through the struts. Katya fixed on a star low on the horizon and flew straight to it. The star made her think about her Papa. Papa and her brother, jammed like kippers inside a tank. Slow, heavy, and ponderous creatures, the tanks. No wind in the face. She smiled; if anyone can make a tank gallop, it's Papa. She sent Valentin letters about her flying; he answered about what life was like trapped inside a can with their father. Her whole family was at war. This was the first time they'd shared the same battlefield; her regiment had spent the winter in the Crimea, Papa and Valya were at Stalingrad. Now she flew at night over their heads. Cossack families always go to war together.

Vera intoned, 'Steady,' the way she always did in the last approach to the target, her calculations almost complete, and Katya pulled her gaze from the star. She felt needles in her stomach; she'd learned over more than three hundred sorties to ignore them. Another minute of engine and wind whipped by. Inside her goggles, a bead of sweat itched beside her nose. Every new second flew alongside, silver and anxious.

Then Vera gave the order. 'Cut engine.'

Katya shoved in the throttle, the engine coughed and died. The propeller blades slowed to a powerless windmill. Now the plane sailed only on its wings. In an instant the feel of the stick and rudders was different; without the propulsion of the motor Katya rode the night air, not demanding but asking for flight, tickling the air for what lift she could draw from it to keep her plane and her mission in the sky. The U-2 was much more alive in her hands; the night was full of invisible gifts and traps and Katya had to find them.

In the rear cockpit, Vera lit two parachute flares and cast them out. Katya banked left to watch the flares drift and lend their incandescence to the moon. The U-2 was down to thirty-five hundred feet now, low and mute enough for her to hear sirens blare below. She saw men run. Some dropped to their knees and fired, muzzles flashed on the ground, jittering under the swaying chutes. A spark struck against the engine cowling. Through the wind she heard a *ping*. A round had glanced off the motor.

'There it is!' Vera shouted in the headset. 'Ten o'clock!'

Katya stomped on the right rudder to skid the tail to starboard, snapped the stick left, and snatched the nose around to the direction Vera wanted. Looking over her wings she saw no holes ripped in the fabric, the gunners hadn't caught up with the U-2 yet. Ahead, a large, fenced compound filled the center of the German encampment. Camouflage netting covered high stacks of crates. This was their target, the ammunition dump.

She dipped the nose and picked up speed, dropping five hundred feet to their bombing altitude of three thousand. The rush of wind grew in the struts. She leaned forward in the cockpit as though across the mane of a sprinting Arabian. Gunfire clapped from the ground.

The ammo dump was thirty seconds away. Katya nudged the stick forward and the U-2 plummeted another five hundred feet through the shreds of darkness left to her. Vera shouted, 'Hold altitude!' but now Katya took over. Vera had brought them here, but she was the pilot and bombardier.

The night split apart, rent by white swords of swinging light. With *whomps* of surging energy, the powerful searchlights of the German camp switched on one by one. The target was still twenty seconds off. Katya kept her course true.

The beams reached left and right, up and down, criss-crossing arms of light that would embrace the U-2 and not let go until the plane and its crew were shot to the ground. Katya's heart pounded in her ears, it took all of her strength – as it always did, it was this way for every pilot in the night bomber regiment – to hold the stick firm, keeping the plane on its beeline to the target. She wanted to dodge the shafts of light, cut and carve the nimble U-2 around them like pylons. But she was here to blow up an ammunition dump, and there it was.

In that instant, a beam flashed across her windshield, making her wince. It vanished, slipping off the U-2 as Katya sped through it, but then another had caught her shape and swung in from the left. This search beam snagged her plane and gripped it. Another raced to its side and Katya was snared in the crossfire of light. She was blinded.

An eruption rocked the air behind her. The flak batteries had opened up. Katya jammed the stick forward. Behind her, Vera knew what she was doing and screamed, '*Go!*'

In the last ten seconds toward the target, Katya shed altitude. Another flak shell roared in her wake. The U-2 rattled, shaken by the blasts and the gushing wind. The plane dove to fifteen hundred feet, almost straight down at the ammunition dump. The propeller, even without the engine powering it, whirled with the mounting speed. Katya swooped out of the spotlights, she left them swishing behind her confused, wondering where she'd gone. But her vision was stung by the powerful beams. She could not fix on her gauges or the ground.

'Vera, can you see?' she shouted into the intercom.

'Yes!'

'Tell me when!'

Letting the plane plunge, Katya put her left hand on the wire release for the four impact bombs. Another light crossed her path; she tore through it like a paper wall. She guessed she was at one thousand feet now, low enough to strike the ammo dump right in the heart and die in the ensuing detonation. In her earphones, she heard Vera mutter, 'Katya ...'

Katya gritted her teeth.

She hissed only, 'When?'

'Jesus, mother of God.'

'When?'

A second, and another, a pounding in her temples, and in her hands gripping the stick and the wire ...

'Now!'

Katya pulled hard on the wire to release the bombs. The plane bounded, freed of the weight. Katya pushed the throttle in a quarter of the way. She fumbled for the magneto toggle, found it and flipped it down. The propeller, already spinning, caught fast. She rammed the throttle full in and wrapped both hands on the stick, laying all her strength and weight into it, pulling the knob back between her legs.

The U-2's engine, reawakened and fueled, howled. The plane leveled quickly but in two more heartbeats this was not going to be enough. She braced herself, waiting for the bombs to ignite the ammunition and wash a pillar of concussion and flame right over them. She shut her eyes and pulled back on the stick. She could feel Vera pulling, too.

The nose of the plane lifted. Katya opened her eyes. Her vision began to clear. Above, searchlights continued to scan, crossing each other like fencing lances. Katya had no prayer to say that would be fast enough.

The bombs struck. She felt the first kick in her tail from the explosion. The U-2 increased its angle of climb, the engine's bellow was lost in the roar of the ammunition dump below.

The next moment, the world became furious red and black. A fireball engulfed the plane. Katya gaped out into a swarming hell in the air around her. Flames lashed her cockpit, heat beat against her bare throat and cheeks, searing them. She flinched but kept her hands on the stick. The plane fought higher, up into the cloud of flame, then burst out of it into the shattered night; the last claws of flame reached for Katya and curled back. Her goggles were filmed with soot, she yanked them down around her neck. Her skin felt slapped. She eased the climb of the plane.

Below, the dump raged. Commas of light shot out of the conflagration as cases of tracer rounds exploded. Magnesium flashes jetted from the stacks like lightning. Vera's voice sounded in Katya's headset. She said only, 'Uh oh.'

Alarmed, Katya shot her gaze around the plane. The engine popped the way it should, the blue exhaust flames were reassuring. No problem there. She looked to the starboard wings and wires. By the light of the blaze below and the searchlights still casting for them, she noted that the upper and lower wings were singed, the percale had a few shrapnel rips. The paint on the U-2 was an acetate-based dope, extremely flammable. The brown and green camouflage pattern had blackened; smoke trailed behind the wing but no fire was visible. The dope had probably tried to catch flame inside the fireball but had been extinguished by their ferocious climb. She swiveled her head to port.

The upper wing there was also murky and smoking from the blast. She shifted to the lower wing.

'Uh oh,' she said.

A foot-long piece of wood protruded from the cotton sheath of the wing. The thing had been shot into the air, probably from one of the blown-up crates, and Katya had flown right into it. The stick was embedded at the far end of the wing. At its tip, sparks glowed. The ember was trying to build a flame in the wind. If this happened, the U-2 would last no more than a few seconds. The dope-painted percale and the wood of the wings and fuselage would catch and burn before she could get the plane on the ground.

She shouted to Vera, 'Hold on!'

Katya snapped the U-2 into a barrel roll. The U-2 responded, spinning wing over wing. She straightened and the stake was still there, kindling, angry at her attempt to dislodge it. She rolled the other direction; it would not be jettisoned.

Vera said, 'Well?'

'Well what? Go get it!'

'Me?'

'Yes! I'm the pilot. I have to fly the plane. We're not out of the spotlights yet.'

'So while I go out there on the wing you're going to be dodging lights?'

'Well, no.'

'Good. Then I can fly as straight as you. You go.'

'Why me?'

'You're the acrobat, Katya.'

What Vera meant without saying it was: You're always playing the Cossack. Play it now.

Katya blew out a breath. She looked at the stake in the wing. It began to lick at itself with a blue tongue.

'Alright! But if this ever happens again, you do it.'

'Go.'

'Hold it steady.'

'Go!'

Katya pulled up her goggles, wiping them clean with her gloves. She unhooked her microphone and tossed it aside. One last look at the gauges told her the plane was level at twenty-five hundred feet, too low, the searchlights and flak and even rifles could reach them here, cruising flat with the pilot walking on the wing. She stood on her seat, gripping the fuel tank above her head, and swung her left leg onto the wing root. With one hand wrapped around a wire strut, she lifted her other boot out of the cockpit and set it on the wing root. This was not like ten minutes ago, showing off for Vera; then, she could sit back down if she wanted. Here, if she lost her balance, she would lose her life.

Out on the wing, the ground looked much farther away, because it was no longer for her a place to land but to fall. The big, round beacons slashed in wild circles looking for her. Balancing on the wing it seemed they were so close and such hard girders of light she could step out onto one and slide down it. A flak shell exploded in front and to the right; she clenched her teeth and sensed the buzz of shrapnel. And then she froze.

She couldn't do this. The prop wash and a sixty-mile-an-hour wind would blow her off the wing. The plane trembled in the shock of the flak, with more to come. Vera wouldn't be able to fly on an even keel for long, they'd be shot down if she did, she'd have to roll and weave. Katya would fall.

She took firm hold of the strut wire with both hands and folded to her knees. For a moment she was stable, the wooden ribs of the wing beneath the cotton held her weight. Katya stared at the stick embedded there, about to bloom into a torch. She was afraid to move, and that was when she knew she must. That's what Papa taught. Fear puts a bitterness in the mouth. The bitterness is your soul, Papa said, come up to see what you're doing. On her eighteenth birthday, Katerina Berkovna had galloped wide open down the main street of her village waving a saber. She'd sliced in half every melon hoisted on the poles, no one else cut as many, not even the boys, and she was the champion *dzhigitka* of the Cossack war game. She'd stood in the stirrups at a rollicking speed and slashed her father's sword, she didn't fall then. Once in a while your soul wants to see a *podvig*, a feat, to prove you're alive.

Belly-down on the wing, she made herself smaller for the wailing wind, before a searchlight glued itself to them and her heroics out here would be wasted on a plane that was being shot out of the sky. She braced her feet against the fuselage. With a deep breath, she frog-kicked across the sooty wing, skidding on her chest, the wooden ribs beneath the fabric bumping her own ribs. She tried to slide straight at the stick but the wind caught her and pushed her sideways; her left leg dangled off the wing, her right side was slipping and she would be gone. Her right hand stabbed up for the wire strut. She missed. She clawed at the taut cotton wing but the dope paint was slick and there was nothing to grab. She felt herself slide.

Vera broke the U-2 into a dive, dipping the front of the wing and flipping Katya back onto it. She reached for the wire strut angled above her head but it was too high and she missed again. Now she skidded headfirst to the leading edge of the wing, digging her palms into the fabric but finding nothing to slow her fall. Her head and shoulders cleared the wing's rim. The ground was cratered with searchlights – giant unblinking eyes; would they see her tumble, follow her, white and garish, to the ground?

Katya held her breath, the edge of the wing was under her chest, there was nothing to hold her. She was beyond belief in that moment, no thoughts or goodbyes, there'll be time on the way down. She went rigid with fright. In that moment, Vera pulled up and the wing tilted again, leveling itself. Katya screamed and lunged with her left hand. She slid backward and snagged the strut wire. The wing was level now. She was only a foot from the stake, which had finally flared into flame. Without time to understand or appreciate her reprieve, she scooted forward one last time, grabbed the burning stave, and yanked it out of the wing. She let it go into the night, feeling flushed and alive again, and hoped to drop the stake on some German's head.

Sliding backward to the cockpit was faster. She knew now she would not fall; fate rewards the bold. The soul had seen its *podvig* and returned to its seat deep in the body, taking the taste of fear with it.

Climbing into the cockpit, Katya buckled on her microphone. She said nothing to Vera but instantly put the plane into a steep climb, then rolled right out of it to bank hard north for home. The spikes of adrenaline withdrew from her flesh, she took what she felt was her first swallow in a long time. She looked back at the ammo dump. The other planes gliding in behind her would have a bonfire to home in on. The U-2 roared, responding with gladness, almost gratitude, for the burning splinter taken from its paw. Searchlights brandished behind them, grasping at nothing but the receding sound of the first of the Night Witches they would suffer before dawn.

They were past no-man's-land and over the Russian lines before Vera spoke.

'Katya.'

She looked down at the gray fields where the tanks had spread. Lanterns were lit, men were digging, the grumble and clank of tanks reached her even through the whine of her own engine.

'Yes, Verushka.'

Vera laughed.
'One day ...'

June 29
0425 hours
Kalinovka aerodrome

Dawn arrived red-rimmed. Katya homed in on the landing lights arrayed beside the short strip of the air base. The lights were nothing more than three grease pots, hooded so they were visible only from a plane on the proper approach to the field.

She was tired to her bones. Even though she and Vera had only flown five sorties that night, the mission had been difficult. The scare she'd had out on the wing meandered in her chest the rest of the night. The flak had been thick and the air over the target acrid with smoke from the fires raging all around the German camp. After the initial raid on the ammo dump, with Vera still ribbing her as 'Katya the wing-walker,' they landed, refueled, re-armed, and waited while their mechanic Masha repaired the rents in the U-2's wings. Within twenty minutes, they were airborne again, this time with the assigned objectives of knocking out the searchlights and anti-aircraft guns. These were smaller targets, and Katya and the other pilots had to glide in low and slow for accuracy. This was nerve-racking work, going right at the things they tried hardest to avoid. In the winter months, with longer nights, Katya could sometimes fly over a dozen sorties before sunup. But this past night was as exhausting as anything she had undertaken.

Katya brought the nose up, killed her speed, and settled the U-2 on the flattened grass. She taxied out of the way as soon as she was down, for the next plane in line behind her would be coming. This was how her 208th Night

Bomber Division attacked and returned: one plane took off and flew straight at the target at a prescribed altitude, the next followed three minutes behind. After dropping their bombs, each pilot returned to base at a different altitude, landed, and was flung back into the air as soon as the plane was ready. The pilots and navigators drank coffee and huddled until the armorers and mechanics – all women in their Night Bombers Division – finished their work and gave the crews the thumbs-up, then they were off again. After the alarms and explosions set off on the first sortie, the Germans knew where the bombers would come from and when. The only way the women would survive was to cut engines and glide through the night, and this was why the Germans named them as they did: Night Witches.

The U-2 rumbled to a halt. Masha ran up as soon as the propeller slowed to chock the wheels. Vera was out of the cockpit and headed for her cot before Katya took her feet from the rudders and pulled down her filthy goggles. The plane shuddered to begin its day of recuperation, and in the raw silence Masha whistled. Katya glanced around her scorched U-2 from the vantage point of the cockpit, now lit by the tincture of sunlight rising above the tree line. The plane was blackened and shredded, tail to rotor. Bullet holes and shrapnel rips punctured the wings, there wasn't a five-foot length anywhere without some hole and ragged cotton.

'I heard you flapping in, you sounded like a pigeon.' Masha laughed, shaking her head at the plane. 'At least you managed not to ruin my engine.' She wiped a stained and knobby hand along the wing, leaving a trace in the soot. The mechanic's days and nights were spent with a wrench and a flashlight, contorted into small, scalding spaces, rapping her knuckles against sharp metal, taping, sewing, and ironing patches over the wounded wings and bodies of planes brought back in wretched shape. Masha was no pilot, she could not fly and did not want to. She was a lover of machines and tools. When one of her wounded pigeons climbed back into the air, she waved her arms like a mother bird. When they did not come home, and the weeping pilots and navigators of the regiment swore revenge, Masha took to her tools to help those crews do just that.

Katya lowered herself to the ground. Her legs were achy and cramped. She tugged off her cloth helmet and tossed it into the cockpit. 'Mashinka.'

'Yes.'

'What's the count so far?'

'Thirty-two out. Twenty-two in.'

For the next twenty minutes, Katya stood by her plane, watching more planes from her division land and taxi. One by one, ten more U-2s made it to the landing strip. Some engines popped, some skipped and struggled, but all ten landed and taxied. Only then did she turn from the field and trudge for the tent. She fell face-first on her cot. Vera was already snoring.

Katya dreamed of smoke and fried flesh. She reared on the cot from her stomach, up through flames the way her plane had catapulted out of them, scorched and in peril. Her ear just missed the side of a tray.

'Ho, ho, calm down, Lieutenant!'

Katya waggled her head, rolling to her side. A plate of steaming eggs and sausage was held by her bedside. Leonid Petrovich Lumanov, Lieutenant, 291st Air Assault Division, sat on a stool, knees together, the tray on his lap.

'Good morning, wing-walker.'

Katya licked her lips. They still tasted of sparks and exhaust.

'Shut up,' she growled. 'I'm going to kill Vera.'

Leonid, a fighter pilot whose squadron was based at Kalinovka alongside the Night Witches, offered the tray.

Katya sat up and took it on her own knees. Leonid was her best friend.

'Kill Vera? Not after she saved your life.'

'She saved *my* life? Vera told you … ?'

Leonid broke into a laugh and Katya felt ill-used. She rang her fork down on the plate.

'Get out!'

'No. Finish your breakfast.'

Katya crossed her hands in her lap to show her displeasure; her courage and danger had been reduced to an anecdote and a stupid nickname. Yes, Vera had acted quickly and well, but it was Katya on the seared wing, staring at the ground over the flying precipice, Katya who almost fell off the back *and* the front of the wing. But the eggs before her still steamed and the sausage glistened. She took up the fork. You'd best laugh at life, Papa always said, because it's laughing at you. Leonid nodded approval.

She glared while she chewed breakfast. This was her way of punishing him, because talking was their favorite thing to do. Leonid flew the plane Katya wanted when she joined the Red Army's Air Force, the sleek new Yak-9. Every day he got to fly high and fast, dueling with German Me-109 fighters and Heinkel bombers at 350 miles per hour, at six miles up, he soared leaving contrails of mist, while Katya *popped* and poked a few thousand feet up, always at night where her passion for flying was dimmed and lost in risk and tension. She had four little bombs, Leonid had cannons that could tear a hole in anything that got in his way. She was a Night Witch, he was a Fighter Pilot.

Katya was qualified for the fighters. When she graduated from the paramilitary *Osoaviakihm* in Krasnodar eight years ago, she was tops in the class, of both girls and boys. A year later, when only twenty, she trained at the Khar'kov Flying School and in her first year became an instructor. Then she attended the Tula Advanced Flying School and graduated with colors. When the war broke out, she'd answered a nationwide call for the formation of women's aviation regiments. She went to Moscow, was trained and tested more, and was certain of being assigned to a fighter assault division. Instead, she was made a night bomber, and there was no appeal.

She'd met Leonid the previous winter, in the fighting around Vorosilovgrad and the Terek River. He saw her standing by the airstrip during the day watching the Yaks come and go, made pleasant conversation in passing, then asked one day if she'd like to go up with him. He snuck her into the cockpit on an early morning and put her in his lap, sharing the safety harness. From that position she flew, blasting through the cold Crimean sky, spinning the Yak like a dervish until Leonid reached around and took the stick from her, shouting in her ear that he had to stop her, anyone watching would know it was not Leonid Lumanov flying, he couldn't do some of those tricks.

Leonid was a city boy, from Leningrad. He was educated and traveled, he'd been to England. He'd never known a Cossack, never been on a horse. In her U-2, Katya flew Leonid to a cavalry company resting in the rear. She put him in the saddle. The horse knew a beginner and took off like a shot. Leonid came out of the stirrups, hollering, What do I do? Katya controlled her laughter enough to shout back an old Kuban wisdom, the first thing her Papa taught her about riding: Don't fall off! A cavalry officer galloped after the fighter pilot and brought him back unharmed and pale as steam.

When their divisions were separated to different fronts, they wrote. With the erratic deliveries of wartime, the letters sometimes arrived to Katya in bunches of twos and threes. It didn't matter if she read them out of sequence, it was good to know that Leonid was well and fighting. The letters had no envelopes; they were simply sheets of paper folded neatly and tucked in, after being read by the military censors. Neither of them ever scribbled of love. Katya had made it clear, she would not fall into a romance during the war. There was no room for that kind of attachment, there was already enough turmoil and grief to fill a heart.

Her 208th Night Bombers had been in combat now for nine months without stop, chasing the Germans westward after the massive Soviet victory at Stalingrad in February of that year. Their division had flown thousands of sorties, against hundreds of targets, in their cloth and wood trainers, in biting winter weather and broiling steppe heat, in open cockpits. Leonid had never been one of the scoffing male pilots, those who thought women had no place in the sky during combat. Katya and the Night Witches had nothing to prove to Leonid. He'd stood beside the runway enough times himself, counting the returning U-2s, watching for Katya, and done the sad math. One missing, two, sometimes three or more, smiling for Katya when there were none. He told her many times the male pilots had to peacock on the ground because they were no more brave than the women in the air, and they knew it.

'If sacrifice is courage,' he said, 'trust me, they know.'

Katya finished off the eggs and sausage. She handed the tray back to Leonid, who took it with the comic attitude of a servant.

'Yes, your highness. What else can I do for you this morning?'

'Come on.'

She unraveled her long legs from the cot, she'd not even removed her boots when she'd fallen into it at dawn. Leonid followed, carrying the tray out of the tent. Scattered around the base were over a hundred planes, U-2s, Yaks, and IL-2 Sturmovik ground fighters. The aircraft received service, fuel, oil, or armaments under camouflage nets and corrugated metal hangars. Propellers fanned in low idle while mechanics checked gauges, fuel trucks skittered every which way, grimy men and women worked side by side; the chauvinism of the skies had not yet taken hold among the tools and ladders. Leonid set the breakfast tray on someone's wing. A mechanic shouted at him, but he and Katya kept walking.

'Grab that bucket.' She pointed to Leonid.

Katya waved to Masha, elbow-deep in another U-2 from their squadron. She stepped up on the wing root of her own plane and paused to admire the patchwork Masha had done. The squares of cotton had even been blotched brown and green to match the rest of the wings. Leonid came behind her and whistled at the number of holes she'd brought back from last night's mission.

Katya climbed into her cockpit. She called down to Leonid, 'Set the prop.'

He dropped the bucket and did as he was told, shoving the propeller into ready position, where the starter could grab it and heave it into rotation. Katya shouted behind her, 'Clear!' and nodded at Leonid. He shoved down on the propeller. The magnetos whirred. The propeller flung itself over once, twice, then the engine caught with a spitting sigh of smoke. Katya sat in the jouncing cockpit, smiling down at Leonid, who stood hands on hips, a handsome, admiring young man.

She let the motor run for three minutes, then shut it down. She climbed out of the cockpit, took the bucket off the ground, and held it under the radiator. Vera came running across the field, holding another empty bucket and a small packet.

'Leonya,' Vera said, shoving the bucket at him, 'be a dear and go fill this with cool water.'

Leonid raised his eyes into his brows and turned to attend to this chore.

'He's nice,' Katya said.

'You own him,' answered Vera.

The navigator unwrapped the paper packet and held up the new bar of soap she'd received in last week's mail. Katya opened the cock on the radiator and filled the bucket with hot water. Big Masha came up, black from her shoulders to her knees.

'You know you're not supposed to keep doing this,' she told Vera.

'Yes,' Vera said.

'You know I have to refill that radiator.'

'Yes, Mashinka.'

'We'll let you wash your hair, too,' cajoled Katya.

'But dear Masha, please, let us go first. There won't be any soap left.'

'This is the last time.' Masha narrowed her eyes at Vera, always the jester.

'Yes, Mashinka.'

'I mean it.'

'We know.'

'Use cold water.'

Leonid returned with the bucket of well water. His boots were sloshed.

'And you,' Masha said to him, spinning on her black heels. Katya looked down, a greasy spot on the trampled grass marked where the mechanic had stood.

'What did I do?' the fighter pilot protested.

Vera took the bucket. She liked Leonid, and encouraged Katya in his direction. Vera had her own boyfriend, a navigator in a Boston A-20 – one of the Lend-Lease bombers from America – based on the northern shoulder of the Kursk pocket.

Katya mixed the hot and cold water in the empty bucket. She pulled off her tunic, down to her green undershirt. She bent over and Vera poured the warm water over her raven hair, cut short above her ears like that of all the Night Witches. Together, the two women washed each other's hair, rubbing in the soap hard, while Leonid sat on the wing watching, saying nothing. Within minutes, several other women pilots were in the seats of their own cockpits, revving their engines, heating bathwater, and arguing with their mechanics. Katya and Vera were the ringleaders; Leonid chuckled at the influence they had in their squadron. Several male pilots walked by, probably, Katya thought, to get a look at the laughing girls in the wet undershirts. A few made snide comments, one said something to Leonid about him being the 'Witches' bath house boy,' but he did not rise from his place on the wing nor even answer. Vera heaved a bucket of cold water in the jeering pilot's direction, and Leonid had to go back to the well.

When the women had washed and rinsed their hair, they combed it flat against their heads and sat in the sun to dry it. Vera produced a small pocket mirror and the comb; the soap and these sundries were gifts from her bomber pilot. Gazing in the mirror, Katya noticed on her forehead and around her eyes her first scars from the war, the fine lines chiseled into her face from the constant strain and concentration of night flying, of wincing into the darkness to spot the smallest glimmers of targets and home, of sopping away tears on rough shirt sleeves. And though she would not admit it, she and every other Night Witch struggled and yearned to win the acceptance of the male pilots, so she flew sometimes harder and more recklessly than she otherwise might. Every one of her black, gliding missions, every friend who didn't reach the landing lights at dawn, every flak burst and averted crash, even the sneers from the male fighter pilots, was etched in her face. Looking at herself in the mirror for those seconds, she relived it all.

Leonid sat on a bucket, kicking out his ankles in a mimicry of the *gopak*, the Cossack dance. Masha rambled back and topped off the radiator without saying a word.

The two women reclined in the sun. Around the base, planes fired up and shut down, some took off, bombers flew high overhead on some mission to worry the Germans before the coming battle. In the command hut, the next mission for the Witches was planned, the objectives often were arrived at by information from the partisans. After an hour of leisure, Leonid left them, then Vera went to write a letter. Katya stood beside her bi-plane, watching Leonid walk to his Yak-9 in his flight suit, watched him take off to fly his shift of patrol duty over the aerodrome. He waggled his wings as he rose, and she knew that was for her.

June 29
2345 hours
thirteen hundred meters above no-man's-land
Voronezh Front

High clouds had moved in late in the day and stuck. There had been some afternoon thunder but no rain. Only pieces of moonlight shoved through the thick cover and the Witches sailed through a darker, better world for their mission.

Katya cruised, the third plane in line. The target was a new supply depot discovered and reported by the partisans. The U-2s' bombs would rip open crates of medicine and bandages, foodstuffs, clothes and blankets. No fireworks tonight, no fuel barrels or ammo stacks. Onions don't blow up. That's what Germans eat, Katya thought, their breath stinks of onion.

She watched the unlit earth slip by below, listening to the engine sounds muted through her quiet headset – Vera studied her maps and the ground in silence, the only times in the day she had her mouth closed – and wondered why she believed this. She had not ever met a German, though she'd bombed them for almost a year. Why was it necessary to hate them for what they ate, or what they looked and sounded like? This was Soviet thinking, Soviet propaganda playing in her head, the barking commissars always lumbering around giving out speeches and pamphlets. It was enough simply to despise the Germans because they were invaders on Russian soil, not for their difference. Katya grew up among men and women of every walk: farmers, riders, poets, brigands, musicians, there were Circassians, Tatars, Kalmuks, Khazars, Slavs, Russians, all came to the Kuban to become Cossacks, difference was the lifeblood. I'll blow up the Germans' onions tonight, she thought, and their breath will smell like mine, then we'll kill as many of them as we can not because they stink but because they are here where they don't belong. And the commissars can lumber off to hell.

She glanced over her shoulder at Vera. Her navigator held a flashlight across her lap, a stopwatch rested in the folds of her map.

'It's quiet, don't you think?' she asked Vera.

'Yes, it's quiet. Leave me alone.'

Katya let moments of engine and wind and night fly past.

'I don't like it. I'm thinking too much.'

'So stop thinking. And while you're at it, stop talking.'

Katya turned around. She surveyed the horizon ahead for the flashes that would be bombs and flak and the white sashes of searchlights. She scanned her gauges and indicators. Everything held trim and smooth, blue exhaust fires blinked and *popped* astride the motor. She felt edgy tonight, and a scan of herself did not reveal why. Was it the mission, destroying medicine and victuals, was it worth the risk taken by the women? Was her jumpiness merely fatigue and stress? If Vera were talking at the moment she would say it was Leonid. If Papa were here, he would tell his daughter to be careful tonight, a Cossack can feel events coming on the wind. Katya fidgeted in her seat, drumming her fingers on the stick.

'Come about a little to port,' Vera said into Katya's headset.

Katya twitched the stick and rudder and the plane flicked left.

'That's enough.'

Moments later, dead off the nose about six miles ahead, a small globe of orange pierced the night. This was the first sortie over the target. Within seconds, enemy searchlights like angry antennae began to wave in the air, looking for the gliding little plane somewhere over their heads, the Witch that had whisked down on them.

Katya held the U-2 steady on the explosions. She would be over the target in five more minutes. She stayed at four thousand feet. Looking over her shoulder again, she saw Vera putting away her maps; there was no need for navigation right now, the supply depot burned and the searchlights guided them in.

Above the target, no flak burst. The Germans must not have figured their vegetables and bandages were much of a target, Katya decided, they've left them bare without artillery. But why, then, are there searchlights?

The second Night Witch released her bombs; another corner of the depot erupted with four small detonations. Beacons rushed back and forth, probing for the Witch, until they found her.

'That's Zoya Petrovna,' Vera whispered, as though the Germans might hear.

Katya watched the searchlights intersect over Zoya's bi-plane. The beams were so strong she seemed to be walking on them, like giant white legs. She's a good pilot, Katya thought, and her navigator Galina Fedotova, she's clever, they'll get out of the lights. Zoya switched on her engine, rolled on her back, and dove at the ground, accelerating, pulling up into an inside loop. Katya watched and admired the maneuver. One spotlight then another slipped off Zoya's skin. Katya lost her in the darkness. Good for Zoya, she thought.

But where was the German flak?

'Cut engine,' Vera murmured. Katya pushed in the throttle and flicked the magnetos off. Vera's voice had been soft, Katya noted. She sensed something, too.

The U-2 began to glide, the propeller spun idly. She bled off a thousand feet of altitude, gaining speed toward the target now one mile away. The rush of wind picked up and Katya leaned forward over her stick as she always did, her galloping position. Her cockpit was lit only by the yellow luminance of the dials. Vera would tell her when to let go the bombs.

'Steady,' Vera intoned. 'Thirty seconds.'

Katya watched the airspeed climb, altitude slipped to twenty-five hundred. She kept her head tucked and her eyes on her gauges. She did not see what made Vera yell, 'No!'

Katya raised her head and saw the tracers, a stream of red darts a half mile away on her port side. At the end of the bullets, being ripped to ribbons, was Zoya and Galina's U-2. Katya jerked at the sight, stunned. She mouthed the same word, No.

'Night fighter.' Katya heard the same fear in her navigator's voice that thrummed in her own breast.

The Germans had a black-painted, night-flying Messerschmitt in the air. They'd never done this before. That's why there was no flak.

Zoya began to burn. A searchlight followed her. She side-slipped, turning the fuselage sideways trying to keep the fire from the plane's engine. Somewhere in the dark the night fighter banked and zeroed in again. Another pounding trail of tracers cut through Zoya like crimson scissors and then was done. Zoya's plane was aflame, green and red signal rockets spurted out of the cockpits, a crazy light show. The plane did not explode but fell, torched. The searchlights abandoned Zoya and Galina and began their quest for Katya, who looked away before the dead plane hit the ground.

'Vera.'

'Damn it!' the navigator cried. 'Damn it!'

'Where are we? Focus!'

Over the intercom, she heard Vera's lungs work, the girl huffed hard to control herself. Katya kept tight reins on her own breathing.

'Vera, stay with me.'

'Yes, yes, shut up! Wait! Alright, stay steady. Damn it. Steady.' The intercom went silent for several wind-whipping moments. Vera's voice returned.

'Alright. Get ready. Five, four, three, two ...'

Katya gripped the bomb release.

'Now!'

She pulled on the wire and thrust her free hand at the magneto switches, then the throttle. The milling propeller caught and Katya blessed Masha. She looked up out of the cockpit and saw something whisk past, straight up in front of her, a blacker piece of the night moving at five times her own speed. She cringed. She heard the roar of the German engine and felt the turbulence of his wash in her own wings. The night fighter had barely missed running into them.

Katya banked left and dove hard for the ground. A searchlight brushed her starboard wings and that was enough for the night fighter. Above her own engine Katya caught the howl of the Messerschmitt zooming down. The searchlight was gone from her plane but the German pilot had a read now on the slow-moving U-2. Red tracers ripped beneath her, she pulled up from her dive, just missing driving straight into the bullets' course. The hammer blows of the night fighter's machine-guns cut through every other sound of the night, the engine, the wind, Vera's curses, Katya's pummeling heart. Then she heard the slower thumps of cannon fire, and she thought this was ridiculous, that the night fighter needed his 20 mm cannons to stop a plywood biplane. The Germans are serious; they want the Night Witches cleared from the sky. And the Russian women made it easy for them tonight, sailing in from one direction, at one altitude. The night fighter was feeding on them like a black shark.

Katya banked hard right, plunging again to avoid the bright tower of another searchlight. The Messerschmitt screamed past. The U-2 rocked in the wake of his wailing engine. The German pulled up and away so fast, he vanished in an instant. Katya aimed at the ground, glued to her altimeter. At four hundred feet she leveled the plane out. The U-2 could fly slow enough to hug the ground and blend in with the earth.

'He's gone,' Vera said. 'Son of a bitch.'

'No, he's not. Get us home, Vera.'

Over her shoulder Katya caught the glow of Vera's flashlight. The navigator was scrambling for her maps, gazing over the cockpit for landmarks now that the night fighter had chased them out of their prescribed track. That track, Katya thought. We're going to have to change our tactics if this is how the Germans fight now. We were prepared for searchlights and flak, but not this. We've got no armor, no radios, no guns. She wished Leonid were here in his Yak-9, blasting back at the Messerschmitt. That would be a proper duel. Not this.

As if to illustrate her thoughts, Katya saw the U-2 in line behind her become snared in the white web of the searchlights. 'No, no, no,' she whispered, beseeching God or whatever power flew with the Night Witches in their ancient, plodding bombers, but her voice was screeched away by machine-guns and engine whine. The red teeth of the black shark bit the U-2 above and the little plane burst in the air, struck above the wings in the gas tank. Not even the death of the Russian girls in their little plane was louder than the bellow of the speeding German, climbing out of the way to wait for his searchlights to find him another morsel.

Katya kept at four hundred feet over the smooth, dark terrain. Vera recited the names of the crew. 'Marina Rudnova. Lily Baranskaya.' This was her need to witness, to talk out her shock and anguish. Katya's witness would be to survive, reach the airstrip as fast as she could, and stop the night's mission before their regiment was annihilated. She flew straight and low over enemy territory while Vera gathered herself and her maps.

In a minute Vera had a direction for them to fly. Katya climbed to two thousand feet, safely away from the killing zone of the supply depot burning behind them. Thirty Night Witches had set the depot on fire, that was their mission. Each one, flying in line, saw the plane in front of her attacked, some destroyed, yet stayed on course, cut her engine, sailed over the target, banked through the lights, and did her job. Katya dreaded the final tally for tonight's German vegetables and bandages. She could not spur the U-2 to go faster and her heart sickened.

CHAPTER 4

June 30
2150 hours
Wehrmacht train moving east
Treblinka, Poland

Luis Ruiz de Vega lifted a hand to snare the attention of a passing waiter. He waved his fingers over his plate, then made a sweeping motion to tell the man to take the dinner away.

'Ja, mein Herr.'

Luis had been asleep over the half-full plate. He'd not touched more than a few bites. The train slowed herky-jerky and Luis opened his eyes. He heard the waiter's German and remembered he was not in Spain, where his dream had taken him. He did not speak to the waiter – white-gloved hands swooped down dovelike and took away the tray of *schnitzel* and wafers – and so did not switch languages in his head, but continued to think in Spanish.

He'd quelled the hunger, but he knew it would return soon. A year ago he'd been shot in the stomach by the Russians, leaving him forever with appetite. His gut had been cut in half, stitched closed in an emergency field hospital to save his life. And such a life it has become, he thought, looking at the hand he'd left dawdling in the air. He could not wear his father's signet ring anymore, his fingers had shrunk too much. His face, his chest, hips, legs, everything but his bones and them, too, he believed at times, had been whittled away, the shavings of *Waffen* SS Captain Luis de Vega must be lying in a trash bin somewhere in the Berlin recovery ward of his previous eleven months.

He flipped the suspended hand over, examining his palm, then set it in his lap. In the way he'd awakened from his dream in Spanish, Luis awoke in his old form, strong and sinewy, five foot ten, the perfect physique for a man. It was the dark body that had earned him his renown, in the bullrings, then in the Civil War, next with Franco's Blue Division, and finally with the SS at the Leningrad siege, his captain's commission and his own company. The feats he could perform in that body earned him praise, women, and his nickname, *la Daga*. The Dagger. He raised the shrunken hand to his waist to finger the sheathed knife he wore on his belt, a ceremonial blade given to him by his division. On the blade was written the SS oath: *Meine Ehre Heisst Treue*. My honor is loyalty. Funny, Luis thought, smiling a wretched grin, the irony of things. Finally I have become *la Daga*. I could stick someone with these hands.

To help wake himself up, Luis dug a knuckle into his eye socket. Both were bony, there was little cushion of flesh to him anymore. The chased-away dream was of the *plaza de toros* and his father: The old man was young and the crimson *muleta* rippled in his outstretched arms, bull, blood, and dust boiled around him, the arena was packed and hot. In those days before the Civil War, Ramon de Vega's picture was painted for posters, tacked up across Barcelona, the *matador*'s son was his best *banderillero,* until the cape of Luis's eyes lifted when the train stuttered to another stop and his father disappeared. He wanted the waiter to bring back the tray of food; he was hungry again. Tidbits satisfied him now only for short periods. He'd lost the old human habit of savoring; still, on occasion the desire for it came back like the echo of a missing limb. Luis swallowed saliva instead and looked out the window. How can anyone get anywhere, he thought, aggravated, stopping like this at every station and encampment?

A Wehrmacht major sat in a seat facing him. The man was overweight, his uniform belt bit into his belly folding into the red velour chair. For all the habits Luis had lost, he'd picked up others. He viewed this major as a glutton, though the man had only a small roll about his waist, and the beginnings of a double chin. Before his wound and long, wasting convalescence, Luis was voracious for women and drink, a Spaniard set loose in wartime Germany; a muscular and hot-blooded Catalonian from the bullrings could have a field day among the cool *fräuleins*. Luis had not had sex in a year, what woman would have him, it would be like coupling with Death himself, white and skeletal? His little stomach could no longer tolerate alcohol or spicy foods. He would not laugh, what is funny to a skeleton? All his former appetites had been replaced by the one, hunger. He ate constantly – no, he nibbled, and this irked him, the memory of great skillets of paella and chilled *jarros* of sangria – and now he had become silent, his Spanish flame banked and his spirit pruned. Luis Ruiz de Vega had not yet become accustomed to what he saw in the mirror, and his hate for the Russians who did this to him smoldered like his hunger, it was never far away.

'Where are we?' he asked the major, not looking from the train window.

'Still in Poland, I'm afraid.'

'How far from the border?'

'Not too far. Northeast of Warsaw.'

The village train station bustled with soldiers on the platform. The town seemed too small for all this activity. Luis brought his head around to gaze out past the curtains on the other side of the train car. Not far from the tracks was a high and vast barbed-wire perimeter. Inside it rose a solid block fence, many watchtowers, and the peaks of a hundred barracks. The place was grim and busy.

Luis looked back to the platform. An armed guard followed three emaciated men hauling a cart filled with the luggage of the debarking passengers. The skinny men wore blue-striped wool trousers and tunics. Their heads were shaven over vacant eyes. Water could have collected in the hollows of their cheeks.

'What is this place?'

The major said, 'Treblinka.'

'A work camp?'

The major chose his words. 'Of sorts.'

Luis watched the three slaves shuffle the cart away from the train. German officers, some of them SS, walked behind their bags, clapping others on the shoulders who'd come to meet them, some saluting higher officers. The SS were *Totenkopf,* the Death's Head Division, the prison camp guards. To Luis they were fat. The slaves were the ones who looked like him.

He was careful to keep his distaste off his face in front of the watching major. There was so little padding to his features anymore, even a wince was a wrenching gesture. This train trip back to the Russian front was a revelation for him, and he did not like what he was seeing.

In 1941, Luis first crossed through Poland into the Soviet frontier as a soldier. He served in the vanguard of the troops, moving fast with the *Blitzkrieg* over enemy towns and cities, gobbling up territory and prisoners until his army hit the gates of Leningrad. There, the assault ground to a halt, and the old city was surrounded and put under siege. Millions of square miles of Poland, Ukraine, and Russia had been captured and occupied by Hitler. Luis did not know then the quality of that occupation. Why should he? He was one of millions fighting at the leading edge of the war. The rear was not his concern.

Then he took his bullet to the stomach, standing beside his tank, one of the lousy Mark IIIs, near Lake Ladoga. A Red sniper got him. As a teenager Luis had been gored by a bull, he'd guessed wrong and the bull accommodated his mistake – his father did not rush out to tend to him lying in the ring; the *matador* came last and not until the bull was bled and worn down, that was the rule, even for fathers – and the Russian bullet did not feel as bad. But Luis's bleeding did not stop and he would die, that's what the medic told him. He asked for a priest, but there were none to be brought to him. And so he faced God alone, and God reprieved him. He woke in a hospital three days after his surgery and began his recovery. He spent four months in that hospital and seven in another in Berlin learning about his new body and withered spirit. He found bit by bit that he'd become almost impervious to passion; that was left behind in the Spaniard he was. He must always have food with him, crackers, cheese, something to keep him going when the small reservoir of his stomach was empty. There was humiliation in this, it was a weakness, and Luis accepted it as his shame, and a small one as shames go. And this new body, with all it had gone through, the stitches and vomiting, so much of itself shearing away like melting ice, was almost unable to feel pain anymore. Luis, though rail thin, sensed he had become even more powerful than the distracted boy, the Spaniard, he once was.

He'd been given a few medals and ribbons and, when he was well enough, a black, tailored uniform and an assignment to return to the Eastern Front on this train as security officer.

Luis stood.

'Taking a walk?' the major asked.

'Yes.'

'I'll come along, if you don't mind. Stretch my legs.'

The major rose and followed Luis down the narrow corridor and off the train. Stepping onto the platform, the waning day was tepid and bland. Polish weather, Luis thought, it makes for an indifferent history. This country has a tradition of being conquered. Luis walked quickly through the crowd, careful not to be bumped by any of the burly bustlers leaving or greeting the train.

He stopped with his back to the warm brick wall of the station. The major stood close, protective, reading Luis's discomfort. Luis stared down the length of the train, twenty cars long. In the middle of the linkage were ten flatcars bearing brand-new Mark VI Tiger tanks. These were painted tan for the coming Kursk campaign, Operation Citadel. The tanks were marked for delivery to the SS *Leibstandarte Adolf Hitler* Division on the southern flank of the Kursk bulge. The machines were behemoths, so broad their regular treads had to be removed and narrower transport tracks put on so they could fit on the train cars. The things were mighty-looking to Luis, they seemed proud and powerful like fresh, angry bulls. They were his to deliver to *Leibstandarte*. The Tigers were supposed to guarantee victory in Operation Citadel and turn the war around again for Germany. This was the third summer of campaigning in Russia. The Reds had not buckled as expected in the first year or two under the *Blitzkrieg;* in fact, they'd held and gone over to the offensive themselves after their big victory at Stalingrad. Even so, the question was never the superiority of the German forces or the power of the tools at Hitler's command, like this Tiger under Luis's protection. No. Germany would beat Russia if given the time, if a breakthrough could be won at Kursk. But the war had dragged on so long, the calendar might soon run out of pages for German destiny. Why?

The Americans. They were coming, certain to enter the war in Europe anytime now. The Americans, powerful, an unknown quantity, like an infant grown too big, were clumsy and unpredictable. But their presence on the Continent would split Hitler's strength in half, he'd have to fight on two fronts. The Russians had to be broken before the Yanks landed, or the war in the East would take a sudden and nasty turn against Germany.

Luis had been given another chance, a rarity in war. He knew he could never win back his old body, the Spaniard; he believed he might surpass it in this new and deformed shape. He would do it in the days coming soon, in Russia, at the battle for Kursk, somehow. If the Americans left him time.

He had placed four armed men on each flatcar with the tanks. The Tigers were safe for the moment in this Polish town of Treblinka. There were no unguarded enemies here.

Without inviting the major to follow, Luis strode along the platform to where the concrete ended. He stepped down onto the blue gravel strewn beside every train track. He walked gingerly, the stones shifted even under his weight. Behind him, the major's boots crunched more assuredly than his own.

'Off to check on your Tigers, Captain?'

'Yes.'

'Quite the brutes, aren't they?'

Luis did not feel this remark required a reply and picked his way along the track. He wished the major would go back to the train and leave him alone.

'You're one of Franco's boys. The Blue Division.'

'Once. I am in the SS now.'

The major sidled up beside Luis with one long, confident stride, then kept pace easily. 'So I see.'

Luis wore the uniform of a *Leibstandarte* captain, except for two small irregularities. He was not allowed to wear the SS lightning bolt runes at the right collar, these were reserved only for Germanic members, and on his sleeve was a depiction of the Spanish flag in the shape of a shield.

The first cars behind the locomotive were filled with troops. Then came a dozen flatbeds, the first and last of them covered by green tarps. Luis strolled along the track to stop beside the first flatcar bearing a Tiger. Two SS guards facing him saluted with extended hands. He waved in the air, approximating the return salute. The two men gripped their machine pistols and went ramrod stiff until Luis and the major passed. The Tiger seemed impossibly huge up there on the flatbed, as though it might crush the supporting train wheels and platform. Luis had spent years fighting in the forerunners of this ultimate tank, the Mark IIIs and IVs. Those were toys, cap guns compared to this brute with its impenetrable armor and 88 mm gun. But the Tiger, like any weapon, had to be put in the proper hands. Luis had been *la Daga,* had once been those right hands.

The major walked beside Luis the length of the ten Tigers. At each, the guards saluted and Luis did no more than nod. He ran his hand along the treads and wheels, sensing the hard thickness of the Tigers, jealous of their girth and purpose. All was in order, the tanks were secure, the men alert.

At the last tank he climbed up on the flatbed. A guard offered him a hand but Luis refused; he was thin, not helpless. The major stayed on the ground, watching him clamber over the tank's treads then to the top of the Tiger's turret, rotated backward for transport. Luis spread his feet and put his hands on his hips. He lifted his chin to the purpling sky in the fashion of his father standing over a conquered bull. But this bull, this Tiger, would be much tougher to put down. The metal radiated strength. The 88 mm gun was the largest cannon carried by any battle tank in the world. Its armor was the thickest. Its design was German. Its purpose was conquest.

Luis felt an old stirring, standing up here. He could wrap a Tiger around his frail body and be frail no more. He would be this powerful, unutterably powerful, thing.

'You look good up there, Captain,' the major shouted. 'You've stood on tanks before.'

Luis looked down on the major, heavy, earthbound. He answered, but not loud enough for the major to hear, only to himself. 'Yes.'

'What can you see?' the major called up.

Luis surveyed the camp across the tracks here in Treblinka. From this height he gazed beyond the concertina wire and over the block wall. The camp sprawled in every direction, a massive place of incarceration. Machine-guns were manned in watchtowers every fifty meters. Guards walked the perimeter with dogs. He looked back along the tracks and saw a separate rail line split off and enter the camp. The train cars inside the camp were not for transporting people but livestock. And there they were, the people of the camp, blue-striped and wilting, shaven-headed, shuffling, beaten, miserable in their final forms. He guessed at the numbers that could be housed in the endless barracks: twenty thousand at a time, perhaps more. A tall brick chimney dominated the camp, rising out of a rectangular building. A wrought-iron sign arched above the entryway to the camp, it read *Arbeit Macht Frei*. Work Makes Freedom.

Luis lowered his eyes to the colossal tank under his boots. Here were the twin faces of the war fought by Germany in Europe. The one face he knew; he'd stared into and embraced it – the face of battle, honor, this face was German in making but Spanish in spirit, hot and glorious. Yes, he'd been wounded and lost so much, but he did not blame war itself, these were the risks you took for the reward if you survived. But this other face, this Treblinka. Luis had passed this way three years in a row: once riding to the attack in 1941, when Treblinka was not the rear but a battlefield; a year later, he returned, flat on his back, sedated in a hospital train and he did not see the way Germany occupied the nations it mastered; and now heading east again, taking Hitler's tanks to Russia, looking over this fence. The smoke from that chimney. Luis spit and watched the white gob fall far to the ground.

'What do you see?' the major asked again.

It did not have to be like this, Luis thought. The Polish people, the Russians, all of Europe, they might have been glad to have us, welcomed Hitler as a liberator from the tyrant Stalin and his atheist Communists. Not now. Not under the pall of that smoke. Now they will fight every inch, with every breath. Now they will all have to be defeated or killed, because they will never stop hating.

Luis raised his eyes one last time to the camp before climbing off the tank. The prisoners were starved, phantoms of men. I know well, he thought, very well how much you can hate the ones who've done this to you.

June 30
2220 hours
Wehrmacht train moving east

Luis went into the bathroom of the train car. He wanted to clean off the sweat of his exertion from walking the tracks and climbing on the Tiger. He needed to wash away Treblinka.

He unbuttoned his tunic, raised his arms and splashed water from the sink under his pits and over his shoulders. He stopped and looked at himself in the mirror. There were the dark eyes of Luis but where was the rest of him? That was his black hair spread across the reflected chest, but where was the muscle? Those ribs, like the naked spars of a boat. He stared at the figure in the mirror, the close walls of the train's water closet rattled around him as the train bumped along. He cupped a handful of water, leaned over the sink, and played the water over his brow and jet hair. He gazed down into the white scoop of the china bowl, waiting a moment, then stood straight and looked in the mirror again. There he was, his image also the white of porcelain. He slicked his wet hair down and considered himself. He raised a hand to the mirror; the gaunt reflected man reached back and they touched. They spoke.

'*Lo jugue, y lo perdí.*'

You played, and you lost.

Cool drips trickled down his chest, he watched them undulate over the corduroy of his ribs. He dried with wads of paper towel and put on his black shirt. When he was dressed again the mirrored man was a captain in the SS. This man Luis touched too, and he reached back, as well.

'*Soy yo,*' they said.

It's me.

Luis returned to his seat. The major was still there. His eyes were closed and his hands lapped over his ample belt-line. He opened his lids when Luis sat. He cheered immediately.

'We've still got a ways to go,' the major chirped.

'Yes, it seems.'

'I expect we'll get to Kiev tomorrow afternoon and Belgorod sometime the next morning.'

Luis gazed out the window. The world whizzing by donned the first shawl of night, it would indeed be a long trip hauling those Tigers into Russia. The major seemed pleasant enough, eager to be obliging. Luis did not know the man's name.

He leaned forward to shake hands.

'SS Captain Luis Ruiz de Vega.'

The officer took his hand. 'Major Marcus Grimm.'

The major made his own voice more comfortable than had Luis, an effort to put the younger officer at ease.

'What division are you with, Captain?'

Luis sat back. '1st SS Panzergrenadier Division *Leibstandarte Adolf Hitler*.'

He'd not been with his division in almost a year. It felt strange to say he was part of them anymore. He was a delivery man at the moment. He did not know what role waited for him in the coming battle after the tanks were off-loaded and gone from the Belgorod station. Would he be sent back on the train? Perhaps. But God had given him this second chance in Russia. He would wait and see, it's all one can do with God.

'And you?'

'Interestingly, I'm with 4th Panzer Army. I'm the liaison officer assigned to *Leibstandarte*.'

Luis nodded. Of course.

'You're here to keep an eye on me,' he said.

'Oh, no,' the major laughed, 'not you, really. More the Tigers than anything else. I'm just here to help. The *Führer* has a lot at stake on those tanks.'

The major smiled, taking in Luis. His eyes made Luis think there was much more to him than the major could possibly be seeing.

'But I do think you bear close watching, Captain. May we talk awhile?'

Luis saw no option. The major was his superior, though he was not an SS officer.

'Of course.'

Major Grimm settled into his seat, his hands layered again over his waist. 'Tell me how a young Spaniard comes to be in the SS. Tell me about the Blue Division. And if it's not still too fresh for you to talk about,' and here the major waggled a finger at Luis, not at his face but at his body, 'tell me what happened.'

The major's manner was kind. Luis and he were riding a slow train through the night, over conquered lands. Luis recalled how he used to love conversation when he was the other man, not the one in the mirror. Over wine and *cervezas,* along the beach and in cafés on the Ramblas, with friends and lovers he would jaw and laugh, he had tales from the bulls and Spanish Morocco and the Civil War. And tonight this fat Major Grimm seemed to see the other man – the young Spaniard, as he called Luis. Not the victim. He saw *la Daga*. For Luis, this was the first time in so long.

'Alright,' he said.

The bull charged into the arena flinging snot, searching, angry, bred to be angry. He lunged at the big capes waved at him in clumsy, hurried *verónicas*. The old *matadors* ran the bull about to charge him up, then finished and dashed behind the boards from the onrushing horns. The *picador* on horseback trotted in holding his lance high, his horse plumed and plucky. He did not wait for the *toro* but assailed it instead. Three jabs between the bull's shoulders began the flow of blood down the shoulder and cut tendons to lower the bull's head, bleeding him but making him wary and madder. Luis's heart pumped with the bull's, waiting for the *picador* and his stunning mount to finish. When the trumpet sounded, the *picador* withdrew, the arena applauded, and the next stage of the *corrida* belonged to Luis.

He leaped out, shouting *Toro, heh! Toro, heh!* He held his two *banderillas,* barbed sticks wrapped in ribbon, close over his head as though they were his own horns. He mimicked the bull's pawing foot with his boot, raising dust and wild clapping in the hot, brimming arena. He took his eyes from the bull and glanced into the stadium, the crowd knew he was the son of Ramon. He'd practiced this move on leather bulls for five years, pushcarts in his father's hands. Finally, this was no barrow with strapped-on horns but a *toro* charging. Luis waited, waited, he felt nothing but the barbs in his raised hands; the *toro* bore down and Luis held motionless. Then he began to run at the bull, at the lowered horns, not dropping his hands and the *banderillas*. Close enough to see into the eyes of the *toro* – they were black and blank with stupidity and rage – Luis vaulted aside, nimble as wind, and drove the sticks into the crimson gash opened by the *picador*. The barbs bit deep, the ribbons unraveled and fluttered and the bull thundered past. Luis thrust his empty hands in the air and galloped away under a canopy of applause. Blood spattered the silver trousers of his *traje de luces,* his suit of lights.

Once the bull was stuck more times by the other *banderillas,* the trumpet sounded again, and Luis retired to the wall to watch his father; for the first time Luis wore the silver while his father wore the gold. Out Ramon came for the *faena,* the last part of the bullfight, to music and shouts, and he butchered the bull. It was the worst performance Luis had ever seen from his father. Ramon de Vega was renowned across Spain for the grace of his maneuvers with the *muleta,* his nearness to the horns, the blood he swiped from the bull onto himself. The cape of Ramon was the passing of the veil of God for the bull, a daring and honorable final act. The *trincherazo,* with one knee on the ground. The *pasa de la firma,* where the *matador* stands in one place and runs the bull around him in a dangerous circle. The *manoletina,* holding the *muleta* behind the body. And the *natural,* where the sword, the *estoque,* is removed from behind the cape to make the cloth a smaller target, tempting the bull to charge at the largest thing it sees in its fury, the *matador*. Luis watched his father hesitate in all these, Ramon failed to engage fully and the bull lost its fury. His father's passes were mechanical, not the flow of the blood and heat that was Spain and the fame of Ramon de Vega. The bull stopped and the father was left with nothing, the unsure crowd sat on its hands. Ramon dropped the *muleta,* pointed the sword, and waited. The bull glowered at him, exhausted and dumb. Ramon ran at the bull. The animal was done with it and stood detached. Ramon rose and drove the *estoque* between the shoulder blades and the bull stumbled at the pain but did not fall; the blade had missed the aorta. This was a disgrace for a *matador*. The art of the bullring was to live dangerously with the bull, then to reward it with a swift and beautiful death. Boos from the cheap seats in the sun hurtled down like thrown trash and Luis ran into the ring, unsheathing his knife. He approached the bull quickly. He measured the place at the base of the bull's skull, in front of the golden hilt of the *estoque* wobbling, useless, and plunged his short broad blade as hard as he could to sever the spinal column there. He was sixteen years old and weeping for his father. The bull buckled and fell. Luis left the ring, the bull's blood sticky in his fist. He found his father inside the *toril*, beside the pen in a corner. The man's golden suit of lights would not go dim, even in the shadows of the pen. Luis held out the knife and his stained hand and said to him, 'Father.'

The man's eyes were as red as the blood on Luis's dagger.

'Father, a de Vega killed the bull. It doesn't matter.'

'I'm ashamed you saw that. I wanted it to be the best bull, for your first day in the *corrida*.'

'Then it was the best bull. Because you wanted it to be. Thank you.'

His father looked at the knife. He sniffled and smiled at once, a wonderful maneuver.

'You were fearless out there,' Ramon told his son.

'Because,' Luis said, 'you wanted me to be.'

An hour later, Ramon de Vega engaged his second bull, the final and the greatest of the six in that day's *corrida*, and he was magnificent. He won the crowd again and was awarded two severed ears from the wonderfully dead bull. Circling the ring, Ramon held up the ears to the roaring crowd. Luis walked behind him gathering off the ruffled dirt the tossed roses, wineskins, hats, cigars, and ladies' fans.

The year was 1934. Luis intensified his apprenticeship under his father, learning all the passes, and perfecting his courage as a *banderillero*. He would become the next generation of great *matadors* in the de Vega lineage. One day he came home and told his father his friends had come up with a nickname for him, The Dagger.

But around him, boiling about his family and the bullrings, across Barcelona and all of Spain, was civil unrest. The elected Republican government had for several years begun to unravel the ancient influences of the Church in Spain. Luis's father despised the Republicans as socialists and middle-class reformers, handmaidens of the Communists. Ramon told Luis many times the government wanted to sweep away old Spain, a society built on Catholicism, monarchy, and the military, buttressed by birthright and honor. The Republicans wanted to reform the country into a little model of Russia, where there was fake equality among men, all were laborers, there were no peasants, no noblemen, and there was no God for anyone.

In Barcelona, a Republican bastion in Catalonia, Luis watched the violence grow. Priests were murdered – he saw a mob force a priest to lie on the ground with his arms spread in the shape of the cross before they chopped his arms off – nuns violated, and churches desecrated. Brawls spilled into the streets, it was the old and the new come to blows. Labor groups became vigilantes in what was known as the Red Terror, they rounded up suspected opponents and held midnight courts and dawn executions. Luis was kept away from the fights and the virulent politics by his father. But revolution was brewing. Even practicing his passes with the *muleta* and his thrusts with the dagger and the *estoque*, Luis saw the revolt coming.

In 1936, the Republican Catalonian governor shut down the bullrings, claiming the events were anti-Socialist. The energies of the people would be better spent building the new Spanish culture, not hewing to old, violent traditions. Ramon de Vega saw no hope for peace; a delirium was in Spain and it had to be thrashed out between the Soviet-backed Republicans and the unyielding supporters of old Spain, the Nationalists. He sent his son away from the bulls, into the Nationalist army, to serve in Spanish Morocco under his old friend, General Francisco Franco.

Within four months, the uprising in Spain erupted. Franco needed his army to come quickly from Morocco, and he got the help he needed from the German *Führer* Hitler. Luis boarded a German airplane with the rest of Franco's loyal army and headed over the Straits of Gibraltar for the mainland.

For the next three years, Luis Ruiz de Vega fought in the armored division. His tanks were supplied by the Nazis and the Italians. They were all lightly protected, creaky playthings and pitifully gunned. Mussolini sent his CV-3s, Hitler his Panzer Mark Is. Neither could withstand a direct hit from the smallest anti-tank guns of the Republicans, and neither stood a chance against the fast Russian T-26s with their 45 mm guns. Luis learned to be sly in his tanks, to come from the flank and behind, to dodge the horns of the enemy, always relying on speed and cunning more than strength. He earned promotions to squad and platoon leader, then company commander, leading as many as a dozen tanks into battle.

In the three years of the Spanish Civil War, Luis became an ace, *la Daga*, destroying more than fifty Republican tanks in the battles for Madrid, Málaga, Bilbao, Segovia, and finally, his homeland, Catalonia. He fought alongside the German Condor Legion, and began his study of their language. Fighting on the side of the Republicans were

English and French, and Luis hardened his heart against these nations for supporting the Communist enemy. Franco's alliance with Hitler led Luis to follow the events outside Spain in greater Europe. In March of 1938, Nazi Germany stormed into Austria. In October, Germany captured Czechoslovakia. Luis had no real love for the creed of the Nazis – their fascism and its required dictator, this would not be right for Spain; his own land needed the Church and its older, perhaps more backward ways – but Hitler had been a good ally and his troops were superb. In March of '39, Madrid fell at last to the Nationalists and Generalissimo Franco assumed power to end the Civil War, reuniting the country. Luis went home to Barcelona and his father. He was convinced that the New Order in Spain was going to flow from Franco; he knew, too, the new face of greater Europe would be Hitler's.

Luis told his father he'd made up his mind to remain in the military. This was where fresh glory for the de Vega family would arise, not from the bulls. Surely Hitler would conquer Europe. How could he not? Who would stop him? The English and the French had not lifted a finger to hinder Germany's expansions. Nor had the Americans. The Russians had been whipped with German help right there in Spain, for all to see. When the European war came, Luis intended to help the Germans. When that war was won, he would return to Barcelona a hero, a powerful man, a de Vega with a debt from Hitler himself. Luis stood before his father a decorated veteran, a man in every right. Ramon took his son into the courtyard, gripped the handles of the old bull-barrow and rushed at him. After a half hour, the *matador* laughed. 'So, you've lost your skills as a *banderillero*.' Ramon gave his blessing for Luis to stay a soldier.

Within five months of the Spanish Civil War's end, Hitler invaded Poland. France and England declared war on Germany. Franco kept Spain neutral. Hitler came to

Spain seeking repayment for the debt of blood won by his legions, his tanks and planes in Franco's service during the Civil War. But the Generalissimo refused even to let German troops march across Spain to attack the British garrison in Gibraltar. After their conference, Hitler was quoted as saying, 'I'd rather have three or four teeth out than meet that man again.' Luis agreed with Franco; Spain had suffered enough in the previous three years. Over a half-million Spaniards had died fighting or by the executions. War had gorged on Spain, it was time to feed elsewhere. That place was to be Russia.

Franco paid his debt to Hitler in another manner. He raised the Blue Division, twenty thousand strong. Their colors were that of the Nationalist Falange Party, they wore red berets and dark blue shirts. By handing the Blue Division to Hitler, Franco averted the threat of Axis invasion across the Pyrenees. The Blue Division, like the soldiers in every army who go to battle on foreign soil, was made up of every kind of man, with every sort of reason. Many were fervid anti-Communists or pro-German. Some were adventurers, others were starving in Franco's new Spain and joined for the food and clothes. Most were professional soldiers in the Spanish army and war was their craft. The youngest ones of these, like Luis, went to invade Russia to coat themselves in glory for their return to Spain, or to find death instead.

The Blue Division left Madrid in July 1941, for training in Germany. Luis, because of his combat experience and ability to speak German, was made a captain. In October, the Blue Division was shipped across the Russian frontier.

Luis fought to the gates of Leningrad. His Latin troops were brave and loyal, but were treated badly by their German superiors. The Blue Division was given poor equipment and worse support in the field, and their strength ebbed. America entered the war after the Japanese attack on Pearl Harbor, and Hitler's *blitz* ground to a halt at the approach to Moscow. By February of 1942, Franco began to press for the withdrawal of his gift to Hitler. The Blue Division became the butt of jokes in Spain while its men suffered on the frozen Eastern Front.

Luis did not want to go home. He believed the war on Russia could still be won by Germany. He needed to hold on to his chance to be as great as his father; he would change from Falange blue to starched black linen and silver eagles, to match the gold suits of Ramon. He would win with his own courage, not applause and flung wine-skins, but power, that was the spoil with which he intended to return to Barcelona, a conqueror of Russia and Europe. He and his father would compare wounds, gored by bulls or bullets, and they would be equals. Luis asked to transfer into the *Waffen* SS, in order to stay in the war when the Blue Division was called home. Luis was accepted into the SS division *Leibstandarte,* retaining his captain's rank, and given a Mark IV tank to command. He served with the SS for six months and in that time became convinced the German soldier was the most potent weapon in the world. They possessed Europe already. And they surely would not lose to the Russians.

Then came his wound.

While Luis lay in a hospital – cut open and closed again, a chunk of him in a bucket and tossed away – the world saw Stalingrad and the Soviet counteroffensive that shoved the German army all the way west beyond Kursk. While he convalesced, the Germans occupied their territories with death camps and slaves and showed themselves brutes, as bad as the Communists. While Luis learned again to swallow and walk, while his body dissipated, the war soured against Germany. He could have left the hospital and gone home, and he might have.

But not the way he healed, not with the flesh and time he'd lost. What did he have to take with him back to Spain? He'd not even told his father yet in his letters what happened to him. No. The only hope for Luis Ruiz de Vega was if the Americans would hold off their invasion in Europe, if the German assault on Kursk would go well, then he could get his hands on what he came to Russia for the first time with the Blue Division, and why he was here again with the SS on this train, rumbling across the border in the pit of night, late, tired, and once more hungry, talking with this fat officer.

To return with honor – to become the hero so he can become again the son and the Spaniard.

He did not say this to Major Grimm. But the German listened keenly and nodded, and knew it.

CHAPTER 5

June 30
1010 hours
a Luftwaffe JU-52
altitude fifty-seven hundred meters above Rakovo, Soviet Union over the German front lines

Abram Breit folded to his hands and knees. He crawled out onto the thick, clear pane in the nose of the plane. Breit wobbled, unsteady even on all fours.

A reconnaissance photographer lay flat on his stomach across the swath of clarity. The man ignored Breit creeping up at his side. A blue and green eternity yawned beneath them. Only wispy pads of clouds seemed to separate them from the planet. Breit laid flat, too, and he thought they looked like riders on an invisible magic carpet.

The photographer snapped pictures of the army on the staging zone below. He plugged his headphones into a jack in the fuselage beside him. Instantly his earphones came alive. He heard the pilot laughing at him.

Breit looked back up the companionway to the cockpit. The pilot quieted.

The photographer took shot after shot, flipping the film advance on his big camera. Breit finally looked down now. His chest squeezed. He laid his palms flat on the big plastic sheet to remind himself that it was there.

The JU-52 flew as high as it could go. Below, a tan and green immensity spread to every compass point; this was the Russian steppe, a vast ocean of grasses. Breit had been told about the dirt of the steppe, how it was rich black beneath the grasses and little forests. Dark telltales of turned soil marred the ground, betraying where German tanks, artillery, trucks, and tractors churned over the Soviet plain. The photographer recorded these scratches in the earth, the telltales of the German movement forward, this unprecedented concentration of men and weapons for Citadel, scheduled to begin in a few days.

Breit had instructed the pilot to fly over the center of the southern shoulder of the Kursk bulge, above II SS Panzer Corps. The three elite SS divisions – Breit's own *Leibstandarte*, plus *Totenkopf* and *Das Reich* – were arrayed side by side across from the dug-in Red 6th Guards Army. Abram Breit had seen these positions many times before, marked on large maps in the war chambers of Berlin, portrayed by little blocks with black or red flags for each unit. He had never before viewed a real army in the field, just in parades, an endless gray wash of men strutting past Hitler standing on high, arms jutted in salute. Breit lay with his chest and legs pressed against open blue space, a flying man, and gazed down for his first look at the loaded guns of war.

He knew all the numbers: as an intelligence officer and a spy, information was his sole value. Germany had nearly a quarter million men on the southern front, spearheaded by a thousand tanks and self-propelled assault guns, thirty-five hundred artillery pieces and mortars. II SS Panzer Corps alone held thirty thousand men, 390 tanks, one hundred self-propelled assault guns. The bulk of the tanks manned by SS crews were Mark IIIs and IVs, with a smattering of captured and repainted Soviet T-34s. The SS divisions fielded no Panthers, and only forty-two Tigers. Abram Breit scanned the ground, slowly becoming oblivious to the discomfort of lying above the clouds on a pane of nothing. He envied the magnifying lens of the photographer's camera, for it would bring him closer to the tiny forces so far below. Breit longed to catch sight of a Tiger tank; from what he'd heard of their gargantuan size, they ought to be visible even from up here. He saw a few wide paths in the dark loam of the steppe, considered they might be the tracks of Mark VIs, and thrilled a little. A new squeeze eddied in his chest, excitement.

The plane kept on course, due north. The photographer raised his head to load another canister of film. For a moment, he tilted his face to Breit, a red bull's-eye circled one socket, then shook his head sadly. The photographer loaded the camera with expert hands and looked down, not into his lens but through the plastic floor, at the vast steppe teeming with weapons and soldiers. He shook his head again in private dismay, then lowered his brow to the camera and returned to his snapping and whirring task.

Hitler had assembled an impressive strike force here in the heart of Russia. To get it, the *Führer* had waited three months, much longer than some of his generals had wanted. But Hitler had to be certain he had in place a big enough hammer to break through the Soviet lines. And such numbers, Breit thought. To see those numbers on the page, then to view them in real life ... remarkable. Powerful. The humanity, the machines, the materials, every bit of it as far as he could see was dedicated, cocked for battle.

The reconnaissance plane droned above a stretch of bare grasses, untrampled land, and gleaming streams. This open band was perhaps three kilometers wide. This was no-man's-land between the two facing armies.

The photographer's fingers accelerated on the camera. He took furious pictures. Breit pressed his nose to the plastic sheet beneath him, to see better what loomed below. Breath snagged in his chest.

'Oh my God.'

The density of the Soviet defense works had been a startling thing to contemplate in Berlin when all Breit saw was facts and figures, intel photos, red blocks on broad map tables. He'd indicated the Red forces many times with long pointers, he'd moved them around like little game pieces. But this colossal network carved into the earth below him beggared his imagination. This was no game board.

Confronting the German armies all across the southern shoulder, the Reds had built a great scab of six hundred thousand men. Nine thousand artillery pieces. Almost two thousand tanks. Breit was aware of the numbers, of course. But he'd never had an inkling that these hordes of Russian men and weapons were so incredibly well dug in. Sprawling to the horizon, trenches and earthworks rived the steppe like the veins behind an eye, uncountable channels splintered the dark dirt. Fat bunkers guarded every approach, anti-tank ditches resembled dry riverbeds in their hugeness, fortress-like berms surrounded clustered artillery. There were men, horses, trucks, everywhere digging, moving earth, stacking mounds, and gouging trenches against the coming of Citadel. Every open piece of land, Breit knew, was girded with mines and wire, presighted by thousands of long barrels, rows of gunnery in every caliber. Deep echelons of tanks were embanked up to their turrets. Under the constant scratching of the Russians, the earth's skin had hived up for them what appeared to be an impenetrable depth of walls and furrows. There was no path unprotected, no meter that would go unchallenged or unbloodied.

The Soviets had put to good use Hitler's wait. While the *Führer* fiddled, stalling for another few thousand soldiers, for a few more Tiger tanks, the Reds had reshaped the earth inside the Kursk pocket.

Breit spoke into his microphone.

'Pilot.'

The answer crackled. 'Yes, sir.'

'Aren't we getting rather far behind enemy lines?'

'Yes, sir.'

The tingle in Breit's chest returned. 'Why don't they stop us? Where are their fighters?'

'No need to worry, Colonel. The Reds don't care. We're not bombing anything. Just taking a look around.'

The pilot laughed again. In Breit's earphones, the sound was tinny and wicked.

Breit's transfer to Citadel had been unexpected, his orders arrived in Berlin yesterday morning by motorcycle courier. This was a promotion, he was appointed intelligence officer for *Leibstandarte* at the front. He was far beyond art and paperwork now, thirty kilometers behind Russian lines. There'd been no time to arrange anything with his Lucy contacts to continue his espionage before he was transferred to Russia. Could he find a way to get in touch with his spymasters even here in the battle zone? Could they find him somehow? From the looks of things below, he'd already done plenty as it was. Perhaps too much? Breit was frightened. He wanted the defeat of Germany, yes. He was committed to this belief – he risked his life every day for it – that Hitler and the Nazis would lead Germany and much of the world to a bad end. But what else had he done by helping the Russians? Had he set the table for Germany's annihilation? The battle that was shaping up below was going to be extraordinary, likely the greatest land battle in all history. How much of Germany would survive it? Would he? Breit wanted a cigarette very much.

The pilot continued, 'Oh, they want us to see this. As much as we can. Half those tanks and field pieces down there are made out of poles and straw.'

He did not believe the pilot, that so many of those guns were fake. Breit had reason to suspect differently.

The plane traced the road headed north to Oboyan. Breit floated above three concentric layers of Soviet strongholds, each more formidable than the last. The photographer whirled through endless rolls of film. Across the window, exposed rolls danced around him on the plane's vibrations. Breit lay on his belly staring in realization and awe at what he had done.

The strongest of all the Soviet forces had burrowed in directly along the Oboyan road, opposite the three SS divisions. This was surely a result of the secrets Breit had stolen and delivered to Lucy. He had coded and dropped them in Berlin trash bins, left them on benches, in newspapers and brown bags, in the Tiergarten, in museums and alleys. And now, grown to inconceivable proportions, *voilà,* there the secrets were.

This was a massive Russian army that knew every move the German generals had made.

This was Breit's handiwork, his painting.

The pilot banked sharply for the German lines. Breit skidded on the smooth pane; under his belly now was nothing but blue air. His vertigo returned. On his hands and knees again, he scooted off the clear floor and stumbled to his seat in the fuselage.

Breit buckled in and closed his eyes. He was relieved that, for a little while, until this plane set down in Russia, there would be nothing more for him to see.

CHAPTER 6

June 30
1030 hours
two kilometers east of Syrtsev
along the Oboyan road

Dimitri craned his neck back and gazed high. A big German plane droned, flying alone above lacy cloud cover. The cross of the plane was far in front of where its sound seemed to come from. Dimitri always resented this illusion of flight; it was a technological marvel created in his lifetime; he was a horseman, a plainsman, and a farmer. He didn't like the trick played on his senses by the plane. But this one dropped no bombs and was not chased away by Russian fighters. This was probably only a reconnaissance flight, so Dimitri saved his curses. The Germans were snapping photos from three miles up of what Dimitri studied from ground level from his roost on a barrel.

He imagined what the German flyers saw. The yellowish-gray topsoil of the Kursk region highlighted every large-scale move made by both sides. The moment you turned the soil here over with a spade, a bulldozer, a tire or a tank tread, you uncovered that black steppe dirt, painting streaks on the earth like ink arrows that could be seen from the air with ease. So the Germans know what we're doing, Dimitri thought, keeping his eye on the lazy enemy plane.

He lowered his gaze to the ground, to the immensity of the scars scratched in it stretching as far as he could see, and thought, I'd go home. I wouldn't attack this.

Three miles below the high ground where he sat sky-watching flowed the skinny Luchanino River. On its banks, one mile to his right, stood the emptied village of Syrtsev. Two miles the other direction was the village of Luchanino. Every silo and home in these places had been turned into a fortification, embedded as part of the 6th Guards defensive works running east-west beside the Oboyan road. The little ghost towns were bristling with weapons and soldiers dug in behind their walls. Now the towns were solid with metal and a vigor that was never given to them in peacetime. Syrtsev and Luchanino, and Alekseyevka two miles to the west on the riverbank, served their greatest purpose now, waiting to be destroyed, to maul the Germans when they came to cross the Luchanino River here. To Dimitri's left was the Oboyan road, the grand prize for the German assault, potholed and shredded but busy anyway with tanks and trucks moving up. Taking the Oboyan road was pivotal for Germany; the poor condition of Russia's transportation system was one of the country's greatest defenses. Germany had to control the few paved surfaces to bring up supplies, fuel, and reinforcements. Sending their trucks overland through the endless bogs, overrunning streams, mud, and fields of this immense country was not possible for them. Russians alone knew how to navigate the eternal muck, endless snows, swelling rains, the vast distances, with horses, wagons, hand-pulled carts, blisters, courage, anger. This is Russia, Dimitri thought. It does not want to be conquered.

Overhead the German plane banked. It's going to circle awhile, Dimitri noted, there's lots to photograph down here.

He kicked his feet against the barrel, dancing his heels

on the canister full of diesel fuel. He smiled, almost merry at the scope of the coming battle. This is how you fight a war, he decided. Historic. Big.

Dimitri did not know the numbers, the actual size of what he saw, and he did not care. It was enough that right in front of him – perhaps ten miles across on this clear day, crammed on this flat tableland of central Russia, from the Oboyan road west past the Pena River – was the greatest concentration of rifles, tanks, anti-tank guns, artillery, mines, barbed wire, blockhouses, and obstacles assembled in the entire war. All the big guns were concentrated and pre-aimed at key points. Over forty thousand anti-tank and anti-personnel mines had been laid in the ten-mile front of his 6th Guards; that was more than a mine per foot, over a million mines across the whole of the Kursk salient, the explosives laid during the spring in bare fields that were now overgrown with maize, wheat, mustard, sunflowers, and steppe grasses to make the mines almost impossible to detect. The defense works had arisen immense and deep. He'd driven his T-34 past these positions, called *pakfronts,* during weeks of drills and scrambles. Sixth Guards alone manned two belts in depths up to ten miles and widths to twenty. And there were thirteen more Soviet armies with defenses just as solid throughout the Kursk bulge, with seven extra armies held in reserve. There were eight defensive belts in all, the first three of which were gargantuan, and every one of them was connected by trenches, there must have been a thousand miles of trenches dug on 6th Guards' front alone. Dimitri shook his head at just what little parcel of it all he could see. When the Germans finally do attack, they'll have to wade through more than hell. Hell will be just their front door.

What kind of force have the Germans put together on their side to believe they can smash through this? It's got to be just as big. Just as historic. Dimitri thumped his heels again on the barrel to let the stupendousness of the idea sink in. He was a part of this history, though just a small and insignificant mote. Beneath the humming German plane come to take his picture sitting on his barrel, Dimitri resolved that insignificance would not be his lot.

He stood from the barrel, his rear was sore and imprinted by the metal rim. He waved to the departing reconnaissance plane. Goodbye, he wished to the German pilot and photographer. I hope you got a good look.

He brought his eyes down to the massive groundworks growing by the shovelful in front of where he stood. The sound of the plane faded, the slips of clouds obscured the wings.

Dimitri stretched and yawned. He looked down the little rise from where his company of tanks sat under camouflage netting. One hundred meters away, a thousand civilians hacked at the earth with shovels and picks to excavate an anti-tank trench. He had been watching these girls, women, and old men work all morning, they dug like people out of the Bible, ancient Jews building something for a pharaoh, they filled buckets with dirt and the dirt was hauled away in barrows to dark piles, and these piles were hauled elsewhere to build protective berms. The ditch had grown to over ten feet deep and wide; it was perhaps a half-mile long. No tank could go into that and expect to get out. These trenches would serve to funnel the enemy attack to preordained channels, directly into minefields or under the sights of Soviet artillery. Dimitri had spent his morning watching these human ants nibbling at the steppe to change it, this was their own fight against the invaders.

'Hey, Andrei!' Dimitri shouted over to the next tank in line.

'Yeah!'

'Keep an eye on the *General* for me.' Valentin was gone

in a company truck to pick up their new crew for the *General*.

Dimitri recalled the Cossack fable about the old stallion and the young colt. The young one said to the old, Let's run down the hill and get us a filly! The old stud shook his great mane and replied, No. Let's walk down and get them all.

Dimitri strode into the steppe grass, the reeds were as high as his waist, the color of bare and untanned skin. He ran an open hand over their tops and recalled the feeling of silk skirts, long, clean hair, and gentle, nervous flesh. It had been a while.

He walked to the lip of the trench and stopped. He was an old horse, yes, but he only wanted the one. He looked down at her, he'd kept a watch on this one all morning from his perch on the fuel barrel. She was one of dozens toiling below his boot-tips at the lip of the trench but she stood out. She would not lean on her shovel handle and gab, she paused only to mop sweat from her brow. She assaulted the soil and heaved great heaping shovelfuls into the waiting buckets, filling them with only three or four loads of her spade. She was not lean like some hungry peasant waif but a woman, with curves and swoops in her figure, she was ample. Around her worked old men in hats and beards with shirtsleeves rolled up, and girls dressed in billowy blouses and patterned skirts with kerchiefs around braided hair. She laughed once at something one of the girls said and he'd heard her through the scraping of a hundred tools and grunts and flopping dirt. He picked up an empty bucket with a rope attached to its handle and tossed it down into the trench. It landed with a hollow thump just where he willed it, at her feet.

Without looking up, the woman righted the bucket. With a few deep stabs of her shovel, she topped it with dirt. She paused now to run her sleeve across her forehead. The bucket did not disappear the way it was supposed to. She followed the slack rope up the trench wall into Dimitri's hands.

'Take it away,' she said.

Dimitri tilted his head at her now that he had her eyes on him. Her voice was like her body, deep and round. He liked it.

'Take it away,' she said again, knowing what the old fool over her head was doing. She made her voice an instruction, a schoolmarm to a stupid student.

Dimitri inclined his head as though she were royalty and tugged up the bucket. He dumped it at his own feet, not on the pile behind him where the dirt belonged, and tossed the pail down to her again. She raised her eyebrows and turned away to another empty bucket. She filled that, and found Dimitri at the rope of this one too, pulling it to the surface to dump the dirt again in the wrong place.

She turned on Dimitri. Even ten feet below him, her eyes were sea green.

'You're not helping.'

Dimitri put his hands to his hips. He pretended to be wounded by her scold.

'You're right,' he said. 'I'm not.'

Dimitri clambered down the slope of the pit. His boots skidded and he almost fell, the ditch was steep. His hurry and lack of balance made her laugh. This was her second laugh for his ears.

Dimitri tugged his shirt tail out of his pantaloons and pulled the tunic over his head. Bare-chested, he reached for the woman's shovel. She did not hand it over. He locked on to her eyes and saw how she took him in.

'What?' he prodded, expecting her to comment on his slim torso.

'You've got no hair on your chest,' she said. 'You've got the chest of a woman.'

Okay, Dimitri thought, good, the filly bucks. He pulled his eyes from hers and slid them down her.

'So do you, my dear.'

She sent her face skyward, shaking her noggin at something up there, her God, a dead husband, something, and said, 'Ha!'

She would not give up her shovel. Dimitri turned to the girl behind him, she was a teenager, and asked her if she needed a rest. The girl sighed in relief and handed over her tool.

Dimitri made a display of his strength and stamina. He dug two to the woman's one, filled buckets, and showed impatience when they were not hauled up fast enough. He worked for fifteen minutes, almost to the point of exhaustion. He finally speared his shovel into the ground and left it. She stood behind him with a ladle of water.

He poured it over his head. He handed it back to her. She walked away to bring him another. Yes, Dimitri thought, she's ample.

She returned with the ladle dripping. He quaffed the lukewarm water and ran a filthy forearm across his lips. Again she laughed at him.

'What's your name?'

'Dimitri Konstantinovich Berko. At your service. And who are you?'

'Sonya.'

'Just Sonya?'

'Yes, Private. Just Sonya.'

She did not smile when she called him Private. This was a hard one, this woman, not a silly girl from the villages. She looked to be in her mid-thirties, a well-preserved lass, even in these war years. She must be, in fact, a teacher or something like that, maybe one of those damned Communists. She was firm in her ocean eyes, even her smiles and laughter were resolute. Dimitri had the instant concern she was smarter and better born than him.

'Yes, well.' He made a face. 'Just Sonya.' He played the clown a bit for her. 'I'm a private in this army. But actually, when there's no war going on, I'm a *hetman*.' He tapped his own chest, in the mud there from the dripping water. 'My father was a *hetman*. And his father.'

Sonya pursed her lips, impressed. 'What is a *hetman*?'

He narrowed his eyes. She doesn't know. Ah, she's too much trouble. One more go-round, then enough. Back to my tank.

'I am a Cossack leader. In my *sietch*, I am the final say.'

'Your *sietch*.'

'Yes, woman. My ... my community. Village. Me. The little private.'

'The dirty little private. Are you a tanker, Dima?' This was the diminutive of his name, the affectionate form.

'Yes. Right up the hill there. Those tanks. The 3rd Mechanized Brigade.'

'You'll be fighting here, then. When it starts. Around this trench.'

'Yes. Along the Oboyan road. The Germans are going to give it everything they've got to take it. But I think this trench alone will stop them. I mean, look at it. You've done a marvelous job. There won't be much fighting for me to do.'

Sonya took a deep breath and looked at Dimitri with softer eyes. He noted the change and heaped on more, this time for sympathy.

'Me and my son. We're in the same tank.'

'The same tank.'

'Yes. It's an old tradition, Cossack families go to war together.'

'That's splendid.'

'And my daughter.'

'Oh.' Sonya smiled her best yet. 'Where is she?'

'Up there. Somewhere.' Dimitri pointed into the sky.

Sonya's face fell.

'Oh, Dima, no. I'm so sorry. *Ay*.' She clucked her tongue. 'To lose a child.'

No, he thought, you goose, Katya's not dead! She's a pilot... .

'How did she ... ?'

Dimitri froze for the moment, raising a hand to wave off the incorrect notion. Sonya touched his shoulder.

'No, no, Dima, it's alright. You don't have to talk about her right now. I understand. It must be so hard for you.'

Dimitri lowered his hand. He drooped his eyes to the dirt and sniffed once, faking. He left Katya unexplained. Sonya patted his neck. Katya would understand, he thought.

She pulled her spade out of the facing wall. Dimitri followed suit. Sonya seemed to want to let some silence hover, to return to work, as though she dug now with a new purpose, for the dead daughter and the brave Cossack *hetman* who would fight beside his son here along the dangerous Oboyan road.

She bent to her shovel. Dimitri, behind her, gave her buttocks a squeeze.

June 30
2130 hours

Dimitri stayed in the trench, digging with the women and old men, the darling of the civilians. When he did not come out of the hole in an hour to return to his tank, Andrei wandered up to the lip to check on him. Below Andrei's feet, he saw Sonya and barebacked Dimitri with a gaggle of women around him. The dairy farmer doffed his cigarette and his tunic, too, and stumbled down the wall of the trench. He was welcomed, introduced around, and handed a shovel. Within the hour, a dozen more tankers were in the trench, sweating and flinging dirt and flirting like it was a holiday. In the early evening, they shared a meal with the diggers.

The air cooled with the lowering sun and the work slacked after the food. The sound of arriving trucks reached them down in the pit, come to take the laborers back to their camp miles to the east away from the front. Andrei got a peck on the cheek from the girl he'd worked beside. Some of the other tankers, unsure bumpkins, backed away, muttering, Nice to meet you, and clambered up the slope. Sonya told Dimitri, Thank you, she hadn't laughed as much in a day for years. Thank you, Dima. He reached both hands into the water bucket and dipped water to splash his face, then grabbed Sonya in a bear hug. Her breasts against his chest stunned him for a moment, it had been all he thought about the whole day hefting the shovel. He wanted to give her something but had nothing in his pockets, so he gave her a truth. My daughter, he said, is not dead. She's a pilot. Sonya did not take a swing at him for his gambit; instead she said, So, you are still a *hetman,* you have a clan. Yes, he said, proud the way she put it. Yes. You're a good woman, he said. I am, she answered, and lingered in his arms, sea-green eyes flowing over his face. And you need to let me go.

This is when Valentin arrived at the edge of the trench.

'Let her go, Private.'

'Your son?' she asked Dimitri.

'Yes. The bastard.'

'Go,' Sonya said.

'A kiss first.'

'No. I don't know you that well.'

'I've earned a kiss.'

Valentin repeated his command. The sky behind him reddened.

'Go, Dima. You'll get in trouble.'

'See. You do know me well! Kiss me, woman, and I'll deal with the trouble.'

Sonya bent her head to his and they touched lips; the kiss was softer than Dimitri wanted but, again, he found she was plenty. He let her pull away first and open her eyes.

'Another time,' she said.

'Another time, Just Sonya.'

He grabbed one more handful of her bottom and clambered away before she could consider taking a swipe at him. He flew up the trench slope to stand beside Valentin.

'You should have gotten here sooner,' he said to his son, looking down at all the women gathering their tools, washing their bare arms in the last of the water buckets. Then he made a face. 'No. Perhaps not.'

June 30
2215 hours

Two boys sat cross-legged on the ground in front of the General Platov. They jumped up when Valentin strode into the glow of their lantern.

'Sergeant!' they said together.

Dimitri came to stand beside his son, who addressed the two newcomers.

'Men, this is your driver. Private ...'

Dimitri stepped forward before Valentin could make any more formal pronouncements. He held out his hand to each. Neither was out of his teens. More sons, Dimitri thought; Christ, more children to take into battle.

'Dimitri Konstantinovich Berko,' he said with each handshake. The boys had acne and nervous clasps. Dimitri felt expansive after his day in the trench with the woman, the digging made him tired in the good, old way of the farm. 'Call me Dima. Tell me your names.'

Both were short, the way tankers must be. One was thick, the other lean. Dimitri guessed the chunky one was the loader, he had to be strong to sling the shells around inside the tank, out of the bins and into the breech. The other would be the hull machine-gunner and radioman, if the *General* had a radio.

'Pyotr Semyonovich Belyayev,' said the stumpy one. His eyes were close-set. Beneath broad shoulders hung short arms. 'I am ...'

'The loader, yes, I guessed. Of course. Look at you. Strong as an ox, I'll bet. Good, good. And you?'

The thinner of the two was the edgy, pinched one. Both boys had buzzed haircuts but this one looked like a match head, there was something incendiary about him.

'Private Frolov.' His name had to escape his mouth as though words were prisoners in this boy's head.

'Private Frolov? I'm not going to call out 'Hey, Private Frolov, shoot those Nazi fuckers for me!' in the middle of a battle. What's your name, boy?'

'Um ... um ...'

'Yes?'

'Alexander Mikhailovich Frolov.'

This one will be fun, thought Dimitri. The quiet ones always are after you put some vodka in them. He guessed the skinny one would be the harder fighter of the two when the time came. Life for the quiet ones is a fight all the time. Good. He'll keep his head.

'Gunner extraordinaire, *da*?' Dimitri clapped Frolov on the back to see how he'd take it. The boy wavered under the smack but looked up and grinned.

'Good, very good. Sergeant, these look like good fighters. Well done.'

Valentin eyed his father.

Dimitri spread his arms, pushing the two boys together, tucking both inside his span as though measuring their collective width and worth.

'Alright! Pasha and Sasha. Yes. And Dima.' He looked back at Valentin. 'And the sergeant.'

Dimitri took up the lantern and carried it to the *General*. He set it on the ground and folded next to it, resting his tired back against the T-34's tread.

'Gather 'round.'

Pyotr and Alexander came to sit about the lantern. Valentin stood apart. This was the third crew they'd had in a year, and Dimitri had gone through this exercise with each. Dimitri walked over to his son and took the boy's arm, leading him away to speak privately.

'Come on, Valya. They're children.'

'They're soldiers.'

'They're fighters, yes. And who are the best fighters in all of Russia? Hmm?'

'Cossacks,' Valentin said with rolling eyes. The answer was their ritual.

'Yes! So, you see. We have to do this, every time. Yes? Come on.' Dimitri steered Valentin by their linked arms back to the lantern, the *General*, and the two waiting crewmen.

'Good. All together,' he said, grunting a bit while descending to the ground again. Valentin took a place up on the tank, close but above the three privates. 'Pasha. Tell me where you're from.'

The broad one said, 'Lesogorsk. Near Bratsk.'

'Ah,' Dimitri clapped, 'a Siberian. Are you a hunter, then? You must be.'

'I grew up shooting ducks on the Bratskoye reservoir. And foxes in the *taiga*. My father and I ...'

'Excellent, wonderful. You'll tell us more sometime. Sasha, you. Where is your home?'

The boy licked his lips. 'Odessa.'

Dimitri looked up at Valentin. 'You hear that! He's from the other side of the Black Sea from us. Splendid.'

'Did you two know the sergeant and I are Kuban Cossacks?'

The boys shook their heads and looked at each other.

'What do you know about Cossacks? Anything?'

Pasha the stump said, 'My mother used to scare us

when we were bad. She'd say if we didn't behave, she was going to call the Cossack and let him get us.'

'What would the Cossack do?'

'I don't know. Eat us, I guess.'

Dimitri chuckled. 'Your mother was a wise woman, Pasha. I might have eaten you and grown very fat myself. But as you can see, I'm skinny, so I never ate any children. Alright?'

Pasha nodded, like a child being assured a scary campfire story was just that, a story.

Dimitri reached to the lantern to turn up the wick. 'Did you notice the name of your new tank? Sasha?'

Valentin, seated on the tank, sighed and this made Sasha take a moment longer.

'General Platov.'

'Yes. Good. I suppose you don't know who General Platov was, so I'll tell you.'

'Yes,' said Pasha, cupping his chin in his hands and digging his elbows into his bent knees. Sasha nodded. This boy did not ever seem to blink.

'Before the War of 1812, Napoleon knew he would invade Russia. He set out to learn everything he could about the Motherland before attacking. One of the things he found out was that the Cossacks of the Don and Kuban regions were the finest riders and fighters in the world. Better than the Mongols, the British, and better than the French, of course. Napoleon needed good cavalry if he was going to build an empire, and who better than the Cossacks?'

Dimitri slapped the tank tread behind him. 'Good old General Platov here was the *hetman* of the Don Cossacks. He got a letter from Bonaparte himself, inviting him to visit Paris to be His Majesty's guest. When Platov got to France, Napoleon and all of his generals kissed his ass like he was a king himself. They showed him all the wonders of Paris, held fancy balls in his honor, even a parade! All this to get their hands on General Platov's Cossacks. And Platov, you see, was no dummy. He knew what Bonaparte was up to.'

The lantern light reached high enough on the tank for Dimitri to see his son listening, knowing the story well but allowing the father's gift of the telling.

'Finally, Napoleon made his move on the General. He sat Platov down in a giant parlor of gold and silk, and said to him, 'General, such a man as you should be a prince in your country. You command thousands of fighters, but you are treated with no honor by your own king. France can offer you this honor, for you and your Cossacks. Side with us, General. It would do you and your people good to become acquainted with the cultures of France and Europe.' The General kept his opinion to himself, that Napoleon had spoken as though, without French culture, his Cossacks were savages!'

Pasha and Sasha laughed. Even Valentin snickered, this was a new line Dimitri threw into the tale.

'Napoleon made his offer. 'General,' he said, 'I would give anything you asked if I could have Cossacks on my side. With twenty thousand of the best cavalrymen in the world fighting with France, no one could stop us.' Platov listened, rubbed his beard, and answered, 'I see no problem. This is a very easy thing to do.' Well, Napoleon could hardly believe his ears. 'How can we do this, General?' he begged. 'Tell me what you require.' The General stood in the grand, golden room of Napoleon and said, 'It's a simple thing. I will bring twenty thousand of my finest young riders to Paris for a few days. You will bring twenty thousand of your prettiest French girls to Paris. We will let Nature take its course, and in twenty years or so you will have your own twenty thousand French Cossacks!'

Dimitri spanked his knees with his hands, relishing the old General's reply every time he told the story. Pasha and

Sasha clapped and Valentin rocked back in his seat on the tank. The slanting lantern light made all their faces merry.

'So, you see,' Dimitri said. 'The whole world fears the Cossack. Including Napoleon and Pasha's mother. And the Germans.'

He leaned into the lantern, to light his face better for this next chapter of the rite. 'My old father. Your sergeant's grandfather. He would be here right now if he were alive. Cossack families go to war together. Did you know that?'

The two lads shook their heads.

'Well, they do. Every Cossack family knows the history of its warriors. The family heroes are remembered with praise, the villains are the cowards or the disloyal ones. When I was your age, I went to war with my father. We wore red-topped caps and black *burka* cloaks with red hoods. We rode in pigskin boots and kept a tea kettle and sacks of biscuits tied to our belts. I had a curved saber, a carbine with a bayonet, and a goathorn full of powder. We rode first against the Romanovs, those inbred European shits. And when we'd won enough battles against their white cavalry all across western Russia, even on these steppe lands around us right now, the Tsar himself gave in. The Cossacks were rewarded with free land, the right to govern ourselves, and respect! Then, after a few years of royal bribes, when it was clear the Bolsheviks would win, we traded in our white flag for a red one. We turned on the bastard Tsar for the new bastard Lenin. Because the Cossack fights for the Cossack. It doesn't matter who invades us. Germans or Russians, Tsars or commissars. Napoleon called us the disgrace of the human race. And he was right, if you look at how most humans live!'

The two boys were rapt. Dimitri understood the rotten training these two had been given before they were shipped to the Kursk bulge for their first battle. They'd been bullied and frightened and given no pay and less than a month's lesson on how to fight in these tanks. Commissars had shouted slogans at them, they'd taken oaths, but no one had talked with them, told them tales of bravery and deeds and mentioned they might have what it takes to do the same, valiant things – *podvigs*. Valentin and his sour ilk were all they'd seen of the Red Army. These lads were considered nothing more than numbers to be thrown at the Germans.

Dimitri knew he could not make them into more. But if he and Valya were going to fight alongside these boys, they were going to *think* they were more. Or they would all die, because few die alone in a tank.

'My father Konstantin was the best swordsman in the Kuban. Did you know a real Cossack sword has no hilt to protect the hand? Do you know why?'

No, they shrugged.

Dimitri cut his eyes to Valentin on the tank. 'Tell us, Sergeant. About the Cossack sword.'

Valentin ran fingers over his pate. The stubble of his short hair made a fizzing noise. Dimitri held up an open hand, to say please.

Valentin cleared his throat. So needless, Dimitri thought, to be uncomfortable talking to men who may well save your life in the next week. Embrace them, Valya, he urged silently, these are spirits, children like you. Valentin gave the answer, continuing to scratch his head.

'It ... um ... it's not made for dueling. It's made for striking from horseback.'

'Exactly. And Pasha, Sasha, I will tell you right now with the pride of a father that your sergeant Berko there was the finest swordsman in all the Kuban when he was your age. Just eighteen, and a champion *dzhigitovka*! In our village, the streets are wide and there's a great central square. That is where we hold our war games. On Sundays and holidays, the streets are lined with saplings, set thirty feet apart. On top of the trees are clay pots. The test, you see, is to gallop full bore between the trees and cut the pots with your sword. And Valentin there ... well, your sergeant there, he was the best. Slashing back and forth, boys, he was a sight! A champion!'

Pasha looked up at Valentin. 'Did you cut them off, like cutting off heads?'

Valentin appeared impatient, not with the query so much as his own past, before he became a sergeant for the Soviets. Watching his son fidget, Dimitri recalled the day when young Valya came to him and said he was going to join the army. 'Wonderful,' he had said, 'we'll go together. Yes! We'll be in the cavalry.' And Valentin answered him, 'No, I want to join the tanks.' The tanks! The metal horses, slow and stupid beasts, with a cannon and armor and dials where there ought to be a pounding heart and lungs and a life under your rear, not a hard seat and a stubborn clutch. A tank instead of a horse. A Soviet instead of a champion son. Dimitri listened to Valentin's response to the boy Pasha, and thought, He sounds like a stinking Romanov up there high on his tank.

'No, Private ... no. A Cossack does not cut off heads.'

'But ...' Pasha seemed to want to be scared, to hear of heads rolling by the dozens on the Cossack battlefield.

'Only poor Cossacks cut off heads, Pashinka,' Dimitri said. 'Not your sergeant. He practiced hard and became a master of the many different saber cuts from horseback.'

'You mean there's more than ... ?' Pasha drew a finger under his neck.

'Yes, yes.' Dimitri got to his knees and made a blade of his open hand. 'There's the one straight down on the shoulder to take off an arm.' He hacked at Pasha, who laughed. Sasha beside him giggled. 'There's this one, to cut open his guts. One across the hip ...' With each description Dimitri sliced at the two boys to make them laugh and understand they were more than numbers now, they were clan with him and, yes, the sergeant.

Dimitri sat back and glanced again up to Valentin. His son smiled thinly at his father's antics. Alright, the smile said, enough. We are who we are, Father. So, enough. Dimitri sighed, and held up a hand for more of their attention.

'The life of every Cossack relies on two things. First, his fellow Cossacks. He must be willing to die and kill for them, to never betray their trust. The second is his horse. The bond between rider and horse goes deeper than words. It is instinct and devotion. And do you know who was the best rider in my village?'

It was Valentin who gave the answer. 'Katerina.'

Dimitri turned to beam at Valentin.

'My daughter Katya. She was a champion, too. There was nothing she couldn't do on the back of a horse. She could leap across a stream and lean down from the saddle to take a drink.'

'No,' whispered red Sasha.

'Yes,' Dimitri breathed back.

'Where is Katya now?' Sasha asked.

'She's a Night Witch. You've heard of the Night Witches?'

'Yes!' Pasha blurted. 'My mother used to tell us the Night Witches would come if we ...'

'Pasha.'

'Yes?'

'Your mother used to frighten you a lot, didn't she?'

'Yes. Well ... um ...'

'Were you as bad a child as all that?'

Sasha laughed first, then Valentin and Dimitri. Pasha took a jabbing elbow from the quiet hull gunner and chuckled, too.

'Katya's a pilot,' Valentin explained, 'my sister is a night bomber.'

'Oh.' Pasha blushed enough to be orange in the lantern shine.

Dimitri asked, 'Now, do you boys want to become Cossacks?'

Sasha's eyes went wide. 'Is that something you can do? Can you do that?' He turned to his mate Pasha, but the thick boy shook his head, skeptical. 'No,' he said, 'Dima's playing with us again. We won't be real Cossacks. It's a game.'

Dimitri kept still, embedding his gaze into Pasha's eyes.

'It's no game.'

Skinny Sasha jutted his nose at Dimitri. 'Yes. Make me a Cossack.'

Dimitri waited for Pasha's face to change. The loader looked up at his sergeant. Valentin nodded to him.

Pasha said, 'Me, too.'

'Listen,' Dimitri said. 'You've got to know the history first. This is the story of the Cossacks. Centuries ago, Russia was different than it is today. Before the Soviets. In the long time of the Tsars. Russia was a collection of little kingdoms, ruled by boyars and landlords. The people were either rich aristocrats or poor peasants and serfs. But there was one place where the gentry didn't run things. My homeland, Ukraine. Even its name tells you how free it was: '*Borderland.*' During this time, Ukraine was a giant and unsettled country, a wild land. There was room to roam, there were fish and grainlands, grasses for cattle and sheep and horses. The first Cossacks were criminals. These were men who wanted their freedom enough to risk their lives to get it. They were running from the law. Or they were sentries from some landlord's army, who got tired of manning a post and fighting someone else's battles and ran away. The first Cossack was an escaped serf. Or he might have been some highborn who screwed the wrong peasant girl or stole another lord's land and came to avoid scandal or being hung. He might have been a Greek or a Turk looking for adventure. Whoever he was, boys, whatever he was running from, his trouble was not going to follow him into Ukraine. He got a clean slate. And while the Russian state to the north and east was getting more and more civilized and tamed, Ukraine stayed without masters. It was a place for the common man, for bandits and fugitives, vagabonds and slaves to remake their lives. These men who skulked into Ukraine became farmers and trappers. They settled the land and raised their families. Everyone was equal.'

Pasha and Sasha watched him, spellbound; with his hands, Dimitri carved for them Ukraine out of the air, made pistols out of his fingers for the bandits, whips across the backs of the serfs, and open, clear fields with sweeps of his palm.

Sasha raised a hand like a schoolboy to ask a question.

'How did the Cossacks learn to fight?'

'A good question, Pashinka. The plains of Ukraine were not empty when the first Cossacks came. Hordes of Mohammedan tribesman roamed there. So the Cossacks were forced to band together. They learned from their battles with the Mohammedans, who were wonderful horsemen. The Cossacks borrowed the best of what they saw and soon became even better riders and warriors. But even when the Cossacks found themselves coming together for survival, they maintained their love for *kazak*, their freedom. They asked little from those who wished to join them. Only three things does a Cossack have in common with all other Cossacks. Three questions, and you have to answer yes to each. Are you ready?'

The two boys hesitated. Dimitri was tickled at the gravity he'd created in them.

'Yes,' both uttered.

Dimitri's legs were tired, his knees griped. But this part of the rite had to be done standing.

'Alright, get up.'

Valentin stayed in his place on the tank.

When Pasha and Sasha were on their feet, Dimitri asked, 'Do you want to become Cossacks?'

Both nodded.

'Say so,' Dimitri prodded.

'Yes!' they said, a bit too loud. Dimitri kept a serious demeanor though he wanted to grin.

'Good, good. Hold it down, lads. Next question. Will you die if you must for another member of your clan, and for your freedom?'

'Yes.' The two boys stood shoulder to shoulder. Dimitri watched them press closer to each other.

'And last. Do you believe in God?'

The two boys Pasha and Sasha answered well. 'Yes. I do. Yes.'

'Good. Bend your knees. Let's pray.'

Dimitri dropped to his knees on the tank-crushed grass. Pasha and Sasha knelt with him. Dimitri did not glance up at his son. He didn't want to know if Valentin was praying or simply watching with his Soviet disdain. Dimitri said a silent prayer for the lives of these two youths he'd been given. He asked God to only take them if they were greatly needed to win the battle. Let them stay Cossacks as long as they can, God, let them be free on the earth. But if You cannot, let them be free in heaven. He asked also for God to protect Valya and Katya. He did not ask for himself.

One of the boys said 'Amen,' finished with his prayer. Dimitri ended his and lifted his head before he realized the 'Amen' was Valentin's. He stood, Pasha and Sasha scrambled to their feet. Dimitri stepped to his son's perch on the *General* and patted Valya's knee. Valya was maddening this way. Dimitri could never be comfortable with his frustration or his pride in the boy. He did not know Valya at all.

'This,' he said to the loader and the hull gunner, newly minted Cossacks, 'is your *hetman*. He is your sergeant and your tank commander, but he is your Cossack leader, too. You'll do everything he orders. Is this understood?'

Valentin slid down from the tank.

'Are we done?'

Dimitri itched to backhand the boy for the sudden swings he caused in Dimitri's chest.

At that moment – because, thought Dimitri, there is a God and He listens and once in a while even if you don't ask He answers – a convoy of panel trucks rumbled up through the dark, headlamps jouncing over the ruts in the field cut by the company of heavy tanks. In the beds of the trucks, lit by the lights of the vehicles in line behind, jostled crowds of old men holding up bottles, and women. Dimitri saw fiddles, an accordion, and even a clarinet.

He recognized her voice. Just Sonya called out for him.

He moved to his son and lapped his arm across the boy's shoulder.

'Yes, Sergeant. We're done. Excuse me.'

Dimitri grabbed his two new charges by their lapels and tugged them away from the lantern, telling them they had an additional duty as Cossacks to perform. They must each take a girl.

'Dima, is this another game?' Pasha asked, lagging at the end of Dimitri's arm.

'Yes,' Dimitri told him, 'and Cossacks play it well. Come.'

CHAPTER 7

July 1
1430 hours
Kalinovka aerodrome

Katya stood beside a dozen other girls from her regiment watching the truck roll closer to the aerodrome. The others hoped longer than she did, asking, 'Is it them? Can you see?' But Katya noted from far away how the four women in the back of the approaching truck held on with both hands to the side rails, how they did not wave their white silk underhelmets in the afternoon. They were not the four Night Witches come back from the dead, but replacements. Zoya and Galina, Marina and Lily were gone. They were not in this afternoon's truck the way they were not in the truck yesterday or the day before. The four dead friends would stay Night Witches forever now, they would never be anything else. That is not such a bad way to die, Katya thought, to remain for all time someone brave. She was the first to turn from the road.

Leonid said nothing. He put his arm around her shoulders and walked with Katya to the big tent her squadron shared. Minutes behind her the other girls did come in from the road, some even saying, Tomorrow, maybe tomorrow. Katya and Leonid opened the four girls' steamer trunks. Diaries and personal items would be sent home to their parents. Unmailed letters would be posted. The four beds would be remade for the replacement pilots and navigators. Katya was moved by the disparity of things she and Leonid pulled from the trunks: stuffed animals and extra signal flares, dried flowers and flight logs.

The other girls milled around the four beds, littered now with items from the trunks. They joined Katya in sifting through the objects, arranging piles, recognizing and weeping over mementos, sitting on the beds remembering many talks. This was not the first time there had been deaths in their squadron, but it was the only instance when two crews had been lost on a single mission. The doubled blow seemed almost too great.

Katya watched Leonid withdraw from the tent; Katya had the others around her now. She rose from Lily's cot. The springs squeaked, a sign of life but not of Lily's, and Katya had to hold back tears over such a small thing.

She went outside. Leonid stood staring into the afternoon sky.

'Today's the first day of July,' he said.

Katya nodded.

'How much longer can they wait?' she asked, gazing up with him. The battle would take place underneath and in this sky; the blue that fell all the way to the horizon gave Katya the sense the battle would be fought in tight quarters, two titanic fighters in a bout, under this ringing blue sky.

'I don't know. It should have started by now.'

Katya was jarred, this seemed insensitive. She wanted to point back into the tent, to the sobbing girls, and tell Leonid it has started. But she knew what he meant. It's going to be worse, far worse, than anything before. So she let the comment alone.

'Walk with me, Leonya, will you?'

She turned and headed for the hardstands where the eighteen U-2s of her squadron sat chocked and waiting. She did not speak along the way.

When they reached her plane, Leonid ran his hands over the patched wings. He patted the engine housing and plucked the wire struts. He chewed his lips in thought. Katya watched him and again felt the sting of resentment. Was Leonid being condescending, the way he looked over her intrepid little plane? He tapped on the U-2 as though he'd never seen one. Then he squatted on his heels. With a finger he drew a circle in the dust.

'This is your target tonight. Show me how you'll attack.'

Katya walked over to sit cross-legged beside the little circle. 'What do you mean?'

'Show me your flight and attack plan.'

She was in no mood to have her squadron criticized, especially not by a free-ranging, fast-flying fighter pilot. Four dead comrades bought her this day free from tongue clucking.

'I want to go back to the tent.'

'And do what? Mourn some more?'

Katya gripped a fist of dirt and flung it at Leonid.

'Yes. Mourn some more. Maybe there can't be enough mourning.'

'That's selfish.'

Katya cocked her head and repeated the word with shocked silence. Selfish?

'Yes. And what do you think I'll do when it's you dead on the ground because you'd rather cry than adapt? Do you think I'll sit on your bed and go through your trunk? Or do you think I'll get back into my Yak and shoot down some more Germans? What do you think, Katya? Which is it for you? Do you want to fight or do you need a fresh handkerchief? Do you want to learn something? Because if you do, you need to do it right now. You have another mission tonight, and there's going to be another night fighter waiting for you.'

Katya clamped her teeth. Leonid had not even wiped

off the dirt she'd heaved on him, the dark bits salted his folded lap.

'Show me,' Leonid said.

Katya made her hand into a plane, spreading thumb and pinky for wings. It was simple. She approached the target at three thousand feet. One mile out, she cut her engine and glided in, bleeding off altitude to twelve hundred feet. Here she lowered her hand over the dirt circle. She dropped her bombs, hit the magnetos and throttle, and got away as fast as she could from the lights and guns. She banked her hand away from the circle and raised it, heading for home. Three minutes behind, approaching the target right about now, was the next bomber, coming from the same direction at the same altitude. Simple, she thought, again watching her hand sail safely away, not a scratch on it. Then she asked herself the question before Leonid could: What if there is another night fighter waiting for us tonight? Will we fly right into his sights again?

Katya made another plane out of her free hand. This was the German Me-109, stalking high above the target for the Night Witches who floated in straight and on time.

Will we do anything different tonight? No. Leonid is right. Who will it be, then, in flames next?

'Do you have an idea?' she asked.

Leonid sat cross-legged with her. 'Do you?'

Katya looked at the two hands she hovered above the circle in the dirt. One was a defenseless bomber, the other was the black German fighter. The German hand licked its chops. He had the speed and gunnery to make a joke of her regiment's standard attack plan. He already had. Then it struck her.

What if both hands were Night Witches?

'Leonya. What if we take in two planes instead of one?'

Leonid nodded. He looked down at the dirt circle with her, picturing the altitude, the light beams searching, flak exploding. She could see the plan hatching in his head even as it took shape in her own. The scheme was just as simple as what their squadron had been doing for the past year. Perhaps that's why it had been overlooked. This new adversary, the night fighter, called for a new tactic. Katya allowed herself an inward smile, even on this sad day.

Two planes will fly in together. The first ignores the target, but instead draws the attention of the searchlights and the artillery batteries. Meanwhile, the other Night Witch glides straight for the target. Once she drops her load, both planes hit the gas, climb, and circle back. But next time they switch roles. If all the dodging plane has to worry about is staying away from the lights, the guns and night fighters, she can do a better job of staying alive. And if all the bomber has to do is bear down on the target without avoiding the lights, she can be more accurate. When the first pair's sortie is over, the next two in line do the same. Yes?

'Yes,' said Leonid, snapping his fingers. 'And make sure you stagger the times between pairs, and vary the direction you fly in from. No night fighter can hit what he can't find.'

Katya worked her two hands over the target, practicing the maneuver over the dirt circle, determining altitudes and patterns so the two U-2s wouldn't collide in the dark and confusion. The strategy made sense. It could work.

Leonid said nothing while Katya worked out the plan. Then he reached above the dirt circle and took one of her hands in his own, as though his hand was flying beside hers over the make-believe target.

'Hey.'

Katya's hand hovered in his. Their eyes locked high above, among the pretend stars.

Leonid said, 'I know you lost four friends. I am trying to help. It's just my clumsy way of doing it.'

Katya gazed at their elevated and linked arms. We're both better up here, she thought, more graceful in the air than we are on the ground. She set Leonid's hand loose.

'It's alright,' she said. She wanted to say more but could not figure what it would be. The firmness of his hand in hers and the concern in his warning, the gentleness of his apology, these were all opposites of the grief and fear rummaging in her heart. Katya felt guilty and tugged at. She sensed risk and vulnerability and so banked hard away from it.

'I'll go and tell the others. See what they think.'

Leonid rose first, taking the cue from her voice. He looked down at her from his height. He said, 'Good luck tonight,' and walked off to his own hangar.

She watched him stride away, his name on her lips. 'Good luck to you,' she mumbled instead to his back.

Katya rose, glum over how she'd left things with Leonid. He'd spoken sharply to her and she'd returned fire, then they'd both retreated before anything could be damaged badly. She shook her head. No, their friendship was too strong, nothing would have been damaged. Gazing into the immense blue sky, where God lived and she herself galloped, Katya wondered, Was it harm Leonid and I averted just now, or was it something else, something secret revealing itself on this mournful day? What would I have said to Leonid if I'd let myself speak? Would it have been ... ? The sky had no answers for her, only endless room for asking. No, she thought. Comrades have died, and comrades can be saved with this new tactic. There's a mission to be flown, and a major battle looming. I have my answer.

She entered the command tent and found the captain of her squadron, Nina Vasil'yevna Smirnova. She told the captain the new strategy. Smirnova was impressed and asked Katya to write it up. Katya would address the pilots and navigators at their briefing in a few hours.

Tonight's mission would be above a rail station deep inside enemy lines. The partisan network had identified a trainload of German heavy tanks being transported to Belgorod. Efforts were being made to stop this train. One partisan cell was planning to attack the train itself. The partisans needed the Night Witches to take out the station, its water tower, maintenance shed, and tracks to slow the train's progress.

Tonight, she and Vera were assigned to fly one of the two lead planes.

July 1
2130 hours

Katya lay inside the tent and did not see dusk settle over the steppe, but she knew it had come when she heard the first Yak-9 fighters tear away from the field. The pages of her report jostled and mingled on her cot when she jumped off it to run outside.

She was too late. Leonid's plane was the third to take off. His climb was beautiful to watch, his sleek fighter rose and Katya thrilled to the engine's power. She saw the top of Leonid's helmet through the clear bell of his cockpit and felt a palpable rising in her chest, as though part of her heart were flying off with him, banking hard in line with the others on night patrol. The rising went into her hand and she hoisted it in a wave he would not see. The last of the Yaks bounded off the grass field. The pilots closed ranks over the airstrip, then flew beyond sight and sound. Once they were gone, Katya listened to the wide silence return under the vast and bruising steppe sky, serrated only by crickets and some mechanic hammering at something stubborn.

Katya trod back to the tent. She completed the report and closed her eyes. Other girls filtered in, squeaking their cots for some rest before the night's mission. No one spoke, a few snored, and Katya drifted away. She awoke a little while later when the other girls stirred. There was a change in her when she sat up. She recollected a vague sense from a dream she must have had while napping. The dream was of her and Leonid. She remembered a closed door between them. She did not recall if the door ever opened in the dream. She felt bereft of him; he'd taken off before she could see him and explore again what she'd wanted to say, perhaps even what she wanted to hear. The door in the dream was closed, she knew that now. Sitting upright on the cot, she rubbed her eyes awake and made a decision, to leave the door open. Vera walked past on her way to the briefing. She stopped in front of Katya's cot.

'What?' Vera asked.

Katya looked up at her navigator. The girl wore a kind and silly grin. She leaned down to Katya, to read something in her eyes as though on one of her maps.

'Hmm?'

Vera leaned down farther. 'What's with you? You've got a look on your face.'

Katya made no response. She stood from the cot and grabbed her report. Vera blocked her way. She called to the other girls, 'Did you see the look?'

'Yes,' a few answered. 'A definite look.'

Katya snorted and spun away from Vera. Laughing Night Witches hooted behind her, 'A look, yes, yes. I saw it.'

Vera caught up with her outside the tent.

'So, Katyusha. Did you and Leonid ...'

'No!' Katya held up the pages she'd prepared. 'We've got a mission tonight. Do you think you could get your crazy brain to focus on that right now?'

'Yes, Katyusha.' Vera feigned shame. 'Of course, my pilot.' She stabbed a finger into Katya's face. 'But you'll tell me everything when we get back, or I'll ask Leonid. We'll see what he says.'

The briefing took an hour. The pilots and navigators discussed Katya's proposal, refined it, then accepted it. Katya received a round of applause. Captain Smirnova sent them out to get ready. Take-off would be in fifteen minutes, at 2200 hours. The sun's long goodbye over the steppe was still in progress when Katya strode outside the command tent. In the remaining glimmer, she spotted the fuselage lights of the first Yak-9 returning to the field. In moments the sound of the plane came within range. The engine sputtered. Something was wrong.

Men ran past Katya to the edge of the grass landing strip. Many carried fire extinguishers, a few hauled medic boxes. Katya kept her eyes in the dimming sky, on the flashes from the oncoming plane. Then the Yak came into view. Smoke trailed behind it, blacker than the congealing night. The engine coughed and the plane pitched, dipping and unsure. Katya crept closer to the field, some of the other girls in her squadron came with her. The fighter came in too steep. Katya's lips formed the words *Pull up, pull up,* and at the last moment the nose of the Yak-9 lifted, the wheels hit the ground but bounced the fighter back into the air. Then the engine cut. The Yak touched down and stayed, running fast over the grass, but the dulled propeller slowed and the fighter turned off the runway in a sharp pivot. The engine was throttled back. The Yak did not taxi to its assigned station but halted where it was off the runway and quit. An acrid haze billowed from the engine until runners doused it with white chemicals. Others climbed the wing, shoved back the cockpit bell, and clotted around the pilot. Fingers touched the back of Katya's fist. Vera stood beside her. Katya opened her balled hand and took Vera's in hers.

More planes landed, none as badly as the first wounded plane; that pilot was hauled away on a stretcher and his plane was pushed by a ground crew to its hardstand. Three more in Leonid's squadron of a dozen trailed smoke when they touched down. The eleventh plane landed and Katya scanned the maroon sky for his green and red running lights. Vera's hand tightened around hers.

'He's coming,' Katya said.

The eleventh and last plane was the squadron commander. Katya watched this pilot park his fighter, climb off, and speak to his mechanic. The sky did not issue another plane for Katya, the only lights were the first winking stars. The commander headed away to make his report. Katya felt her dread swell with every passing second, each step the squadron leader took was another thing that would make Leonid's failure to appear final. Without thinking, she released Vera's hand and ran across the field through the warm smells of exhaust and burned oil. Weaving through the wings she saw the bullet holes ripped into the planes.

'Captain,' she called, 'Captain, please. A moment, sir.'

The grimness of the officer's face was plain when he turned to her. Katya ran up beside him but he did not stop. She stepped into his path.

'Captain, please. Lieutenant Lumanov. I didn't see him land.'

'No.'

This single word tore through Katya like one of the bullets through the Yaks.

She fought for her composure. 'Can you tell me, sir, what happened? Where is he?'

'Who are you, Lieutenant?'

'Katerina Berkovna, sir. I'm with ...'

'Yes, you're one of the Night Witches. I know. Leonid tells me about you.'

'Captain, please.'

'There was a dogfight over Tomarovka. He was shot down, Lieutenant.'

Katya seized up, her lungs seemed to bite at her from inside her ribs.

Before she could speak, the Captain laid a hand on her shoulder.

'I flew over his crash site. He sent up a white flare. He's alive. But he's pretty deep inside German territory. I don't have any way to know if he's injured or how badly. He's a clever lad, Lieutenant. I suppose you know that.'

Katya muttered, 'Yes.' The word was a relief, better than another wounding No, but the comfort was cold. Tomarovka was six miles south of the front line. Leonid might have been badly hurt in the crash. Yes, he survived, but for how long? Until he bleeds to death, or a German patrol captures him?

The Captain studied her face. She did not know or care how much she showed him.

'We'll alert the partisans in the area. They'll try to get to him first. That's all we can do, Lieutenant. You understand?'

Katya nodded. Leonid had been shot down. She'd imagined this fate for herself with every mission over the past year, she'd suffered with her mates when this fate fell on others in her regiment, she'd seen it happen in the sky more than she cared to remember. But never once had she prepared herself for this to happen to Leonid.

But the worst had not happened. He was still alive.

The Captain cleared his throat. 'I've got to make my report. Good luck. Lieutenant?'

'Yes, sir.'

'I'd like to tell you something. Leonid has made me appreciate you Night Witches. I ... wanted to be sure you knew that.'

The praise was spoiled. Katya wanted to beat the man's chest: Why didn't you bring him back?

'Thank you, sir.'

The Captain sidestepped her. Impulsively, Katya reached for his arm.

'Captain? West of Tomarovka? East?'

'East, Lieutenant. Two miles due east. In a small field beside a dry creek.'

'Thank you, Captain. Thank you.'

Katya turned to hurry away, but this time the Captain stopped her.

'I hear those broomsticks of yours can set down almost anywhere. Is that true?'

'Yes, Captain. Anywhere.'

July 1
2340 hours
over no-man's-land
Voronezh Front

Leonid was on the ground. This notion wrapped Katya as tightly as did the flying night. She tried to keep her mind on the mission, on the train station far inside enemy lines, but like a disobedient horse her thoughts shied from her instruments, away from the wind in her wings. She tightened her mental reins and brought her own head around to attention on the raid.

Only a wedge of moon glowed behind soupy clouds. She and Vera cruised southward at four thousand feet. Far to port, the other U-2 belched little exhaust fires from its engine. The plan was for that crew, Olga Sanfirova and navigator Olga Kluyeva, to attack the station first while Katya and Vera diverted the defenses, then they would switch roles. The darkness tonight was dense enough for them to hide in its folds. Katya kept one eye on the popping blue fires from the Olgas to avoid drifting too close to them. Vera remained quieter than usual in Katya's earphones. Something was unsaid between the two of them. This added to Katya's sense of burden in the cockpit. Leonid was on the ground. Katya chugged through the air, distracted and scared, and Vera, never a mystery, was silent.

The air currents were smooth and the flight was even. Vera's direction brought them in range of the target only forty minutes after take-off. The rail station lay fifteen miles south of Belgorod in the village of Oktabrskaya. The tracks ran alongside the Lopan River, and Vera brought Katya and their bombs down the slim waterway to the lights of the village. They were deeper tonight behind German lines than they had yet flown. Katya checked the two Olgas. They were dead even to port.

'Cut engine,' Vera said.

Katya pushed in the throttle and switched off the magnetos. The plane began to sail, and under her gaze the two Olgas disappeared, their motor shut down, too. Katya began to drop altitude, gliding and accelerating to the target. The Olgas would hold up here at four thousand for a count of ten, then begin their muffled dive. Katya looked out through the flipping propeller, the whoosh of wind mounted, and she thought, Leonid, I must leave you for a few moments, please hang on.

'Steady,' Vera intoned. Katya grabbed a flare and readied it. No searchlights lashed out yet, their approach was fast and unspoiled. The air she slid down was silken and beneath the rushing wind everything was hushed. The ground below slipped by, wary and dangerous.

Then, high over her head, she heard a snarling deep and unseen in the dark.

The night fighter circled. The Germans had success with this countermove once, so they tried it again. There would be no artillery tonight, just lights and the game of hunter and quarry. Katya licked dry lips. It was time to find out if the quarry's new tactic would work.

Her altimeter read twenty-five hundred feet. Vera whispered – she'd heard the howl of the night fighter, too – 'Drop it.'

Katya struck the flare and tossed it out of the cockpit. For a second, the bottom of her upper wing jittered white from the bursting flare, then she banked away. The train station of Oktabrskaya was made garish by the sparks floating down under the tiny parachute. The flare glittered against the roof tiles and the vacant steel rails. In the next instant, everything was punched out of Katya's sight by a hard white fist of light.

A searchlight beam drove straight into her face. Katya slammed her eyes shut and whipped the stick to the left, ramming hard on the left rudder to swing the U-2's nose around in a snap turn. Behind her eyelids the blackness was alive with a starburst of electric swirls and hues.

'Level out, level out!' Vera shouted in the intercom.

'I can't see!'

Katya felt Vera's hands on the stick, but the girl was not a pilot, the stick waggled directionless and panicky.

'We're in the lights! Katya, come on!'

Katya tried to open her eyes but the world was a morass. She shut them again.

'Vera, let go!'

'What! We have to ...'

'Let go!'

Katya felt Vera release the U-2. She laid her own hand on the stick and sensed her plane, the speed and gravity of her flight. A thousand times she'd ridden in the saddle with eyes closed, wearing blindfolds to do tricks, as a child she could do a handstand and canter in the ring with Papa at the center, her horse on his long lead. She lifted her chin, tilted her head, and knew she was rolling left. She twitched the stick back and to the right and the nose came up, the starboard wings dropped and trimmed out. She ducked her head into the well of the open cockpit, out of the searchlights, and opened her eyes. Her vision was stained but the gauges reappeared. She was flying level, at nineteen hundred feet.

Without hesitating, Katya whipped the plane into a steep corkscrew left, diving and twisting away from the powerful beams. In that instant, scorching red tracers flashed in her wake. The roar of the black Me-109 blasted behind her tail, the German's engine screaming to pull the fighter out of its dive. Katya followed the sound in a swooping power arch behind, then beneath, then in front and above her, cleaving through the air like a scythe. The noise was wicked and mesmerizing, fusing every bit of Katya to it so that she didn't notice she'd slipped out of the searchlights. She turned to look back at the station and every search beam was trained in her direction, away from the two Olgas. Katya blew out the breath she didn't know she'd been holding. Her strategy was working, even though the night fighter had missed her and Vera by inches!

Katya's altitude was down to twelve hundred feet. Her vision cleared. She glided into a slow wide turn in time to see the bombs hit the station. The little building erupted and even sailing a half mile past the target Katya saw brick and tile shards and burning timbers flung in the air, lit by the explosions. She flicked the magnetos and the propeller caught. She throttled power to gain more height for her bombing run. High above, the deadly night fighter skulked in circles. Behind her, the Olgas switched on their motor and together the planes gained altitude in a tight spiral. At three thousand feet the two Olgas cut power and glided away. Katya held back until she saw the searchlights sweep the night, watched them miss the dancing Night Witch, glance her, then lose their dazzling grip. The night fighter was too fast for its own good; it couldn't spot the slow and mobile U-2s as long as they stayed out of the light. The German would have no prey. The two Olgas swung left and right, riding the creases of darkness between the swaying beams. Katya followed them in. She put her nose dead on the burning train station, cut power, and one minute later blew the Oktabrskaya tracks into scrap.

July 2
0055 hours

'Vera.'

The navigator did not answer right away. Moments later, Katya said again, 'Vera.'

'Just a second.'

Katya turned to look in the cockpit behind her. Vera's flashlight swept over her lap, across a flapping topographical map. Vera made notes on a pad strapped to her leg. She leaned her head out over the fuselage and took some mental snapshot of a landmark below, then entered it on her notepad. She trained the flashlight on her stopwatch.

Off the tail, three miles behind Vera's bent head, the second flight of night bombers was over the target. The searchlights sliced back and forth, a good sign, they could not find the Witches working in tandem. The burning station made an easy bull's-eye.

Katya pivoted to face forward. Off the port wing flew the Olgas, their U-2's signature blue flames a halo around their engine.

'Any time, Vera.' Katya noticed her own tone was impatient.

'Now.'

Katya drew out the fuel mixture knob slowly to lean out the gasoline and increase the air flowing to the engine. She teased the motor just to the point of choking, then goosed the mixture. The plane coughed and sputtered, dipping in altitude. Katya rode the control to make the plane spit as loudly as it could.

The two Olgas swung alongside. Vera waved her flashlight at them to signal distress. When the other plane was close enough, Katya pushed in the control to smooth the engine. Her little U-2 caught and rose. Vera lowered the flashlight, and Katya slid out the knob once more. The engine hacked. Katya let the plane stumble in the air. The Olgas stayed by her side, matching her rise and fall. She reached for the flashlight. She shined it on herself, to make a signal to the Olgas that she was having engine trouble but she would be okay. At that moment, she pulled out the throttle all the way to shut off the fuel, flicked off the magnetos, and let the engine quit. She cut off the flashlight, banked hard beneath the two Olgas, and vanished from their sight.

Vera guided her. 'Come to port a little more.' Katya tweaked the gliding plane to the northwest. She felt a twinge that her fellow Night Witches were surely flying mad circles behind them, looking for a struggling plane or a crash landing. After a minute of silent running, having spent only a thousand feet of altitude, she struck up the propeller and powered the U-2 back to four thousand feet.

'We should cross the Udy River in about eight minutes,' Vera said. 'At this speed, we'll be over Tomarovka twelve minutes after that. Two miles east, right?'

'Yes.' Katya put fingertips on the stick. The U-2 was marvelously stable.

'Verushka?'

'What.'

'Thank you.'

'Don't thank me.'

'Yes, thank you. Leonid will thank you.'

Vera did not reply. Katya kept the plane on a straight heading. Leonid had been on the ground now for just under two hours. Enough time for German patrols or the partisans to get to him, enough time to bleed to death. Katya's plan was simple, because it was the only move she could make. She hoped to fly close enough to Leonid in the dark for him to recognize the popping Russian engine. If he was still alive, he would send up another flare to tell her so. She and Vera would set down in the nearest clearing, scoop him up, and lift him to safety. She'd brought along an emergency medical kit in case Leonid had wounds. She carried a pistol strapped to her belt; Vera did not, the girl knew nothing about firearms. They would have to locate him somewhere east of Tomarovka, set down in an unknown pasture in the dark, then gather him up and take off across this same field, missing ruts and irrigation ditches, creeks and stumps. If he could not walk they must carry him somehow to the plane. They had to reach him before the Germans, who may have seen the white flare Leonid fired for his squadron commander, and they must get out ahead of their guns. They had to fly low and very slow to find him, above an untold number of enemies. There was not a single step of the plan that was not dangerous. Katya wanted to talk some more about what they were facing but Vera stayed stony. This was a reversal of their natures.

It occurred to Katya that Vera was scared.

'Vera, we have to do this.'

The navigator did not reply.

Katya kept talking. 'We'll be alright. He's alive. I know he is.'

'So are we.' She noted Vera's heavy sigh in her earphones.

'There's no one else who can do this! It's up to us.'

'The partisans. You said the partisans were in the area.' Vera took the same harsh tone, the intercom made both their voices thorny.

'Yes, they are. But they're going after the train tonight, who knows if they'll send help after a downed pilot? The Germans will definitely go after him.'

More silence. Katya tried to fix her mind on the black flying and the rescue ahead but she required more, she needed forgiveness for bringing Vera into this extra peril.

'You're being very brave.'

In response, Vera almost barked. 'Don't we do enough?

We risk our lives in these shitty little airplanes they give us. Leonid risked his, too. He knew this could happen. We do enough, Katya.'

Katya wondered, How can I answer her? How can I say, No, we don't, we never do enough so long as a friend is in trouble. How do I tell this girl, my good friend, that I would die to find him? I can't do otherwise. She knows this. She agreed to come. She's just frightened.

'If he's not there, we'll go on. I promise, we'll only look for a few minutes.'

'And if we find him?'

'Then, Verushka, you have to trust that I'm the best pilot you know and I can land this plane on a ruble.'

Vera made no response. Behind Katya the flashlight came on. Vera was checking her maps.

'There's the Udy River. Straight now, twelve miles. Damn it. Let's get him and go home, wing-walker.'

Katya chuckled. This was her absolution from Vera, the bond and honor between them was stronger than the danger. The U-2 bumped over an air current, and this was a signal to focus on their task. Leonid was on the ground, and the Night Witches were coming for him.

They flew over the heads of a hundred thousand enemy soldiers. The Germans drew back a hundred thousand bolts, stuffed themselves deeper into their helmets or holes, winced, and eyed the night sky for a glimpse of the Russian plane droning past in the dark. They knew the sound of the U-2's puttering engine. But none would know it better than Leonid, and none would be happy to hear it but him.

The village of Tomarovka lay where the Vorskla River crossed an east-west rail line running to Belgorod. Vera located the tracks and kept Katya over them, headed west. The area where the fighter captain had said Leonid was down should be within two or three miles of these tracks. When Vera whispered they were five miles east of the village, Katya began her descent. She had to fly in low enough to be certain Leonid would hear her. And if he did send up a flare, Katya and Vera would need to get on and off the ground fast.

At two thousand feet, the potshots began. Katya did not hear the reports from the rifles and machine pistols, but muzzle flashes like a carpet of orange sparks blinked in her path. She could not glide over these men and guns, the motor had to keep running, that was her signal to Leonid. One ragged hole appeared in the port wing. She kept the U-2 flying straight; it made no sense to dodge, these were blind shots. She settled lower, to fifteen hundred feet, and leveled.

Tomarovka sat three miles to the west, dead and invisible. So close to the front lines, the occupying Germans hunkered without lights. Vera found a bend in the rail tracks that matched her map. 'Start circling,' she said. Her voice was firm and this gladdened Katya. She took the plane into a soft bank, dipping the port wings to look down at a velvet black earth. She prayed for Leonid to hear her. She asked that he be in a smooth field, that he not be hurt, that the Germans not know he was there until she had taken him away. She felt that God heard her better when she was in the air. She was closer to Him, to His domain, mimicking His angels. Katya muttered, 'Amen.' Vera said, 'I don't know what you were asking for, but Amen, too.'

Katya swept in a wide arc, staring at miles of nothing, as though down an eternal well, the earth was so featureless. Her engine *pop-pop*-ed. She flicked her eyes once at the gauges to make certain of her attitude and height, then did not pull her gaze from the deep, horizonless ground. She drifted lower, to make her engine louder. The propeller and pistons shouted: Leonid, Leonid! It's me!

For long minutes, Katya flew and scanned. The red winks from the ground grew fewer, the Germans got tired of shooting at a noisy but fleeting shadow. She banked right, to change her pattern to a figure eight and fly closer to the fortified village. She leaned so far out of the cockpit the wind almost whipped the goggles from her face.

She began to hear her own heartbeat louder than the engine. One more minute churned past. Vera's voice came from far away, behind the motor and wind, the pounding of her heart, and the silence of Leonid.

'Katya.'

A white sparkle punctured the even darkness on the ground. Her first thought was someone was lighting a fuse, as if to fire an old-fashioned cannon up at them. She turned the plane broadside to the light and banked to circle it just as it vanished. She kept her eyes on the spot; seconds later, the sparking flash came back, disappeared again, then returned.

Was this Leonid?

Katya whipped the plane directly at the light and it flicked on and off once more. It must be Leonid! Of course! He couldn't send up a flare, a German patrol would spot that, too, and home in on him. He was flashing a flare on the ground, covering it with a bucket or something. Katya checked her altitude: one thousand feet. She pushed in the throttle and flicked off the magnetos. The engine coughed and quit.

'What are you doing?' Vera asked.

Katya did not answer. She let the U-2 glide for ten seconds. This was the hallmark – the broomstick – of the Night Witches. Leonid, if it was him, would know and answer.

He did. The flare appeared, then blinked out.

Katya fired up the propeller, the plane had fallen to eight hundred feet. The flare glimmered from a mile away to the west. Leonid must have left his wrecked plane, to hide in the fields. He'd known she would come.

She tried to keep her vision glued to the spot in the dark

canvas where she believed he was, but taking her eyes from the ground for a moment to check her dials, Katya lost the location. Vera, the steady navigator, did not lose the bearing.

'Left. More. More. There! Straight ahead. Go get him, Katya.'

Katya's mind raced with the plane. Leonid would have moved to a field he knew would be suitable for her to land in. She had faith in this; he was a pilot himself, and like his captain said, a clever lad. The U-2 needed very little runway, less than four hundred feet. She could swoop in, stop, bring him onboard, then turn and roar out for safety. Yes! They would do it! There, a half-mile ahead, was another flare. This one did not blink but glowed fiercely, a landing light!

Katya swung the U-2's nose right at the beacon. She dropped altitude for a fast and abrupt landing. There was no time to do a fly-by and check out the conditions of the field; she had to trust Leonid for that. Her heart climbed into her throat with the approaching ground, five hundred feet below and closing. One hand juggled the stick, the other adjusted the throttle; she put out her senses to determine the direction of the wind, it seemed light and at her back. Her feet stayed ready at the rudders.

The flare gleamed straight ahead. This close to the ground, she could discern the shapes of trees to her left and right, and behind the flare spread a flat dark swath of ground. Leonid had done his job. Now she did hers.

At three hundred feet off the field, she was still coming in hot. She had time to bleed off the last of her speed in the thousand feet before she lifted the nose and laid down the wheels. She pointed at the white flare, aiming to touch down just past it, Leonid would have set it at the leading edge of the runway. She felt a thrill, not just for the return of Leonid but for the heroic feat of all this, the *podvig*. Her hands and toes kept the plane reined tight, she leaned forward in these last seconds, into the mane of the airplane.

In that moment another, smaller flash lured her eyes away from the flare to her extreme right. Blinks of crimson glittered from a stand of trees silhouetted against the night. In that one swift glance, Katya knew. A German patrol had followed the sparking flare and the pops of her engine. Enemy soldiers were running at her, firing.

She sped past the flashes; there was still time to get on the ground, collect Leonid, and get away. The flare was ten seconds ahead. She slipped in the throttle, easing her airspeed, then pulled on the stick to lift the nose and slow her approach, but instead of responding the stick surged on its own to the left. The plane dipped and banked. She lost a moment in surprise, then hauled back too late and not enough, now the plane's descent was sideways and too steep.

'Vera, let go!' she screamed into the intercom. 'You'll make us crash! Let *go*!'

The stick did not free into Katya's struggling hands. She shouted at Vera but no answer came into her ears or her straining grip.

Katya was afraid to take her eyes off the expanding ground but she had to see why Vera was gripping the stick. There were only a few seconds remaining in which to right the plane. She whirled at her navigator. The girl was slumped. Her head lolled against her chest. Vera's body was crumpled in her harness and her leg lay across the stick, shoving it to the left. In the right wall of the fuselage, lit by the little green light of the dials, a diagonal line of holes was punched through the fuselage. Each was matched by a black rip in Vera's flight suit.

Katya screamed again, 'Vera!' The feat that had lain only seconds away became a panic. She could not reach Vera's body, could not take her hand off the stick even for a moment, the ground was too close, her speed still too great. Frantic, she shoved against Vera's bent head. The dead girl would not lay back. She had no time to mourn; battling the stick and Vera's weight against it, Katya fought her shock and the dread rising in her fast with the ground.

If she could level out and pull up, Vera would fall backward off the stick. Leonid would hear her fly off, he'd run from the Germans to another field. She could circle and come back.

If.

Katya looked at the rising dark earth. She yanked a final time on the dead stick. No, she thought. No. She went rigid in the cockpit against this fate.

The port wings grazed the ground first, cartwheeling the fuselage. The left wheel touched down, then bounded into the air. The tail leaped behind her, the propeller and engine smacked the earth, drilling into the soft loam and snapping to a halt. Her goggles went blank with dirt, her brain curtained black with concussion. One last thought streaked through the collapse of her life: Vera is dead, Leonid is lost, and I am dead; goodbye to Papa and Valentin. She felt dismay that it all could be summed up and done so quickly.

She opened her eyes. No sound or light told her she was alive until one of the U-2's wire struts broke with a comic *sproiiing*. Her head was too heavy to lift. She faced the ground, which jumped with uneasy shadows. Katya turned her throbbing head enough to see a flare on the ground, and the curtain parted, memory pierced her. The U-2 had not been pulverized in the crash but somehow had come to rest standing on its engine like a dart flung into the earth. She was suspended in her harness. Vera was dead in the cockpit behind her. Ah, Vera.

Leonid's flare hissed, she tasted its smoke blown at her. Where was he?

Katya's chin hung against her chest. The number of her

predicaments flooded in on her; riding this awareness came pain. She fumbled with her safety belts but could not muster the strength in either hand to pull the catches. Both shoulders felt wrenched out of joint; her head seemed ready to snap off her body from the ache rising through her neck.

The flare began to fizzle, its time almost done. Katya sensed the weight of Vera dangling at her back. She tried again to get out of the wreckage, pushing back her pain to work her hands on the buckles.

In the last sizzles of the flare, a knife appeared beneath her throat.

The German patrol! They'd come to finish off the Night Witch! No, no, Katya thrashed her head and arms, she kicked her feet in horror, the pain in her body forgotten. No!

'Calm down, calm down,' a male voice urged. The words were Russian. It was Leonid! 'Sit still, damn it!'

The blade withdrew. A strong hand went into Katya's hair and yanked up her head to see. The face that slid close to hers was dirty and unshaven, yellow teeth flickered in the dying flare.

'I'm going to cut you out of here. Do you understand me?'

Katya tried to speak but her throat stayed clamped in hurt and the ebb of her terror. She tried to say Vera's name.

The face issued an order to someone else. 'Kick some dirt on that fucking flare, fast!'

Instantly, the white light went out. The hand that gripped her head by the hair let go. Katya heard a snipping sound, several hands pushed up on her in the cockpit and she was released into them past the shreds of the slashed belts.

'Can you walk?' The hands lowered her out of the cockpit. They tried to put her on her feet. Her knees buckled. Dark shapes did not let her hit the ground.

'Her,' she mumbled. 'Get her.'

'No time,' the voice answered. 'You two carry this one. Let's go.'

Before she could protest, she was dragged away from her plane. The tops of her flight boots scraped over the ground. The three men smelled of wool, sweat, and grass. The sourness of gun oil rose from their backs, where their carbines were strapped.

'Leonid. Where ... ?'

The man hurrying on her left, short and burly under her arm, answered. 'He ran away before we could find him. We weren't expecting you to swoop in like that.'

No, Katya thought. Leonid wouldn't have done that. He would have run to the plane the moment it crashed, he would have gotten me out of the wreck. He would have gotten Vera out.

'He ... ,' she forced the words out, to defend Leonid, ' ...wouldn't run away.'

She felt the partisan's heavy shoulder shrug under her weight. 'Then the Germans got him.'

CHAPTER 8

July 2
0120 hours
Wehrmacht train
north of Khar'kov,
near the Ukraine-Russian border
the Russian steppe

A knock sounded on Luis's compartment door. He snapped awake. His sleep was never deep anymore, this frail frame he despised needed only shallow rest.

'Yes.'

'A message for you from the engineer, sir.'

Luis pulled his heels off the bench across from him. He stood and arranged his uniform. No trooper would see him in disarray, he was a *Waffen* SS Captain. His father had always told him the power is in the performance.

He slid the cabin door all the way back. The soldier seemed surprised, expecting the door to be only cracked at this time in the morning, not to encounter such alertness.

'Give it to me, Private.'

'Yes, sir. Good morning, sir.'

Luis took the folded sheet without looking down, keeping his eyes glued to the young grenadier's face. Was there any hint of surprise on the boy at the gaunt white form who'd opened the door? No. Good. Luis nodded and the soldier clicked his heels in attention. Bearing, thought Luis. Bearing. This soldier could snap me in half if he had a mind to, but I can make him jump off this moving train with a word.

Luis opened the page. The private waited.

He read the one-line message, then looked the soldier up and down. Strong boy, he thought, big blond lad. But the soldier was not German. The insignia on his collar and sleeve revealed he was Czech. He and Luis had this in common, they were non-Germans serving in the SS. Because of their massive losses, the SS was recruiting outside Germany. Standing here on this rattling train deep in Russia, blond and dark, were two samples of the reach of Hitler's ambitions.

Luis patted the boy's arm.

'Tell the engineer to stop the train.'

The soldier set his jaw, a love of taking orders was clear. Looking at him, Luis thought: This boy has not been to Russia before. The soldier said, 'Yes, sir!' and left. Luis reached back for his cap, nestled it on his head, and walked to the next compartment. He knocked.

'Major Grimm.'

Behind the door, a sleepy throat snorted and coughed.

'Yes. Yes, who is it?'

'Captain de Vega.'

'Captain. What time is it?'

'Open up, please, Major.'

'Yes. A moment.'

The major slid back the door only inches, disheveled, the plat of hair he combed over his wispy pate hung below his ear. Luis saw he was barefoot and in his undershirt.

'Do you have a sidearm, Major?'

'What?'

'A weapon, sir. Do you have a gun with you?'

'Yes, yes.'

'Please strap it on and come with me.'

The fat officer sighed, then nodded, resigned. 'Give me a …'

The major started to close the door to dress but Luis gave him a displeased glance, that he would not care to linger outside a shut door, waiting. The major slid the door full open and turned to his task.

The car jerked to the squealing of brakes, the train slowed and stopped. Under the gasps of steam from the locomotive, the officer donned his pants, tunic, and boots. Out of a travel case he took his Luger pistol and holster and buckled them on. He asked no questions.

Luis led him down the hall to the passenger car door. He spoke over his shoulder. 'As ranking officer on this train, I thought I should alert you, Major. I've received a radio message that the tracks are broken ahead at the Oktabrskaya station. We cannot get through just yet. I've ordered the train to a halt.'

Luis stepped out of the train onto the rail mound. The major clambered down behind him.

'Why are we stopping out here in the middle of ...'

'Shhh, Major. Please.'

The train stood still, the locomotive continued its heavy metal breath, waiting for the order to continue. On either side of the tracks stretched a field, without trees or bushes. His ears caught nothing, not the rustle of a leaf or the shush of a breeze, so vast was the open land, just a flat earth black with unmown grasses.

'They won't come here.'

'Who won't come here?' the major asked.

'The partisans.'

'Partisans?'

'They're trying to stop this train, Major.'

Something in Luis's flat tone kept the major from further queries. The officer's bare head pivoted up and down the empty tracks, he seemed suddenly aware he was alone outside the train car with only a skinny SS captain and their two pistols. The notion of partisans was a fearsome one, bearded wild men in civilian clothes who fought with abandon, with vengeful crudeness and animal cunning. They were natives who knew every inch of the land and had the local populace to abet them. But there's no danger right here, Luis thought. He'd seen enough ambushes, set a few himself, to know when and where they were likely. Not here, without cover to attack and retreat. No, they're waiting somewhere ahead. There will be trees beside the tracks and they'll come out of them.

Luis lifted his nose, sipping the night air, calculating. The major asked, 'How do you know this?'

'The SS has received reports over the past few days that the Russians would try to bomb the Oktabrskaya train station. This they did tonight, apparently quite well. Blowing up the station was just a delaying tactic, Major, to slow the train in case the first partisan attack fails. While we wait for the tracks to be mended, they'll have time to organize another ambush.'

The major fidgeted. 'Another ambush?'

'Yes. After the one tonight.'

'Tonight?'

The major was repeating things again, but Luis grew patient now that he knew what was going to happen. The engineer had followed his instructions and alerted him when the train approached Slatino, ten miles south of the Ukraine border with Russia, twenty miles south of Oktabrskaya.

Luis eased his voice and said, 'Yes. That's why I'm here.'

The officer cocked his head at Luis.

'You may get back on board, Major. I'll join you shortly.'

Major Grimm turned on the sooty rocks. He climbed the steps back into the passenger car.

From the steps he asked, 'How did you know, Captain de Vega?'

Luis nodded into the vast darkness of the Russian steppe.

Yes, he thought, let's begin, and he harkened back to the huge silence of the *plaza* when the bull first enters the ring.

'I know, Major, because we have infiltrated the partisans.'

July 2
0200 hours

Luis ate only half of the bratwurst sandwich. He offered the rest of it to the engineer. The man declined, making a face to indicate he was too nervous to eat.

Luis looked around the locomotive compartment. It was not unlike the innards of a tank with all its dials and handles, everything made of metal and glass, but roomier. He admired the power of the big, pulsing machine to pull the immense weight trailing behind them. With a smile he considered how easily any one of his Tiger tanks straddling these tracks could shoot this locomotive into the ditch. But he did not say this, he was not feeling competitive. The engineer was executing his job well and with discipline, doing what Luis told him to do. The man did not also have to be brave.

Luis kept watch on the terrain beside the tracks. Major Grimm had wanted to wait until morning to continue but Luis made the decision to keep going the rest of the way under the cloak of night, a trainload of new Tigers would be ripe for a Soviet air attack. Besides, this was his train, his first assignment back on active duty, and it was going to arrive at Oktabrskaya at sunup, as scheduled, even if the station there was in shambles.

'That's enough,' he told the engineer. The man worked his levers and cords and the train slowed with a tremendous sigh. When it was stopped, Luis climbed down onto the rails, his Luger in one hand, a flashlight in the other. From one of the troop cars, a soldier climbed down and waited. Luis flashed his light at the soldier once, the soldier flashed back.

Luis walked ahead. The train panted in stillness behind him. He trod the rail mound leaving the flashlight off, fixing his gaze on the tracks; this was the third time in the twenty kilometers since Slatino he'd escorted the train through a passage of trees lining the rails. The scanty body he was trapped in made almost no sound walking the ties, his balance was so good he could stay on a single rail for a hundred meters before stepping off. His night vision was remarkable. He was sharp, like his nickname, cutting through the night.

The partisans will come with fifty men, he thought. That was the SS intelligence.

Somewhere close to the Ukraine border. He paused and turned back to the unseen train a half mile behind him now. He blinked his flashlight twice. He knew without seeing that the soldier he'd stationed a quarter mile between himself and the train was signaling with another flashlight for the train to move forward. In response to the signal, Luis heard only a distant heave of steam.

The phalanx of trees was at least another mile long. The woods appeared to him as a jagged edge of deeper night, like the blackest paper roughly torn and pasted beside the tracks. He walked, head down, considering the partisan plan, filling in the gaps of his knowledge with what he would do in their position. Fifty men with smallarms, on foot, would wait in the trees. They'll expect the train to come barreling past. When it does, they'll blow the track under the locomotive or perhaps under one of the troop cars. The train will derail and the partisans will rush in a single wave out of their cover, across fifty meters of open ground on either side. Many cars will be upended, the garrison will be stunned or injured. They'll engage in a quick and fierce firefight. In the midst of the shooting, they'll head for the tanks with more explosives to spike the cannon barrels. Then the partisans will melt back into the steppe, and Luis will make his return to his SS division *Leibstandarte* by reporting the death of the ten Tigers that were under his protection.

Luis stopped. He turned a full circle on the rails and tingled. He'd walked into the place where he would have set the snare were he the one lying in ambush. A curve in the tracks. A band of trees on both sides of the rails. Wide fields behind them, no villages close by. Luis cast his gaze into the brush and branches left and right, and peopled the dark with twenty-five dirty faces per side, breaths held, fifty fingers on triggers. He walked another dozen quiet steps, sensing the Russians' anger; in the darkness he pitched his own wrath against theirs, and in the spark that was made when the two met and struck, he saw the explosive.

He froze on the track. The train was far back and puffing, waiting for his signal to come forward. The partisans would be waiting just ahead, expecting the train's momentum to carry it past the point of the tracks they intended to blast, toppling the cars in front of them. Perhaps they haven't heard the train yet; Luis himself could barely make out the huffing locomotive.

He hoped they hadn't seen or heard him, either.

He bent low, approaching the mine with five careful strides. Wedged sideways between the tracks was a fat log, like a damsel tied there in the night. Luis knelt beside it, feeling the bark, listening into the darkness for the sound of boots coming to draw a knife across his scrawny neck. With exploring fingers, he determined the nature of the bomb. Jammed between one end of the wooden trunk and the left-hand rail were two bars of C-3 explosive, two and a quarter pounds of the stuff smashed between the wood and the steel. Luis skimmed fingers across the putty lumps of plastique, feeling for the blasting caps; there would be two, wired together in case one failed. He found them and pulled his hand away; blasting caps were notoriously volatile, far more than the C-3 itself.

Luis admired the cleverness of the partisans. The section of tree trunk had been laid between the tracks as tamping for the explosive. When the C-3 blew, only one track would be severed, the one on the inside of the curve. This rail would break to the side, not up. The train cars leaning around the bend in the tracks would derail to the inside of the curve, and because one set of wheels would be lower, the cars would spill over.

Luis saw the single electric cord running to the blasting caps. The slender wire ran left, straight into the trees in front of him. This was not good. The partisans were right there, forty meters away. Slowly, he put his Luger pistol in the hand holding the flashlight, and reached his empty hand into a tunic pocket for his wire cutters.

He dropped the Luger.

The thing clattered, metal tattle-tale on the big granite stones of the rail mound. Luis wasted not a second. He clutched the wire cutter and snipped the wire, felt the wire coil away from the blasting caps, then pulled the caps out of the C-3 as quickly as he dared. Once the explosive was disarmed – the detonators were out in seconds but to Luis it seemed an hour – he jumped to his feet and took this new physique of his on its first flat-out run.

He turned on the flashlight and blinked it three times into the darkness that swallowed the train. This was a different signal. Then he threw the flashlight away and drove his arms and legs as fast as he could. It was good to hear his boots were not always so silent; this time they tore down the rail ties with blaring purpose.

The first shots sounded in the trees. He could not tell how close the bullets came to him, he was running and huffing so hard he would have to get hit by a bullet before he would know if they had a bead on him. He ran down off the rail ties into the grass; it made no sense to race straight down the tracks, it made him too easy a target. More reports cracked out of the trees on both sides. Luis reproached himself for a clumsy ass, dropping the pistol like that. He ran on, exhilarated, laughing with manic gasps at every shot fired behind him that missed; he was too thin to be much of a target.

The waist-high grass beside the rail mound did not slow him. Like running on the moon, he thought, pumping his knees and elbows; whipped-up pollen flew in his face, a night breeze brushed his puffing cheeks. But what speed, he thought, where is the gravity of the world now?

He lost count of the shots the partisans fired at him. He wasn't worried about being wounded, they never got a clear look at him in his speeding black uniform. He just wanted to get back to the train fast, before the partisans could repair the cut wire and blow the track anyway, settling for that little victory and making their escape. Luis had more planned for them.

The soldier shined his flashlight at Luis coming up out of the grass. Luis stopped and turned back up the tracks. He controlled his breathing as best he could to be quiet, to hear if they were still shooting or even following. He heard nothing.

From the other direction came the train, rushing to where they stood. This soldier had done his job. When Luis flashed him three times, he was to summon the train.

'Captain, are you alright?' the soldier asked.

'Yes,' Luis huffed. 'They ... uh ...' he took a deep breath and blew it out, ' ... they spotted me. But I found it. I cut the wire ...'

'Are they following you, sir?'

'I don't know.'

The soldier unshouldered his submachine-gun.

'You go back to the train, Captain. I'll keep them off you.'

Luis took one more moment to look this boy over, the Czech one who'd delivered the message to his compartment an hour ago. This is why the SS is running out of men, Luis thought.

'No, Private. Stay with me. You'll get your chance in another minute.'

The train rumbled up to them. The two ran alongside. Luis climbed onto the ladder to the locomotive. He stuck his head into the compartment. 'Keep this speed, no faster,' he shouted to the engineer. Then he dropped off the ladder and let the train haul the first of the passenger cars to him. He beckoned the Czech grenadier to follow, then matched the pace of the car and jumped aboard.

He entered the car. Fifty SS troopers huddled in the seats; helmets, boots, belts, and barrels creaked and rattled with the joggling of the slow-moving train. Several of the soldiers snored.

'Up,' Luis said. A few leaped to their feet; the jangling noise animated the rest.

'Now,' Luis said.

In seconds the men lined up like paratroopers in an airplane to leap from the passenger car doors. Luis turned to enter the next car.

'Up,' he said.

When he had done this in all four cars, issuing two hundred trained grenadiers onto the rail mound, he jumped down the tracks, the Czech soldier at his heels. The train engineer, though a fearful man, had not sped the train up one jot.

When his own passenger car rolled past, Luis saw the major peering out the open window of his own cabin.

Luis waved. 'You're going to miss the fun, Major.'

Grimm held up both palms to Luis and shouted down,

'Wait!' He disappeared from the window. Luis envisioned the fat officer scrambling in his dark compartment for his socks and boots to scoot off the train before it reached the partisans and their booby-trap.

The train ambled by. When the flatbeds carrying the Tigers came up, he called to the guards on the first car: 'Ready.'

Two of the guards jumped from the flatbed over to the connected car, which was covered by a tarp. With Luis and the Czech private watching, the guards slipped the ropes holding the canvas sheath. The tarp flapped in the moving wind and fell away from a sandbagged machine-gun position. The two guards leaped in behind the gun, primed the ammo belt in the breech, and slid by toward the partisans, pivoting the barrel left and right, ready just as Luis had commanded and planned. When the last car in the train rattled by carrying the second tarp-covered pillbox, Luis gave the same signal. The soldiers sprang to their assignment.

Luis and the Czech stood behind the slowly receding train. The major trundled to the end of the steps and held on, hesitant to jump down to the moving ground, then hopped off, almost stumbling on the rocks. Luis looked at the Czech. The boy was eager like a dog, to fetch, to chase.

'Go,' Luis said, releasing him with his voice and an open hand. The boy ran off behind the train, to get his portion of the kill.

Luis strolled behind the train, over the tracks he'd run across just two minutes before. He walked over to the major, caught his elbow and walked him forward along the tracks.

'Shouldn't we stay back here?' the major asked, confused and apprehensive.

'It's safe, Major.'

To punctuate this, small-arms fire erupted out of the

night from up the tracks. Luis walked beside the officer, listening and calculating when the train would pass beyond the partisans' defused bomb. Gunfire spurted on both sides of the rail line, automatic weapons unleashed their *rat-tat-tat,* then gave way to single reports, then nothing. It was over. The train was safe.

'What did you do?' Major Grimm inquired. The man walked with both hands clasped behind his back, buttoned and belted belly out. His double chin hid part of his collar. Luis felt a twinge of vexation at this Wehrmacht officer, who carried on him as extra all the weight Luis had sacrificed, who cowered in his compartment until even that became unsafe, while others – SS men all – ran ahead into the dark to engage the enemy.

'Once I found the place where the partisans wanted to blow the tracks, I cut the wire to their explosive. Clever idea they'd come up with, to wreck only one rail and spill the train on its side. They spotted me at the last second and I ran back to the train.'

'Those were the first gunshots, then. Them shooting at you?'

Nothing was said about the dropped Luger. Luis caught himself drawing up his posture, gaunt shoulders back, he took longer strides, the peacock walk of the *matador*. He had lain in hospital beds for months, tottered with canes for more months, suffered in sanitary surroundings through seasons of battle news from the front, and now this night marked his return to the war. Luis preened and strolled and talked.

'In addition to escorting the Tiger tanks, I'm also bringing a company of reinforcements to *Leibstandarte*. Once I was sure where the partisans were located, I sent each of the four platoons ahead. Two platoons were ordered to take positions between the tracks and the trees. Two more were to penetrate the woods and come out behind the Russians in the fields. The train drove between them. The Tigers were protected by twin machine-gun redoubts on rail cars.'

'The tarpaulins.'

'Yes.'

'Ah, I wondered what was under those sheets.'

'Guns, Major.'

'Yes, of course. Well, this is a war. What does one expect?'

'Once the train was safe, the first two platoons entered the trees to flush the partisans away from the tracks and back toward the fields. When the Reds ran out from cover to disperse, the second platoons were waiting.'

'It sounds like a quail hunt,' the major said with approval.

'Actually, a pincer action.'

'Yes, well, it doesn't matter. The tanks are safe. And so are we, I assume?'

'Yes.'

'Good. Good.' The major clapped Luis on the back, celebrating his own closeness to danger and his survival in the graces of this little SS captain. There was something condescending in the slap on the back, Luis thought; it carried the flavor of a German officer thanking a Spaniard for a job well done in the service of Germany. There was also a hint of surprise, as though Luis were too much a runt to be this brave and effective.

They approached the place on the tracks where the partisans had set their bomb. The log was still smeared with the gray explosive on one side, the blasting caps and wire were helpless deposits beside the rail. Major Grimm studied the set-up and clucked his tongue.

The locomotive sighed in the dark around the bend. As per Luis's instructions, the train halted a half mile away. Dawn would overtake them in another hour. Luis would roll with his Tigers safe and on schedule into the ruins of the Oktabrskaya station. The rails there would be repaired before the day was out. The tanks were too valuable to leave them at a rail station thirty miles from the front.

The two hundred SS grenadiers he'd unleashed into the woods began to return to the tracks. They came crashing through the underbrush carrying the bodies of dead partisans, as they'd been instructed. One by one, the carcasses were tossed like sacks onto the slope of the rail mound. Luis walked along the line of bodies, the Germans laid them out spaced neatly. The partisans would be found like this. Their ruse to blow the tracks was discovered and averted. They might suspect they have a spy in their cell and tear themselves apart looking for him. Perhaps not. No matter. Even if they found the informant, he'd be easily replaced. The Gestapo were masters of persuasion.

He walked the line of corpses. He expected to see many forms of one man, the simple Russian peasant roused to fight the European invader, knobby-handed laborers, shaggy beards and moustaches under close-cropped hair, tattered clothes and savage expressions even in death. These freshly killed ones were civilized, and Luis found that odd. These partisans were not starved, their clothes were not ragged. The weapons collected by the grenadiers were first-rate, front-line rifles, oiled and loaded. A handful of the partisans had been young men, perhaps soldiers slipped into the conquered lands to provide the partisan cells with professional training and leadership. Most were older, with determined looks frozen on them in repose. Luis kicked the boots of one; these were new boots, good leather all around.

Major Grimm came to his side.

'They're getting stronger,' the major observed.

Luis nodded. He'd been briefed that the Russian partisan movement was disorganized, tattered. These corpses gave the lie to that intelligence. These men lying shoulder to shoulder on the gravel had been supplied, supported, led, emboldened. Their kind of fury was fed by the harshness of Germany's occupation, the stench from the death camps, and the lunacy of taking these people lightly, something Luis had sworn long ago he would not do again.

Thirty-six bodies were lined up. Luis saw the determination and efficiency of the SS troopers daubed somewhere on each one, each corpse a quick tale; a short run to somewhere ended in being shot down. A wound in the neck, several in the chest or abdomen, many coats had no rents, their bullets were in the back. At the end of the row of partisans lay one SS soldier. Over him stood the Czech private.

'Your friend?' Luis asked.

The young soldier nodded. The dead grenadier, too, had the Czech flag on his sleeve. One stained rip dotted the dead boy's jacket, the hole darker than any night.

'Go get the train,' Luis ordered the soldier. 'Tell the engineer to come back.'

The soldier said, 'Yes, sir.' With what seemed like no effort he reached down for his comrade and slung the corpse across his shoulder. He walked off down the rail ties with his cooling burden.

A sergeant from one of the platoons presented himself to Luis and the major beside him.

'Report, Sergeant,' Luis instructed.

'A few got away, sir, no more than four or five. But we've got these here who surrendered.'

Behind the sergeant stood three partisans. These men hung their heads, making Luis think of a bull when he and the *picadors* were done with it. But these men were captive and afraid and for Luis that was their difference from the bulls, animals that were never afraid. He moved close to the three. They smelled. He curled his nose at fear and dirt, cheap wool and vodka. He never hated the bulls when he fought them, he and every man inside the ring respected and loved the beasts for their courage and how hard they died. He tried to keep his anger from quaking his hand when he held it out for the sergeant's pistol. The soldier laid the gun in Luis's palm.

'Turn them around,' he directed the sergeant. The soldier obeyed.

Luis barely looked at them. He'd had more curiosity for the dead ones lined along the rail mound, the ones who died fighting. These three surrendered.

Luis dispatched the first one. The single shot to the back of the head pitched the partisan forward. The report flew off into the fathomless night. The partisan crumpled across the tracks. One of the grenadiers hauled the body back by the feet, aligning it tidily with the rest of the corpses.

The second partisan whimpered. Luis stepped back and shot him from an outstretched arm, to put as much distance between himself and this weeper as he could. This one did not even tumble forward but collapsed at the knees, so weak was he. Another soldier straightened the body.

Luis walked behind the third. He raised his pistol. The man turned around to face him, not lifting his eyes to the Luger aimed at his forehead but glaring deep into Luis's sockets. Luis saw a sneer; the partisan was enjoying what had been done to this SS man he now eyed, the flesh stripped off him by the war made on Russia. The partisan licked his lips, dry, under clean-shaven cheeks. He was old, this one, he'd seen enough life, time to balance it out with death. He challenged Luis by turning around. He mocked him by speaking.

'Rodina,' the partisan said.

Luis felt alone with the partisan, enfolded by night out here on a stretch of Russian rail. The man had said 'Motherland.' His eyes were final, not just for himself but for Luis and the whole war. Luis held the gun steady between the partisan's eyes.

Slowly, with even more sureness than the partisan had mustered, he shook his own head. No, he told the man with the gesture; the finalness is yours alone.

He lowered the gun, handing it back to the sergeant. No one else moved, not the major nor any of the watching grenadiers.

In a flash, Luis grabbed the hilt of his SS knife. The blade leaped from its sheath. With a backhand stab, knuckles up, Luis drove the dagger into the side of the partisan's neck. The knife embedded where it was intended, missing the carotid artery and striking between the vertebrae to slice the spinal cord. Luis yanked the blade out and the partisan fell like a puppet with its strings cut. The glare on the man's face was wiped away.

Luis looked to the sky. The sun was beginning to rise. He knelt to swipe his knife on the partisan's pant leg, then slid the blade back into its scabbard.

He issued no orders for the soldiers to follow, but walked away past the line of bodies, toward the waiting train. The men tramped after him, wordless, rifles clanking in their arms and across their backs. He didn't look down at the partisans, there was no more curiosity, death made every man the same.

Major Grimm caught up to him at the head of the company. Luis still felt the life of the defiant partisan throb in his hand, a powerful sensation, like a heartbeat. The major wanted to talk, it seemed, but Luis did not oblige. He reached into a pocket for a packet of crackers to appease his hunger.

CHAPTER 9

July 2
0210 hours
west of Tomarovka

Even half conscious, Katya could still ride.

The three dark partisans who'd cut her from her downed U-2 had horses tied at the nearby farm of a peasant. Four mounts waited, the spare was to have been for Leonid.

She needed help climbing into the saddle. Her ribs and hips all felt clobbered, every muscle seared. The old peasant looked her over while handing a bag of food up to one of the partisans. He asked, 'Is this the pilot you came to rescue? A woman?' The partisan took the parcel and replied, 'No.'

One of the men grabbed the reins to guide her horse. Katya drew the leather back into her own hands and told him, 'Ride.'

The three partisans wheeled their mounts. The peasant continued his distasteful glare at Katya, as though he'd risked his life stashing these horses for the partisans to salvage nothing more than some fragile female. She managed one good kick in her horse's ribs and lit out behind them into the darkness.

They rode for an hour, stopping at every sound in the night. The horses were well trained, accustomed to stealth, they did not nicker or stomp. The three men did not talk to Katya, they seemed angry with her. She did not ask questions. She was in a new slipstream, swept off in the current of unexpected events and people. She clung to the horse by instinct, for her hands and knees could barely clutch. Her mind staggered between blows: in one moment pain, in the next dead Vera left behind, in another Leonid lost or captured, then fear, then again pain.

One of the partisans was the leader of their little group. He rode in front and set the tone and pace. They stayed out of the open fields and away from every building, creeping along the gaps between tree lines. The Germans in this area kept themselves murky, only a few distant campfires were spangles on the darkness, one set of headlights on a far-off dirt road glimmered and vanished. The four riders came to a stream. The leader raised a hand for them to stop. He dismounted and waved the others from their horses. Leading his horse, he moved into the calf-deep water. Katya swung her leg across the saddle. She heard herself moan, the ground became the sky, galaxy-filled. She fainted.

July 2
noon
in a field south of Borisovka

Rain dribbled on her forehead. Soft light played over her eyelids. The grass beneath her back felt soft and damp. Papa knelt beside her – was it Papa? – smelling of horse and steel, and close too was the youth of Valentin, an energy she could feel without seeing. A horse pawed, a leafy branch strayed between her shut eyes and the sky. She was home.

Katya opened her eyes. Gray light dodged through wet branches low over her face. She blinked, and that movement tripped off the pain in her joints. She groaned and turned her head.

'So, this is a Night Witch.'

The voice tumbled from a squatting man, his elbows across his knees and his boot heels off the grass. His voice was deep, but no deeper than the eyes which were set in his sockets as if at the back of caves. They were black eyes under black brows, over hollow grim cheeks fletched with silver stubble. But he smiled and reached down a hand. Each finger was filthy with half-moons of dirt under the nails. He wore a charcoal wool suit coat and brown slacks. His shirt was forest green.

Katya took a deep breath; her ribs protested, making her wince. The squatting man shook the hand he held out. Katya took it. He pulled gently and she sat up.

'There,' he said. 'All better, yes?'

'No.'

She looked about. In addition to this stranger, thirty others sat oiling guns, eyeing the surrounding fields through the dripping leaves, or napping. An equal number of horses clustered around the trees where they were tethered.

'Where am I?'

'Three miles south of Borisovka. In a stand of trees. On your ass, where you've been for the last nine hours.'

Katya remembered stopping at the stream. Swinging her leg out of the saddle. The burst of stars.

'I ...'

'You passed out. They brought you in across your saddle.' The man pointed at three men standing behind him. 'You're a sound sleeper, Night Witch. What's your name?'

The three came to loom over the kneeling partisan. She recognized them through the haze of her recollection; last night's leader was an old one very like the man beside her, hardened, something vicious under the skin. The other two were younger, probably soldiers found behind enemy lines. One was thin, the other heavy. The skinny one was cold-eyed, not much more than twenty yet he looked wicked, a killer. The heavy one might have been her age, twenty-eight, with a blushed, full face like a red rising sun. This one's manner was mercurial, with fleet eyes and a nervous, jiggling neck. Katya knew either of them, any of them gathered under these trees, would stick a dirk in her heart if they believed she was a threat to their unit.

'Is there any water?' she asked, holding her voice steady.

The heavy one handed down his canteen. He smiled with the gesture, then like a fish the smile darted from his lips.

She drank, then answered the kneeling man's question. 'Katerina Dimitriyevna Berkovna. Lieutenant, 208th Night Bomber Division.'

Katya tried to stand. The kneeling man stood and helped her. The fat one lent a hand, too. The other two held their ground and watched her struggle upright.

Once she was erect, before speaking, she made her peace with the wracking in her body. No bones were broken, but she knew beneath her flight suit she was a storm cloud of bruises.

She addressed the three partisans who'd saved her from the plane and the German patrol. 'Thank you.' They nodded, and the unspoken clung on their faces, a show of their dismay that it was Katya they had rescued and not the fighter pilot they'd been seeking at Tomarovka.

The deep-eyed man spoke for them. 'I'm Colonel Plokhoi.' This partisan called himself *Colonel Bad*. 'You're with a *druzhiny* of the Hurricane Brigade. Last night our cell had a radio alert that a Yak-9 was down in our region. My men went to bring the pilot back. They were about to meet him at the assigned location when you showed up to save him instead.'

'Leonid Lumanov.' Katya said the name so Leonid would not be known as 'him.' These partisans were like untamed bits of the earth itself, gloomy and weathered. She hurt a great deal standing here but not so much that she would drop her defiance and become the disappointing woman these four believed they'd lugged back. She was a pilot, like Leonid.

'Lumanov,' the colonel allowed her, nodding. 'Well, when Lumanov struck his flare for you to land, the Germans saw him. As a result, you got shot down. Your pilot friend disappeared. And your navigator got killed.'

Katya winced. She wanted to say Vera's name, too, to lay a grave marker on the cool words of this partisan. But Plokhoi was right. If she had stayed away, Leonid would be safe. Vera would be alive.

Katya fought the urge to hang her head in grief. Instead she kept her chin and her gaze firm; neither Vera nor Leonid would want her to show regret to these men. Vera had encouraged the rescue, her last words were 'Go get him, Katya.' And Leonid had lit the flare, preferring to be rescued by Katya and her little U-2 instead of the partisans. Yes, she was sorry for what happened, the loss and death, but for nothing more, not her own effort, not the bravery of Vera, not the faith of Leonid.

The three partisans who'd brought her back turned away now that she was awake and standing. The heavyset one allowed a sympathetic smile before walking off. His thinner mate went to sit with some comrades, men who made no noise other than the sound of several whetstones under swirling blades, a hiss that blended with the patter of the rain.

Plokhoi jerked a thumb over his shoulder at his platoon. 'They'll be fine. Actually, they've got plenty to thank you for. We get a lot of supplies dropped to us by you Night Witches. By the way, were you in on bombing the station at Oktabrskaya last night?'

'Yes.'

'Then, you'll be glad to know your part of the mission went well. The station and the tracks were wrecked, and the German garrison was hit hard.'

What did Plokhoi mean, 'your part of the mission'? Then she understood. Plokhoi's *druzhiny* must have been the partisan group assigned to work with the Night Witches to stop the German tank train.

Something had gone wrong.

'Last night,' Plokhoi said, 'I had seventy-two men. I sent fifty of them after the train. Today I've got thirty-one left. The Germans were ready for us. The train got through to the station. It'll reach Belgorod by tonight after the rails are fixed. And I don't have enough men to go after it again.'

Katya rammed her thoughts through the crash, back to the mission over the Oktabrskaya train station. The night fighter had been waiting. As it had been three nights before that, at the sortie above the enemy supply depot. Again, the Germans had known the Night Witches were coming, where and when; the night fighter was there, too. Her Night Bomber squadron received its targets from intelligence gathered by the partisans. And what about last night's attempt to rescue Leonid? A German patrol had been closing in at the same time Katya and Vera and the partisans reached him. Now Plokhoi said his partisans had been anticipated last night by the tank train. Their ambush was damned before it started.

She said nothing to Plokhoi about these facts, or her sudden suspicion that there might be a traitor in their number. Plokhoi must be aware, if he himself was not the traitor. She didn't know the man from a stranger before waking up to him five minutes ago. A cold feeling seeped down her spine, as though raindrops had dripped into her flight suit. She cast her eyes over the surviving partisans. Which one was it?

Outside the copse of trees, the day was leaden. These partisans huddled like trolls from the daytime. The steppe must be a poor landscape for guerilla fighters, not like a mountain wood or a swamp, where it would be easier to hit and disappear. These men had not many places to hide in the Kursk region, a few dispersed villages, some small forests, but the rest was flat, ranging farmland. Secrecy was their survival. Katya knew in an instant it would be hers, as well.

Plokhoi offered a cigarette. She shook her head.

'We'll get you out of here tonight,' he said, looking up through the leaves, invoking darkness, the only time his cadre could move. 'I'll radio your Witches to come pick you up.'

'No,' Katya said.

She didn't trust this Colonel Bad and his radio. More important, she didn't know Leonid's fate. She and Vera had come looking for him, and she hadn't yet found him. He might have been captured, but he might still be free and close by.

And if there was a spy in this partisan cell, she had a debt to pay him. For the four dead Witches. For Vera. And maybe for Leonid.

Besides, the partisans had horses.

She said to Plokhoi, 'I'm staying.'

July 2
1915 hours

Plokhoi assigned the three who'd rescued Katya to stay with the Witch. He would not call her by her name or rank. Katya did not insist. She let it go – after all, she thought, this was a person who'd anointed himself Colonel Bad. She wondered what kind of man he'd been before the Germans invaded. A professor, perhaps, or a gentleman bandit. The dirt on him spoke of stamina and ruthlessness, this was not a man who led from behind. He was charismatic; the others nodded when he spoke and never broke their eyes from him. Colonel Bad reminded Katya of a quieter version of her father.

The three partisans introduced themselves, then let her rest in the deepening shade for the whole of the afternoon. When she sat up, the rain had ended, leaving a spongy humidity under the trees. The thin one brought her water. His name was Daniel. The heavy one approached with a tin of dry biscuits. His name was Ivan. The older man, their squad leader, tossed a pair of men's trousers, a wrinkled tunic, and a thin wool coat on the ground to replace her green flight suit. He walked off and sat near but with his back to them, gazing out through the trees. Josef was his name.

Big Ivan settled next to her and took a few of the biscuits for himself. Daniel folded like a jack-knife, his long legs tucked under him.

'I'm sorry for the men you lost last night,' she told them. Both lowered their eyes. Ivan muttered that he was sorry they couldn't get the body of the other Witch out of her plane.

'The Germans,' he explained. 'No time.'

What will happen to Vera? Katya wondered. The Germans will take her papers and maps and leave her body to rot. Villagers will come along to scavenge things from the wreck. They'll bury her, and after the war there will be a memorial to Vera on the spot of the crash, a bust and a marble garden.

Katya thought, too, about the members of this fighting group killed in last night's raid against the train. More than half of this *druzhiny,* gone. She wanted to ask if there'd been any word about what happened to Leonid, but she put that away for now. This was not the time to ask any of these men to address her concerns.

The mood under the trees was somber, even the horses stood still and dulled. So many lives taken all at once. The partisans sat without talking. Katya was tempted to warn the two young partisans who'd warmed up to her that their dead comrades might have been betrayed. She wanted to tell them how she, too, had lost friends to a possible traitor in their midst. She bit all this back. Daniel and Ivan carried the water and biscuit tin to Josef. He waved them off and kept his eyes on the patches of steppe showing through the wet branches.

Until dark, Katya sat alone. She changed into the new baggy clothes. Then she let her body rest, let Vera's death sink far enough beneath her surface so she could continue on. That was what these partisans seemed to be doing, burying their dead in their hearts, making themselves accustomed to a world that was suddenly without their comrades. Silent and grieving, she watched the partisans sharpen and clean their weapons.

They were twelve miles from the front lines, but no enemy convoys or patrols came near their stand of trees. All daytime activity by the Germans seemed to have stopped. Plokhoi interpreted this to mean the battle would start soon.

After full night fell, Plokhoi led the remains of his band out of the trees. Katya hoisted herself gingerly into her saddle. The moon was shunted deep behind dense clouds as they rode, a shrouded midnight.

Katya rode in the thick of the pack, surrounded by Daniel, Josef, and Ivan. Her horse was sure-footed and strong, well fed. These partisans were obviously receiving supplies, with support and food from both the villages and the Night Witches' air-drops. The men bristled with weapons and ammunition. Colonel Bad even had a radio, something very few partisan cells could boast. This must be a key group, and a good one, to operate right under the Germans' noses like this. For them to fail so badly as they did against the tank train, something was rotten. Plokhoi must be aware of that.

They rode west, away from Borisovka. Daniel whispered to Katya that they were going to the villages to recruit, to regain their strength.

Somewhere in the night, Katya heard planes high up in the quilted clouds. Her spirit leaped for a moment, she closed her eyes to listen to the engines. These were not the popping motors of her night-bombing squadron on another mission. These were bigger planes, American-made Boston A-20s, and fighters, Yak-9s in escort.

Katya and all the partisans reined in their horses to watch the restive black world around them. Colonel Plokhoi sidled up next to her, a wild look in his eyes. Then, no more than five miles behind them, around Borisovka, the night blistered into orange and yellow flashes. She kept a tight rein on her horse, but the animal did not flinch at the bomb blasts and firelights. The horse was used to this.

Plokhoi wheeled his mount around to see the Soviet air raid better. He shouted over the explosions, unconcerned he might be heard by any Germans in the area.

'Are you sure you don't want to go home, Witch?' He leaned closer to her. 'I can smell it, you know, I can tell you!'

The partisan leader raised one arm into the air and shook a grimy fist.

'Goddamn!' he bellowed. 'Goddamn, here it comes!'

CHAPTER 10

July 3
0700 hours
Vladimirovka
beside the Oboyan road

Valentin's boot tapped on Dimitri's left shoulder. Then the hard toe nudged the nape of his padded helmet. Dimitri hauled back on the left lever and shoved the right one forward. The tank spun into a left-hand turn, slipping slightly, Dimitri sensed the mud under his treads. He brought the tank out of the turn and stomped the clutch, jamming the shift knob into fourth, the T-34's highest gear. The transmission grumbled. Dimitri leaned down for his hammer but the *General* did not like to be struck and complied, the gears meshed. Dimitri floored the accelerator and the tank bounded along the ridge at thirty miles an hour, top speed.

All hatches were closed. Dimitri peered into a gash of gray-green and bouncing world through a small periscope. The designers of the T-34 didn't put much stock in the discretion of the driver. His little, horizontal, mirrored view of the road made what bits he could see look like he was driving through a toy world. For the most part, the driver was forced to rely on his commander to tell him when and where to turn. Even the commander's vision was limited; he sent his tank charging into a battle he, too, could barely observe. The commander peered through a periscope or a telescope, which provided him no more than a fourteen-degree-wide outlook, pressing his forehead and eyes against poor rubber pads that did little to keep light out of the optics. In addition he had one small armored port at shoulder height and a pistol port below that. Buttoned up like this, the T-34 was a collection of blind spots. Running this morning shut tight as a tin, the *General*'s insides were humid and smelly, piquant with perspiration and temper.

Valentin rested his feet on Dimitri's shoulders, guiding the tank with his heels and toes because he was busy using the intercom for other duty. He was yelling at the loader Pasha.

'No, no, no, the other bin! The other bin! I want AP! AP, Private! Get three ready. Now, do it, go, go!'

Dimitri kept the tank barreling ahead straight, listening to his son holler at the burly teenager while the boy scrambled for the ammunition. Pasha struggled on his knees, stripping back the neoprene matting that lay across the floor bins, digging down in them for the correct shells; this time Valya wanted solid-shot armor-piercing rounds. Somehow Pasha had managed to grapple from the floor the wrong ammo, a HEAT shell, a high-explosive anti-tank round. The T-34 carried seventy-seven rounds: nineteen of armor-piercing, fifty-three of high-explosive, and five of anti-personnel. Only nine of those rounds were easily accessible, on racks located left and right on the turret wall. Once those shells were expended, the loader had to root around under the floor mat into the eight storage bins beneath their feet. When the tank was moving at full speed, swaying and hopping the way it was now, the loader's job was very difficult.

Valentin's foot crunched into the middle of Dimitri's neck. This meant stop, fast. Dimitri down-shifted and hit the brakes. He brought the *General* to a skidding halt. No sense aggravating his testy son any more than he already was.

Valya's voice swelled in the intercom. 'Load AP!'

Behind and above Dimitri, Pasha rose from his knees to slam a shell into the breech. Valentin hit the electrical traverse and the turret began to whir and pivot. The turret walls, the dials, sights, and controls, the thick breech of the big main gun, all began to swing to the right. But Valentin's and Pasha's seats did not move. Valya's feet left Dimitri's shoulders, he had to stand and dance with the turret whenever he swung it around. This was a major design flaw in the T-34; the seats for the commander and loader were not mounted to the turret itself but to the ring of the chassis, so that the two had to skitter around with the swiveling breech and the firing controls whenever the turret was turned. Dimitri looked over his shoulder to watch his son. The boy contorted himself to keep his eye on his range telescope and at the same time twirl the elevation flywheel to raise the main gun to match his range to the target. At Valya's feet, Pasha was folded again into the floor of the tank, he had the rubber mat in a shambles looking for two more AP rounds to satisfy his sergeant.

Metal clanged and the big boy began to rise with a shell cradled in his arms. Valentin lifted his right boot and laid the foot in the middle of the boy's spine, forcing him back inside the bin.

Valentin had two foot pedals beneath his position, the left one for the 76.2 mm main gun, the right for the machine-gun mounted co-axially to the cannon. He kept his brow pressed against the padding above his telescope, his foot on Pasha's squirming back. He turned the elevation wheel one more round, then stepped on the left pedal.

The big gun fired. The tank jolted with the blast, Dimitri wasn't ready for it and knocked his padded head. Inside the tank, the breech rammed backward in its recoil, the metal slab just missed smashing Pasha's head into pulp. A scalding casing popped out of the breech and clanged on the exposed bins. Valentin pulled his boot off the boy's back to let him up. The casing rolled near Pasha's cheek and he yelped, dropping the AP shell he held, making him dig frantically back into the bin to retrieve it. Sulphurous smoke backwashed down the breech into the cabin. The *General*'s ventilation system sucked at the fumes but with all the hatches secured drew them outside too slowly. Everyone coughed a little; quiet Sasha, crammed beside Dimitri at his gunner's position, gagged.

The tank sat apprehensive, the diesel engine idled waiting for an order. Sasha kept his face at his own machine-gun vision block, a mirrored slit no bigger than Dimitri's. Pasha sat up with the AP shell clutched to his chest, looking up at Valentin from bended knees. The turret traverse whined, spinning the main gun to face forward. Valentin glared tight-lipped through his optics to see if he'd hit his target, pirouetting with the green turret walls turning around him.

Dimitri gripped the handle over his head. He turned it and shoved the heavy metal hatch up. Sodden air tumbled in on him like a wet dog. He stood into the drizzly morning.

'I need a piss break. Anyone?'

He laid his hands flat on the dripping armor and curled his feet up under him, to slide off the glacis plate to the trampled ground. The tank stank of exhaust, fumes from the fired AP shell still trickling out of its long muzzle, black diesel puffs issuing from its rear. Dimitri walked beside the T-34 and opened the fly on his coveralls. He waited for Valentin's hatch to lift and a stream of abuse to fly at him. Instead, the floor escape hatch beneath the gunner's position fell open and thin Sasha crawled from between the treads. The commander's hatch rose. Valya climbed down the side of the tank and hopped off the treads. Round little Pasha followed. The four of them peed into the ground. The *General,* surrounded by its keepers, purred.

Dimitri finished and kept his eyes out over the steppe. Craters and scorched spit-up ground dotted the crest of a low hill a mile off. This spot was where the tanks of his 3rd Mechanized Brigade came to calibrate their cannons and season their new recruits, their own Sashas and Pashas. All the land here on the southern shoulder of the Kursk bulge rose slightly to the north, favoring the Russian defense; here, the steppe was so flat that even a slight elevation was an immense advantage. The Germans will have to run uphill in their opening assault. Another tank on a nearby crest let loose with a shell, the thing whistled and struck, blasting into one of the holes already scarring the ground out there. Dimitri let his imagination create the coming battle on the field and hills below. The thunder and last pattering rain from the fading storm, plus the crash of gunnery from the other tanks in his company, made a grim and real fabric with his conjuration of havoc and punctured metal, screaming shells and geysers of metal and men.

Valentin came beside him.

'They'll get us killed, Papa.'

'I'm glad to hear you say that,' Dimitri kidded. 'I was afraid all you Communists put no value on your own lives.'

Valentin ignored the jab. He fixed his eyes where Dimitri looked. Did Valya see the images? Did he perhaps see himself there, broken in the carnage?

'I'm serious. These two got shit for training before they were sent here. They'll get us killed.'

Dimitri expelled a breath. He winced up into the falling rain to release the vision of the battle, the image of his son dead below. Pasha and Sasha walked up.

'I'm sorry, Sergeant,' the loader said glumly. The boy

had his sleeves rolled up above husky forearms. His skin was scraped raw from digging into the jiggling bins, several nails were blue from getting pinched between the jostling shells.

'The sergeant says you're going to get us killed, Pasha. You're a Cossack now. Would you do that?'

The boy's reaction pleased Dimitri. He didn't cower or mutter, nor did he erupt into shocked shame. He firmed, like something made harder by fire. He lifted his head and inflated his chest.

'No,' he said. Pasha considered his answer under the eyes of the others, his little clan, then repeated it. 'No.'

'There,' said Dimitri, laughing into the rain. 'I knew it! Pasha won't get us killed at all! It'll definitely be a German who does it. Right, boys?'

At this Dimitri spread his arms and turned the two teenage soldiers back to the tank. He urged them to the *General* with a shove. The two boys climbed into their hatches and took their seats.

Dimitri looked at his son, and saw the young man wondering what to do with his impudent father. Dimitri reflected back to his own father, how many times the old man had taken the flat of a sword to his buttocks, the flat of a palm to his cheek, how many lessons handed down with a blow or a barb. He'd hated the old man too many days, and loved him here, now, long after the man was gone, for those lessons. He did not want to be hated by his own son, but how else could he teach, what other way did he know?

There is a straight line, Dimitri thought, from grandfather to son to grandson, like a saber skewering us all. Impatience, demands, love given too late. And now there is another war on; when would Dimitri have a chance to do it better than his father did?

As though reading his mind – this was Valentin's mother surfacing again in the boy, she could do that, answer questions Dimitri asked only in his head – Valentin said, 'I'm trying.'

Dimitri wanted to tell the boy the time was long past for trying. The biggest battle in history was going to start in a day or two, their tank company had orders to defend the Oboyan road with their lives, and it would be Valya's trying, not Pasha or some lucky Nazi bastard, that got them killed. It was high time to quit trying and start doing. Valentin whined and sought forgiveness for getting it wrong. His anger and distance with his men was not leadership, it was just authority. None of the Communists seemed to understand this point. They preached that every man was equal, and so looked down on all men, explaining their mistakes that led to the deaths of millions as *trying*.

'Thanks for the piss break,' he said instead.

July 3
0905 hours

Valentin left for a meeting with the other commanders in their company. Before he disappeared, he ordered the crew of the *General Platov* to remove every one of the shells from the bins and racks left after the early firing practice and lay them on the ground beside the tank. He told Dimitri his reason: he wanted to get rid of some of the heat rounds and add more solid-shot shells. If they were going to face Mark VI Tigers, there'd be little chance they could penetrate the mammoth tanks' armor with the *General*'s 76 mm main gun. So he was going to target the Tigers' treads and wheels for mobility kills. A still Tiger is a lot easier to surround and destroy. Plus, knocking out one Tiger takes out two, because it takes a Tiger to tow a Tiger off the battlefield. For that, the *General* needed more AP rounds. heat rounds were best used against light armored targets, not tanks. And they were less accurate at ranges outside eight hundred meters, requiring more trajectory. This all made sense to Dimitri and he said he'd take care of it. Valya went off with another sergeant. Dimitri watched his son and the other man, both the same age and rank, walk away together, smoking and speaking as equals. He was glad Valya had men to talk with, since he clearly didn't have much to say to his own crew. He wondered what his son was like as a friend and comrade. Probably quiet and earnest. Likely a follower. These would make him acceptable, perhaps popular.

With Valentin gone, the gray morn had them sweat to do their work, a sauna under the camouflage netting. Pasha dug into the bins and passed the heavy rounds up through the commander's hatch. Dimitri hoisted them out of the tank and handed them down to Sasha, who could barely handle the shells' weight. Still, the boy laid them on the ground in a meticulous way, in rows of five, by ammunition type; he turned red as autumn in the process but never slacked. Dimitri's muscles drank the exertion, and his worries were submerged in the dampness of the day.

When all the shells were on the ground, the three men lay beside the rounds to gaze into the low scudding roof of cloud. Dimitri lit a cigarette, sensing the wet ground seep into his coveralls and not caring; being clean and dry was something he'd long ago said farewell to. Dimitri smoked, gazing up – the boys were resting – tapping his fingers on his thighs and wanting darkness, another quick dawn, and the following day to come, knowing that it, or the next, would bear the battle with it.

He was fed up with waiting. There wasn't much more the Soviets could do to fortify the Kursk salient. How many more artillery pieces and tanks and mines and barbed-wire bales can there be left in the world after what had been jammed into these five hundred square miles? How many more times could he flog his tank over the grasses and untended crops to fire at make-believe targets, how long until fate stopped flapping her wings over Kursk and descended to them, to sort them all out one by one? Crouching behind these thick layers of defense, letting the enemy choose the timing of the battle, was making Dimitri edgy. A Cossack was by nature a charger, and this was what the Red Army had become since Stalingrad, pounding the Germans backward, slapping them reeling, back toward Poland and out of Russia. Now, he thought, we wait for the Nazis to call the tune. He sat up and looked south, the enemy lines were thirty miles away. He cast his thoughts over the drab rim of the world, above the heads of the million defenders between him and the enemy, and called the Germans curses in his head: cowards, bastards, godless, anything to anger them and make them come now.

Dimitri stretched out to kick Pasha and Sasha awake.

'Do you know,' he asked the boys when they were sitting up and bleary, 'the difference in these shells? What each one does?'

Both shook their heads, no. Dimitri thought as much; the training these new replacements had been given was – as Valya had said – shit.

'The HEAT shells hold a warhead called a shaped charge. Inside the nose-cone here is an upside-down V of explosive.' With his finger, Dimitri sketched the *V* on the shell, drawing the line, a mirror image of the point of the shell, so that a diamond was made starting at the tip of the shell. 'When this hits, the charge ignites,' and he drew his finger through the center of the diamond toward the tip, 'and makes a jet of molten metal and superhot gases that will burn a hole through the armor. The crew inside is blinded in the first split second, then everything inside the tank is set on fire.'

'Everything?' asked Pasha, blinking, not comprehending what there was inside a tank to burn. There was nothing in there but metal and glass, and a little rubber padding.

'Yes,' Dimitri said. 'Everything, including the air.'

The two boys gaped, wide alert now.

'Then the ammunition cooks off, and boom!' Dimitri spread his hands, there was nothing between them but a fiery vision.

Next, he nudged with his toe one of the AP armor-piercing rounds. These, he explained, were solid shot topped with a soft metal cap. When this shell struck, the cap splashed against the armor, giving the hard, sharp metal core a better surface to grip, lowering deflection and improving perforation. Once the arrow-shaped penetrator broke through the armor, it would blast a blizzard of shrapnel over the crew from its own break-up and the hole it drilled in the tank wall.

Pasha and Sasha marveled, only dimly imagining what kind of death one met inside a tank.

'It's fast,' Dimitri said, knowing it was that and much more but choosing only to describe the speed.

Sasha asked, 'Do the Germans have these?'

Dimitri couldn't contain his laugh.

'Yes. Plenty of them. All pointed at us, my boys.'

His other two tank crews had been boys like these, not much better trained, not much brighter, all awed by war and the responsibility they'd been given by Stalin and his mouthy commissars to stop the Germans. The first crew had died in the Cauldron outside Stalingrad, while the Red forces were finishing off the last of the encircled German 6th Army. Some plucky, sneaky bastard jumped up on the tail of the first *General Platov* and jammed a magnetic mine under the rear overhang of the turret. When it blew, Valya had been standing in his commander's hatch. He was rocketed straight into the sky like a Roman candle, his clothes shredded and on fire. Dimitri was just as lucky; the turret was lifted right off its ring and he found himself sitting in a convertible tank chassis, watching his smoking son drop out of the sky twenty feet in front of him. Half of the loader beside Valya was still in the turret. The gunner in the seat next to Dimitri had been smashed by the lifting turret. And three months ago, when the Germans retook Khar'kov, the second *General* had been immobilized after an anti-tank gun hit one of its treads. Dimitri knew whoever fired it had a bead on them, and they had to bail out in the time it took to reload that gun. He shouted, 'Get out!' and flung open his hatch. Dimitri heard the crack of the incoming shell while he dove shoulder to shoulder with his son into a crater. The other two boys were slower. The incomer was a HEAT round fired from a Mark IV no one had seen. The second *General* rocked, and the tank with its two scrambling boys left inside disappeared in blaze and smoke.

Dimitri said none of this to Pasha and Sasha. The other four boys had their graves, they needn't be buried fresh inside these two. Instead he handed them both cigarettes. A soldier ambled by carting a wooden crate of bottles, a daily ritual for the Red Army. Dimitri held out his hand and the soldier filled it with a clear bottle, a liter of vodka stoppered with a cloth cork. Sasha reached for it but Dimitri held it back.

'The commander gets the first swallow, Pasha. Always. We'll wait.'

Dimitri laid his back against the wheels of the T-34, making his cigarette glow. The clouds were not parting, the day would be dark. The three of them sucked on their cigarettes and Valentin walked up to the three red dots. Dimitri handed up the bottle. Valya tipped it well, then returned it to Dimitri.

The crew of the *General Platov* ate a late morning meal, meat hash with black bread, and the vodka. Another ordnance truck came and swapped shells for Valentin, it was the commander's option to carry into battle what ammo load he preferred. After the truck left, Valya unzipped his coveralls and bare-chested helped reload the bins and racks. Then Valentin ordered them back into the tank for more drills the remainder of the day.

That night, Dimitri was the last of the crew to go to sleep. He sat on the closed hatch above his driver's seat and watched the stars slip into the sky by degrees. Well into his second pack of smokes, he looked down the line of tanks and saw the breathing embers of other cigarettes, other sleepless men. He noted for the first time there was no traffic going on around him. Not a truck delivered soldiers and supplies, no tank rumbled off on night maneuvers. Nothing more was being done in the short dark hours away from the Germans' surveilling eyes. The preparations to defend the Oboyan road were finished. He spit and the taste of tobacco was like gunpowder.

In another hour, the southern horizon flared scarlet. The dark flowed back in, but another jittery dome was bitten out of the night. Dimitri watched and the flashes increased, a fever.

From far off came the thumps, the gavel of war, the commencing.

CHAPTER 11

July 3
1240 hours
Oktabrskaya train station

The beat of pickaxes and sledges lulled Luis. His passenger car sweltered. His train had been stopped since last night at the ruined Oktabrskaya station. The brick station house had no roof left, just scored beams, and all its sills were marred with black brows of soot from the fire. The Red night bombers had done nice work. The garrison billeted at Oktabrskaya would be without quarters for a while. But more vexing, the rails were broken in several places. Luis and Major Grimm sat as they had all morning, staring out their dripping windows at a dreary drizzle, waiting for repairs to be effected.

The major sweated profusely. An hour ago he'd begged Luis's pardon and stripped down to his white blouse. Luis watched him mop his head repeatedly. Porters ferried water to the major but there was no ice left on the train to cool it for him. Luis did not undo the first button of his SS uniform; his body had so little excess on it that he pitied the corpulent officer melting in the seat across from him. The two had spoken very little since the major came to sit down. Luis took long, languorous blinks, wishing to nap in the heat. But the major would not sit still and rustled the fabric of his seat every few minutes.

'Perhaps a walk in the rain,' Luis suggested.

'No. I don't want to climb back into that damn coat.' The major held up his soaked hanky. 'This is my first time in Russia. I thought it was supposed to be cold.'

'I think, Major, Russia is only supposed to be inhospitable.'

Major Grimm nodded and smiled, wiping sweat from his upper lip. The look on his face seemed an appreciation of the man who made this jest, one who'd bled a part of his life away into the Russian soil.

'I think I will put you in for a medal.' The major spoke under the dabbing kerchief. 'You're very clever, you know. Your preparations saved those tanks. And the way you handled those partisan scum.' The major pretended a shudder.

Luis had waited all morning for this statement from the officer. But Major Grimm had slept late, peeping out of his compartment only when the lunch trays were brought around. Luis contained his smile; this was the first step in the vision he held of his return to Russia and warfare. He would cover himself in medals and distinction on the Eastern Front, and go home to Barcelona as blinding to the eye as the sequins on his father's golden *traje de luces*.

'Thank you, Major.'

The officer leaned forward to pat Luis's knee, the puffed hand silly on his puny leg. 'You deserve it, Captain.'

Luis waited a moment while the major toweled himself. Then he stood, taking his leave to inspect the tanks, the men, and the progress of the repairs. He needed to do none of these. He simply knew it was a good moment to walk away. When the bull is down, walk the ring once, then stride away under the applause. Luis had gotten what he'd wanted from this officer. He'd made sure the man saw everything he did last night, held back the surprises of his tactics the way a *matador* hides the sword beneath the cape. Luis kept concealed until the right moment the tarp-covered machine-guns, his signals to the train's engineer, his orders to the company of grenadiers. He could have sent someone else up the tracks to locate the explosive on the rails but he went himself. Knifing the last partisan was an inspired stroke. The major was enamored of Luis Ruiz de Vega, *la Daga,* the white Spanish blade.

He stepped off the train into the sultry summer sprinkle. Luis drew himself up and let others notice him, the painfully thin SS man, unmindful of the rain, the one who'd put down the partisan; yes, they were talking. Moving only his eyes he caught someone point him out. Luis had been comfortable under the gaze of thousands in the *plaza de toros,* just the way he was accustomed to the feel of blood on his hands. Walking these tracks in damp Russia was nothing as far as performances went.

Fifty meters in front of the locomotive, new rails were being laid by gangs of workers. The old, bent rails lay aside like giant tusks. The laborers were local Russians pressed into service by the occupation force, guarded by soldiers with machine pistols.

Luis approached a sergeant.

'*Schneller,*' he said. Faster.

The sergeant took a step forward and struck one of the workers with the butt of his gun. This worker – elderly like the rest of them, there was little but dregs left of Russian manhood in the towns, all the youth were gone to fighting – crumpled under the blow. Luis watched the man wobble to his feet without help, the other Russians along the rails kept their heads down. He did not see an appreciable increase in the rate of work, but the sergeant seemed satisfied and stood back. Luis did not watch. He'd made his appearance and his point. Again he wondered at the German mind, the strange calculation that striking a human was the best way to make him obey. Perhaps this worked in Russia. It would not, he thought, work so well in Spain. The bull just gets angrier the more it is stabbed. When this war is over, he intended to be one of the men who saw to it the Germans took a more civil approach in his country.

When he returned to his passenger car, the rain had not slacked. The major receded into his compartment and Luis was able to sit alone. He ate a bit of bread and cheese, always surprised by how quickly he felt full. More than half of what had been brought to him remained on the tray. He tossed the rest out the window and left the empty set of plates in front of him. When the porter came to clear them he gave Luis an approving wink. Luis closed his eyes and listened to the Russians work, the clink of hammers and spikes. The rain had washed away some of the day's close heat. He slept, and did not awaken until the train lurched into the gray dim afternoon.

July 3
1845 hours
Belgorod station

At Belgorod, Luis's mission dissolved around him. The rain stopped, too.

The company of grenadiers filed from the train and was met by its new captain. They marched away. The locomotive uncoupled and chugged off on a different line to lug another train back to the west. Major Grimm disappeared and did not say goodbye. Luis was not greeted by anyone, though the station bustled with people in uniform. No one came to congratulate him for arriving with the Tigers safely. He felt deserving of attention but was unnoticed.

The train yard was large and not ruined at all by bombs. He stood on the platform waiting, making himself easy to find should someone be looking for him with new orders and a pat on the back. He gazed over the skyline of the small city. Onion domes, crosses on spires, and water towers were visible against the overcast sky. Solid brick buildings without adornment made the character of the town humble and strong, Luis sensed it was very Catholic, and he liked Belgorod at the end of his long journey back into Russia. He thought this boded well for him. He cheered up and walked to the rear of the train to supervise the off-loading of the ten Mark VI Tigers, and the change from their narrow transport tracks to their wider combat treads.

He knew this work to be back-breaking; he'd watched the tan-colored Tigers loaded onto the train in Germany, and now the process had to be reversed. Crews of mechanics from *Leibstandarte* clustered around the tanks on their flatbeds, local rail operators assisted by uncoupling the cars one at a time. One mechanic lifted himself into the driver's hatch of the Tiger at the end of the train. He cranked the engine, black exhaust spat from the pipes, and the thing roared and shook the whole flatbed car, so powerful was it even in starting. Others scrambled to lay reinforced ramps at the end of the car; somewhere deep in the Tiger's guts the transmission clanked and the tank shuddered. It was like watching a behemoth come alive. The sprocketed wheels began to turn, the treads squealed, the flatbed flexed under the rolling weight, and the tank kicked forward with a cloud of smoke and metallic whines. Men stood back while the tank crept ahead toward the ramps, afraid the giant might stumble and fall on them. They stood admiring, heartened. Luis felt even better, because he'd brought the Tigers here to Russia, he had saved them from the partisans.

The Tiger crept down the ramps, screeching and belching, surrounded and welcomed. When it was flat on the ground, two pairs of mechanics hammered at the tracks on either side, to knock out one of the pins that held the transport track sections together. The mammoth stood fuming under their blows; the small sledgehammers insignificant against what this tank's armor could withstand, the hammer strikes like petting strokes.

While the pins were hammered out, the crew assembled the Tiger's wider battle tracks on the ground at a spot twenty feet in front of the tank. Each cast-steel link weighed seventy-five pounds; the assembled tread would weigh well over a ton. A dozen men wrestled each link from the flatcar and hefted it into place, then pounded its pin in to join it to the whole. Luis sat on a fuel barrel watching the mechanics; when their Tigers roll over a mine in combat, or lose a track to an enemy shell, these mechanics would have to effect this repair on the battlefield, under fire, or lose the Tiger. No one was better at this than the Germans, Europe's greatest machinists.

Once the pins on the transport treads were beaten out, the tank rolled slowly forward, allowing the unhinged tread to spool out onto the ground. The tank rolled across the earth on its bare wheels for a few meters, then crept up onto the new combat tracks. Mechanics on both sides guided the tracks over the sprockets with come-along rods. When the new tracks were in place, they were joined with the pins bashed back into place. The transport tracks on the ground were hooked to a tractor and dragged off. The first of the new Tiger tanks stood ready, leaving behind an exhausted crew staring at nine more groaning flatcars.

Luis watched the off-loading of the second tank, wondering if the mechanics would be able to get them all on the ground and re-treaded by dark. The tanks had been his charges for several days, he'd risked his own neck to protect them, and he felt little pangs when they were started up, refitted, and driven off without him.

While the third Tiger was idling on its flatbed, another SS captain walked over from the train platform. He leaned against a steel pillar beside Luis's perch. The man was impeccably outfitted, every buckle and strap gleamed. A cigarette was pasted on his lips, his pale blue eyes were hooded and sleepy. He folded his arms and crossed his boots, standing on one leg, spewing smoke, rakish.

'What do you think?' He spoke without taking the cigarette from his mouth.

Luis turned to the man, the only one to talk to him in the hours since the train pulled in. He was one of the German SS, wearing the lightning bolt runes at the collars. Between the collar tabs hung an Iron Cross First Class. This captain was close to Luis's age, the blond, lithe Aryan of posters. Luis felt something pleasant he'd missed for most of a year: He was drawn to another human. This captain was disdainful, confident with a cool carriage, the manner Luis considered best for soldiers and bullfighters. The man cut the figure that Luis imagined he would have without his wound.

'About what?' Luis answered.

'The Tigers. What do you think? Are they worth waiting for? We've been putting off the attack until they got here.'

Luis couldn't tell how to respond. Was he being baited into saying something negative? He didn't know this captain; what was the man's interest in the Tigers? Or in Luis?

He watched the next tank amble onto the ramps. The thing was huge, its cannon so powerful, the chassis and turret girded with the thickest armor of any tank ever produced. It would be operated by SS-trained crews. What did the Russians have to counter the Tiger or the SS? Luis envisioned the fire belching from the big cannon, Russian tanks bursting before it, Russian villages burning, his own hand – the old hand, the fleshy one – on the trigger.

Luis had arrived with the Tigers, defended them on the

rails, and they remained under his protection until they were off the train and driven away. He felt loyal to these tanks. He would not criticize them simply to curry favor. And he would not utter anything good about the Russians. Is that what this captain wanted him to do? Luis watched the man grip his cigarette between long, elegant fingers. He noted the band on the captain's left cuff, the words *Leibstandarte Adolf Hitler* emblazoned in silver thread. He was still drawn to this captain but now he felt competitive. He was in *Leibstandarte*, too. He felt the life of the partisan throb again in his knife hand. What has this captain done? Has he done that?

'Yes,' Luis said, 'yes, of course they're worth waiting for. Look at them. They were designed to be better than any tank in the world. What other tank has an .88 for a main gun? The Russians have just got 76s. Pop guns. The Tiger can sit back at two thousand meters and pick them off. What have the Russians got to match that?'

The captain puffed, not looking at Luis but at the growling Tiger being shucked of its transport treads.

'What the Russians do have is twenty-five T-34s manufactured for every one of these Tigers,' he told Luis. 'When the Kursk battle starts, we'll have Mark IIIs, IVs, Mark V Panthers, Mark VI Tigers, all of them mixed together. How do we expect to keep spare parts available for so many models? Tracks, transmissions, engines, wheels. But the Reds, they were smart, you see. They put only one tank on the field. The fast little T-34. If something breaks, there's plenty of parts laying around for it. And every one of their soldiers knows how to fix the damn thing, it's as simple as a wind-up toy. The Russians make one tank and they produce thousands of them a month. But do you know it takes over three hundred thousand man hours to build one Tiger? Yes, the Reds. The *Untermenschen*. They are smart about this.'

The captain brandished his smoky fingers while

extolling the intellect of the enemy. Luis frowned at the suggestion that the Russians had out-thought Hitler.

'That's crap. What does it matter, when none of them can stop a Tiger? I don't care how many T-34s the Reds have got. Each Tiger is worth a hundred of them. The armor is so thick... .'

'One hundred twenty millimeters on the gun mantlet, one hundred millimeters on the hull front,' the fetching young captain interrupted. 'Eighty millimeters upper-hull sides and rear, sixty on the lower sides. Turret front has one hundred millimeters, turret sides and rear, eighty. Twenty-five millimeters all horizontal surfaces. Impervious to the Russian .76 gun at distances greater than four hundred meters. Impenetrable by Russian tanks at any distance head-on.'

Luis paused. This man knew the tanks' specifications. Luis nodded at the captain, though the man's blue eyes stayed fixed on his tanks. And they were his Tigers, Luis realized. He was the one who'd come to Belgorod station to claim them.

The captain stood away from the pillar. He dropped his cigarette and trod on it, walking toward the grounded tank and the hammering mechanics. He raised a hand to point out his observations, assuming without looking that Luis was behind him.

'Look at the armor. See how it's straight up and down, like a giant shoe box? Hitler told his designers he wanted nothing of Russian design, those *Untermenschen* and their tanks. So instead of sloping the armor, which would have added a great deal of protection, the Tiger is a collection of flat faces. If the plating had been sloped like the T-34, the Tiger could have been made twenty to thirty percent lighter. Lighter means faster. Better range and maneuverability. But this big bastard is too heavy for its engine. It's ponderous even under the best conditions.'

The captain walked to the rear of the Tiger, inhaling its

engine fumes like the scents of a woman. He knows these tanks, Luis thought. He's fought in them, he's lost them and seen them killed and is furious with their flaws because he loves them. He knows these tanks must save Germany. And look at him. He wants a few more medals for himself. So he knows, too, the Tigers have to do their job before the Americans intervene, or there'll be nothing left to win in Russia but your own life.

The captain talked on, breezy.

'Look at all this back here. Exhaust covers, air filters, it's a trap for shot. And this eighty-eight-millimeter gun you're so in love with. That's the reason why this damn tank is so gigantic, just to carry it. There's a new, long-barreled seventy-five on the Panthers that will do the trick. But Hitler wanted the eighty-eights, and so here they are. Do you know what the mileage for a Tiger is?'

Luis shook his head. The captain was showing off.

'Point eight miles per U.S. gallon on roads. Less than half a mile per gallon cross-country. With a one-hundred-and-forty-two-gallon fuel capacity, that's four to five hours of battle running.'

'That's not good.'

'No,' the captain laughed, 'it's not good.'

The man reached out to the idling Tiger and smacked it hard.

'But so far, it's been good enough.' He thrust the hand at Luis. 'Captain Erich Thoma. 1st SS Panzergrenadier Division. Pleased to meet you, Captain *la Daga*. Major Grimm sends his regards.'

The captain's clasp was warm and enveloping. With the mention of his nickname, the partisan's life beat harder in his bony mitt, there inside the handshake between the two SS captains.

'Captain Luis Ruiz de Vega.'

'Sí,' Thoma said. *'Gracias por traer mis Tigres.'* Thank you for bringing my Tigers.

'You were in Spain?'

'Yes,' Thoma said. He cast his eyes over Belgorod's fading skyline. 'I wish we were there now. I much preferred fighting in Spain. Beautiful country.'

Thoma left the handshake and tapped Luis in the arm with the gibe. The gesture was manly, between warriors, with no concession or notice of Luis's painful thinness. Thoma put his hand between Luis's shoulder blades.

'Come on,' he said. 'Major Grimm wants to see you.'

July 3
2115 hours
Belgorod

Thoma's and the rest of the cars ran without headlights to get to their posts before the steppe darkness grew total. Luis rode beside Thoma in the front seat of a Mercedes convertible staff car. Belgorod was a small German city at this point, almost no Russians were visible on the streets and sidewalks. Soldiers manned sandbagged positions at every corner. Not a single window let light seep into the gathering dusk, all were shaded by blackout curtains. Horse-drawn carts clip-clopped through the town headed north to the lines. There was something medieval about the sight of soldiers leading animals on tethers over cobblestones.

Thoma drove and talked about his tanks, acknowledging Luis's background in them, updating him on changes in the armored divisions during the time he'd been in the hospital. The old Mark III light tanks were too small to be of much good anymore. The turret ring wouldn't take any of the bigger guns. They were obsolete. Their production had been halted in June of this year. Even so, Germany still had over four hundred Mark IIIs around Kursk, in infantry-support roles. The 50 mm gun could still kill a

T-34 at five hundred meters, but, Thoma opined, most Mark IIIs would be dead before they could get that close.

The workhorse of the Wehrmacht remained the Mark IV medium tank, with 850 of them around the Kursk salient. The design had been upgunned since Luis had commanded his Mark IV outside Leningrad. The tank now featured a long 75 mm cannon with a greater muzzle speed than the T-34. The Mark IV, in Thoma's estimation, had superior cannon and fire controls, and a better three-man turret. The Soviets possessed superb mobility and armor, but held only a crew of four, putting a lot of pressure on the commander/gunner.

'Both can wipe the other out at standard battle ranges. There's no real technical advantage between the T-34 and the Mark IV. So the dead and the living, you see, Captain *la Daga,* will be determined by tactics and training.'

The Tigers, Thoma declared, were not designed to be offensive weapons. They were too slow for that, they had eight forward gears and four reverse, with an average overland speed of thirteen miles per hour. The range of the Tiger's main gun was too long to be used solely in tight fighting, where the advantages of distance were dismissed. No, the heavy Tigers were most lethal when used in defense. But Kursk was not to be a defensive battle. The tank that was ordained to become Germany's standard offensive weapon was the new Mark V Panther. Luis had never seen one of the Panthers, though he'd heard much about them. Sloped armor, medium weight, a long-barreled 75 mm main gun that could penetrate any Soviet armor, as nimble as the T-34s, the Panther was reputed to be the master of the Russian tank in every category.

'But,' Thoma said, wagging his long fingers again, 'the Panther's going through some teething pains. The transmissions and engines don't seem ready, the things blow up on their own. Hitler hurried them into production to get them ready for their debut here. Two hundred were delivered to 4th Panzer Army but we don't have any of them in the SS Panzer Corps. They're on our left flank with the 10th Panzer Brigade. To tell you the truth, I don't hold out a lot of hope for the Panthers in Kursk as anything more than smoke bombs.'

'That leaves your Tigers,' Luis said.

'Yes. That does, doesn't it?' Thoma smiled. 'Poor out-of-place monsters. They'll just have to make do.'

The car pulled up in front of a four-story brick building rising beneath a tarnished gilt dome. Thoma and Luis slammed their car doors to the convertible, they were two young men with long strides in black uniforms, gliding alongside each other up the steps. Inside, they dodged men with sheaves of paper in the hall, other young, shining soldiers in the service of the generals directing the coming battle from these rooms. The eyes of those men hurrying by sometimes snagged on Luis, so odd-looking was he beside the hale Thoma, and he began his accustomed descent into contempt for those without scars. Thoma saw this – how could Luis hide it? – and slipped his arm under Luis's elbow.

'They wouldn't know which end of a gun to fire,' the captain said without lowering his voice.

Thoma laughed, he and his Iron Cross, and Luis felt his own discomfort ease. Thoma ushered him into a high-ceilinged room off the main corridor. Under an impressive muraled ceiling lay a vast map of the Kursk region, resting on the tops of a half-dozen tables shoved together. Positioned all over the map were painted wooden effigies, like game pieces on a wonderfully large board. There were carved tanks and artillery guns, squares and circles with flags standing over them denoting armed units, colored black or red, German or Russian. Two young orderlies waited along the rim of the table with long poles to push the pieces about; it was shuffleboard with machines and lives as pucks.

Thoma led Luis to the edge of the carpet and halted, heels together. Luis copied this posture of attention, making his boots click. On the far side of the room stood Major Grimm speaking with an SS colonel. The fat major looked better now in a fresh shirt, he'd had a bath and a shave.

'Captain Thoma. Good, good! Come in.'

The two young captains advanced around the long perimeter of the table. Walking beside the map, Luis glanced down to it. The map held far more red figurines than black.

'Colonel,' Major Grimm said, 'this is the young man I told you about. Captain de Vega, this is Colonel Breit. He's the intelligence officer with your *Leibstandarte* Division.'

To Luis's eye, Colonel Breit was the epitome of a general staff officer. The man was slender, with a close-cropped head of dark hair, flecked with white. The colonel was pale and seemed uncomfortable with speech, the opposite of the energetic and verbose Thoma. Breit wore a War Merit Cross with swords on his breast. This was not a battle citation but the sort of medal won by administrators, for non-combat contributions to the war effort. The only tank this one has ever handled, Luis considered, is on these maps. Breit welcomed Luis with a handshake and a curt, tight-lipped smile. Nothing on the man's face betrayed any thought about Luis's appearance. He's the brainy sort, Luis decided. He doesn't care about anything that's not on these tables.

'Captain de Vega,' Breit said. His tone was clipped. 'Thank you for coming. Major Grimm has been telling me you're an impressive young man.'

Major Grimm piped up. 'You should have seen him, Colonel. His planning was impeccable.'

Grimm said nothing more. There was no mention of the killings by the rail mound. Luis supposed they had been covered earlier by the major. But Breit held on to Luis's hand for a longer moment, nodding into Luis's eyes, seeing something there he approved of. There was much unspoken about this SS colonel.

Breit let go of Luis's hand.

'Captain, let me bring you up-to-date on the situation around Kursk.'

The staff officer turned to indicate the giant map and all its pieces. Thoma came to stand beside Luis, Major Grimm sidled around to the Soviet side of the chart.

'As you know,' Breit said, 'Germany has spent two summers now in the Soviet Union. We have not succeeded in destroying the Red armies as we'd planned. In fact, now in our third summer here, it has become unlikely we will do better than a stalemate on the Eastern Front.'

Luis stiffened at this candidness, smacking of defeatism. Breit cocked his head and smiled in his taut way again.

'Captain de Vega, don't be shocked. You've been away from the war for a year now, recuperating. The situation here in Russia is common knowledge, at least among the general staff. We keep up appearances among the men, of course, but we are officers here. You understand?'

This was the first time Luis had heard this view expressed as an official stance. He knew the coming entry of the Americans into the war made it urgent that Germany win in Russia this summer, at this battle. But now, to hear there was no victory to be had at all in Russia, simply a stalemate? What would happen after the Americans landed in Europe to his chances of returning home a conqueror? What will they say on the Ramblas in Barcelona to a tie? A million dead and ruined, for this? The notion lay rancid on his tongue. The bull must always die. When is it allowed to call a draw?

Thoma laid a hand on Luis's shoulder. The touch said, Don't worry, brother. These are not fighters like you and I. We will be the ones to decide, not them.

Luis swallowed. He indicated the map and Colonel Breit.

'I apologize, sir. Please continue.'

The colonel resumed. 'The question has been, what strategy will achieve for Germany the best political solution of the war? Our defeat at Stalingrad last winter cost us more than just men and weapons. Germany lost the initiative. Some of our allies have been looking for the back door out of their support for us. Romania and Italy have both contacted the Allies with peace feelers. Turkey is sitting on its hands and has decided not to attack the Soviet Union in the Caucasus, though they had agreed to do so. Japan is up to its neck with the Americans in the Pacific and is therefore upholding its non-aggression pact with Russia. And Finland has made entreaties to Stalin for a separate peace. Under these circumstances, Captain de Vega, you can see why Germany cannot sit back this summer. For both military and political reasons, we need an offensive on the Eastern Front to reclaim our momentum.'

Luis asked, 'Sir, tell me about the Americans in Europe.'

'Italy,' Breit answered, shaking his head. 'The Americans will invade Italy, most likely Sicily, and they'll do it soon. This summer, certainly. When they do, the only place the *Führer* will be able to find troops to fend them off is here, the Eastern Front.' Breit pointed down to the map, speaking to the German black blocks now, as though urging them. 'If we haven't broken through to Kursk before the Americans land in Europe, Hitler will almost certainly call off the attack. He will bleed off units from Citadel and send them to Italy. To Mussolini.'

Breit left his finger dangling above the map, contemplating the impact of such a thing.

'Then,' he said, lowering his voice and his hand as though lowering a flag, 'I can make no predictions for Germany's future.'

The colonel dug into his jacket for a cigarette. Major Grimm took over now. He raised one arm, a counterpoint to Breit's deflated half-mast, and moved his flattened hand over the map's terrain like a scudding cloud.

'But we are going to attack, gentlemen. It will be fast and it will be magnificent, with more force than Germany has ever assembled. And the Americans can go hang. Right?'

Colonel Breit's quiet face flared behind a flickering match. Thoma filled the void, responding with 'Right.' Luis said nothing and Thoma raised his eyebrows at him. Grimm said, 'Take a look here, at the front line, stretching from Leningrad to Rostov. It doesn't take much to see the best place for us to strike.' He turned his flat hand into a pointing finger, as if the cloud had released one large drop of rain.

'Here,' he said, looking up at Luis. 'Our target is Kursk. Operation Citadel.'

Luis brought his gaze down to the map and saw how right Grimm was, how easily the decision must have been made. The Soviet lines projected into German-held territory as though kicked into them by a mule. On the northern border of the bulge sat the city of Orel, in the south lay Belgorod. A straight axis drawn between the two cities met in the middle of the bulge, at Kursk.

'We'll attack from the north out of Orel,' Grimm said, 'and out of the south from the area west of Belgorod. If we can meet at Kursk, we'll have wiped out two Soviet front armies.

'After a successful pincer action on Kursk, we'll be able to straighten our lines, shortening them by a hundred and fifty miles. These are men and matériel we will need elsewhere. As Colonel Breit mentioned, the Americans are expected to land soon in Italy. Once we have Kursk, we can send our forces south to fight off the Allies for Mussolini.'

Colonel Breit sucked loudly on his cigarette. Grimm stepped back and Breit trod up to the map.

'At first, it was discussed that our forces should wait on a Russian summer offensive. We would grind them down and then go on the offensive ourselves. Take them "on the backhand," Field Marshal von Manstein has called it. But it's been decided by Hitler that we will be the ones to go on the attack. The "forehand," so to speak. And so ... ,' Breit swept his own hand over the map, '... here we are. Looking at the same chart the Russians are looking at. They know exactly what we intend, and where. History, it seems, will have it no other way.'

The four officers stood around the huge map, sombered by the notion that they stood at a pivot point in world events. Luis looked to Thoma. The young officer seemed to be calculating the coming clash, his eyes shrewdly tagging the positions and strengths displayed in red and black blocks. He did not appear to Luis to be daunted, though some of the devil-may-care and dash in the set of his spine was gone.

Thoma spoke to Breit. 'Colonel, may I?'

The officer nodded.

Thoma turned to one of the orderlies. He took from the boy the long stick. The tank captain addressed Luis.

'The Reds have about one and a half million men inside the salient.'

He reached out the stick and tapped several red bits and flags inside the bulge, bearing the names Voronezh Front, Central Front, and Steppe Front.

'We've got eight hundred thousand men. That's a two-to-one advantage for the Russians.'

Thoma took in all the German positions with a wave of the stick like a wand. The ebony blocks were spread north, middle, and south, while the crimson ones concentrated in the middle. The blocks were clotted in each color, crowding each other for space on the map.

'We've got ten thousand artillery pieces,' Thoma said. 'The Reds have twenty thousand. Two-to-one again. Facing our twenty-five hundred tanks and self-propelled assault guns, the Russians have five thousand.' He lowered the stick and grinned at Luis. 'I believe the math speaks for itself.'

Major Grimm began the long walk back around the table. 'So you see, Captain de Vega, those ten Tigers you delivered to us are crucial. There are only a hundred and thirty-three of them out of all our tanks in Russia.'

Colonel Breit stepped to Luis, laying a hand to his arm.

'You did a great service seeing those Tigers through. We don't have a numerical advantage against the Russians. The *Führer* is counting on these tanks to even the score. Yours was the final shipment of Tigers. Captain Thoma?'

'Yes, *mein Herr*?'

'Captain Thoma here commands one of *Leibstandarte*'s armored companies.' Colonel Breit kept his hand and eyes on Luis. 'Out of the forty-two Tigers in the SS Corps, we have fourteen in our division. Sixty-two Mark IIIs. Thirty-three Mark IVs. And ... how many T-34s, Captain?'

'Twenty-five.'

'Twenty-five Russian tanks we will turn against their former owners. So. There we are. Captain Thoma here will find you suitable quarters. I am assigning you to my staff, Captain de Vega. I assume you have no pressing orders requiring your return to Germany?'

'No, Colonel.'

'Good. From what Major Grimm tells me, I can use a steadfast manner like yours around this table. Settle in and report to me here at oh-five-hundred.'

'Yes, sir.'

Colonel Breit nodded to Thoma and left the room. Major Grimm gave both young captains an approving nod and followed in the colonel's wake. The two orderlies went behind them. Thoma hung on to the long stick.

'Well,' he said, 'good for you.'

Luis was conflicted about the assignment to Colonel Breit's tactical staff. How much of the battle would be fought in this room? Real lives won't be taken, real ground won't be gained on this colossal paper plate. Standing here during the battle he might win for himself one of the merit badges worn by officers like Breit. But what he craved was the Iron Cross worn by Erich Thoma.

'Tell me something,' Thoma asked him. 'How did you get to be called *la Daga*? As soon as Major Grimm told me I said: Now that's a wonderful nickname. Tell me the truth. Was it some bullfighting thing you did?'

Luis folded his arms, reluctant, but Thoma's grin fanned a spark inside him. He had not had a friend in almost a year. He'd been an invalid, a recovering patient, surrounded by nurses and doctors who'd marveled at his willpower to heal and return to the war, but no one had dared enter the bulging eyes and white, straining frame to see if the heart and soul of the Spanish soldier had shrunk, too. They had not. Thoma stood now cajoling Luis, wanting a secret, something from beneath the flesh to share, something only for the two of them to know.

There was not much room anymore in Luis, he admitted this. He looked at smiling Erich Thoma and found there was enough for a friend.

'No. It wasn't from bullfighting.'

Thoma grinned. 'And?'

'In Barcelona, there's a long boulevard through the old quarter down to the water, *La Rambla*. Gypsies used to walk along the stalls and mix in with the tourists. They taught me how to come up behind tourists and slit their pants pockets with a razor.'

'Why?' Thoma's face was incredulous.

'To get their wallets.'

'Gott im Himmel,' Thoma cried. 'You're a pick-pocket!'

'Shhhhh.' Luis waved his hands at the laughing captain. Thoma pretended to compose himself, then burst out guffawing again.

'That's better than any bullfighting story! That's beautiful. You stole wallets!'

'Alright,' Luis said. 'Alright. Get it out of your system.' He looked about to see if anyone else could hear this outburst from Thoma, but they were alone. Luis admired the wellspring from which Thoma laughed, it all seemed so rooted in him, so confident and authentic; at the same time, Luis was sorrowed by the knowledge that he no longer had such depths himself. Erich Thoma was the man Luis would have been.

'Now it's your turn. Tell me something. The truth, as well.'

Thoma cleared his throat and smoothed down his hair, worn longish for a combat officer. His face crinkled.

'Citadel.' Luis gestured at the campaign map. 'I want to know about the battle.'

Thoma stepped to the map, lowering the long stick like a lance.

'One thing's for certain. It's going to be one for the record books.' He hovered the stick over the map. 'All the great generals are here.' He tapped the stick to a set of black blocks on the northern shoulder of the bulge. 'In the north, running the show, we've got Field Marshal von Kluge. He's not so sure about the operation and has said so. Hitler, I think, has more confidence in General Model.' He laid the stick to a collection of blocks in the north bearing the 9th Army signet, Model's force.

'Problem with Model is, he's the one who's been dragging his feet, making us all wait with his demands for more and more armor when we should have jumped off months ago. It's July now, and he's got his tanks and guns, but in the meanwhile the Reds have used the time to dig in like ticks.'

Luis took in the thickness of the red blocks. The analogy was apt, the map seemed bitten and swollen ruby by them.

Thoma swept the stick over the southern shoulder of the bulge.

'In the south we've got our genius Field Marshal von Manstein. For the most part Citadel is his brainchild. And the best fighter in the bunch is down here, too, with 4th Panzer. Papa Hoth. Next to us here ... on the SS right flank is Army Detachment Kempf. It's an ad hoc collection, really, strong enough on paper but Werner Kempf has never commanded this many men before. He's got to keep up on our right.'

'How about the Russians?'

'Oh, yes,' Thoma chuckled, touching the stick to the hillocks of clustered red blocks inside the bulge, north, middle, and south. 'They've brought out their top guns for this one, too. Central Front is under Rokossovsky. Voronezh Front under Vatutin. In reserve at Steppe Front, Koniev. And over all of them is Georgi Zhukov, who kicked our asses in Moscow and Stalingrad. I can't wait to meet Georgi.'

'Thoma.'

'Yes, de Vega.'

This was the first time either man had not called the other 'Captain.'

'What do you think? Personally?'

'Me? I'm just a soldier, I don't have my own block. But I'll tell you this. The Reds have got more of everything, men, guns, tanks, planes, we've hemmed and hawed long enough to give them all the time they needed to get ready for us. There's aerial photography for every foot of the salient, but it's been hard to estimate the Reds' strength. They're so damn good at disguising their forces and using fake positions. Even so, hanging over all this is one big fact that every one of these blocks is aware of, red or black. Up until now, in every German offensive, the Soviets outnumbered us then, too. But you know what? Not once have they stopped a German advance before we got far behind their lines. We'll go deep on this one, too, you can count on it. The question is, will we get to Kursk? And will we get there before the Americans hit shore in Italy and Hitler pulls the plug on Citadel?'

'Where are you?' Luis asked. 'Where's *Leibstandarte*?'

'In the heart of II SS Panzer Corps.' Thoma dabbed the stick in the center of the southern lines. 'Right here, to the left of *Das Reich* and *Totenkopf*. We're going to be in the vanguard. *Leibstandarte* will make straight north. Right along here. Citadel jumps off in two days.'

Luis leaned forward to read the map under the point of Thoma's stick. Red blocks crowded along the path.

'The Oboyan road.'

Thoma laid the stick to the Russian positions. 'Right across from us is 6th Guards Army. They were at Stalingrad, so they're battle-tough. Behind them, in front of Oboyan, is 1st Tank Army. Vatutin, here on the Voronezh Front, has put his best forces along that road, figuring Papa Hoth was going to dive straight for Kursk through Oboyan. Instead, 4th Panzer is going this way, northwest to Prokhorovka, around their best force. We'll take on this group here, 5th Guards Tank Army, kept in reserve. We'll deal with them, then swerve back west toward Oboyan and Kursk. As long as Kempf keeps up and protects our right flank, we should be alright.'

Luis was galvanized by the map. It was almost impossible for him to translate his combat experiences to it, to reduce the memories to such a tiny scale. But there it was. Head this way. Deal with this force. Turn and go that way. Where was the carnage? Where was the wound in his gut, where was it on the map?

'Come on.' Thoma clapped a hand over Luis's shoulder. 'We need to find you someplace to sleep. You look like hell.'

Luis did not take exception to the comment. It was not meant the way it came out.

He decided to smile at Captain Thoma.

He said, 'I know.'

July 3
2320 hours
Belgorod

Thoma heard the bombers first. He raised one hand, cigarette poised between fingertips, and listened. Then Luis heard them, thrumming from the north. It was easy to imagine an Asiatic horde in the sky, riding down on them, the engines sounded like hoofbeats, the ground shook under the thunder.

Thoma threw away his smoke. It landed at the bottom of the steps of the storefront where Luis was billeted.

'Good luck to you, *la Daga*. I've got to go.'

'Take me with you. I want to see the division.'

'Can't. This might be the opening bell, and you need to be here in the morning. I might not be able to get you back. We've both got our orders.'

'Thoma.'

'Yes?'

'Look ... Thanks.'

The captain smiled and was at that moment a heartache for Luis. He suffered under Thoma's round and full face, the strength in his handshake; the bit of battle was between Thoma's teeth, and Luis was to be left behind beside a map, a stick in his hand.

'Go.'

Thoma nodded and gripped once more hard, then let

go Luis's hand. He turned and leaped into the convertible's front seat without opening the car door.

'Thoma?'

'Yes.'

'I'm going to push the *Leibstandarte* blocks all the way to Kursk.'

'Maybe you'll do a lot more than that, *la Daga*! See you!'

Thoma wheeled away at the flashing western sky with his headlamps off. The roar of the motorcar disappeared into the pounding of bombs and high-flung engines. The Reds were targeting the German front lines, trying to soften up the Panzer Corps arrayed in a seventy-mile row across from them. The Russians must know the attack is coming soon.

In two days, Thoma said.

Luis stood on the sidewalk beside the abandoned cigarette. He looked around the darkened city of Belgorod, without lights or people, then pivoted a circle on his boot heels. Buildings lifted like an arena on all sides, but empty, without audience for him. When he came around to the west, the horizon above the roofs flickered orange, body blows to the three SS divisions in a row there, where Thoma sped and Luis belonged. With each fiery glimmer, Luis remembered his hatred better; he grew angry at Erich Thoma for making him forget, even for a few hours, what he was.

Luis watched the bombs falling somewhere else and retreated inside himself, into his wretched, ugly body. He did not have far to go.

July 4
0500 hours
SS *Leibstandarte* situation room
Belgorod

At dawn, Colonel Breit greeted Luis over the map. The colonel mentioned that this morning marked Independence Day in America.

'I understand,' the colonel said, 'they celebrate with fireworks. An appropriate metaphor for our own endeavors, eh, Captain?'

This proved to be the extent of Colonel Breit's attempts at conversation. That was just as well for Luis, who'd awakened from his hard cot beneath a deserted millinery shop in a simmering mood. Breit set about his work at keeping the gargantuan map updated and fed, the thing changed and shifted like something hungry and restless. In the apartments and corridors of the building, radio operators and couriers collected the latest words from the front lines and ferried them to the map room. No grand strategies would be crafted here in Belgorod. The city was too close to the front; the German generals of Army Group South made their decisions at an airfield twenty miles south, in Prud'anka, where they could fly in and out and confer. Colonel Breit's orders were to follow battlefield developments, study the configurations on the map, then wire the information to the command center at Prud'anka. He fretted over his paper landscape and lorded over those lesser deities than him in charge of helping him keep the map thriving.

The windows to the situation room remained opaque behind blackout curtains, and the morning grew stifling. The rains of the day before left a sultry residue in the air. Weather reports came in, Luis wrote their contents on a chalkboard: low cloud cover, threatening thunderstorms across the area, hot and steamy along the ground. Major

Grimm entered the situation room soon after sunup and began his sweating, mopping ordeal. Colonel Breit would not let the major lean over the map for fear he would dribble on it. Colonel Breit did not comment but Luis was aware the officer took note of him standing bolt upright in his buttoned jacket beside the table, seemingly untouched by the rising heat and tension of the room.

Every communiqué transmitted to the building was to come through Luis. He arranged the reports for urgency, compared and vetted them for accuracy, then handed the reliable accounts to Colonel Breit, who translated the sheets into movements on the board. Their main task was to keep track of the three SS divisions in the middle of Army Group South and the opposing forces, the Soviets' Voronezh Front. Major Grimm shuttled in and out of the map room, Luis heard him on the radio with his superiors advising them of SS actions. Luis had never observed the eve of battle like this, from the lofty perspective of a god. Here, detached voices whispered the intents and fates of two million soldiers. Each of the black blocks was five thousand or more men, clustering right now under ground sheets out in the drizzle, perspiring from heat and nerves, not a one of them with the vantage point of Luis, who looked down on the sheer weight of the red blocks across from their force, the Reds packed in, waiting, ready. This was the battle that history books would tell, the scope of this map would be recreated, embracing hundreds of miles of conflict and never the bloody personal skirmishes and the screaming seconds where one man killed an enemy or was killed. Luis knew he was not a coward, far from it, though he suspected the others dashing in and out of the room and those caressing the map were. He'd been a warrior not long ago but right now he was one of them, the message takers. The clean battle of wooden blocks was appealing, and Luis felt the tug of fighting this way, like gamesmen. But the map room was not the arena and bulls are not cut of wood.

The dawn warmed to morning, and the messages from the southern lines began to flurry in from 4th Panzer. Companies of sappers had spent the night removing mines in front of their positions; for six hours several hundred engineers dug up almost a mine a minute. Luis and Breit plotted the cleared areas. Major Grimm said something was up. The attack, Operation Citadel, was not supposed to start until 0300 hours tomorrow morning.

At noon, Luis began to receive messages from General Hoth's headquarters. Papa Hoth had made the decision to move up into the no-man's-land between his forces and the Reds', to improve his position for the jump-off in the coming morning hours. They needed to eliminate enemy forward strongpoints and observation posts, and find the exact location of the Soviets' first line of defenses. The black blocks of 4th Panzer began to tighten. At 1445 hours, couriers from the bowels of the building ferried in a burst of messages: An air raid had begun over the Russians around Butovo, near the center of Hoth's line. The first thrust of Citadel had begun. One of the quiet stick-handlers around the table laid a small carved airplane over the Russian town.

Another ten minutes passed. Luis handled another page: An artillery barrage followed the planes, conventional artillery was joined by *Nebelwerfer* rocket batteries to pummel and unnerve the Soviet advance positions. Then the middle of Hoth's line rushed forward at the Russian strongpoints of Gertsovka, Butovo, and Streletskoye. Luis watched one of the stick-boys shove the black blocks to the north.

When the attack was less than fifteen minutes old, the sky opened with a blinding rainstorm. The map room shuddered under the thunderclaps, barely muffled by the heavy curtains and thick brick walls. The messages kept up a steady stream into Luis's hands and the pieces on the board made their way north, into the Russian defenses, slogging over the dry map. Luis knew the sounds of combat, he knew the suck and slip of mud under boots and wheels and treads. The whiz of a bullet is different when it slices through rain to get to you, you hear it coming sooner and you hear it pass longer. None of these were on the map with its charging black bits and the reeling red pieces, nor were they on the faces of Breit or Grimm or the stick-boys or messengers quick-stepping in with the news. The sounds were only in Luis's ears. He imagined himself standing in the turret of Erich Thoma's Tiger, leading the assault, and it was bitter for him waiting for the blocks labeled *Leibstandarte Adolf Hitler* to move ahead. So far the three SS divisions had stayed out of the initial stages of the fray.

The afternoon hours passed, too, this way, quieter once the thunder rolled off, leaving the shuffle of feet and pages, the dry slide of wood pieces over paper. The attack was taking place fifteen miles west of Belgorod, stretching another ten miles to the west. Luis followed events with a tension in his chest he fought to hide. German forces struck the defenders between Berezov and Streletskoye, surrounding a Soviet battalion and driving off the rest. A fierce fight took place for control of Gertsovka. A German battalion commander was badly wounded and one-third of his men were hit, including the commander's replacement. At 2100 hours Gertsovka was cleared but at a high price for both armies. Butovo to the east was taken, the Soviet garrison was driven off, but not before Russian riflemen put up a seven-hour brawl that left all of their number dead. Their epitaph was a black block pushed into Butovo over their bodies.

The three blocks of the SS Panzer Divisions did not move throughout the day, while the rest of the German lines improved their positions. Luis wanted to ask Colonel

Breit if he might go out to observe firsthand the situation, but instead bit his tongue and dealt with his task. Sometimes you have to go to the bull, but often enough it comes to you.

After midnight, at 0115 hours on the morning of July 5, Luis handed a message to Colonel Breit detailing the entry into battle of the three SS Panzer Divisions. Within the next hour, these divisions destroyed half the forward outposts of the Russian 6th Guards Army and forced many others to withdraw. Luis himself slid the tank icon of his *Leibstandarte* comrades into the Red lines.

Luis was exhausted, he'd been at his station for twenty-three hours. Colonel Breit slipped out of the situation room, Major Grimm was long gone. Luis was left in charge. He told the stick-boys he would be back in a minute.

Outside, rain pelted the street, peals of thunder pounded. Operation Citadel had begun in this, glimpses of the enemy came in split-second flashes from lightning, the explosions of shells were lost in Nature's din. The world had been torn open here around Kursk. Luis said a prayer aloud in Spanish. This was his father's practice before the bulls and in the last five years Luis had made it his own custom against men. He asked for victory. His words trudged out into the downpour like soldiers.

THE STRONGEST FORTRESS IN THE WORLD

The German Supreme Command was committing exactly the same error as in the previous year. Then we attacked the city of Stalingrad, now we were to attack the fortress of Kursk. In both cases the German Army threw away all its advantages in mobile tactics, and met the Russians on ground of their own choosing. Yet the campaigns of 1941 and 1942 had proved that our panzers were virtually invincible if they were allowed to maneuver freely across the great plains of Russia. Instead ... the German Supreme Command could think of nothing better than to fling our magnificent panzer divisions against Kursk, which had now become the strongest fortress in the world.

Major General F. W. von Mellenthin
Panzer Battles

CHAPTER 12

July 5
0330 hours
Vladimirovka

Dimitri tugged the tarp tighter under his chin. He'd made a makeshift hood and poncho out of the oiled sheet and let the rain tumble over him. The heavy drops pattered over his covered shoulders and crown. Even with the chattering of the rain in his ears he could hear the explosions.

The German and Red armies traded blows in this hour before dawn, preparation and counter-preparation. A thousand artillery pieces on both sides lofted shells, one at the other, like arguing spouses, while the earth, a sick and sad child between them, shivered under Dimitri's boots. He leaned against his tank, alone it seemed, under the rain, watching and listening to the beginnings of the battle. His son and crew were in their covered foxhole riding out the storm. The rest of the tankers in the brigade were buttoned up out of the rain, too, inside their two dozen tanks or holes. Dimitri was glad to be alone with the thunders of God and man for these final minutes before the war came back to him. He said a few prayers for himself and his children. He didn't know where Katya was. He could help God protect Valentin, but the daughter was off on her own, up in the sky doing who knew what. Dimitri had never been in a plane, the highest his feet had ever risen from the ground was sitting on a seventeen-hand horse. He didn't know what to pray for her protection, he had only poor images of her dangers. He prayed for Katya that she remember she was a Cossack, and figured that was protection enough.

Lightning coursed overhead. He lifted his eyes to it and caught rain on his face. In the next minutes the rain eased to a drizzle. He walked to the hole where his crew slept and peeled back their tarpaulin.

'It's started,' he said.

The three had been lying on their sides curled in the dirt like piglets. Pasha and Sasha had slept well, they yawned and slowly roused. Valentin was first to his feet. His eyes were rimmed, his mouth downturned.

'Orders?' he asked Dimitri.

'Not yet. They're coming, you can bet.'

Pasha and Sasha came up, the four of them in a row in their gray tanker's coveralls. They faced south, checking the dripping sky. Then Dimitri heard not the boom of artillery but droning engines, higher than where the thunder had been. Soviet and German bombers and fighters were stepping into the fight, each side trying to pummel the other through the air before the clash of men on the ground. The four crewmen of *General Platov* leaned against their tank and gazed upward.

For thirty minutes a terrific dogfight took place over their heads. Even from three miles up, behind the thunder and lightning, the roars of German Me-109s streaked in twisted combat with Soviet bombers and Yak fighters. The Red Air Force and the Luftwaffe were testing each other the way the artillery did with their opening salvos. He felt the hard tank at his seat, the shoulders of boys pressing against him on both sides, and he knew they were next.

A blazing plane plummeted out of the clouds, trailing flame like a comet, lighting up the mist; burning pieces of it broke off and fluttered beside it until it all rammed into the ground. The plane was too far off and too engulfed by flame to tell if it was German or Russian. But the looks on the faces of Pasha and Sasha revealed this was the first war death they had ever seen. Dimitri stared at the fire in the cratered plain, and said one more quiet prayer for his daughter.

The rain stopped before the breakfast wagon creaked past at 0430. The men were given all the portions they wanted of warm porridge and powdered eggs. Sasha and Pasha ate with appetite, Dimitri and Valentin picked at their plates and did not talk. He watched his son and thought how little there was left this morning – the morn of the battle – of their blood relation. They'd sagged into becoming more private–sergeant than father–son. That is wrong, Dimitri thought. Again he did not know what to say or do, and the closer the war came, the more urgent and less capable he felt. He clamped his lips around his fork and pulled his eyes from Valya. Sasha and Pasha were dim boys, Dimitri knew how to negotiate them. But Valya, so intelligent and moody, he was a complexity beyond Dimitri's ken, like a woman with his hurt feelings all the time. Always there was something beneath the surface brooding or baking. Christ! Dimitri thought, let it go, boy! Look at the battle flashes coming closer, look at that poor cooked bastard in his crashed plane out there flickering on the steppe, *tick tick tick*, it goes so fast, Valya, slow down, lick some honey, laugh, and shed tears. Dimitri shoveled his eggs into his mouth but spit the last bites out. He grew edgy. He wanted the fight for the Oboyan road to be here now. Something he could get his hands on, like a plow or a sword, two leather reins, the steering levers of his tank. Something he could handle. Valentin, he could not.

He smacked Pasha in his meaty shoulder.

'Come on, big one,' he said, 'let's take one more look at

the shell bins and be sure where everything is. Sasha, you oil your machine-gun, count your ammo belts. Up, lads.'

Dimitri slid into his hatch and started his engine. The *General* awoke for him.

The morning passed this way, scrambling over their machinery, going over drills and tactics. Valentin joined them after a while, climbing into his seat and barking orders to Pasha, the boy on his knees on the rubber matting. Valentin spun his turret, checked his optics, tested the intercom, arranged his maps. The crew of four filled the tank with flurrying activity, the crackle of voices in earphones, and pretend enemies. Dimitri nodded at the progress of the two new boys. Valentin handled them with precision. All was ready.

At 1015 hours, word came down the echelon of tanks. The Germans had indeed burst out of their positions north and south. The push for Kursk was on. The initial reports here on the Voronezh Front were that the German 4th Panzer Army had a head of steam into the advance trenches of the first defense belt, manned by 6th Army. Third Mechanized Corps, with its ten thousand men, two hundred T-34s, and fifty self-propelled guns, was ordered to rush south to their prepared positions outside Syrtsev, stretching west for eight miles through the village of Luchanino to Alekseyevka on the Pena riverbank. The Germans would likely punch through 6th Army's forward positions and reach the river by tomorrow morning. They'd be bloodied and angry by then. Dimitri and the other tanks of his division were assigned to bleed them some more at the second defense line.

The Corps' commanding officer, Major General Krovoshein, issued a terse statement to his fighters, flyers were handed out down the line by runners. The simple sheet read: *The road to Oboyan must be defended. The Germans are coming with everything they have. The battle for Kursk is the Nazis' last hurrah. See to it they break their damn necks.*

Dimitri slipped through his hatch and settled into his driver's seat. Red-faced Sasha nestled next to him behind the machine-gun. Pasha sat above, to the right of Valentin's place in the cramped turret. Valya stood with his head out in the air behind his raised hatch cover. The *General* idled, a glint of sun diced between parting clouds and fell through Dimitri's open hatch. The T-34 in line to his left rolled in front of him. Dimitri did not wait for Valya's order to move out. He loosed his new tank, willing it silently to do well, to honor the name it bore, it had brave ancestors. Metal and men all across Dimitri's narrow horizon lurched forward into breaking daylight and clumping mud.

July 6
0240 hours
Syrtsev

Only the dead slept this night.

There was nowhere to drive. The *General* sat hull down in a defensive trench with only the turret showing, and Dimitri's nerves keened. The tank's nose was buried; in front of his driver's hatch loomed the dirt wall of the berm, obscuring his small slitted aperture. Drifting in from Valentin's raised hatch, falling down the boy's shoulders like dust, came a darkness ruptured with the roar of artillery and falling bombs. This was all the light to reach Dimitri beyond his own green glowing dials. The interior of the tank jittered with flashes that were no longer far on the horizon but dead in front of them. Dimitri's ears and the quaking of the seat under him told him the bursts were on all sides in the earth.

Valentin and Pasha worked the big gun, taking part in

the barrage, the punch and counter-punch exchanges with the Germans only a few miles away. Dimitri glanced over at Sasha, also with nothing to do but wait and put up with explosions. The young gunner smiled at him, to show he was brave. Dimitri was in no mood for dull gallantry; he despised sitting still, waiting for a lucky German artillery round or night bomber to slap them on the back in this hole. The air in the tank was rank with propellant fumes, the night was warm and the dank ground sweated out the rains of the past two days. This was not how a man fights, he thought, hiding in a duck blind, trading shots like poltroons cowering behind cover.

The Germans had breached the first defense lines of 6th Guards. Tonight the enemy caught their breath south of the second defense belt, lofting shells to keep the Red forces across from them pinned down in their positions while sappers cleared lanes through the minefields. Valentin and the rest of their 3rd Mechanized Brigade fired at muzzle flashes, to keep heads down on the other side, too.

Several cramped hours passed and Dimitri chafed in his seat.

When enough racket and rattling time had passed, just minutes before Dimitri could boil over and jump out of the tight tank just to breathe some clean air, Valentin's voice ordered him and Sasha to help replenish the *General*'s ammunition from the bunkered ammo they'd buried a week ago near their position. Dimitri thanked God and rose in his open hatch to hoist himself out.

Dawn had come. Beside the tank, Dimitri gazed over the disrupted, smoking plain. The day would be dry judging from the dawn sky, the earth slippery. In a wide band behind him among the splotches of craters were the dug-in positions of the 90th Guards Rifles. Arrayed left and right was his own brigade, and stretching beyond them to the Pena River the rest of his mechanized corps.

Spikes of gun barrels large and small bristled in every place his eyes lit, out of foxholes and tank holes and artillery bunkers. He turned his eyes south, down from the high ground where he and his brigade were dug in, and there they were, black barbed dots two miles off, the Germans with the same needles poking out of the earth, aimed at him. In the past forty-eight hours, the Germans had already fought their way ten miles north from their jump-off lines. This morning they had one prize in mind: the Oboyan road, the artery to Kursk and the latchkey to German victory. Now they sat behind a river two miles south, meaning to come get their road. Dimitri stood in the way.

The lull in the firing lasted the remainder of the morning. Valentin pitched in and the *General* was soon reloaded. Dimitri was done with chatter among the two new boys – they had their jobs and their destinies and he had his. Valentin was quiet as usual. Bordering the few miles between their second defense line and the Germans was the once-narrow Luchanino River; this was normally a summer creek, just a branch of the larger-flowing Pena. This morning the Luchanino was swollen with the past few days' rain. It was no longer an obstacle the Germans could merely step across, they would need to bridge it. Between the villages of Syrtsev and Luchanino, the ground on both sides of the river was flat terrain, mostly carved into cornfields. The crops had been spared the bombardment of the night, the shells had arced over the tall stalks. According to Valentin's maps, these were dense minefields. Dimitri tried to imagine a place in the world that was not mined or armed. He could not, because every place he'd ever been in his life was today at war. The cornfields, simple and honest stands of maize, had at this moment enemy sappers crawling on their bellies to burrow at the roots. The little village of Luchanino, not much different from his own village in the Kuban, was today glutted with guns to beat the enemy away from the river. The river, rippling and oblivious, would run scarlet before the day was up.

Dimitri looked over to the tank trench dug weeks ago by Just Sonya and her citizens of the steppe. He wondered where the woman was right now. Quickly he added her to the list of people he asked God to protect, and wondered if he wasn't taxing God's patience somehow, there must be a million men asking for the same right about now.

His son, standing in the turret, spyglasses up, screamed, 'Down!'

Dimitri dove to the rain-soft ground one second before he heard the whistle. A round hit twenty meters behind him, rocking the soil, spraying a black shower distressingly high.

'What was that?' he shouted up to Valentin, clambering with Pasha and Sasha for their hatches.

'Tank.'

'Tank? Jesus.'

A Tiger, he thought. An 88 mm cannon. It must be. *It's here.*

'Jesus,' he said again to himself, diving into his driver's seat.

Behind him Valentin dropped into his own seat and buttoned his hatch. Boots came down to Dimitri's shoulders. Both toes tapped in fast unison. *Crank the engine.*

Dimitri pushed the starter and the *General* shuddered. Valentin on the intercom ordered Pasha to load an anti-personnel shell, and Dimitri again stared into the blankness of the dirt wall. He wanted to ram the gears into reverse and get the hell out of this ditch but first the German assault had to come closer, the T-34s had to stay hidden and protected to get off the best shots against the enemy charge.

Dimitri worked himself into a sweat, flexing his hands in and out of fists, rapping his knuckles against the hard, close armor around him. Sasha never took his eyes off him. Dimitri fought the urge to yell at the boy to take his red face around or catch a smack on it. Valentin and Pasha worked well in the turret, firing another dozen shells in quick succession. They were aiming at German artillery positions or troops advancing down to the river. Lobbing rounds at armored tanks from this distance would be a waste. Valentin, his foot on the firing pedal, his eye to his periscope, muttered to himself: 'Hang on, hang on, hang on ... safety off ... and ...'

The tank shook with the report.

'No.' Valya had missed. 'Five degrees left.'

The turret whined, Dimitri heard his son's hand ratchet the long gun's elevation wheel. 'And ...' Another shell exploded out of the barrel. Dimitri reeled in his seat. 'No. Shit. Another round! Now!' The turret rotated one or two degrees. Pasha rammed another shell into the breech, then scurried in his racks for the next round.

This went on for minutes. Valentin and Pasha fought the war while Dimitri ground his teeth and glared at green gauges and dark nothing. Sasha wrapped himself in his thin arms and collapsed into his space. The motor idled with restive energy, the *General* wanted to get moving, too. A tank was not designed to be motionless, it was a mobile platform for a big gun. Dimitri idled with the *General*, popping, joggling and anxious.

Explosions jarred the ground around their T-34. Valentin and the rest of their tank squad buried on either side of the *General* continued to trade shots with the German big guns across the river. At last, in the wake of a few very loud and close shells, Valentin gave the order. The words were accompanied by the dancing of two boots on Dimitri's shoulders.

'Let's back up. Fast. They're getting our range.'

Dimitri jammed the gear shift into reverse and hit the accelerator. The tracks spun and everyone in the tank pitched forward from the backward speed he used to get out into the daylight. In a second, a shaft of sun glowed in Dimitri's vision block. He leaned his forehead into the padded periscope and through the rectangle of glass watched the tank shed its dirt sheath.

When the *General* was on level ground, Dimitri caught his first glimpse of the battleground before and below him. The cornfields on the southern bank of the Luchanino were trampled under the feet of many thousand running soldiers. They ran in a wide column; their sappers had cleared a big channel for them through the mines. German fusiliers ran to the riverbank to secure it for their pioneers to bring up bridging equipment. Across the river from the attackers, on the north bank, the village of Luchanino was lost under a pall of Soviet gunsmoke, a thousand steel throats screamed at the Germans to go back! Behind the men rushing to the fattened stream, Dimitri saw tanks rolling forward. At this distance the enemy were little more than dots against the ripped-up earth of the steppe. But the rounds falling on all sides of the *General* shook the ground with awesome force, and this from miles away!

Valentin shouted, 'Driver, right!'

Dimitri jammed the tank into first gear. Valentin headed him west across the ledge of high ground looking down on the river villages. Valentin opened his hatch to stand in the shattering morning. Dimitri leaned forward and propped up his own hatch, widening his view. His jaw hung at what he saw.

Five of his brigade's tanks were in ruins, smoking charnel even in their protective ditches. The German cannons had reached out and blown them to pieces. Two of the tanks were in flames, shafts of greasy fumes throbbed into the heating day. The others were just dead, crumpled like paper boxes into themselves, a gaping hole in each askew turret knocked from their fittings. This was why Valya had pulled the *General* out of its redoubt, to get back the tank's best defense, to become a moving target.

Dimitri charged ahead along the ridgeline. The other four tanks in their squad plus a half-dozen others had dislodged themselves from their dirt casings and were doing the same, back and forth like giant picnic ants around a stomping foot. What now? The T-34's 75 mm gun couldn't even dent the German tanks across the river, the *General*'s main gun barrel wasn't long enough to generate the shell speed needed to penetrate their heavy tanks, not from two miles, not even from one mile! But even from this distance those big, unseen Tigers and Panthers had the power to sit back and knock a T-34 out. The morning was a shooting gallery for them, and all Valentin and the others could do was hunker and fire spitballs or dash around in a dither. This is our first meeting with Hitler's new tanks, Dimitri thought, and judging from the results, the little Austrian bastard was right to wait for them!

A round landed twenty meters in front of Dimitri's path. The earth geysered.

'They're finding the range,' he said into the intercom. 'We're getting bracketed.'

Valentin made no response.

Dimitri downshifted. He yanked back on the left-hand steering lever and shoved the right forward. The tank hauled into a left turn. Dimitri shifted up into third gear and sped straight down the hill.

'What are you doing?' Valentin shouted. A boot pressed between his shoulder blades, and when Dimitri did not stop to the order, the boot heel kicked him.

'Load up,' Dimitri called back, ignoring the pain beneath his neck. Through his open hatchway he watched the green field tear up beneath his tracks. 'Check your maps, make sure we don't go through a minefield.'

'What? Turn around, turn around!'

'Valya, listen. Don't fucking kick me again! We can't do a thing up on that hill. I'm going to take us down to the river. Signal the squad to follow. We'll make a pass at top speed, I'm going to get you a shot in close. You're the best gunner in the company. Take it, and we'll get out.'

'We don't have orders to do that!'

'You're the squad commander. *Give* the damn order!'

Dimitri glanced over at Sasha. 'What do you think, Cossack?'

'Go!' the boy hollered, a nervous thrill in his eyes. 'Go!'

'Hang on,' Dimitri called into the intercom. 'Valya, wave your hanky. Pasha, kiss a shell!'

Valentin barked in Dimitri's headphones, 'Damn it!' When Dimitri did not slow or veer off, he grabbed up a banner from behind his chair back. He unfurled the blue flag and stood in his open hatch, waving the pennant over his head, the signal for the four tanks in their squad to follow the *General Platov*. Only command tanks in their corps had radios, the rest had to make do with smoke canisters and pennant signals. When the other T-34s had formed up into a column behind him, Valentin ducked down and buttoned his hatch. Dimitri smacked his lips and thought, That's more like it, charging with your son and comrades under a battle flag. That's how a Cossack fights.

The slalom down the long slope was fast and careering. Dimitri snaked left and right to stay out of any German's range finder. The world through Dimitri's open hatch was divided in half, the upper portion blue and clean, the bottom was all battle shroud and flying bits of crop and dirt. He yanked the *General* side to side, knowing it was impossible for Valya to find and target anything in the turret on this kind of wild ride. He'd have to do it at the bottom of the hill, and fast. Right now, Dimitri could not slow.

A shadow raced over the ground beside the *General*.

Dimitri didn't hesitate: He skidded the tank into a tight turn away from the dark shape flashing across the smashed cornfield. Twin rows of soil bounded into the air in the path he might have taken. The bullets stitched away, then quit, and the siren of a diving Stuka screamed through the clank of his tank when the plane tore past. The Stukas had learned to come at Red tanks from behind, trying to score a hit with their two 37 mm anti-tank guns on the engine compartment, which sometimes blew up and took the tank and crew with it. Dimitri's forearms were beginning to smart from the exertion of swinging the levers back and forth over the bumpy, speeding terrain. He thought one more time about his daughter, and marveled again at the enemies she had to face in the air. Too fast for him; he preferred the ground, hooves and tracks. That Stuka will be back. Dimitri shifted into fourth gear and let the *General* roll as fast as it could, straight down the hill.

The demolished buildings and silos of Luchanino began to fill his restricted vision. He caught a glimpse of the sun glinting off the swollen river. Tracers and small-arms shredded the flowing water, trying to stop the German engineers floating across it on pontoons to establish a beachhead on the north shore. Behind the ducking, paddling pioneers stood a phalanx of four tanks, all Mark IVs. Every cannon seemed to point at the rushing *General,* Dimitri had no idea if the other four tanks in their squadron had kept up the frantic pace down the slope. The four German tanks were painted in the same camouflage tan scheme.

'See them?' Dimitri called into the throat microphone.

'Yes.'

'Sons of bitches. Where's their big brother? Afraid of you, Valya, I'll bet. Best damn gunner in the Red Army.'

Valentin laughed. His feet came back to Dimitri's shoulders, a gentler touch this time.

The field just outside the village where Dimitri raced his tank was filled with dug-in men and weapons. Soviet anti-tank gunners with their long-barreled weapons lay belly down behind dirt embankments, machine-gunners squatted in shallow foxholes, and fresh, hot craters were filled in seconds with men looking for cover in the earth. Dimitri scurried his tank in and out among them, angling closer to the buildings at the water's edge, waiting for Valya to give him the signal to turn and stop for him to acquire the Mark IVs and fire. The armor close to his head rang with the *pings* of small-arms fire banging against the *General*'s side. The lineup of German tanks must be going crazy waiting for this column of mad careening Red tanks to come to a stop.

'Range, one thousand meters,' Valentin intoned.

'Closer?' Dimitri asked.

'Closer.'

Dimitri gunned the tank farther down the hill, his padded head took a buffeting in his hard driver's space. He aimed the *General* at the remains of a barn along the riverbank. He intended to nestle behind it out of the sight of the German tanks. Their platoon of five T-34s could group there and decide on their attack. The Mark IVs would be less than five hundred meters away. That ought to be killing range.

Dimitri executed a sharp swing to the left. One more 'S' turn ought to bring them down to the lee of the barn. This time through his open hatch he saw the Stuka coming. The last two tanks in the platoon had not turned yet, their tails were still facing the path of the low-rushing German buzzard. Sasha saw the Stuka, too, and squeezed his machine-gun, the gun shook his whole body trying to keep it steady and aimed on the plane, but the fighter-bomber bored in behind his own bigger, raging guns. Dimitri watched the last T-34 in line, the tank driven by the other old man in the company, the Caucasus goatherder Andrei, take the hits. The chassis of the tank bounced under the tank-killing bullets ripping up its back, as though some giant stood on the tank and jumped up and down. The Stuka roared past, banking hard into the sky, a sort of coward, thought Dimitri, rushing away from the men and machine it left still and smoking, all dead.

Now they were four against the four German tanks. Dimitri sent a curse trailing after the rising Stuka on behalf of friendly Andrei, and in answer to his damnation a Sturmovik fighter swooped into the German's route. The two planes gnarled in the air, fighting to the death on equal terms. Dimitri wanted to watch the Stuka get his desserts but the two planes left his vision. He returned his attention to the wreckage of the barn. The four Mark IVs had not issued a shot. Dimitri drove the *General* in fast behind the barn, Valentin's boot told him to stop there. Valya flung open his hatch and stood. The three remaining tanks in their squad pulled up behind him.

Valentin leaped out, was gone for thirty seconds, then spilled back into his hatch, snapping his helmet into the intercom and kneeling low. He called out the orders to his crew over the idling *General*'s rattling hum.

'We're going to go first, Slobadov's tank will be right behind us. As soon as we clear the barn, Kolyakin and Medvedenko are going to emerge going the other direction. We're going to split their attention four ways, right and left. Papa, I need speed. This close to the Germans, if we run straight sideways to them, we'll need to make it hard for them to keep us in their sights. Once we've gone far enough, you hit the brakes. I'll take as many shots as I can, then you get us back up that hill.'

This was a dangerous tactic. Running sideways to the Germans exposed the T-34's tracks and its weakest armor, the side plating. Every tank is designed to have its thickest armor in the front. But this sideways run also would get

Valentin and Pasha at an angle to the Mark IVs, at their own vulnerable sides.

It was going to come down to who was better in his range-finder, and who was fastest on the trigger.

Dimitri closed his hatch. He reached up to crack his fist on Pasha's boot.

'Pasha, kiss that first shell and name it Katya for me.'

'Sure, Dima.'

Dimitri caught Valentin looking at his loader, assessing the boy coldly, as if Pasha were metal, and Valya wondered only if the loader might break down under stress. Valentin saw whatever he needed, then returned to his seat. Pasha smiled down at Dimitri, assuring the old man he would not break, then got into his place, too. Sasha swung himself back to his machine-gun.

Above Dimitri's head, the turret whined and pivoted. Valentin and Pasha walked around the rubber matting to stay behind the swinging gun. Valentin brought the cannon around to the right, past ninety degrees, where he thought he'd be taking his shot once the *General* galloped out of cover.

'AP,' Valentin ordered. Pasha hefted an armor-piercing shell. Dimitri heard the smack of his lips in the intercom.

'Go get him, Katya,' the boy said to the round before slamming it into the breech.

'Sasha?' Valentin called.

The machine-gunner answered, turning away from his gun portal. 'Yes?'

'What's your mother's name?'

Sasha grinned at Dimitri, as though telling the old driver that his son, their sergeant, wasn't so bad, see? He was a good *hetman* after all.

'Tamara.'

'That's our second shell, then. Ready? Papa?'

Dimitri told himself he was rarely ready for the things his son displayed. But there wasn't time to ruminate over it right now. If they died together in the next minute, he could wrestle Valya all the way to heaven until the boy made sense to him. But now …

'Ready. Good luck, my boys.'

Valentin paused, like the moment before horse and rider were cut loose in the village war games. Saber raised, melons strung from trees …

'Go!'

Dimitri popped the clutch and hit the accelerator, the goosed tank spun up a cloud and took off. Dimitri was in second gear even before the *General* cleared the barn walls. Over the rumble of bounding steel Dimitri heard a ringing report; one of the Mark IVs had taken a pot-shot at them when their nose appeared around the building. The German missed, Dimitri's revved-up *General* was too quick. But that was only for the first round, they were certainly loading another, and there were three other enemy tanks.

Now Valentin fired. The *General* heeled over onto the left track from the concussion of the blast, with the cannon fully sideways to the chassis and the treads bumping over corn rows. Jolted, Dimitri kept his hands and feet pressing more speed out of his machine, shifting into third gear even before the *General* could get both tracks back on the ground. Pasha fumbled the second AP shell, Dimitri heard it clang on the floor, but the boy scooped it up and got it into the breech in time. In his ear, Valentin urged, 'Go, go, go …'

Dimitri wound the T-34 as far as he dared take the transmission. He watched the rpm's shoot past the point where he should have shifted, he begged the *General* to mind him and hold a moment more with the building speed. His prayers were lost in the rising whine of the engine. He waited, then stamped on the clutch, threw the gearshift into fourth, and the *General* heaved forward, relieved and running for all it was worth. He looked at nothing, not through his small slit, not into his periscope, just at the jumping green walls around him; he reached out with his senses five hundred meters to his right, across the river, to the four German tank commanders, wishing them sudden blindness and palsy.

Then Valentin yelled, '*Now!*'

Dimitri's foot smashed on the brake. He downshifted as fast as he ever had any machine in his life, in his heart a horse reared its head at the suddenness of the pull on the bit but dug in its hooves, heeding its rider. Dimitri leaned back in the saddle and pulled harder, the horse came still, the grinding tracks of the T-34 settled and dust flowed over them. They were motionless and in the open, broadside and six hundred meters from four enemy tanks.

Dimitri's pulse pounded in the single second before Valentin moved. He looked over his shoulder to watch his son. The boy laid his left foot on the firing pedal, the turret slipped a few degrees more to the right and Valentin hopped on the other boot to keep up with the rotating cannon. His eyes were locked in to his periscope. Pasha stood beside the loaded breech, another shell cradled in his arms. A further second pounded inside the tank as though it had come from a blow against the armor. Valentin's hand turned the elevation wheel.

'Yes,' he muttered, 'come on ...'

Dimitri wanted to reach his hand up and push down the firing lever himself. Christ, boy! he thought, shoot! We're not measuring them for a new fucking suit, we're trying to kill them! Shoot!

Valentin's boot toed the firing pedal: The cannon erupted. The report was thunderous, the breech shot back and the smoking casing flipped out, but before it could bounce twice Pasha had the next round in the big gun and Valentin made a small adjustment to the elevation. He toed the pedal again and the tank rocked, another immense bang shook the tank and the breech spit another shell. The compartment stank with the gases but Dimitri had no time to wrinkle his nose, he had to dodge his face away from Valentin's oncoming boot, the signal to get the *General* running, and fast.

Dimitri worked the levers and gears to the sound of Pasha and Sasha shouting, 'Go, go, Dima, come on! Go!' Bounding away, Valentin traversed the turret around to face front again, for better balance and speed.

'Well?' shouted Dimitri. 'Well?'

Valentin made no answer for a few moments. Dimitri guessed he was turning his periscope back to the Mark IVs, to read the damage while speeding away.

'Two Mark IVs burning. One smoking. One missed.'

'What about our tanks?'

'Medvedenko,' Valentin said. 'Disabled. The crew got out.'

Dimitri drove hard, swerving up the hill, but he hadn't gotten out of second gear yet. His shoulders and arms ached from grappling the levers.

'What?' he asked the frowning face of Sasha.

'We go back. Right? They're alive.'

Dimitri had been too busy flailing the tank back up the hill to consider this.

'No,' answered Valentin over the intercom. 'We do not go back.'

'But ...'

'I'm not risking three tanks to rescue four men, Private. They'll have to fight where they are.'

'You said so, Dima.' Sasha addressed Dimitri now. 'You said a Cossack will die for someone in his clan.'

Dimitri grinned at Sasha, even through his mounting fatigue. The *General* swung and accelerated up the hill.

'Yes. I did say that.'

Pasha piped up from his loader's position. 'They're in our clan, Sergeant. They're tankers, aren't they?'

'Yes,' Dimitri answered before his Soviet son could.

'And we're the Cossacks,' Sasha implored.

We're the special ones, Sasha was saying. This freckled boy understood.

Dimitri spoke up. His voice shook with the effort in his hands maneuvering the tank. He'd brought them halfway back to their lines.

'Valya. We vote to go back.'

Valentin spluttered in Dimitri's earphones. 'You ... you don't vote! I said no.'

Dimitri whipped the tank to the right, to circle back down the hill. Sasha held on while the tank jolted, shaking a skinny, childish fist at Dimitri in approval. Dimitri aimed the T-34 down the hill, grabbed the gear knob to shift into third, then froze. The blunt barrel of a pistol appeared beside him, in Valentin's hand.

Dimitri gazed at the gun. He thought, Well, let's see if the little shit is man enough to make it stick.

He flung the gearshift into third. The *General* plunged ahead. Dimitri posted a stupid grin on his face.

'Yes, Valya, I see it! It's a lovely pistol, but I don't think we're going to need it just yet. Put it away and get your big gun ready!'

The pistol hung in front of Dimitri's face for another second, then withdrew. Dimitri shook his head in a small, rueful rattle at the shame of this.

The tank lumbered into the air, bounding off the lip of a crater, then crashed down and kept running. Everyone jarred. Dimitri knocked his padded head and wondered if this constant banging of his noggin was going to make him silly one day when he got old. He balled a fist, hollered, 'Faster, *General*!' and laughed. Death was everywhere, in the Germans' waiting tanks, in his son's mean cowardice, in the sky with its stinking Stukas. And Dima Berko was alive in the middle of all of it, shaking his fist and howling.

'Are the other three still with us?' Pasha asked.

Dimitri didn't know. He had to keep his eyes forward to get back down to the river and the barn. Valentin was the squad leader, and *General Platov* was the lead tank. The others were still under Valya's orders. They'd be to the rear. Valentin would have to find them through his rotating periscope.

'Yes,' Valentin answered. 'All three.' Reluctance stained his voice. Dimitri considered: His son was no coward. No, the boy was a Communist. Three tanks for three men. Valya was right – it was a rotten risk – and he was so wrong.

Two hundred meters away, smoke curled from both sides of the river. The burning Mark IVs were in full flaming bloom, their fuel and ammo had been set off. Gray trails billowed from the engine compartment of the third tank but it was rolling. The fourth patrolled back and forth along the riverbank. To the right of the barn, Medvedenko's T-34 was ruined, its left-hand tread shot off and lying in pieces behind it. The tank smoldered, black smoke boiled out of the open hatches. One of the remaining Mark IVs had put another round into the Red tank to be certain it would not be rescued and repaired later. Dimitri drew closer. At one hundred meters, flinging the *General* to and fro to keep the German tanks from drawing a bead on him, he saw Medvedenko's crew, hunkered behind their blazing T-34. Only two men squatted, waving at Dimitri's onrushing tank. Two others lay on the ground.

'They've got wounded,' Dimitri called into the intercom.

A burst of small-arms fire from across the river tattooed the glacis plate around his hatch door, *p-tang-ting-tang*. Dimitri angled the *General* to run alongside the bank. His wrists ached, the veins in his forearms were as swollen as the river. At top speed he brought the T-34 between the downed tankers and the river, then shut down his pace, broadside to the still functioning and dangerous twin Mark IVs. In the turret, Valentin was already acquiring a target, mincing in his small circle with the traversing gun. Pasha on his knees raked in his racks for shells. Dimitri shot a glance at Sasha.

'Go.'

The boy did not hesitate. He reached down between his legs and yanked the handle to the escape hatch. The door lifted and the thin lad slithered out between the treads, then pulled shut the hatch. Close by the *General*, a report boomed. One of the T-34s in their squad had gotten off the first shot. Dimitri couldn't see the result. In the blue steppe sky, white scrawls displayed the ferocity of the air battle taking place. Below, for miles running west along the river, every meter of the battlefield bore guns and men exchanging fire, wisps of smoke showed where triggers were pulled, shells struck, lives were taken. Here, almost privately on this small plot of cornfield and river beside a shambled barn, the two Mark IVs and three T-34s defined the war, a rescue and a fight to stop it.

One of the T-34s pulled ahead of the *General*, Kolyakin angling for a better shot at the roaming Mark IVs across the river. Dimitri kept his own tank still, shielding Sasha while he helped Medvedenko's crew climb on the *General*'s back with their wounded. Valentin poked his head out of his hatch to check on the progress of the scrambling men and boys. Dimitri heard him holler down at them, 'Get on, get on!' The turret swiveled again, Pasha shoved in another shell, Valentin toed the firing pedal and the tank recoiled. Something across the river took the hit, Dimitri heard a terrific metal din.

'They're on,' Valya yelled. 'Go! Get out of here!'

Dimitri floored the gas. Kolyakin's T-34 in front of him began to roll out of his way. Then, with a wrenching *clang*, Kolyakin's tank was hit so hard it reared over, almost flipping on its side. The turret ripped off the tank's body, a ball of fire gushed from the beheaded chassis. The noise was horrific, a gutting. Kolyakin's turret rolled like a boulder behind his devastated tank, spewing flames and black fumes. Dimitri was stunned in the handful of seconds this obliteration played out in his hatchway. He muttered to himself, 'Tiger.'

Valentin screamed it. 'Tiger!'

That jolted Dimitri into action. He rammed on the brake, shifted the *General* into reverse. He swung his tail around fast, putting the rising hill behind him now, and laid on every bit of backward speed the tank could give him.

He faced the Tiger on the far shore. The thing was mammoth, the first heavy German tank Dimitri had ever seen. Its main gun was so long the tank seemed to want to tip forward onto it. The Tiger was boxy, its armor not slanted like the Soviet tanks. But it looked solid, terrible and lethal.

Dimitri ran backward up the hill, keeping his thick frontal armor facing the Tiger, and presenting the T-34's smallest profile as a target, a broad triangle. Valentin shouted to Pasha, 'AP! Now!' The boy must have already had one of the armor-piercing shells in his hands because the breech was loaded in an instant. Dimitri kept his foot smashed on the accelerator. Anyone behind him had better fend for themselves, he would not see them to dodge. His eyes were fixed on the Tiger, needing to anticipate the movements of the huge 88 mm cannon to stay out of its lethal path. He thrashed the tank left and right, and hoped Sasha and Medvedenko's crew were still clinging to the *General*'s deck handles. To give them a smooth ride right now would kill them all.

Valentin managed to rotate the *General*'s turret around to face the Tiger. The other two tanks in their squadron were tearing away from the riverbank and the scorching pyre of Kolyakin's tank. The Tiger opted for the easiest of his three Russian targets. Slobadov made a wide, circular turn, choosing speed over evasion. The Tiger let go one round, a fountain of dirt rose at Slobadov's rear. A perfect smoke ring spit out of the big German gun. The Tiger adjusted its aim to Slobadov's flight. The turret waited, drawing the proper lead. Slobadov wasn't swerving enough, Dimitri knew, and the Tiger's gun yowled. The big tank barely rocked with the report, the thing was so immense. Slobadov's tank was hit in the right-side chassis, above the wheels, by an armor-piercing round. No flames or explosion blew from this dead T-34. The tank ran another twenty meters, swung toward Dimitri's retreating window, then stopped. A hole the size of a bread loaf gaped in the armor; Dimitri knew there was little left inside the tank that would resemble a man. The Tiger puffed out another perfect smoke ring, some kind of infernal hallmark.

The Tiger's turret paused, still aimed several degrees away from them. It appeared to be admiring its kill. Dimitri had propelled the *General* eight hundred meters from the river. In another minute, they'd be far enough out of range to turn around and run up the hill in forward gears, faster to safety. He hit the brake.

'Take a shot, Valya.'

His son was ready. The T-34's turret whirred left, the gun was depressed a few degrees to the riverbank below. The one surviving Mark IV had moved behind the Tiger, like a handmaiden to the hulking queen.

Valya fired. The *General* shivered behind the shell. The blast kicked up a dust cloud, and Dimitri hit the gas again, not waiting for the roiled dirt to settle. Backing away, he caught a glimpse of the Tiger. It stood impassive, haze drifting off its face where the AP shell struck, unhurt and swinging its turret straight toward Dimitri.

'Shit, shit, shit,' Dimitri mumbled to himself. He desperately needed speed. He could spin the *General* around pretty fast, but fast enough?

Before he could act, another shadow grazed the ground, streaking over the crushed stalks and upturned earth. 'Shit!' That was all that was missing, another Stuka.

But it was not a German plane. The guns roaring at the Tiger and her attendant on the riverbank told Dimitri that this was a Sturmovik. The pilot came in low and hot, blazing away at the Tiger, lifting a veil of torn-up ground and hot metal between the *General* and the massive German tank. Dimitri stopped the *General* and spun around. Shifting gears, he heard Sasha and Medvedenko outside the tank raising their voices in an 'Urrah!' One last glimpse at the riverbank showed the two German tanks withdrawing. In their wake were seven dead vehicles: three Mark IVs and four T-34s. The *General Platov* was the sole surviving member of their squadron.

Dimitri ran the T-34 up the hill as fast as he could. Infantrymen cheered and raised their rifles when he sped past their positions, they'd watched the entire confrontation from their holes. Valentin said nothing, gave no orders to Dimitri but sat stony while the *General* crossed into the second Russian defense belt and hurried to an aid station at the rear.

Away from the front line, Dimitri shut the tank down. He leaped from his seat to lend a hand lowering the men off his tank. Aid workers rushed forward with stretchers. Dimitri and Pasha both put their arms up to receive little Sasha down from the turret. He yelped when Pasha took him by the arm. Sasha had been winged, his first battle wound, a bullet had nipped his left biceps. His tunic was torn and stained with blood, but his eyes were clear and his color remained that of a carrot. 'Get that looked at,' Dimitri told him. 'We'll wait. Pasha, go with him.'

The two boys followed the stretchers. Medvedenko walked up to Dimitri. The young sergeant was white-faced from his adventure down the hill. He was unshaven and unnerved.

'Where's Valentin?'

Dimitri jerked his thumb up at the *General*'s turret. Valentin had not come out yet.

Medvedenko looked at the *General*, it was undented. He patted the fender, as though the tank were a talisman of luck. 'I've got to go find another tank and a crew.'

'Alright. We'll see you when you get back.'

'Tell him I said that was fucking brave.'

'Of course.'

'I mean it.'

Dimitri pointed behind Medvedenko to Pasha and Sasha, headed for the medical tent. 'Tell them.'

The sergeant nodded and walked off after the two boys. He'll get his spine back soon enough, Dimitri thought. No shame in being scared when you think you're going to die beside a river, naked outside your tank, unmanned like that. No shame in thinking Valentin Berko is a brave man. What does Medvedenko know? Only what he sees. The *General* came back for him.

He gripped a handle and hoisted himself up onto the T-34's deck. Gore from the wounded slicked the armor. The new *General Platov* was blooded now. It had performed well. Dimitri patted the tank's warm turret, then stepped around the stains.

Valentin's hatch was open. Valentin sat on his commander's seat, his soft helmet doffed, a map spread across his lap. He lifted his eyes to the shadow falling over his hatch. He looked up into Dimitri's face. The boy's cheeks were filthy, black outlines marked where his goggles had been. The grit made him look older, seasoned.

Valentin lowered his eyes back to his map. He said nothing.

Dimitri could reach down and grip him by the throat, pull him up out of the tank like a salmon out of a river, he could do it, man or no man, this little Communist piss-ant. It felt stupid, leaning over like this, his head only one foot above Valentin's, the two of them not speaking. Dimitri wondered, Is he mad at me? What was I supposed to do out there, wave goodbye to poor Medvedenko and his crew, wish them luck there beside the river with ten thousand Germans making ready to cross? Won't risk three tanks for four men! What the hell does he want, how does he expect to fight this damn war? Waiting for orders, doing only what he's told, dying on the Soviets' schedule?

Dimitri sat on the fender, dangling tired legs. Valentin stayed inside the *General*, silent armor separated father and son. After several minutes, Dimitri saw Pasha and Sasha returning from the aid tent. Plucky little Sasha's arm was wrapped in fresh white gauze. Both boys waved to Dimitri. A jaunt was in their steps, veterans now, one of them wounded. Dimitri turned to look again down into the hatch, into the pool of shadow where Valya sat, head bent over his maps.

He may not be a Cossack, this boy, he thought; the Communists may have undone that.

'Hey,' he said down into the hatch.

Valentin did not lift his head at the word. His hands plopped onto the map, crinkling it. 'What.'

Dimitri squatted on his haunches, closer to the opening. 'Medvedenko said to tell you he'd follow you into hell. Said you were his hero.'

Valentin made no response.

Dimitri reached down to pat his son's shoulder. He climbed off the *General* to hear Sasha brag about his first bullet and his bandage.

CHAPTER 13

July 7
2350 hours
outside the village of Stepnoe

Thirty-two horses stopped in the darkness when Plokhoi hauled back his reins. The leather of saddles and boots creaked and the metal jangle of rifles eased. At the head of the pack, Plokhoi spoke to one of his lieutenants posted at his side. A black mile off, across an unhindered plain of field, a village glowed with the pallid light of lanterns, winking stars, and a quarter moon.

Katya had named her partisan horse Anna, after her favorite Tolstoy novel. Anna was the name she'd given to the first pony Papa presented her when she was only ten; she figured this horse might prove to be her last in this life, so why not go out where you came in? Anna was quick and responsive to Katya's touch, even though the animal showed little affection for her new rider. Despite the lack of nuzzling, Katya trusted this horse, and thought how quickly trust blossoms in wartime. You trust the person ducking in the hole with you, you trust the ones wearing the same uniforms, and the ones you do not know who give the orders. You may not even know their names; they share an enemy with you, and that's all you ask in war. But in this rag-tag collection of farmers and lost soldiers she rode with tonight, she knew there was a traitor, and so trusted only Anna, the knife in her belt, and the loaded rifle across her lap.

Plokhoi turned in his saddle. The little light made the man's deep eye sockets look empty.

'Witch.'

'Yes.'

'Up front. Josef, you too.'

Katya nudged Anna to the front, beside Plokhoi. Josef rode up from the edges of the group.

Plokhoi pointed to Stepnoe village with his nose.

'You two reconnoiter. You're father and daughter, if anyone asks. If there's trouble, head west. We'll wait here thirty minutes.' Josef wheeled his mount away and trotted off to the village. Katya nodded to Plokhoi. The colonel returned the gesture. She spun Anna to follow.

Josef rode well. He knew his way around a horse. Katya told him so. The man made no answer.

'If we're going to be father and daughter, we ought to talk, don't you think?'

'Plokhoi said if anyone asks.' Josef did not turn his head. 'No one has asked.'

'Why are you mad at me? What did I do?'

'You chased off the pilot.'

'Lumanov.'

'If that's his name.'

Katya wanted to defend herself; she hadn't chased Leonid off! She'd come to rescue him, just like Josef had. Things went wrong, it wasn't ...

Josef swung his weathered face to her. 'The partisans is no place for pretty girls on a lark. Do your job, Witch. Stay out of my way.'

Pretty girls? Did this dirty farmer know anything about the Night Bombers, their battle, their rickety planes puttering over enemy targets in every kind of weather, facing night fighters and spotlights and flak, the plummeting deaths in flames? She could ride circles around this old mule Josef and scream at him for all the Witches he'd just insulted. But Leonid had told her, sacrifice is courage. She clamped her teeth. She would sacrifice her anger right now and be silent, there was a mission to do in the approaching village. She had a job, as Josef had snarled at her. She'd do it. And like the pretty Night Witches had shown the male pilots, in every theater they'd flown, about courage and sacrifice, she'd show these partisans here on the ground.

They entered the village. It was arranged around a central dirt street, lined with three dozen small houses. Every house had a tiny garden plot behind it, fenced in with chicken wire and moldering boards. Even in the wan light, Katya could tell the single-story shacks were done up in pastel colors, their porches and cornices decked with gingerbread flourishes. These were steppe peasants, folk who lived their entire lives in three-room homes, toiling in the rich fields where ancestors had done the same and now watched from graves nearby. These were the farm districts collectivized by Stalin in the decade before the war. The people in these houses were starved and threatened, brutalized by their leader, until they accepted his methods. They gave up their lands to the State, and worked in their private gardens only when their long days in Stalin's fields were done.

Katya and Josef rode down the middle of the road. Other horses tied to posts or in stables whinnied at their arrival, but the partisan horses – like Josef – were determined to remain quiet and surly. Wagons leaned on empty traces in the street; there were no machines, no tractors or cars. All these would have been requisitioned by one army or another long ago.

Katya noted curtains eased back in several windows, lit eyes watched them wandering the village. No one greeted them, no one was even outside the houses. In the far distance, over the northern horizon, the booms of the battle coated the clopping of their hooves.

The Germans had been here, that was clear in the earth. Tracked vehicles had left gouges on the lone dirt road, and in the fields, crops were crushed. But no sign of the occupiers showed in Stepnoe tonight.

'I'll go get Plokhoi,' Josef growled at Katya. 'You wait here.'

With that he pivoted his horse into the dark and galloped. Katya eased forward in the saddle, stopped. A door opened in a nearby house. An old woman stepped out from a yellow interior. She came right up to Anna and stroked the horse's brow with fingers like dried twigs.

'You are with the partisans,' the woman said.

'Yes, mother.'

'Please leave us alone.' She said this to the horse, as though she knew beseeching Katya to be useless.

'It's not my decision.'

'We have only a few men here. They are old, too, but we need them to work the fields. If they don't we will starve.'

The woman did not lift her face to Katya. This was the way of the Russian peasant, beaten and badly used by Tsar and Soviet alike. The war had brutalized this little worthless village as profoundly as it stalked the battlefields twenty miles to the north. These people were killed, too.

Katya carried some dried meat and crackers in her pockets. 'Are you hungry?'

At this the old *mamushka* lifted her head. 'No,' she said. 'But I think I shall be tomorrow.'

Other doors opened. Villagers edged into the street, the little houses contained a surprising number of people, perhaps a hundred, two-thirds of them were women. The men wore cloth caps and dark jackets, even on a warm summer night, the women came in white blowzy dresses and decorative aprons. There were no bare pates, all heads were under hats and scarves, these peasants covered themselves to go outside, even in front of their own homes to beg a stranger. Every face was wrinkled, every eye a sad witness.

They clustered around Katya. Anna held still. Katya, high in her saddle, felt like another plague sent down among these people, come to skim away the last of their vitality. She looked the gathering crowd over and knew right off which ones Plokhoi would take, that one and that one, those two look like brothers, yes, and there; there might be twenty or more who looked strong enough to mount the final few horses left to this village and ride off with the partisans to fight. And what would be left? She looked down at the first old woman to come outside, the bold one, still caressing Anna's soft muzzle.

The village people said no more to Katya than 'Please,' and 'We can't.' She had nothing to say in response. She sat in their midst for the minutes until Plokhoi rode into the street. In ones and twos they worked their way to her boots in the stirrups, some stroked her leg, others the horse. None looked up at her. Anna heard the pounding of the many coming hooves before the old folks. She stamped a foot once and the people stepped back.

Plokhoi and his partisans rode into town looking like a band of brigands. They advanced tightly packed, their dark horses rubbing shoulders, the riders grimy and slouched in the saddles. There was little military bearing to them, even though many of the men had been soldiers before they joined Colonel Bad and his cell. The villagers edged back to the side of their dirt road.

The mounted cadre stopped. Katya and Anna stood between the two crowds. She backed her horse out of the way.

Plokhoi's mount strode forward. He spoke, a black voice on this pallid night.

'Where is your *starosta*?'

A snowy-bearded old man stepped forward. This was

the village elder. Even he was straight-backed and strong; the times in this land were harsh and they formed hard men to live in them.

'Here, sir.' The peasant took off his hat and would not look up at Plokhoi.

'You know who we are?'

'Yes, sir.'

'Good. You will send ten of your able-bodied men to come with us.'

The elder's hands worked his hat in a circle, turning it by the rim. 'Please, sir. Please.'

Plokhoi's horse shifted under him, an impatient movement from the animal. His voice matched the horse's gesture.

'Please what?'

'Sir. I am sorry. This we cannot do.'

Plokhoi's horse moved out of the pack of dark partisans. The animal came close to the *starosta* and tossed his head. The old man made no move to back away, but the turning of his hat quickened.

'Please?' Plokhoi repeated from high above the peasant.

The elder clutched his hat now, stopping his hands. He spoke but could not raise his head to answer, as if Plokhoi's boot were on it.

'Sir. The Germans. They've ...' and the old man quit.

'They've what?' Plokhoi demanded over the elder's bowed head to the rest of the village. 'The Germans have what? Have they been such good masters to you in the two years they've occupied your land that you won't rise against them now?'

Plokhoi slung his legs down from the saddle. He walked away from the horse, leaving it untethered, and the animal stood still. He strode to the middle ground between the villagers and the mounted partisans. He lifted both arms.

'We greeted the Germans, didn't we all? We met them with bread and salt. They were supposed to be our liberators from Stalin and his henchmen, they were the ones to set us free from the tyranny of the Communists. Hitler couldn't be worse than Stalin, we said. We were all hopeful.'

Plokhoi lowered his hands. He nodded to the people.

'I was, I know. I hated Stalin. I saw the steppe fill with the graves of starved women and children, next to wheat fields that should have fed them. I watched comrades be jailed, exiled, or shot for raising their voices against the repressions. So I was first in line when the Germans came. I waved my arms in the air.'

He walked past the *starosta* to an old woman. Flesh hung from her face, in the quarter light of the night Katya could see her hunger. Her neighbors stepped away from her now that the partisan came close.

Plokhoi reached for her hand. 'How many of your men have the Nazis taken, mother?'

The woman lowered her chin, but with his free hand, Plokhoi lifted her face to his.

'How many, mother?'

'Half.'

'Half your men.'

'Yes.'

'I've lost half my men, too, mother. Should I tell you about it? They were left beside a railroad mound, unburied, to rot like cabbage.'

Plokhoi held the old woman's hand for a long moment, then let her loose gently. He stepped back to address the villagers.

'Your men, the ones the Nazis took. They were executed. Two of your men for every one of theirs killed by the partisans. I know this. I've seen the bodies hung outside this village. I've seen it in other villages, too. You were ordered by the occupation police to let them hang for two weeks before you could cut them down and bury them. Two weeks!'

Katya imagined the gallows of corpses dangling in the middle of this little collection of pastel houses, the people shuffling past their husbands, brothers, cousins, friends, watching them turn blue-black and crow-pecked. She saw the bodies piled beside a railroad. Her mouth went dry.

Plokhoi raised his voice.

'And others. They were taken to Germany as slaves. I know this, too. I was captured from my home in Poltava. My brother, as well. But I escaped. My brother's in Germany somewhere, starving worse than you, beaten every day, spit on. Instead of a gun, he carries German slop buckets.' He unstrapped his carbine and with one hand he hoisted it over his head.

'I carry the gun.'

He held the rifle high for several seconds, a statue of dark resistance; in Katya's mind he stood beside the gallows, defying it, equaling it. Then with a clatter he lowered the gun and strapped it back over his shoulder.

'So will you.'

Silence descended in the village, broken only by a shifting horse, a squeak from a saddle.

The *starosta* linked his knotty hands in front of his face. He held them up to Colonel Bad, as a counterweight to the gun, a prayer perhaps to equal the partisan's command.

'Please,' the old man said again. 'I ask you to let us alone. My people have ...'

So much was on the old man's tongue. He wanted to tell all to this partisan gang come out of the darkness, all the stories of his village's sufferings. But Katya knew Plokhoi would not be moved by suffering. And the *starosta* knew this, too, for all he could say was 'I beg you, please go away.'

'No, father. That is something I cannot do.'

Plokhoi pivoted to his waiting horse. He stepped into the stirrup and mounted, rising again above the peasants and their plea.

'Ten of you. Get your horses and come with us. Now.'

No one moved. Plokhoi sighed and shook his head. He doffed his cloth cap and ran a hand through his hair. A bead of sweat trickled down Katya's back. Artillery thunder from the north filled the moments until Plokhoi returned his hat to his head and spoke.

'Father.' The partisan folded both hands over his saddle pommel. 'Which is your home?'

The *starosta* pressed his hat closer to his chest. He hung his bare head.

'Go to it,' Plokhoi told him, 'and bring me all your food.'

The elder did not move.

'Old man. I will pick a house.'

At this, a woman in the crowd bolted up the street with a swish of skirt. She was the elder's wife, sister, it didn't matter, she obeyed when her man would not. Nothing moved in the minutes while she was gone but the jittery horizon.

Katya watched Plokhoi and his band glare down on the villagers. Plokhoi wanted to save these people, and to do this he would hurt them. Three years ago, Plokhoi had chosen Hitler over Stalin, until the one became an even greater monster than the other. Tonight the villagers chose, between the German invaders and these looming, dangerous partisans. None of the choices for Plokhoi or these peasants had come to them with mercy.

If Leonid had been saved by these partisans instead of her, would he sit here on a horse and watch like she was? Or would Leonid speak up to defend the old village, to ask that they be left alone as they pled? She tried to imagine Leonid blank-faced and grimy, one of Plokhoi's men, she tried to imagine him cruel, and could not.

Carrying a woven basket, the old woman ran back up the street. Now, breathing hard, she offered up the basket to the partisan leader. Another partisan rode forward to take the food. Katya saw a few loaves and leafy vegetables, a pittance of victuals to fill the stomachs of a household. Plokhoi did not acknowledge the basket or the woman. She looked surprised, then frightened. Plokhoi rode away from the crowd and his motionless cadre to a nearby barn. He dismounted, took a square bale of straw, then walked along the dark street where the woman had gone.

Moments later, the windows of a house began to flicker. Plokhoi emerged from it and walked back to his horse. He climbed into the saddle, carrying something. He rode forward. The house behind him glowed brighter until it was clear the lapping light was flame. Plokhoi rode up to the *starosta* and handed down to him a lantern out of his little house. The lamp was unlit and, Katya knew, drained of fuel.

The elder and the crowd did not know what to do. Heads turned to the burning house, then crept back to the partisan on the tall horse gazing down on them. The old man slipped his hat back on his head. His role as leader for the village was over. He stepped away from Plokhoi. No one spoke to him or touched him. The woman stood rooted in the street where she had handed up her basket, hiding her face in her hands, sobbing beneath the crackle of burning wood.

Plokhoi's demand rose above the fire and the murmuring villagers.

'Ten men! On horses!'

The elder did not raise his head to select the men. Katya couldn't tell if his burden was loss or shame. Again, it didn't matter; neither had come to him mercifully.

The men from the village chose themselves. More than ten of them assembled in the street on horseback. Three were told by the others to stay behind, with muttered instructions of care for the women and the work to be done in the village with ten fewer backs tomorrow. The burning house collapsed on itself, spewing sparks and smoke high while the men gathered and said goodbye. The new riders hurried, Plokhoi didn't have to say a word to them. When they were ready and lined up, Katya saw the resolve on their faces. They'll hate Plokhoi, she thought, but they'll fight the Nazis. These old men will get the chance to die not as foreign slaves, not strung up as reprisals, but fighting. They have been given the chance to live. That was the choice Katya herself made when she joined the war as a Night Witch, and again when she decided to stay with the partisans.

Plokhoi wheeled his horse, forty-two others turned with him. Katya guided Anna to the rear of the partisans riding off into the starry fields. The yellow light of flames from the burning house flickered across their backs.

July 8
0130 hours
the village of Vorskla

Five miles away in a neighbor village, Plokhoi collected fifteen more fighters. He did not have to burn any homes there, he left the place dim and intact. The village *starosta* himself stepped forward and joined the partisan band. Standing beside Plokhoi, the elder announced it was time to rise. His followers, most of them family, brought along rifles they'd cached from the battles of the past year or stolen from careless German garrisons in the area. These men mounted good horses and rode away from their wives and peasant lives with a flair that struck Katya as both brave and comic. The new recruits raised the spirits of the ten farmers Plokhoi had commandeered from the other village an hour before. Katya rode in the middle of the expanded pack. These newest men surrounded her, the only woman in the cell; it seemed natural for these farmers who were riding off to be heroes to protect a woman, even a partisan woman who rode away with them.

Plokhoi led the cell into the center of a vast bean field, away from any village or road. Far off, on the edges of the field, the lights of a vehicle or two bumped over dirt trails. These were German security patrols making a half-hearted effort, none of them wanted to encounter a partisan group in the dark. None of the riders made a sound or lit a cigarette, the new men picked up the clandestine ways quickly. Plokhoi dismounted, carrying his box radio.

Colonel Bad squatted in their middle, hidden by the many haunches and hooves. The radio came to life and Plokhoi's features glowed lime by the dials. He held a receiver to his ear, a microphone to his lips, and muttered, talking with partisan headquarters somewhere. She could not hear him, she only caught him saying one thing: 'I have a *druzhiny* again.'

Plokhoi finished with his radio and took his seat in the saddle.

'We have orders,' he said. 'North of us, the Germans have broken through between Syrtsev and Alekseyevka. They're stepping up their rail traffic to keep supplied. We're to move to the Borisovka line and break the tracks in as many places as we can.' He checked his watch. 'We need to move if we're going to get it done tonight. Ivan, how much wire have we got?'

The heavy-set partisan reached behind him to pat his saddlebags. 'One,' he said. Two others in the crowd did the same and counted off.

'Three reels, Colonel,' Ivan concluded. 'Who's got the C-3?'

Five men sounded off.

'Caps?'

Another five said yes.

'Alright,' Plokhoi said. Without another word, he urged his horse out of the center of the riders. The partisans fell in behind him. Plokhoi did not break into a canter, he kept his band at a brisk walk across the bean field. They moved with eerie quiet for fifty-seven riders, like a moon shadow. Katya had no idea that for days she'd been riding with men carrying explosives, blasting wire, and caps. She didn't know much about such things, but she guessed these were dangerous things to gallop with in your saddlebags. This partisan cadre wasn't just stolid men with rifles roving the countryside: They were a bunch of disassembled bombs waiting to be put together, aimed, and exploded. Riding in their dark core, with them spread out on both sides of her like wings, she felt a little like a pilot again, part of a dark shape gliding through the night, loaded with bombs, heading for the target.

Skinny Daniel, big Ivan, and glum Josef were never far from her. Plokhoi must have assigned her to them, since they'd rescued her instead of Leonid. A punishment, perhaps. That would explain Josef's instant dislike. She pushed Anna through the crowded partisans, to pull alongside Plokhoi.

'Witch,' he said.

'Colonel. Has there been any information about Lieutenant Lumanov? On your radio?'

'No.'

'Have you asked?'

'No.'

'Colonel ...'

'I take orders. When I'm told to pick up a downed pilot, I send men to do it. When he disappears, I send men to do something else. Watch the sky tomorrow, Witch. There's a downed pilot every two minutes. What do you expect?'

There was no coldness in the man's voice. He expressed what all of them knew and feared most, that each was expendable in the higher goal of defending Russia. So what did Katya want more? To search for Leonid or to stop German supply trains from feeding the enemy's armies? She wanted to say *Leonid;* Katya thought, Couldn't it be that way, just once?

Plokhoi watched her with an intent expression.

'Tonight I'm sending two teams, five men in each. I can't risk more than that. You'll go with …'

'I know. Ivan, Daniel, and Josef.'

'What's the matter, Witch? You don't like your bodyguards?'

'I don't need bodyguards.'

'We'll see. I'll send along one new man with each team. You take the *starosta*. He's got spunk, that one.'

Katya knew she could trust the *starosta*. He could not be the traitor, none of the villagers could, they'd just joined the partisans tonight. But what about Plokhoi himself? Why doesn't he want her to find Leonid? What is he afraid of? Is Colonel Bad himself the informant? If she finds Leonid, will she find the secret to the spy in their cell?

Katya nodded. She glanced at the radio, the size of a bread box, strapped to Plokhoi's back alongside his carbine. The metal box was the only way to find Leonid, to speak into it and beg for whoever was the power behind these murky partisans to send more men to find him. The radio voice, the unseen authority in the air, would ask her, What do you want, Katerina Berkovna? What would she answer?

Plokhoi said, 'Go back, Witch. We'll be splitting up in ten minutes.'

July 8
0245 hours
four kilometers north of Borisovka

Big Ivan lay in the dirt beside Katya.

'Pour some more,' he urged in a whisper.

Katya tipped the little bottle of vegetable oil and dribbled it over the man's meaty hands.

'See,' he spoke with the voice of a purring bear, 'the C-3 is hard like a brick when you take it out of the wrapper. You got to do it like this, like bread dough, to make it soft. That way, you can shape it any way you want. Here. You do it.'

Katya did not reach for the gray explosive clay. Ivan held it out to her.

'It's not going to blow up, girl.'

Ivan smacked a fist into the lump. Katya jerked. Nothing happened.

'It takes an explosion to make it go off. That's what the caps are for. Here.'

Still, Katya hesitated. He stuffed the clay in her hands. Under the cast of a slim moon dicing through the leaves overhead, Katya noted Ivan's palms were stained. Kneading the C-3, her own hands began to turn gray.

'It makes your skin yellow,' Ivan said, grinning, showing teeth that were gray, too, under the moon and branches.

While Katya and Ivan molded the explosive, Daniel and surly Josef re-wrapped the long coil of electric detonation cord out of Ivan's knapsack. The *starosta* knelt, peering through the bushes where they hid. The village elder's name was Filip Filipovich Platonov. He had a son – also Filip – fighting somewhere with the Red Army. The boy's letters had stopped a year ago, and the elder knew nothing more. Katya guessed how old the man was, probably more than sixty. His face had collapsed around his hawk nose, he had high cheekbones and a brow like a white awning to make his face sharp, years of hunger and labor had rooted in his flesh. Many of the men from his village who'd joined that night carried the same lean look, the same predator's nose.

A hundred meters away, the Borisovka rail line ran over flat ground. To make the tracks easier to protect from partisan sabotage, the Germans had mowed down a wide swath of trees beside the tracks for miles in every direction. Tonight, two-man patrols walked the rails with flashlights. The guards ambled past every four to five minutes, shining their lights down at the rail ties. Filip watched them without blinking, with a bird-of-prey focus.

Ivan wiped his hands on his jacket. The C-3 became malleable in Katya's grasp, she was excited by the danger, the peril of rolling a powerful explosive in her fingers. She imagined them all going up in a red burst out of her hands.

Ivan breathed, 'Daniel?'

The thin one came close. He and Ivan had both been regular army soldiers, privates. Each had been captured by the Germans and escaped, and both had been found separately wandering behind enemy lines by the partisans. Daniel had been born in this part of the steppe; he told Katya that Plokhoi had stopped him from going home. With the partisan band they risked their lives just as much as they had fighting on the front lines, but now in civilian clothes they enjoyed more status – now they were considered even more as military men. Plokhoi had made them leaders.

Daniel brought out from his jacket pocket two small wooden cartons. He handed them down to Ivan, who took the boxes with uncharacteristic gingerness. The big man set one aside and opened the other for Katya, as though showing her a gem. Inside, on a bed of cotton, lay something that resembled a copper bullet casing with antennae.

'Blasting cap,' she said.

'Definitely.' Ivan raised his grin to Daniel, squatting next to them. 'They say I'm the dumb one, but I'm smart enough not to carry these damn things around.'

Daniel didn't mind the gibe. He brought down a slender finger to the cap, such a clean and comfortable thing, in bed in its little wooden home.

'These babies have a bad temper. Ivan's too clumsy to carry them. He falls down a lot. You do that with one of these in your pants, you don't get up the same man.'

Katya snickered at this, drawing a shush from Josef. The older man kept himself apart while spooling the long detonation wire around his arm.

Daniel continued, unchastened. 'Here's how it works. The C-3 explodes at a rate of about twenty-five thousand feet per second. To detonate it, you need to make a faster explosion. That's why C-3 won't blow up if you just burn it or hit it. That's where the blasting cap comes in. You push the cap into the plastique, hook these two wires up to the electric firing cord, send a current down the wire, and the cap goes off just a little faster than the C-3.' He raised both hands. 'Boom.'

'Boom,' repeated Ivan, savoring the word and the concept.

Daniel lifted the little cap off its cotton pillows. He fingered the twin slender wires sticking out of one end. The wires were crimped together in the middle by a tiny round tab.

'They're very sensitive, these bastards. Anything can set them off. So once you got the C-3 stuck to whatever it is you're going to blow, and you got the wires attached, you make sure you take off this little piece. This keeps the two wires touching, see? To short them out. Once this is gone, the cap is live.'

Daniel returned the copper detonator to its case and closed the lid. He reached down to scoop up both boxes. Ivan took the doughy C-3 from Katya's oily and stained hands. She wiped them on her pants, like Ivan. When they were clean, Daniel handed her the two boxes.

'You and me, Witch.'

Katya hefted the twin cartons, almost weightless in her palms. She waited for Daniel to tell her he was kidding. 'Me?'

'Why not? At this point you know everything the rest of us know about this stuff.'

Josef stalked forward. 'You and Daniel are the smallest and quickest. You'll go.'

The urge pulsed in Katya to mount an argument, that she'd never done anything like this before. But she looked around at ox-like Ivan, crotchety Josef, and ancient Filip – the elder gazed at her with a 'you want *me* to go?' shrug – and clamped her lips. Suddenly she missed her U-2 and the thousands of feet she used to have between her and the Germans.

'Fine,' she whispered. Josef finished with the firing cord and checked his watch. He laid the wire on the ground and crept to the edge of the bushes to join Filip. Daniel grabbed up the long black loops and hoisted them over his shoulder, they hung almost to his boots. He found one loose end and handed it to Ivan. The large man dug in his knapsack for the handheld detonating machine and set about stripping the firing-cord wires. Katya held the blasting-cap boxes one in each hand, very aware of keeping them cozy and still. Her palms began to sweat, and she wondered how sensitive these temperamental caps were to nerves.

They waited for another five minutes. No one moved, except Josef, who glanced up and down from his watch to the strolling, then disappearing, German guards and their flashlights. Katya knew there was another five-man demolition team waiting a mile south down the track. The plan was simple for each squad: two in the team set the charge; one stays on the detonator; two slither out and try to bag a prisoner for Plokhoi to interrogate. This was the Battle of the Rails, fought throughout the occupied territories, designed to disrupt the flow of German trains to the front. The Russian road system was so primitive the Nazis had no choice but to rely on the railroads to supply their men and weapons. The partisans knew this and carried the fight to the enemy here. But tonight, Katya hoped, there would be no fight, just a quick strike. The Germans had lax security at this point in the Borisovka line. At other spots – bridges, bends in the line, downhill runs, all places where the partisans were most likely to hit – the Germans maintained garrisons and watchtowers, and even this was a partisan victory because every enemy soldier safeguarding the railways against the guerillas was one more German soldier not battling on the front. Plokhoi may be a madman, he may even be as bad as his *nom de guerre* implied, but he was clever and disciplined. He hewed to the partisan motto: Attack the weak, fly from the strong.

Katya held the two cap boxes apart as though they might react even to each other. How could Daniel carry them around like they were candy bars? She looked at her partner kneeling beside her. He was reed-thin and chewing a blade of grass. He nodded to himself, some song or pulse playing in his head. She had seen her horses do this at the starting line years ago in the *dzhigitkas,* champing, bobbing, ready to bolt. Ah, well, she thought, Papa, another *podvig*. Where are you? You used to love to watch me race. So, watch now. Here we go.

She sensed the starting moment come, and it did. Josef lifted his face from his watch and whispered, 'Go.'

Daniel moved first, lugging the long links of cord. Katya stumbled out of the bushes; her heart leaped into her mouth, she started to use her hands to catch herself but couldn't because of the caps. She struck a knee to the ground and expected to explode. She didn't, and heard Josef cluck his tongue in disgust.

Daniel lit out for the rails, she followed in his wake. The moonlight out on the flat, cleared ground was milky, just enough of a silver wash to discern shapes at close range and no more. To their right, about fifty meters past them, a two-man patrol had already gone by, playing their beams on the rail ties. Skinny Daniel skittered bent at the waist, the loops of the cord dragged the ground and Katya was afraid of the noise they made scurrying to the rails. She ran awkwardly, too, with both hands before her, still wary of offending the blasting caps. But the guards continued to move off on their rounds and the two reached the tracks. They collapsed on their bellies beside the rails, catching their breaths, trying not to betray themselves from the exertion of the run.

Daniel mopped his brow. Even in the measly light Katya saw the beads of sweat glisten around his eyes. She sat the twin cap boxes in the dirt, relieved to let them loose. Daniel dug into his jacket pocket for the slippery lump of C-3. He handed it over to Katya. Her hands smeared with the oiled stuff again.

'Push it against the track,' Daniel breathed to her. 'Make it stick.'

She worked the explosive clay against the closest rail, molding it to the smooth warm contours. Daniel busied himself with the blasting caps, easing them from the containers. When he had them both out, he waited seconds while Katya finished forming the C-3 to the rail, then pushed both caps into the putty, leaving the tips and wires exposed.

With his knife he cut a short piece from the end of the firing cord, then stripped away the waxy sheath to expose bare wires at both ends. He twisted the wires to connect one cap, then the other, they were now hooked in sequence. Katya guessed the second cap was a backup in case the first one didn't blow. She watched him strip the end of the hundred-meter cord and wire it to one of the caps, astonished at the speed with which the partisan could do this minute work. His long fingers were precise as a musician's, playing over the little wires on this dark and dangerous ground. Daniel connected the caps in under a minute, working on his stomach with precious little light. Katya kept her ears open, and heard nothing but the pitter of Daniel's knife and his elbows in the dirt. The last thing Daniel did was remove the crimps from the blasting-cap wires. The caps were now live.

'Let's get out of here,' he whispered when he was done. He lifted the circles of cord over his shoulder again and got to his feet, still backing away from the rails, unraveling the first loop onto the ground. Katya had no work to do, her hands were free. She wanted to run for the shelter of the bushes and her comrades, but she stayed beside Daniel while he laid loop after loop on the ground.

Katya watched for the guards to turn and come back their way. She listened for any unwelcome sound, her skin prickled with every crunch of her boots and the complaints of the unspooling wire. Daniel, a lean young man, began to huff with the effort of carrying the wire. Katya was hyper-alert and scared. She looked everywhere into the night, except where she was walking. She tripped over the wire under her feet.

She did not catch herself, that would make more noise, but folded into a ball and rolled to her side on the earth. Daniel made an angry grunt. They were halfway between the rails and cover. Daniel froze in place. Katya lay still, petrified that her stumble had betrayed them to the strolling guards. Daniel looked up and down the tracks and saw no reaction from the sweeping flashlights. He shook his head at Katya, then resumed his careful backward gait. She rose from the ground, humiliated at her clumsiness, knowing she would hear it from Daniel if they survived that she was an even bigger oaf than Ivan. What if she had done that while carrying the blasting caps? A cold tingle bristled over her shoulders.

The load across Daniel's back lightened with every unleashed coil. He quickened his pace and Katya stayed to the side, letting him play out the last lengths of wire. When they reached the bushes, he had only a few loops left. Big Ivan slipped out of the shadows to take the remaining cord.

'What was that?' he growled at Daniel.

'Our ballerina here.'

Katya slid into the bushes behind exhausted Daniel. Josef and Filip were gone into position to do their part of the mission and nab a prisoner. Relieved not to have to bear an angry stare from Josef or a bemused grin from old Filip over her tumble, she hunkered behind a thick bush and peered out to the tracks.

Ivan bared his wrist and raised his watch to a sliver of moonlight so he could read the time. He lifted the small, boxy blasting machine into his lap. With a knife he stripped the sheathing from the end of the blasting cord and fastened the bare wires to the terminals of the box, then screwed in the T handle. Earlier, Ivan had explained to Katya how the detonation machine worked; the box was nothing more than a magneto. When the handle was spun fast, a pulse of current – forty-five volts – shot down the blasting cord to the caps and set off the explosion. Ivan completed the detonator assembly, set it between his knees, and fixed his gaze on the dim hands of his watch.

The German guards were far down the track now. They would amble forward another minute, then turn and follow their beams back this way. Katya wondered where Josef and Filip were. Would they act now, while the night was tense and quiet, or wait for the C-3 to go off and make their grab in the echoes and running confusion?

Ivan whispered to himself. Katya turned her attention to the big man curled behind her. The detonation box lay tucked in his abdomen, the wire led away from his gut. He counted, looking at his watch, '... four ... three ... two ... one ...'

Ivan twisted the handle. Katya whirled her head around, eager to see the blast.

Nothing.

She heard Ivan twirl the handle again, and again, but the curtain of the night stayed down. Then, from far off to their left, a boom gushed up the rails. The other squad. They'd blown their track.

Daniel spun an angry face at Katya.

'It's you. You tripped on the wire.'

Ivan cursed behind them. He turned the handle one last time, then set the detonator hard on the ground. He scrambled up to Daniel and Katya. 'Now what?'

Daniel glowered at Katya. 'Yes. Now what, Witch?'

Katya fought to stay calm. It was her fault, but it was an innocent mistake. Just a stumble, anyone might have done it, it was dark, the wire was black, she'd stayed by Daniel to be helpful ... she wanted to plead this to the two furious faces so close to hers. She was humiliated and frightened all at once; their anger crackled in the air while the explosion farther down the track died. They had failed because of her.

She looked out to the tracks. The German guards held their spots down the rails, unsure what to do; should they rush in the direction of the sound, should they keep walking, or hold still? They cut off their flashlights and melted into the dark. They knew there were partisans around. Katya sensed they were as scared as she was.

Daniel's breath soured in her nostrils. Seconds had passed since the other squad's explosion.

'Well?' Daniel tilted his head. Ivan swallowed so

loudly, Katya heard his throat work.

Daniel hissed, 'We have to blow the tracks.'

Katya was crowded, by the blaming hot eyes of the two partisans, by dread leaping in her chest. By the thought of facing Colonel Plokhoi without wrecking these tracks, and being the one to blame. I'm not brave, she said to herself, I'm not this brave.

A horse pawed the ground. She must quiet the horses before they made the situation worse. This gave her a reason to get to her knees and crawl away from Ivan and Daniel. The two men said nothing when she pushed past them. Do they think I have a plan? she wondered, hurrying to the animals. I don't.

Then, looking at the horses milling nervously, she did. It would be a *podvig*, the greatest of her life. Likely the last of her life.

Katya flung herself at the first horse in line, scrabbling to unstrap the girth to slide off the saddle. She risked noise to work fast, calling Daniel and Ivan over to help. The two hurried to her side.

'Get these saddles off. Move, move. And the harnesses. Everything.'

The three stripped the horses of saddles, blankets, reins, and bits, piling them all on the ground with as much quiet as haste allowed. The six horses stood freely in a bunch, laying shoulders to each other, questioning the humans' dire energy and the removal of their bonds. Katya took the harness last off Anna.

She stroked her horse's muzzle. 'We have a job to do, girl,' she whispered.

Katya swung herself up onto Anna, bareback.

'What are you doing?' Daniel asked her.

'I'll be back,' she said. 'Wait as long as you can.'

Katya kicked Anna with a heel to turn her out of the bushes. Daniel and Ivan stepped away and faded in a second behind her under the sound of the six horses cantering in the open. Katya clung to Anna's mane, tugging left or right in play with her boots to lead her clever little horse and the following pack across the hundred-yard plain, to the rails.

Her instincts were right. The partisan horses were unaccustomed to being ridden alone, they'd always traveled in the band of men, never less than in a small group. Tonight, even without tack, they collected tight around Katya and Anna. Their run made no human noise, there was nothing of leather or metal about them in the darkness, they were just a tiny herd of spooked and naked horses that had jumped some fence, frightened by the blast a minute ago.

She rode low, hugging Anna's neck. She'd been the best bareback rider in her village, better than Papa even. Valya had no peer with a saber but she could always outride him. Anna snorted, excited to be in the lead like this, her rider so close as to be part of her.

Katya kept her head inside Anna's flying mane. She sent her eyes up the tracks, seeking to spot the guards somewhere in the night. Where were they? The tracks were fifty meters away, another twenty seconds.

A flashlight popped on, a white sword swinging at the sound of the hooves. Katya slid to her left, away from the patrol, down Anna's midsection. She squeezed both arms hard around the horse's neck. In straining fists she clutched the mane and flattened herself to Anna's galloping ribs. When she was a girl she could pick a fallen hat off the ground at full gallop. The horse running alongside bumped against Katya and loosened her grip, nearly knocking her off. Katya gritted her teeth. Her arms and knees burned, Anna's breath and the other horses' snorting nostrils and whipping legs filled her senses, blending with the pain in her muscles. Between Anna's pounding hooves the ground flashed, lit by the sweeping flashlight. The light stayed on the running horses for seconds, then moved away. Katya used most of the strength she had left to hoist herself up just enough to glance over Anna's bounding back, up the tracks. The flashlight remained on, but had returned its gaze down to the tracks. The two-man German patrol was headed back this way.

She kept Anna running straight, cuing the horse with pressure on her neck. The other partisan mounts jostled her, her grip waned in her horse's mane, her calves and hips burned. Every ache from the crash of the U-2 came back to scream under her skin to let go! Katya growled deep in her throat, a savage sound of will and terror and anger.

She could hold on no longer. Her hands were slipping from Anna's neck, her legs unwrapped and Katya began to slide off. Smart Anna sensed her rider's release and slowed. Katya's boots dragged, then her fanny and shoulder hit the dirt, and she was down. She skidded, biting back a grunt in the kicking dust. Anna galloped unleashed in a small circle, then came back, leading the others to where she'd dumped her rider.

Katya lifted her head, muzzy from the fall. The horses stood around her, panting and pleased, snorting and bobbing their heads. She laid a hand to the ground to roust herself, she couldn't just lie here, no matter how much her body hurt. With a surprise that was too great to be mere relief, almost a shock at her luck, her fingers brushed on the black firing cord, running beside her to the tracks only ten meters away.

She shook her head: She needed to be clear-headed, or she would be dead in minutes. Scrambling to her feet, she crouched behind the horses. She took Anna's muzzle and walked her and the other five horses the last steps to the rails. Holding Anna by the mane, Katya shooed the others away, smacking one on the rump to make them skitter off and grab the attention of the coming guards, leaving Anna and Katya behind at the C-3.

She pressed flat beside the rail. Fifty meters off, the guards' flashlights glanced up at the pack running away from them, then lowered to the tracks again. Anna stood still, disguising the dark form of Katya fumbling with the wires.

Katya's hands felt racked and unruly, her fingers rejected any fine movement. She pulled back from the blasting caps for a moment, to catch her breath and gain control of herself. Her heart beat thunderously in her ears. The guards strolled closer every second; now she could hear their voices, their boots on the gravel beside the rails, their flashlights were the brightest things under the lack-luster moon and stars. Now, she thought. Or, really, never.

She leaned into the C-3, close enough to smell Ivan's vegetable oil. She could not stop the tremble in her fingers so she let them hover above the caps, gingerly touching the wires until she found the place that had come undone. The firing cord had been pulled away from the first cap by her stumble, the stripped copper wire stuck straight up, cooperative and easy to repair if the sun were high and her hands did not quaver like a divining rod and an armed German patrol was not bearing down on her. Katya pulled her hands away again from the task. She commanded them to be still and obey. She filled her lungs with the steppe night and held it. Anna bent down to see what her rider was doing in the dirt. Katya pushed the probing muzzle away. This touch – an old and familiar feel, a horse to her hand – brought her a moment of calm and remembrance. That was all she needed.

German voices sped her hands to the wires. She grasped the loose antennae of the blasting cap, pincered the copper length of the bared firing cord in her other fingertips, and twined the wires together, two, three, four turns. She couldn't be certain the contacts were good, but there was no more time. The first daubs of a flashlight's beam trickled at Anna's hooves.

Katya stood. She grabbed a handful of Anna's mane and started to run. Anna broke into a trot. Katya hopped and bounded onto Anna's back, tucking low to meld with the horse's silhouette. She ducked her head and gripped the horse hard with her weary arms and legs, sliding down again to ride unseen away from the patrol.

She was less than ten meters from the rails when the C-3 blew.

Anna reared. The horse stumbled and neighed, hurt. Katya felt the blast through the animal's muscles, Anna was lifted and smashed down by the explosion. Katya held on by instinct, not thinking to let go. Clinging to Anna's ribs, Katya screamed. The horse seemed broken in the middle, she collapsed as two horses, the upper part wrenched in agony, the lower half still running.

Anna lost her balance in a few wild steps and crumpled over, hitting the ground on top of her. Katya tried to scramble out but her legs were trapped. The weight was too much, Katya couldn't even kick at the horse. Anna convulsed, screaming, grinding Katya into the black dirt. Katya cringed at the agony of the shuddering animal across her thighs and ankles but couldn't make a sound: The German patrol might hear her. She gritted her teeth and blew slow breaths. The patrol had shut off their flashlight at the blast. Through the red haze in her eyes and the injured horse's terrified breathing, she no longer knew where the Germans were.

Struggling to sit up, she looked over Anna's heaving side. The horse had been ripped open at the abdomen, intestines spilled on the ground and lapped across her trembling shoulder and flank. The moon stole the color of Anna's workings, her guts were gray and pulsing, blood ran black. Tears ran down Katya's face. Her horse was in agony. The report of the explosion had faded away now and Anna's cries would bring the guards right to where Katya and she lay. They'd put a rifle to Anna's head to finish the poor beast, then do the same for Katya, the trapped partisan.

Anna shivered. Her hooves crawled in the dust, not understanding what had happened, believing that the answer was to run, always the state of a horse's mind. Katya could do nothing for her horse but to die alongside her. She lay back down, looking at Anna's panicked eye, unblinking and beseeching, You are the rider, you can lead us away from this. Katya stroked her neck and lifted her gaze from the dying horse to the stars. Her vision had cleared, the pain in her legs had gone numb. Anna breathed fast, in deep gulps, as though she were indeed running.

Why did the C-3 go before Katya was clear? What happened? Too late, she thought, it's too late, she would die with questions. She tried to think of Papa and Valya and the war, how would they turn out, where was Leonid? The universe of stars and moon and the years of her life focused down to a pinpoint, a single dark mote here on the ground, Katya, living her last bits second by second in the dust. Enough. To end with a horse seemed right, a horse had been the dearest thing in her life, so this was proper, it was better than an airplane, after all.

The guards spoke out of the darkness. Katya heard the metal slap of a rifle bolt. Anna answered with a nicker, an absurd last appeal to the new human voices, maybe they will be better riders. Boots crunched in the gravel. Katya sat up again.

She drew the knife from her belt sheath. She would not let the Germans finish her horse, this was the Cossack's final responsibility. With her left hand smoothing Anna's ears, she slid the blade deep into Anna's throat to open an artery. The horse did not jump at the new sting. Blood flooded over Katya's fist and the horse's head relaxed in her hands. The wild eye closed. She lay the horse's unsuffering crown back to the earth.

The guards approached. The tracks had been blown fifty meters from them. Partisans were near, danger lurked, so they crept forward with caution.

Katya had only a few more seconds before the darkness was not enough to hide her. Anna's blood dripped warm and sticky in her hand. She gasped, like a woman coming up from under water, then shut her mouth. She knew what to do.

She untucked her tunic. With the knife she cut a hole in the shirt above her belly. Sitting up as far as she could, careful to make no sound, she reached for a handful of Anna's intestines, sorting fast through the wet morass to take only the small bowels. When she had a wet gob of them in her hand, she sawed the blade of her knife through the guts, slicing a portion away. She stuffed the entrails into the hole in her tunic, like stuffing a scarecrow, leaving a length of them dangling out. With both hands, she cupped blood out of the horse's gaping cavity, fighting a need to retch at the heat of Anna's bowels snuggled against her own warm skin and at what she was about to do. Holding her breath to keep her stomach from pitching, she smeared the blood over her face and neck to the sickening smell of copper, she cupped more and splashed blood around the hole in her shirt and Anna's bulging bowel. Urgency and fear carried her past what she was doing, wallowing in gore, salt blood on her tongue and matting her hair. With only seconds before the creeping Germans were near enough to discern more than a dead horse, she drove her knife into a bulging section of Anna's large intestine. The bowel burst at the prick with a gassy pop and a stench blew out that made Katya retch; she caught the vomit halfway up her throat and fell back, eyes closed, a silent prayer on her blood-painted lips.

'*Ach*,' said one of the Germans. The voice came from about ten meters away. Their boots stopped on the gravel.

'Was riecht so faul?' The voice was nervous, and disgusted.

Another few wary steps.

'Das Pferd.'

The dead horse across Katya's legs began to hurt her again. She kept her breathing as shallow as she could, to still her chest, to play dead. She opened her mouth and put an agonized grimace on her face. The boots left the gravel by the rails and scraped in the dirt, coming closer to the horrid mound under which Katya lay pinned. Anna's blood began to cool on her cheeks and neck.

The flashlight clicked on. Behind her lids Katya sensed the beam play over the dead horse. The light washed over her.

'Partisan.'

'Ja.'

'Sie sind nahe.'

The two guards walked in a wide circle around Anna's carcass; behind her lids Katya watched the beam move and fall on her. The stench of the open bowel was keeping these two at bay.

'Ach,' one said again, *'der Geruch.'* He cleared his throat and spat. *'Sheisse.'*

The boots halted a few meters away. The flashlight played full on Katya's face. She needed to breathe, her chest burned. The light searched her.

'Genug.'

A pistol cocked.

Another step was taken in the dirt.

Katya longed to scream, to sit up and scare them away, bloody ghoul, suck in a great breath and call for help, something, anything except lie here posing as dead with her last moment! A bullet was aimed at her brain. No, no, she thought, panicking without moving a muscle, no flinch marred her brow, but her body was coiled to spring up and surrender, she held it back, she was a catapult, every fiber tensed to rise up and fling her hands in the air and shout No! She fought herself, she willed her body to stay rigid as the dead.

'Nein, Hans, nein. Partisanen. Die werdeu uns hören. Shhhh.'

The light stayed pressing across her eyes. The world was at an end inside Katya's yellow glowing lids.

The boots near her head stepped again.

'Ja,' the pistol said, *'ja, sie ist tot.'*

The flashlight clicked off.

The guards' boots moved back to the tracks, crunching again in the gravel. Katya's body sagged with relief. She kept her eyes closed and sipped a long, greedy breath through her nose. She heard the Germans murmur, they were looking over the rail that had been severed by the blast.

She lay marveling that she was still alive. The blood coating her hands and face grew tacky, the odor of the popped intestine renewed itself in her nostrils now that she was breathing again. She could not imagine a way out of her predicament and did not waste her attention trying to figure, she waited in amazement that the clock still ticked on her life. She listened to the guards curse the partisans for the shattered rail.

One of the guards sounded as if he might puke, he made heaving noises behind a clamped mouth. The other voice went mute. Katya heard a brief scuffle on the gravel, something laid down. She kept herself still, she fought the strong urge to look, her only chance of survival was to be dead.

The bootsteps stayed near the tracks. Then, after a short silence, they tromped near her, two sets. They stopped on either side of her head. She kept the veil of a tortured death mounted on her face, the congealing horse blood began to itch. Her held breath burned in her lungs. Above her, a tongue clucked. The man standing over her sighed.

A call – a loud, raspy whisper – issued from down the tracks. *'Was ist los? Gibt's was?'*

The one who'd sighed answered. *'Nein, nein. Alles klar. Es gibt ein totes Pferd.'*

Katya trembled inside her frozen flesh. This was not the voice of either of the guards. This man was older.

The set of boots on the other side of Katya's death pose made a nauseated sound, 'Pfew.' In Russian, the voice whispered, 'Leave her.'

The old one murmured, 'No. We can carry her.'

'She stinks.'

Katya's fear did not release easily. She recognized these voices, but cracked her eyes slowly, just enough to peer out under her lashes, to stay dead.

She saw boots. Russian boots. And there were jackets and dark civilian shirts, and yes! Filip, and nasty Josef. They'd come!

Katya gulped a deep breath and fought to sit up.

The two leaped away from her, old Filip staggered backward and fell to his knees, crossing himself and muttering to Christ. Josef recovered first, he stepped to her and without a word dug his hands under Anna's spine to raise the horse off her.

'Come on, old man,' he growled at the *starosta*.

'Witch?' old Filip mumbled, still on his knees.

Katya turned to Filip, knowing how ghastly she must look. 'Filip, help me get up.'

Josef grunted again, 'Old man.'

Filip helped Josef heft the horse from Katya's legs. Katya plucked the dangling intestine from her ripped shirt and tossed it aside, callous now for Anna's death, her sorrow dismissed by the thrill of reprieve. She sucked down air and thought it sweet, blessed it, felt the honey of her own blood rush back into her feet, then reached up for Josef's hand to stand on her own. Only minutes had passed since the C-3 exploded, that was all, and she had lived a lifetime in them, and a death. She wanted to hug both men, even Josef.

The two left her wobbling while they went to the tracks to collect the German guards. The blown rail was curled in the air like a beckoning steel finger. Josef and Filip hoisted one man to his feet, he'd been unconscious until Josef kicked him to wake him. The soldier's hands had been tied and his mouth stuffed with a sock. In the moonlight Katya saw the shock on his face, his pupils wide and white at her standing before him, a blood-covered zombie partisan. The other guard did not rise. His throat was slit. The gash was gaping enough in his neck for Katya to see it from where she stood, blood had poured and pooled in the crannies of the gravel and across rail ties. Katya felt nothing at the sight.

Josef held his knife to the bound German's throat and gripped him under the elbow. He led the soldier away into the hundred open meters between them and cover. The prisoner walked off with his eyes fixed on Katya.

'Sei still,' Filip hissed to him, and drew an index finger under his own chin to make sure the German understood that Josef would kill him if he made a sound.

Filip took Katya under the arm. Together they hurried away behind Josef and the prisoner back to the trees.

'Where are the horses?' she asked.

'Ivan and Daniel got them. They're waiting. You had a close call, Witch. You scared me so bad I almost filled my britches. Well done. Are you alright?'

She ached down to her marrow, not just from the fall of her horse but from the tempest of fear in her veins; it had withdrawn, but not without leaving its mark in her.

'Yes.'

Limping across the dark ground on Filip's arm, she prepared herself for her return to life, to the war and Plokhoi's partisans, this long night and tomorrow's day, and her place in it all. Why did the C-3 go off before she was clear? Where was Leonid? Who was the traitor?

How does old Filip know German?

She asked him.

He answered out of breath, lugging her across the open ground. They were almost to the shrubs. Katya spotted the outlines of Ivan and Daniel saddling the remaining horses.

'My mother was a Sudeten Slav,' the old man replied. 'My six brothers and I grew up speaking German.'

'Did all your brothers come with you to Plokhoi?'

'Yes.' The *starosta* hesitated. 'All but one.'

'Where is he?'

'He stayed in the village. He's ... he's not welcome.'

Katya slowed, even before reaching the safety of the copse and the other partisans.

'Why, Filip?'

The *starosta*'s whisper vented through tight lips, baring shame. 'Nikolai works for the Nazis. He's an interpreter. For their interrogations. One day the village ... No, my brothers and I, we'll put a stop to it.'

Katya tugged Filip to a halt. This was a calamity in the old man's family, a collaborator. She saw shame on Filip's face, but could not pause for it. She needed to ask something fast, outside the hearing of the others. Of all the partisans, she knew Filip was not the spy.

'Did he ever question downed Soviet pilots?'

Filip cocked his weathered head at this. 'Yes. Why?'

A prayer raced through Katya's heart. 'Did Nikolai ever travel to Tomarovka?'

'Last week. They came and took him to Kazatskoe, three kilometers away.'

Her heart cartwheeled at this news. Before she could explain, Daniel and Ivan tramped out of the bushes to them. Katya whispered to Filip, 'Please, don't tell anybody about this. Talk to me alone. Filip, please.'

'Yes,' the *starosta* beamed, glad at her urgency, he was

needed for a secret with the Witch, the bloody partisan woman come back from the dead, 'of course.'

Daniel and Ivan recoiled when they came close. Daniel gaped at the sight of her. Big Ivan was uncowed, he gathered Katya in his arms.

'It was Daniel,' Ivan bent low to her ear, 'he said it was alright to blow it. I swear.'

'I heard your horse take off, Witch,' Daniel said. 'I didn't know you were still close to the tracks. The Germans were headed your way. I'm sorry.'

'Shut up,' Josef barked, with no interest in whispering. 'Saddle up. Daniel, you ride with the prisoner. Up.'

Daniel made a helpless gesture at Katya, then grabbed the German soldier by the wrists and shoved him onto a horse. Ivan whined, 'I told him to wait. But the guards got so close. Witch, are you alright?'

Katya moved beside an open saddle. The blood on her face and hands was drying to a rusty cake. She was a resurrection and a fright for the partisans, even Josef winced looking at her. With ease, without pain, she toed the stirrup, rose from the earth, and spurred the new horse away.

CHAPTER 14

July 8
0450 hours
SS *Leibstandarte* situation room
Belgorod

With every telegram he handled, the partisan's heart pumped in Luis's hand. He took the pieces of paper, some yellow, some blue for urgent, and walked them to the map. The battle was a game, fleshless and compact. It was a slow-moving tide, black German markers inching toward the red sandcastles of the Soviet defenders. Luis did not let himself begin to hate what he was doing, presiding over numbers and stratagems, sliding blocks with shuffleboard sticks, breathing tobacco smoke and not the fumes of gunpowder and gasoline. Hatred was a commodity he would not waste on this map room and these clean liverymen of staff around him. He'd nibbled morsels throughout the first and second days of the battle, he'd slept no more than an hour at a time, sometimes on his feet leaning against a wall. He never unbuttoned his collar. He hoarded his hatred, refusing to squander it on wooden armies. The throb in his knife hand reminded him of actions far beyond a paper field and a toy war.

Luis was naive on his first morning beside the map, the opening day of the battle. He did not understand how the black German blocks of Papa Hoth's 4th Panzer Army could fail to push through the Red ones. The black had everything: air support, momentum, powerful new weapons, expert and experienced leaders at every level. Luis wanted to simply reach down to the map, sweep his arm through the red bits and push them aside, that was what Hoth was certain to do on the battlefield, what was so difficult? Those were Russian blocks, they were the ones that always were defeated, *verdad*? But by the end of the first day, he'd read out eight separate messages from the 48th Panzer Corps, fighting on a fifteen-mile front alongside the Oboyan road, to the left of II SS Panzer Corps. The 48th was trying to keep up with the spectacular northward sweep of the three SS panzer divisions; *Totenkopf, Das Reich,* and *Leibstandarte* had fought their way thirty-five kilometers from their jump-off positions, north past Smogodino and Luchki, through the Soviet 6th Army's second defense belt. The 48th's job was to protect the SS left flank by crossing the Luchanino River and taking Syrtsev and Alekseyevka, then reach the Psel River by nightfall. Eight times Luis watched the black blocks of the 48th charge across the green line of the Luchanino at the little red battalion blocks of the 3rd Mechanized Corps. Eight times, he hid his growing astonishment when the attacks had been repulsed, the red blocks had held, the road to Oboyan remained in Russian control. The reports spoke of flamethrowers and dug-in T-34 positions, of deep echelons of unyielding defenders and close-quarters combat, of dozens of Tigers and Panthers destroying opposing Russian tanks by a score of seven to one throughout the day. Hundreds of Red tanks were wrecked on an afternoon in just one part of the greater battle, and still those Russian blocks held.

On the right-hand side of the SS advance, battle group Kempf was also lagging, staggering far to the south, running behind every schedule and plan. *Totenkopf, Das Reich,* and *Leibstandarte* were outpacing their mates, exposing their vulnerable flanks left and right, like a spear stabbing alone through the Russian defenses. Major Grimm could find nowhere to bang his fist, the game board would have been upset, so he pounded the walls. Breit showed no emotion, only a keen raptor's eye for information. The entire first day and into the evening, Luis read the messages in a calm voice, supervised the long sticks, and kept his own counsel, absorbing the others' anger and frustration to feed his own.

On the northern shoulder of the bulge, Colonel General Walter Model achieved nothing to match the penetration into the Soviet defenses by the SS divisions in the south. The lines on Luis's map in the northern salient resembled more a sag, like a wet ceiling. First, Model was bogged in the town of Ponyri, a blazing battle of tanks and infantry, then he'd been stymied outside the town of Ol'khovalka right at the tip of his advance. The movement of Model's 9th Army across the big map was globular and slow, not the lightning flash of *Blitzkrieg* at all. Luis gazed over the little blots of red that held back the unprecedented might of Germany. The reports streaming in to the situation room told the story in bald detail. Model was safeguarding his tanks, keeping them away from the points of attack, using infantry instead to punch through Russian lines, exploiting with his tanks only when there was an opening. This was not working and could not work – Luis realized this first, hours before Grimm began to bleat about it – not against the immense depths of the Russian defense belts. Infantry on foot were getting chewed up in those thousands of miles of trenches and millions of mines. Tanks, he thought without speaking, watching every flow and recoil of the black blocks in the north. Look at what the SS has done there in the south, look at the pace and ferocity of the assault. The SS uses the bludgeon of the tanks: Mark IVs in the lead in wedge formation, Tigers in the center, this is the *Panzerkeil,* the armored battering ram. Infantry follows closely, neutralizing the trenches, swarming into the breaches cut by the tanks, holding the gains while the tanks move on. That's how you cut the Soviets to pieces, that's how you smash those red blocks into splinters. Tanks, he thought, and the SS. And hatred.

On the second and third days of Citadel, the tendencies set out on the map in the first morning of the German attack played themselves into themes. In the north, Model had advanced his 9th Army no more than fifteen kilometers, then ground to a stop after sacrificing fifty thousand men and four hundred tanks. By the morning of July 8, any possibility of reaching Kursk lay only in the south, with Papa Hoth and his 4th Panzer. But on Papa's right, Kempf continued to drag behind. The three SS divisions at the vanguard of the assault turned increasingly to the northeast, toward Prokhorovka and away from Kursk, to face the Soviets hacking away at their flanks. *Totenkopf* was ordered to fall back, given the task of protecting the right flank where Kempf's army should have been, thus subtracting one SS division from the crest of the advance. On the SS left flank, the 48th Panzer Corps finally broke across the Luchanino River, made progress along the Oboyan road, and linked up with *Leibstandarte* and *Das Reich*. But slowly they, too, began to face difficulties. Over the hours it became clear that they could not keep up with the hard-driving SS. Germany's elite SS Panzer Divisions became more exposed with each kilometer they took. Every incident, attack and counterattack, advance and retreat, all the high ground gained and lost, casualty counts, tank and field-gun losses, repairs, air assaults, every meter of battleground wrested from the Russians by the dying flowed through Luis's thin touch. He stood by the sprawling map watching the developing carnage and defeat for Germany. Through three short nights and long hot days, all of it vicious for the mounting cost, he handled every message with increasing dread, not only for the miserable news the pages brought to the map but afraid the next sheet would announce the American invasion in Italy, and that would toll the bell on his chance to enter the battle; his second time in Russia would end as fruitlessly as did his first, without a wound this time but also without honor. Luis was helpless, and this was a silent misery for him because he felt strong, growing in power even while Germany struggled, even sleepless as he was, the beat in his hand nudging him, to do what? He was forced to stand by and watch the bull be butchered, knowing if he could only run into the arena he could achieve something, save something, perhaps the day, perhaps Germany, certainly his dream of glory. The map of war was not war, and he knew God did not have a map in mind when He brought Luis back to Russia.

At dawn of the fourth morning beside the teetering chart, Luis took in the message that unleashed him.

Erich Thoma lay in a Belgorod hospital, a bullet through his neck. The note was written by Thoma himself, asking Luis to come.

Luis did not relay this information to the two intelligence officers grinding their teeth beside the map. Major Grimm was a mess, untucked and occasionally forced to leave the map room just to mop his anxiety and restore his uniform to some military decorum. Slipping the location of the hospital into his pocket, Luis approached Major Grimm.

'Major.'

The heavy man raised his gaze to Luis; eyes and cheeks and chin were swollen as though Grimm were a sponge and all the failure on the map was soaked into him, to seep out his pores in the Russian summer. Luis felt like an icicle beside this bloat.

'Captain.'

'I would like an hour, sir. May I be excused?'

'No!' the major snapped. He shot a hand at the map.

'Look. Look for yourself, Captain de Vega. Where is there an hour for you to take?'

'Go.'

Colonel Breit spoke from across the room, behind his cigarette, a dispassionate voice drilled through the tobacco cloud above the map. 'He's been here more than both of us combined, Major. He wants an hour to breathe some air not spoiled by the two of us. Go, Captain. Nothing will get much better or worse in an hour.'

Major Grimm nodded in apology to Luis, overruled. 'I'm sorry, Captain. Of course, take an hour. Take a walk. I can read bad news as well as you can, I'm sure.'

Luis spun on his boot heels, and left the building. Outside, the slanted sun whitened his skin in the first daylight to hit him for four days. The time was only 0500 but high overhead planes streaked every direction, the cobblestoned street in front of him was clogged with armored vehicles clanking past, ambulances sputtered by, a frenzy of noise and motion assaulted him outside the tense cocoon of the situation room. He stopped only for a moment to take it all in, to absorb this, the senses of real battle, the way Grimm had sopped up the disasters of the map, then moved on, blade lean and ready.

He caught a ride to the hospital in a careening, beeping staff car. When he told the driver he wanted a lift to the hospital, the soldier thought it was because Luis himself needed care, he looked so bad. He asked if Luis was alright, and was told in a curt voice to drive. The man took off.

At the hospital, Luis picked his way through hallways jammed with squealing gurneys and the hurly-burly of medical heroics. This was the place where the road split for a thousand soldiers this day, onward to life or curving away to death, and Luis was unimpressed, he'd crossed this way a year ago and ended up where no man was supposed to go, in the middle, off the road. He dodged surgeries in the hall, blood on the linoleum; doctors and nurses shouted and scurried like the walls were trenches and death was the enemy pouring over the ramparts down on them. Luis neither admired nor respected any of the wounds in the hall; none, not even the fatal ones, were as bad as his. He kept himself erect, disdainful even, when he looked into the scared eyes of the soldiers on the tables, slumped in corners, bleeding in chairs.

He searched for half an hour – the hospital buzzed, a hive of moaning – until a harried nurse led him to Thoma. The man lay in his tailored black SS uniform, on a sheetless bed in a corner of what once was the cafeteria. There were no food smells here, just the clean odor of gauze and the brown smells of soldiers and the dirt they'd fought in. Thoma lay with his hands arranged beside his hips, composed. A collar of bandage swathed his neck, marred only by a red coin of blood below the ear. Thoma was dead.

Luis stood beside the bed.

'Sniper.' A grenadier in another cot sat up, his leg was wrapped in a log of gauze. 'A sniper got him. I heard him say it. A little while ago.'

Luis did not acknowledge the soldier except to pivot his head to the man, then turn away, back to Thoma. Yes, that would be Erich. He would be standing in the turret during the attack, bravado, charmed. Luis lay his hand over the still fingers. Thoma had gone whiter than Luis. He was no longer the man Luis might have become; they'd switched roles. Thoma was now the pale thing.

That's why Thoma sent word for Luis to come. To make the exchange, to give his blessing.

Luis lifted his hand from cool Thoma. The Iron Cross at Thoma's throat was not covered by the bandage. The soldier in the other bed had continued jabbering, about the combat, about Thoma perhaps and his exploits, that he might have been a hero. Luis walked off, past the yapping soldier's bed without exchanging another look. The man gabbled as Luis cut past.

He left the hospital, purposefully. The faster he walked, the more he gained the sense of shedding the failures of the wounded there, the boundaries of the dead, he was alive and hungry and hailing a car. One stopped for him and he got in the back seat, slamming the door with a sound that only the halest of men can make. He rode through frightened Belgorod. The scales of the battle were not tipped just yet, there was still time for Luis Ruiz de Vega to add his weight. Yes, he thought, my weight.

He entered the situation room. The morning was an hour older and nothing had changed, there were no bodies scattered about the carpet, just wooden blocks prodded back or forth. They ought to move this map to the hospital, Luis thought, that's what Grimm and Breit should have as their backdrop. He walked to Colonel Breit.

'Sir.'

'Yes, Captain. Refreshed, I hope.' The officer's voice was bland, without sentiment. He's draining, Luis realized. In a day or two he'll be as white as Thoma.

'Sir, Captain Erich Thoma is dead.'

Breit reacted with a bland face. He nodded and reached for his cigarette pack. Major Grimm muttered a curse and set both palms flat on the board to resume his gaze at the pieces. Thoma was nowhere in this room, he was off the board, and the board was all that mattered. Luis reproached himself for tolerating this for the four days he already had.

'Sir.'

Breit had turned from Luis, expecting the captain to go collect his dispatches and get about his work, stoking the map.

'Sir.'

'Yes, Captain?'

'I request permission to take over Captain Thoma's command.'

Breit kept his eyes fixed on Luis for several moments, long enough to tug a cigarette from the little carton, pulling his eyes away only to match his lighter flame to the tip. He sucked deep lungs of smoke, eyes on Luis, then peered through the gray, long exhale. The partisan's heart pulsed in Luis's hand. He wanted to hold it out to Breit, have him feel the beat for himself. He'd know then.

On the far side of the map, Major Grimm said nothing. He was a protruding and indulgent man, Luis did not want him to speak, not even on his behalf. Breit was a colonel in the SS. Luis stood in front of this officer wearing the same black uniform, the one Thoma wore, the one worn by the only men defeating the Russians on that map.

Breit spoke.

'How long since you've been in combat, Captain?'

Look at me, Luis wanted to shout. I'm in combat every fucking day. Instead, he kept the gush of temper out of his face and voice.

'Almost a year, sir. Before that, I had five years' service in the armored divisions of Generalissimo Franco and Adolf Hitler.'

Breit dragged again on the cigarette. The corners of the colonel's mouth flicked. 'What do you know about the Tiger tank?'

'I know, sir, that if we win this battle, it will not be because of German weapons but because of the hands they've been put into. And I know that we need to reach Kursk as soon as possible.'

'Yes,' Breit said, billowing smoke with the words, 'the Americans are coming.'

'Yes, sir. The Americans.'

Breit glanced back at Grimm, who echoed his nod.

'*La Daga*, hmmm?'

The name of the pickpocket, and the *banderillero*, and the tank commander. A hero's name.

'Go,' Breit said.

July 8
0710 hours
the Oboyan road

Luis rode alone in the bed of a troop carrier on the Oboyan road. He'd hitched a ride in a convoy headed to Luchki to deliver fuel to *Leibstandarte* and fetch back the wounded. The road itself had weathered the battle well, it was not too torn up by tracked vehicles or bombs. But the land east and west of the highway had been scourged into a vista of destruction. There was hardly anywhere Luis could look that did not display man's ability to blacken.

Luchki lay fifty kilometers north of Belgorod. In the two hours he spent bouncing on a bench in the back of the four-ton truck, Luis saw a thousand charred vehicles: tanks, self-propelled artillery, personnel carriers, supply trucks like the one he rode in now, ambulances – there was no preference of army, both iron crosses and red stars alike blistered on their burned aprons. The ground had been torn up by mine blasts and cannons, creviced with abandoned trench works, and charred under the gusts of flamethrowers. Unattached wheels and spent shell casings were common on the ground, so were the dead, every human or mechanical bit of them seared murky by the heat of the fighting. The battlegrounds bumped past and Luis was surprised at how the natural colors and contours of the earth had been sooted over, as though the black German blocks of the big map were actually here pressing their shade into the world. He rode amazed at how even the immense steppe sky could absorb so much of man's stain that it lost its own blue; it was blotched by the streaks of fighters and bombers, smoke from ruined villages and smoldering fields, flak burst in its deepest reaches. He recalled Breit's cigarette cloud over the map and thought, Yes, that's here, too. Calm hovered here in the aftermath of the fighting, but it was uglier than any battle, a scorched peace. Luis held on to the truck's panels, eager to rejoin his division, where the battle took place and everything was not already settled.

In Luchki, he dismounted the truck. The Soviet farming commune was unrecognizable as having ever held the roofs and beds of people. It was a junkyard now, a vignette of the power that frothed when the two battling armies met on the field. Three silos lay on their sides, crumpled, riddled tubes. Fences and sheds, porches and painted windowsills, were strewn flat in a jumble and crushed, nothing of the village stood higher than a hitching post. Luis smelled the battle perfume of petrol and gunsmoke splashed over the smashed slats that had been homes and barns.

Luchki was in the rear of *Leibstandarte,* in the shaft of the salient thrust like a pike into the Russian defenses by the SS divisions. The front lines were only eight kilometers away on three sides, surrounding all but the south where Luis had come from. Rumbles stomped back to Luchki from these fronts but the early morning had not yet erupted. Luchki filled with supplies of fuel and medicine for *Leibstandarte*. A battlefield armor repair station was set up next to an aid tent. Luis made himself known to a passing lieutenant. The subaltern directed Luis to the repair area.

Luis walked past men of every mint, clusters of fresh-faced replacement grenadiers just trucked up from the rear, filthy SS fighters slumped around their weapons. Outside the stuffed aid station were men cut in pieces, sometimes in half, groaning on stretchers. Soldiers in undershirts, white-skinned Aryans of long muscle and bone, formed bucket brigades behind the convoy to off-load supplies; officers in still shiny boots spoke in gaggles about what they'd survived out there on the battlefields. Luis overheard one of the officers curse Kempf for not protecting their eastern flank. Another wondered how the campaign in the north was going. Luis walked among them, knowing none of these men and everything about the dispositions of the battlefields around Kursk, not just Kempf but Hoth and Model and von Manstein's progresses and failures. He was freed from the map room at last, but had not yet shed the knowledge of the map, the vast perspective, like a god sent down among mortals.

He approached the repair area, arranged beneath a hasty camouflage tent. Several tanks were under repair here, two dozen mechanics ministered to them, banging and yanking, clanking the blocks and tackles of mobile tripods to hoist heavy parts. In the center of the shop, four mechanics in rolled sleeves leaned on the fat handle of a jack to raise the immense side of the only Tiger tank under the tent. Luis walked close. He was astonished again at the size of the Tiger, while the four stout mechanics labored over the jack to raise the left-hand tread a few centimeters. One of the twelve interwoven bogie-wheels on this side had taken an anti-tank round. The mammoth Mark VI must have limped into Luchki to have it replaced. But the Tiger had to be lifted first; these mechanics heaved together, counting *'Eins, zwei, drei ...'*

Luis walked around the Tiger, counting in its thick armor the scoops and punches from Soviet shells. The tank had weathered an excruciating number of hits. The whole exterior had been covered with *zimmerit*, an anti-magnetic paste made from sawdust that dried like concrete, to keep the Red infantry from attaching magnetic mines to the chassis once the giant tank broke through their lines. He read the markings painted on the Tiger: on the left glacis plate beside the machine-gunner's portal was a horizontal bar topped with two vertical bars, the special signet designed by the SS to denote the battle of Kursk; on the turret was painted the vehicle code, S21. The 'S' signified a heavy panzer, the numbers denoted it as part of the second platoon, the first tank out of four. Luis thought this might be one of the Tigers he delivered to Thoma last week. He recalled the sight of the huge machines on their flatbeds, they'd been new and awesome, bearing the promise of victory. Now, to look at this Tiger after only four days in battle, it seemed to bear the scourges of a thousand guns.

When the mechanics had struggled enough with the jack, two of them stepped off to dab their brows while the two others wrestled with the bolts on the hub of the damaged wheel to release it. Luis was noticed now. A mechanic crammed his kerchief into his overalls and executed a quick dash over to Luis.

'Yes, sir, *Herr* Captain.'

Luis could not break his recent habit of searching the eyes of every new man who looked at him for the first time, to ferret out what that man thought of the chalky apparition, the Spanish SS officer in front of him. This mechanic did not react to Luis's gauntness. Good, Luis thought, excellent. The soldiers up here at the front are different from the cows in the rear. They don't flinch.

'I am Captain Luis de Vega. I'm taking over Captain Thoma's company in the 1st Panzer Regiment.'

The mechanic nodded. 'Yes, sir.'

Luis paused, to let the mechanic instruct him further, where to go, where the other Tigers of *Leibstandarte* were. The man said nothing.

Luis asked coolly, 'Where is Captain Thoma's regiment?'

'They're just south of Sukho-Solotino.' The man turned to point northeast. 'It's about ...'

'I know where Sukho-Solotino is,' Luis said. The mechanic lowered his arm and set his jaw. Luis did not care to mollify his tone. 'This is one of Captain Thoma's Tigers, isn't it?'

The mechanic shrugged. 'Yes, sir, you might say that.'

Luis saw insolence and was about to correct it, when another voice came through the hammering in the tent.

'This *was* Captain Thoma's Tiger.'

Four men advanced through the loose parts on the ground and the other noisy repair crews. They came dressed in *Waffen* SS blacks under cloth caps, slim and purposeful young men, walking abreast. Their strides as much as their insignia identified them. *Leibstandarte* tankers.

They stopped in front of Luis. All four presented the Hitler salute, that outlandish thrust of the arm. Luis returned the salute and felt asinine, the five of them forming an arbor of upraised hands. He lowered his hand first, the others followed suit. The tallest of them stepped forward. He appeared to be the oldest of the four, as well, perhaps twenty-two.

'Sir. I am Sergeant Balthasar. We were Captain Thoma's crew. Are you the new company commander, sir?'

These boys were stolid, Nazi dogs of war. Luis did not bother to scrutinize their reactions to him. Every chin jutted above the SS runes at the collar. These German lads knew their place well enough for Luis to have no need to put them in it. Yes, Luis thought, these fellows are of the right makings. Steel-eyed, puffed chests, godless hearts, each one of them was as deadly as a bullet, and Luis was now in charge, the one to aim and fire them. He was back in command.

'Sí,' he spoke in Spanish deliberately, to announce to his new crew that he was different, he was exotic, he was not Thoma nor did he care to be. Thoma was dead.

'Ja,' he corrected himself in German. 'Captain de Vega.'

Luis added nothing more for a moment, a little test for the four crewmen. Who would speak if not spoken to, who would scrape his feet with impatience? He cast his eyes up and down their line, their mouths stayed shut and awaiting, and he was again satisfied. Thoma had whipped them well. Luis mounted a cruel sneer for them and nodded, his first performance of leadership; the boys surely saw him as a bizarre-looking, extraordinary man. He let them have a first glance at the new power he brought to them, and to this scarred, apparently indomitable Tiger they controlled.

The next step was to show them his physical vitality; though he was reed thin he was still nimble and strong. He turned from the crew and swung himself up on the tilted chassis, leaping easily from the ground onto the fender, then climbed up to the turret. There was an element of swagger in his swift motion, the crew were all young men, he drew hints of smiles. He started to step down into the commander's open hatch, to lower himself into the Tiger, to give the appearance of inspecting it, leaving the four to wait on him until he popped back up. Luis had never sat in the commander's seat of a Tiger. He would not tell the crew that, or describe the thrill spreading into his hands and ruined stomach. The tank was a brute – the crew were brutes, too – and they were all his. Outside this clanging repair tent rang the battle and the war and his redemption.

The Tiger reached up to embrace him with an oily, dark aroma. The jagged, close quarters welcomed him. In the padded seat of the commander, more than anywhere else in the world, Luis was not wounded, he was not ugly or woeful. He felt his lost wholeness returning.

He reached up to close the hatch door, to enclose himself in the Tiger and imagine what lay ahead in the warming morning. Above his hand, something was splattered in the workings of the round raised door.

Thoma's blood.

Luis did not hesitate. Thoma was off the board. He

wrapped his fist around the smirched handle and pulled the heavy door down. He'll take Thoma's blood back into battle for him, gain some measure of revenge for the man. This felt right. Luis sat alone inside the Tiger, with the mechanics pounding at its side.

As he expected, the Tiger was far roomier than the last tank he'd sat in, the Mark IV. His commander's seat was secured above the massive breech of the main gun. He set his feet on the turntable and could almost stand erect. Inside the cupola, his head was ringed by five thick glass vision blocks, each with a padded browrest. He leaned into them one at a time and peered into the tent, forward, to the sides, and back. There was his crew, in their tight little chorus line, still black-clad and disciplined. This added to his delight.

Below Luis's feet were two more chairs. Directly in front and to the left was the gunner's position, with all its firing controls and sighting and aiming systems. This was one of the great advantages of the Tiger, for German optics were the finest in the world. The gunner was expected to hit a stationary target inside twelve hundred meters with his first round, at two thousand meters with his fourth round, and a moving target under twelve hundred meters with his third round, each shell aimed and fired within thirty seconds. The gunner had at his disposal a hydraulic turret traverse and a handwheel for the final few degrees of accuracy. The commander's position had only a manual traverse flywheel in case the hydraulics failed, but no access to the power traverse control. The designers made it plain that operating the cannon was the gunner's job.

Below the gunner sat the driver. Luis craned himself lower to see into the driver's position. The main features there were the steering wheel and poor visibility. The driver was only allowed to see the outside world through a narrow glass block visor and a periscope. No provision had been made for him to drive with his head out of the chassis. At the driver's feet were conventional pedals for brake and clutch. To the right, across the bulk of the transmission and a shelf for the tank's radio, was the position for the bow gunner/radioman. The bow gunner had a 7.92 mm machine-gun and a telescope firing sight. The odd thing here was a metal headpan, an upside-down cup at the end of a rod designed to rest on the bow gunner's skull, so that he moved the direction of the muzzle with his head. When the bow gunner was not firing, the radio to his left was his priority.

Luis straightened his back and sat up in his commander's seat. Beside him, on the right-hand side of the big breech, was the loader's position. This chair faced the rear of the turret. The loader had the most room of any of the five-man crew, with superb access to the many rounds of the tank's ammunition. The shells were mounted on horizontal wall racks in the compartment, five dozen rounds within easy reach. There would be more in bins beneath the floor. The rounds were huge, the sharp teeth of this Tiger, bigger than anything the Russians could hurl back at him. Luis tried to take one in his arms and almost dropped it out of the rack. He put it back gingerly, a little embarrassed, he'd almost fumbled it and let the crew hear him knocking around inside their tank. It appeared the Tiger had been reloaded, with a full complement of rounds divided equally between AP and high-explosive.

He leaned into the forward vision block, to stare along the magnificent length of the 88 mm gun. He relaxed in his chair, just for one more private minute, and breathed in the cave of the Tiger's innards. He liked the arrangement in here; unlike the Mark III and the Russian T-34 where the commanders were also gunners, every crewman in the Tiger – like the older Mark IVs, with a five-man crew – had a well-defined task. The radio, all guns, the driving, each had its station. The commander had only to command. Luis, even without experience in a Mark VI, knew he could do that. He'd led tanks in battle many times. Command was his nature, and as soon as the mechanics repaired the wheel, it would be a nature unbound. He'd never had this kind of force at his fingertips – not in another tank, not in the *corrida* holding his *banderillas* over his head, not even in his fast knife hand. He caressed the Tiger's thick hide from the inside, where he and his men would be the Tiger's courage and anger. The partisan's heartbeat still throbbed in his hand, but different now, encased in steel.

He drew a deep breath and put his hand to the bloody hatch cover. He shoved Thoma out of the way and stood in the commander's cupola. The four crewmen below had not moved. He glanced down at the mechanics, they'd gotten off the bad wheel. The Tiger would be rolling inside the hour.

Luis climbed down and stood in front of Sergeant Balthasar.

'I'm sorry about Captain Thoma. I knew him only a little. But he must have been a fine commander to bring you through like this.'

Luis expected this sentiment would dispose of Thoma and finalize his taking of the Tiger and crew. Balthasar said, 'Yes, sir.' The others made memorial faces. Luis changed his tone.

'Now, Sergeant. We'll leave for Sukho-Solotino as soon as possible. Which is the driver?'

'I am, sir.'

A teenager with a big gap in his front teeth spoke, a corporal. He lisped his name and Luis did not remember it a second after it was said.

'Make certain she's properly fueled. Any problems with the transmission, the engine, anything the mechanics should look at while we're here?'

'No, sir.'

'I'll rely on that.' Luis dripped a hint of threat into this remark. 'Radioman?'

Another of the four straightened. Luis asked again if all was well. He repeated this query with the loader, Are we fully armed, machine-guns and main battery? Luis listened to perfunctory replies, marking each man in his head by role and not by name or rank. Driver. Loader. Gunner. Radio. There was no need for them to be men. They were tasks.

'Gunner,' he said to Balthasar. 'Walk with me.'

Luis led the young man away from the tent. The sun climbed in the morning but it was not yet even eight o'clock. Luis spoke.

'The crew,' Luis said. 'Tell me right now anything I need to know.'

'They're the best, Captain. Every one of them.'

'Again, I'll rely on that.' Again the threat on the pallid lips. 'You understand.'

The sergeant took this in. Luis saw and savored the impact.

'Yes, sir.'

'The rest of the regiment is in Sukho-Solotino. What's the condition of the other tanks?'

'We're down to thirty-one Mark IIIs, thirteen Mark IVs, and seven T-34s.'

'What about the other Tigers?'

The sergeant hesitated.

'You don't know, sir?'

Luis was aware only of what the map and messages had told him, the progress and location of wooden block armies.

'Know what?'

'We're the last Tiger.'

'In the company?'

'No, sir.'

The gunner drew himself up, like a schoolboy ready for punishment. 'In the division.'

Luis went stock-still, to keep from the gunner how this rocked him. He was about to join an armored division that four days ago had thirteen Tigers. Seconds stretched out while he stared at the sergeant. The wreckage of a dozen Mark VIs, invincible machines, would not play out in his head. Something was wrong. Luis couldn't believe it was the Tigers themselves but the hands that guided them, into minefields, into ambushes, into indefensible positions. Yes, the Tigers were slow, and certainly there were mechanical problems cropping up here and there. But to lose all but one to the Russians in four days? No. Luis could not blame the machines.

He looked back across the littered and busy ground to the repair tent, recalling the beating that brave tank had taken, the last Tiger in *Leibstandarte*. He had only that one left, to put into battle at the head of Mark IIIs and IVs and captured Soviet tanks. He brought his eyes around to the gunner, who'd helped keep this one giant tank alive for him to command.

'Good,' he said.

July 8
0830 hours
Luchki

Luis was not in the tent when the mechanics lowered the Tiger. A lieutenant from *Leibstandarte*, alerted by Major Grimm, came to greet him with orders. He was instructed to proceed in his Tiger immediately northwest to Sukho-Solotino. *Leibstandarte* was assigned along with *Totenkopf* to reorient away from the northeast, to mount an attack in the direction of the Oboyan road, then plunge directly at Kursk. The third SS division, *Das Reich*, was to hold down the right flank instead of Army Group *Kempf*, which had barely gotten out of the gate east of Belgorod and was continuing to lag. Receiving his orders, Luis cast his thoughts back to the map room, to fat Grimm and chain-smoking Breit pacing beside the board. He saw the map and how these orders made sense. He thanked the lieutenant and jogged back to the repair tent, excited now, envisioning the long sticks pushing *Leibstandarte* into position at Sukho-Solotino and then the Oboyan road. One of the black blocks moving against the Red defense line across the road would be his.

Even before he saw it he heard his Tiger's howling engine in the center of the village, bellowing for him. Beside his tank was a Mark IV that had also been repaired. The Tiger was almost twice the size, its revving engine distinct, the pocks on its surface testaments to the fight in its hide. Men walking past gave the tank a wide berth, like a bull run into the ring belching steam and snot and spoiling for blood. Luis ran to it and climbed the turret to his open hatch. He dropped his legs into the open cupola. The loader handed him his padded helmet, he strapped it on and attached the throat microphone. The Tiger waited, vibrating around him. Luis pulled his goggles down over his eyes, to ride standing like Thoma over the barley and wheat fields, to crush the sunflowers and mustard stalks between him and Sukho-Solotino. He glanced at Thoma's blood and spoke into the intercom, 'Driver, forward.'

July 8
0920 hours
8 kilometers south of Sukho-Solotino

The sun was unstinting, a Spanish sun over the fields that would become battlefields this morning. Luis gazed north across a bland expanse of steppe grass and patchy greens where young crops had not yet been stamped on. Ten kilometers to his left, the flat reach was split by the ribbon of the Oboyan road, his objective. In his way was the defended town of Sukho-Solotino. Behind Sukho-Solotino was the last of the three principal Soviet defense lines, the most dangerous and desperate of the Red barriers. Behind those positions, idling on the steppe, was a full-strength Russian reserve army waiting to engage the SS forces now draining themselves in the trenches and minefields on this path to Kursk. Luis's fight would be here, across this broad and dangerous field, in this tiny piece of the arena.

Below the ridge, two grenadier battalions of *Leibstandarte* – worn down to a thousand men each – had dug in, turning captured Russian defense works against their creators. A dozen batteries of anti-tank artillery were leveled at Sukho-Solotino. Sappers crawled through the crop stalks to pull mines out of the ground. Farther out in the grasslands, T-34 hulks smoldered; apparently there had already been a Russian attack at dawn, repulsed.

A soldier flagged Luis down and pointed him into a position in the middle of five other tanks, all Mark IVs. The gunner said in the intercom that this was their command platoon. Luis barked to the driver to bring the Tiger into place, then shut down to save petrol. A sergeant-major climbed up on the deck to salute and welcome him. The man was in his forties, flat-nosed, and badly shaven. Luis could tell he was very glad to have a Tiger back in the regiment, and didn't give a damn that the man commanding it was a frightful-looking chap and not Erich Thoma.

'Captain, well done. You got here just in time.'

Luis aimed his chin at the battle detritus in the field, and beyond to Sukho-Solotino. 'What happened?'

The sergeant-major shrugged, hardened by carnage.

'Nothing much. They made a halfway charge at us this morning at sunup. We knocked out twenty T-34s with no losses of our own. They ran straight into the infantry, and the anti-tank guns did the work. The tanks didn't even leave the hill. You know the Reds. Twenty of their tanks dead, and they got nothing for it. It just winds them up and makes them madder.'

Luis liked that phrase 'You know the Reds.' It said to him, Fellow soldier.

'We figure they'll hit back anytime now,' the sergeant-major continued. 'After we scatter this next attack, we'll move down and take the town.' He struck a palm against the Tiger's turret. 'Having this big son of a bitch back in the lead will make it go a lot better.'

Luis took a moment to unstrap his soft helmet and pull it off. He ran a bony hand through his hair. 'This big son of a bitch will not be in the lead, Sergeant-major. Your tank will be.'

The man reared back at this, pulling his face away and wincing, as though Luis had disappeared and another had popped into his place, a coward.

'Captain, I don't think ...'

'I didn't ask what you think, Sergeant-major.'

The man was expected to close his mouth and say no more, but he did not, perhaps, Luis thought, because he was an older fellow and believed he knew best, that is what happens with every year.

'Captain, if I might. Captain Thoma ...'

Luis interrupted again; his voice was that of a man slapping the hand of a reaching child.

'Captain Thoma commanded an armored company in a regiment that lost thirteen of its fourteen Tigers in four days of fighting. Captain Thoma and others lost those tanks to improper use and unnecessary risk, and was lucky not to have lost this one, as well. Captain Thoma, you will also note, is dead.

'Sergeant-major, the Tiger tank was not designed to be trotted out in front at the first sign of trouble. It is the ultimate weapon of the panzer unit, and from now on will be used solely in that role in this company. When the assault begins, this platoon will form a *Panzerkeil*. You and your Mark IV will take the point. I will follow inside the wedge. The three other platoons will form *Panzerkeile* as well and take up positions to our front and sides. You and the other Mark IVs will protect this Tiger from mines and infantry assaults. When the Soviet tanks appear and the decisive moment in the battle arrives, you will then have a living Tiger beside you and not a dead one. Do you understand?'

The sergeant-major had gone stiff. 'Yes, sir.'

'The Tiger was designed with one purpose, Sergeant-major. It was brought to Kursk for that purpose. To meet and defeat the Russian tank on the battlefield. No other target warrants my attention.'

'Yes, sir, Captain.'

'Instruct the other platoon leaders that I will see them here in ten minutes.'

The sergeant-major did not approve, Luis knew this from the blank face he mounted while listening. The man said, 'Yes, sir,' and clambered off the Tiger. Luis watched him go. The sergeant-major would tell the three other platoon leaders and nudge them into dislike of the new captain, and his tactic, as well. No matter, Luis thought, and not to be unexpected. They've had the maverick Thoma and fourteen Tigers charging to the front, taking their hits for them and delivering massive blows to clear the way. In the process Thoma squandered all but this last Tiger, and stopped a bullet for good measure. Luis had no intention of rolling over an undetected mine or losing a tread to a cheap Soviet round in the flank. This last Tiger was a gift: It would not be frittered away while in his hands.

He let his crew lift their hatches. Four of the five positions in the Tiger had their own escape doors, except for the gunner, who had to follow the commander out. A Tiger was expected to be evacuated in under twenty seconds. He slipped a tin of crackers from his pocket and chewed. He could not imagine himself giving that order to evacuate.

The sergeant-major returned with the other platoon leaders, all sergeants. Luis gave them instructions without coming down from his turret. He was not Thoma, he was not going to pat shoulders and cajole. The men returned to their tanks with orders, not encouragement or rationale. Luis watched them walk off. His eye snagged again on the underside of the Tiger's hatch door, on the brown spatter there. At the first opportunity he'd have Thoma's blood scraped off. He didn't like the dead man keeping such a close eye on him anymore. It was not Thoma's turn any longer. It was his now.

The Russian attack started at 1000 hours. Puffs and flashes rose from the plain in front of Sukho-Solotino. The Red infantry moved up beside their tanks. Luis slipped his headgear back on and snapped his throat microphone in place. He ducked into the hatch.

'Driver,' he shouted down, 'start engine.'

The Tiger's great Maybach motor roused with a vigor that sent a thrill up his legs. Everything came alive with such power, the hydraulics yowled, the exhaust pipes spit black as though the Tiger were clearing its throat, every metal muscle flexed; standing motionless the thing exuded more strength than any tank Luis had ever seen running at full bore.

'Radio.'

The answering voice crackled in his headset. 'Yes, sir.'

'Tell the platoons to hold fire until my command.'

All the Tiger's hatches were lowered and secured, except where Luis stood in the turret. He raised his binoculars. Eight kilometers away, the Russian assault began to flow across the fields, met only by the popping of mortar fire and mobile artillery. The sky was clear of fighters and bombers, this morning was to be a pure ground battle. The two *Leibstandarte* grenadier battalions showed discipline and stayed in their revetments, on the defense for the moment, winnowing the creeping Soviets as best they could. The grenadiers waited for their tank support. Luis held it back.

He counted forty T-34s streaming out of Sukho-Solotino, outnumbering his four tank platoons three to one. The Red tanks barreled over the open ground away from the Oboyan road, outdistancing their own infantry. At that rate they'd be on top of the grenadiers in ten minutes, firing flat trajectories into the trenches, softening the German resistance for the sweep of their following horde. This was the moment when Erich Thoma would have charged down the incline into the melee, for the dramatic rescue, superior enemy numbers be damned, there was style to be considered. Luis shook Thoma off. He waited, gathering in the panorama, the Soviet rush, the line of tanks under his command, the Tiger pulsing beneath his feet, smoke and flame on the plain. He would let the dug-in grenadiers absorb the first blows of the T-34s, have them slow the Soviet charge with anti-tank fire, perhaps some of the more intrepid soldiers might hop out of their foxholes and board a few Red tanks with magnetic mines and grenades. He liked the power of his denial, of holding back and watching the Soviet tanks close in on the grenadiers, he relished the uneven clash of raw men below against the charging machines and knew the entire panzer company strained for his command to enter the fight. Thoma would have let them go by now, but Thoma was dead, and so were a few grenadiers to make Luis's point. He licked all this power out of the morning for his hunger, swallowed it like morsels, and tasted the last of his bitter wounded year, it had come to an end. A new time was begun, a new and stronger hunger took over. *Ahora mismo*. Right now.

'Gunner.'

'Sir.'

'Range.'

The turret whirred and swung a few degrees to the right while Balthasar acquired a target.

'Twenty-eight hundred meters and closing.'

The big gun elevated.

'Loader.'

The response was immediate. 'AP round loaded and locked, Captain.'

With the binoculars pressed to his sockets, Luis paused ninety seconds to let the T-34s close in to the killing range of the Tiger.

Balthasar said, 'Captain.'

'Yes, gunner, one moment. Distance.'

'Twenty-one hundred meters.'

'Patience, Balthasar.'

Luis lowered his binoculars. He liked the dust clouds under the Russian tanks. He smelled the morning, to remember it.

'Range.'

'Sixteen hundred meters, Captain.'

'Fire at lead tank.'

Luis ducked inside the turret just before the cannon erupted. The tank jolted backward. The noise, even through his helmet, was pulverizing. The breech rammed back and ejected a hot casing into the turret basket. The loader moved like lightning, stuffing another shell into the breech almost before the tank could settle, then he shoved the spent casing into an empty bin and hefted another large shell into his arms for the next shot, all this in seconds. Luis did not speak or stand to look into his binoculars to peer through the whipped dust to see if the target was hit. He kept in his seat and watched his crew work.

The gunner twirled the elevation handwheel half a turn, paused with his brow pressed to his optics, then calmly said into the intercom, 'Away.' Luis braced. The gunner toed the firing pedal. The long gun woofed again, the tank shuddered, a smoking casing spat from the breech, and the loader was there kneeling beside the gun with another cradled shell. The gunner's voice sparked in Luis's helmet.

'T-34 burning, sir.'

Luis shook a fist that the gunner did not see. The crouching loader caught his eye. The young soldier grinned. 'Keep firing. At will, gunner.'

'Yes, sir.'

In five minutes the Tiger racked up four more kills at ranges of two thousand to fifteen hundred meters. Luis kept his head down, his eyes fixed in his own vision block. The first three Red tanks had to be bracketed with shells before they were hit, the fourth was a single shot to a T-34 that had hit a mine and ground to a stop. Gunner Balthasar snapped the turret off the Soviet tank like breaking a French loaf.

The Russian tanks charged through the spouts of flame and dirt flung up by the Tiger. They had to. At this distance, their 75 mm guns could barely dent the frontal armor of the German tanks aligned on the ridge. Against the Tiger itself, their cannons were useless even at point-blank range unless fired from the side, where the Tiger, like all tanks, was vulnerable. So the Reds gunned forward, relying on numbers and speed to survive until they could get within one kilometer, their lethal range against the Mark IVs. Luis was in no hurry to help them close the gap. He held his tanks at bay on the ridge.

The frontal elements of the Russian attack slowed when they neared the grenadiers' first defensive positions.

The Red tanks had outpaced their infantry by at least a kilometer. The *Leibstandarte* grenadiers fired anti-tank guns and small-arms but there were too many T-34s for them to stop. The Russian tanks slammed explosive rounds and machine-gun fire into the scrambling infantrymen. The Tiger's driver revved his engine, a subtle signal that he considered now to be the time to get going, fly down the hill, and take on the Red tanks. Still Luis waited, to let the ground troops absorb the first brunt of the tank attack. 'Gunner, lead T-34' was all he said. The gunner drew a slow and careful bead on a tank in the van of the Soviet assault. The long cannon whined, lowering to a level trajectory, pointing a damning finger at the Russian tank. Luis asked, 'Range?' The voice answered, 'Fifteen hundred meters.'

'Fire.'

The gunner muttered, 'Away,' and blasted the T-34 with a round that Luis heard strike like a blacksmith's anvil. This was what Luis waited for. The Russians were now in range of the Mark IVs.

'Radio. Tell the platoons to open fire.'

With a single earsplitting cannonade the fourteen German panzers hammered at the Soviet charge. When the salvo was away, Luis stood in his turret to assess the blow. He had to wait several seconds for the dust and powder smoke to swirl away on the concussive wind. When he could see through the battle haze, he raised his binoculars to a field of black geysers. Smoke poured out of a fourth of the Russian tanks. The odds were better now, two to one.

Luis restrained his Tiger and the Mark IVs on the hill for another minute, to further sap the Soviet attack. In that time his company fired over fifty rounds, destroying another ten T-34s. The *Leibstandarte* grenadiers were out of their holes now, gaining the flanks on the Soviet tanks. The Russian infantry had not caught up yet, they still ran at least two kilometers behind. It seemed to Luis they were losing their verve for rushing into a battle that had swung against them even before they'd entered it.

The enemy was confused and hurt. There were no trumpets to announce it, but Luis knew the time had arrived to send the *banderilleros* away. The moment had come for the *matador*.

'Driver. Forward.'

The Tiger was not swift but it did not have to be. Its frontal armor was impervious to anything the T-34s could hurl at it, and for the first five hundred meters of their advance down the hill so were the Mark IVs. His tank formation never exceeded ten kilometers an hour, but with every meter they closed, the Red tanks grew larger in his gunners' optics. Luis buttoned his hatch and trained his eyes on the terrain and the conduct of his company. The Mark IVs lumbered on his sides and in front, moving in wedges the way he'd ordered. He shifted in his seat, glancing left and right through the vision blocks in his cupola, communicating over the radio with the platoon leaders to keep them in formation. At a range of one kilometer from the lead T-34, the fourteen *Leibstandarte* tanks were a formidable blazing force. The Tiger stood at the center braying the loudest and killing the surest.

Rumbling in his commander's seat at the heart of the charge, Luis felt quietly exultant. The Tiger paused once a minute for the gunner to aim and fire, then lurched ahead with the pack. Luis had not dreamed of this kind of power at his control, he'd never imagined it from his hospital beds in his white-washed convalescence. How could he? Now, a year later, dust and smoke parted for him, small-arms fire hardly made *pings* against his rushing armor. Luis selected targets, the gunner blasted them, the radioman issued his orders, the loader fed the breech, the driver jolted the Tiger at his direction. In every angle of his vision, German tanks under his command fired and chased the Russians backward. He held on in the Tiger's belly and pressed the counterattack.

The Russians were routed. The T-34s were quick, and when they scattered it was impressive. The Soviet tanks were nimble, running wide circles to gain flank angles to the German wedges, or to get away back to Sukho-Solotino to set up a final defense line there. Luis kept his attention on three T-34s coming at him in a zigzag. Three Mark IVs fired at this bold group and missed, or their rounds glanced off the T-34s' sloped armor. These Soviets had spotted the last Tiger tank and wanted it dead.

Luis gave the order to halt.

The Tiger dug in its claws and ground to a stop. The Russian tanks advanced, cutting left and right. Luis admired their agility. They moved faster than the gunner could traverse, the Tiger's hydraulics whined but could not keep up. He watched them approach, inside seven hundred, then five hundred meters.

The first of the three T-34s came to a standstill. The Tiger's gunner swung the turret at the tank, but Luis knew his cannon would not be fleet enough. Head-on, the T-34's angled design made it a green triangle on treads. In the center of the figure, the enemy's main gun smoked. Faster than Luis could flinch, the shell struck. He was kicked back from his vision block by the blast, everyone in the Tiger shivered. Paint chips snowed down on him; the shell had smacked the turret directly in front of his position and the thick armor held, another scar for the Tiger. His ears rang from the clout, but not so much that he could not hear the gunner holler, 'Away!'

The Tiger rocked again, now to its own cannon. Luis did not bother to see if that T-34 was finished, at this range the enemy tank would have filled the gunner's sights. The loader fed the breech in an instant, the driver kicked the clutch, and the Tiger turned to find and face the remaining two T-34s. When Luis aimed his eyes back outside the Tiger, he found those two T-34s in burning ruins. One Russian crew was bailing out of their tank's billowing hatches. The Tiger's driver swung his nose at them so the machine-gunner could finish them with one long burst.

Luis lifted his heavy hatch door. He ignored Thoma's blood there. He reared up into the late morning, the air greasy now with a black mist from dying machines. On his right and left flanks, the barrels of five Mark IVs steamed. A hundred meters away, the flat-nosed master-sergeant shot him a salute from his own turret. Luis returned the gesture.

Across the fields, the Russian force retreated at full clip. Their assault had been executed badly, piecemeal, tanks without infantry, without air cover. The pageant of this morning was nearly complete. The bull had been prepared, worn down, the *matador* had danced with it, allowing the horns to pass near, luring the danger close enough for gasps. The *muleta* had blood swiped on it. Now the *matador* must lay the cape aside. Time for the sword and the final pass.

Luis gave the order. He did not use the radio to talk to the platoon leaders. They were all in their turrets, looking over at him, some through binoculars. Instead, he raised his white saber of an arm and stabbed it forward at Sukho-Solotino.

CHAPTER 15

July 8
1830 hours
SS *Leibstandarte* situation room
Belgorod

The battle flowed through Abram Breit's hands.

Citadel streamed past on flimsy pages, like comic illustrations on a pad: Flip the pages fast and the figures move for you. The reports were carried to him by couriers, men who stalked up out of the outlying reaches of the room beyond the map table. Breit read the sheets – always terse statements that belied the frenzy and rage, the smoke and the dying; field commanders seemed to have an ethic about this, writing only cold words for their plights – and turned them into black or red twitches on the table. Breit gazed at nothing but the reports, the shifting board and blue match flames to light his cigarettes.

In the dim, big room, lit by one bulb swaying low over the map, Breit studied the map as a living canvas. With arms folded, seeping smoke, he watched Citadel take on its shape and colors. He was mesmerized by the paint that was flung onto the table, lives. Break enough lives here, paint it black. Not enough here, paint it red. Hourly he forwarded action reports to SS headquarters. For the generals, Breit separated the battle into its vital measurement: numbers. Every soldier, minute, meter of grass could be caught in a number, a brush stroke of math. His calculations spoke terrible news: After four and a half days of fighting, three hundred Germans were being killed or wounded every hour. For the Russians, the number was six hundred. Every hour, a dozen German tanks were knocked out of action. For the Reds, twice that. Seven German airplanes were shot down. Ten for the Soviets. Every hour, night and day. No one could count the number of artillery rounds fired, or the bullets and bombs it took to make these mounds of bodies and wreckage.

Breit computed a ratio of losses per territory gained. In the north, where Colonel-General Model fought, German progress had been stopped. Though the fighting was still vicious, there was no longer any way to break through to Kursk out of the north. The Reds had held there. The casualties per kilometer for Model would be enormous, over twelve hundred men for every one of his fifteen kilometers of penetration into the Soviet lines.

Here in the south, only the three SS divisions had made significant headway. *Totenkopf, Das Reich*, and *Leibstandarte* fighting together had blazed almost forty kilometers up the Oboyan road. They'd done this against the stiffest Soviet defenses in the whole Kursk salient. Hourly losses for the SS units averaged less than a dozen men and two tanks. Sometimes with quick repairs the tanks were replaced the same day. Not so for the human casualties. The keepers of the map watched the black blocks of II SS Panzer move north along the road, globular and inexorable like water creeping over the map. Each time another Soviet unit was absorbed or shoved aside by an SS division, the mood in the room flared, little bursts of hope, like heat lightning. Abram Breit smoked and stayed apart while Major Grimm and the others clapped and paced, shouting at the table like fans at a cockfight. Soon more news would enter from other dark chambers, from the radio and code rooms, about other units, their dire struggles and failures against the Reds and the costs they were paying. Then the map room would take another long, slow dunk back into the quiet mire of dismay.

This was Citadel, passing through Breit's hands.

In a calm moment, he wondered about the Spaniard who had left this morning to replace Thoma. For a while he'd thought perhaps young Captain de Vega with his wounds so visible might have been a Lucy contact, secreted somehow to Kursk to keep in touch with their star spy, Breit. The skinny boy was secretive, as silent as Breit himself. The Spaniard had the false look of a man living two lives, with two faces, two everything. Though de Vega proved not to be from Lucy, he was plainly more than what he appeared, a quiet and hurt boy. Breit glanced down at the black block for *Leibstandarte* beside the Oboyan road, noting the ten kilometers of road de Vega's division had already captured that afternoon. Breit feared he may have sent out into the battle a fierce one and given him a Tiger tank.

Standing beside the map, Breit handled another page. He did not look up at the face of the messenger who loomed in and out of the gloom ringing the table. The Spaniard had been the only distinct one, the rest were simply staffers. Breit was one of them, too, lean and scholarly, unscarred by battle. He looked at his own white hands holding this latest page, recalled the remarkably thin hands of the Spaniard, and marveled how different a man can be from his appearance.

Breit scanned the report. He expected it to be like the hundred others handed to him today, another mosaic of news in the battle. He lifted a finger to beckon one of the stick bearers, to have the staffer push some block forward, and another one backward. He lowered his hand. Behind him, boots retreated. Breit read the page again, slowly.

Leibstandarte had taken the town of Sukho-Solotino.

Another seven kilometers of the Oboyan road had fallen into German hands.

Breit digested the facts on the page, the casualty count, matériel lost, enemy losses, current status and location of division.

One word occurred over and over in the report. It dawned on Breit that this word had stood at the head of every report of every successful action the Germans had mounted since Citadel began.

Tiger.

In the fighting in the north, out of the six hundred tanks in Model's 9th Army, none were Mark V Panthers and only thirty-one were Mark VI Tigers. Model had not used his few Mark VIs well, he had not put them into the fight at the right times and places. He'd been too cautious, too impressed with the Tigers to spend them. So Model was *kaput*.

Of the one hundred Tigers assigned to the southern front of the Kursk bulge, fifty-seven served in the three SS divisions and the *Grossdeutschland* division of 48th Panzer Corps. Every one of those tanks had been used in the battle for the Oboyan road, in the middle of the most brutal combat in all of Citadel.

The Russian T-34s often ran away from the Tigers when they encountered them. Good thing, too, because no single T-34 could ever hope to best a Mark VI in combat. Even so, the Tigers were being lost at an alarming rate, to mines, to misuse, to asking them to do too much, or too little. Right now there were no more than six Tigers total operating in all three SS divisions. But the behemoths were hard to knock out of the fight for good; at night, German mechanics towed the wounded Tigers off the battlefields and often repaired them by morning. The Tigers were a single-minded priority for the SS's mobile repair stations. Tomorrow, Breit knew, the number of Tigers in the field could double.

The reports in his hands did not lie. Every time a Tiger appeared – in any amount, one to a dozen – and was utilized the way it should be, the battle swayed its way. The map table showed the results, revealing the difference these tanks were making. All three II SS Panzer divisions along with *Grossdeutschland*, each with Tiger battalions, had ranged far out in front of their flanking units, spearheading the drive to Oboyan and Kursk. Other units without Tigers failed to keep up.

Abram Breit dug fingers into his brow. He should have seen this sooner. But perhaps not, perhaps it took these five days of fighting for the numbers to congeal and this fundamental truth to appear. Perhaps he'd caught it in time. In any event, he knew he was right.

Stop the Tigers, or you will not stop the German offensive.

The Reds had to change their tactics, they had to engage the Tigers at every chance, at any cost. Find them, charge them, and don't just knock them out. Kill them. Then the Soviets' numerical advantages can assert themselves. But so long as Tigers stay on the battlefield, because of their power, armor, and their raw reluctance to die, and because they have been given only to crack units, the outcome of Citadel will hang in the balance.

Abram Breit carried in his head something more powerful than any tank, or any weapon at Kursk. He had all the German information for the battle neatly memorized. He possessed the numbers for every SS and Wehrmacht division, their troops, artillery, armor, air power, casualties.

With what he knew, Breit could thwart Citadel.

He called for the stick-bearer now. A tall, bald lad moved forward. The staffer shoved the Reds backward out of Sukho-Solotino, retreating up the Oboyan road. Then he pushed *Leibstandarte* – and the young Spaniard riding his Tiger – in.

Breit lit another cigarette. He watched the curls of his smoke spread over the battle map.

He stubbed out the butt when he knew what to do.

'Major.'

'Yes, Colonel.' Grimm attended him quickly.

'Arrange a flight for me to Berlin.'

Grimm hesitated, baffled. 'Yes, Colonel. May I ask why?'

'I need to report to the *Führer*.'

Major Grimm looked down at the map table, uneasy. Everything seemed in order. What had come up so suddenly that Abram Breit needed to fly back to Berlin to report to Hitler?

Breit handed the page to Grimm. Let the major deduce what he will about Hitler. Breit would concoct something for that madman's ears, make it sound urgent and vital.

'Within the hour, Major.'

Abram Breit left the map room.

July 8
2010 hours
Slatino aerodrome

Breit was coated in dust.

Grimm had not found a staff car quickly enough to suit Breit. Instead, a motorcycle courier was given orders to carry the colonel to Slatino's aerodrome as fast as possible. Perhaps this was the major's way of giving Breit back a fuck you. For the eighty-kilometer journey, Breit had ridden in an open sidecar over busted roads, pontoon bridges, and dirt tracks. He wore goggles and held on with white knuckles. He could not smoke for the entire insane trip, the driver was determined to make the best time and showcase his motorcycle skill to the colonel.

Now, Breit stood from the idling sidecar. He looked

down at his uniform, matted with dirt and grease kicked up by the wheels of vehicles the motorcycle passed. Pulling the goggles from his eyes, he felt a seal of grime and sweat break on his cheeks. He imagined himself to be the image of the German combat officer, filthy, a man of action, like a picture of Rommel.

The driver was doubly dirty and grinning. He'd gunned the motorcycle right to the steps of the waiting Heinkel 111 H-16 bomber. The plane's motors fired the moment the motorcycle stopped. The props began to spin, the sound of the cranking engines drowned out the motorcycle. Breit let himself be amused at how much Germany assisted him in duping her.

The courier saluted and spun away. Breit stood in the prop wash, hoping some of the dust would blow off him. A pilot appeared in the doorway, waving him up. Breit nodded and climbed the steps.

He took his seat. The crew left him alone in the belly of the plane. Breit carried no briefcase or papers with him. This helped give the impression of a top-secret mission, that the information could only be carried safely in his brain. In truth, there was nothing he needed to haul back to Berlin to show Hitler and his staff. Breit would simply give the *Führer* a progress briefing on Citadel, almost a courtesy call. He might get scolded for taking Hitler's time, perhaps not, and would simply hop a plane and fly back to Belgorod and his map table.

First, he would visit the museum.

The flight to Berlin would cover two thousand kilometers and take five hours. Breit would arrive after three in the morning. Time to have his uniform cleaned, catch a few hours of sleep, then go to the Reichs Chancellery. Perhaps Hitler would not even be in Berlin when he got there. The *Führer* might decide to head for East Prussia in the morning. Who knows with that man? He had too much power, too many people around him saying 'Yes.'

Hitler lived in a fantasy world, a world of conquest and German hegemony. Sometimes from the looks of him he seemed to live in hell. It was perverse that Abram Breit, the spy, was the only person Hitler could talk to for the truth about the war and what was happening to Germany. The lone man in his presence Hitler could trust was one who was betraying him.

The bomber revved and rumbled to the runway. The plane shook its rivets and sprinted ahead, lifting off. Breit gazed out his window over the wing at Russia letting go. He felt no allegiance to this land he was helping, this backward, unfinished place. He was a German, and what he was doing, he did for Germany. Russia was nothing but a tool for the changes he and others saw must come about.

Breit sat back, listening to the droning, rising plane. He lit his first cigarette in over an hour. The bomber gained altitude. The country below became immense, tinged crimson by the coming dusk. Breit looked away. It was too much, to think that he was affecting all this, to a thousand horizons.

July 8
2025 hours
Heinkel 111 H-16 bomber
altitude three thousand meters
above L'ubotin

A German bomber, flying west without escort. The Russian hunting pack must have licked its chops.

The Heinkel bristled with gunnery. It bore twin turrets in the belly, one in the nose, and one up top. Every barrel raged at the streaking Soviet fighters. Breit pressed his face to the window. He couldn't get a count of the Yaks, they banked so tightly and blasted back in, they seemed to be everywhere. He guessed there were three or four, no, five, then cursed his own need for numbers. The bomber's engines wailed and his seat tilted steep, the bomber's pilot rolled the plane hard to the north, back toward the Slatino airfield and closer to air cover. Breit's breathing scraped in his throat, his lungs worked so hard they made his eyes and head hurt. He'd never been shot at before. The noise was deafening, there were machine-guns and cannons barking, roaring engines on all sides, baying around him like wolves at night. Breit didn't know what to do – hold on, grab a gun, scream – he locked his eyes on the sky and the ripping contrails of the Soviet fighters' wings.

The bomber dove for the ground, trying to gain speed. Breit's seat dipped and rolled. Vomit soured on his tongue. Over his head a sound like a freight train and a buzz saw all at once made him raise his eyes from the slanting floor to his window. The silvery cross of a Yak fighter leveled at him and came straight up the bomber's wing. He watched the sparks of the fighter's cannon wink at him, a wry death. The pass was over in a second but he had time for horror watching the fighter stamp holes in the bomber's wing and blow up the starboard engine.

The Heinkel rocked and dipped. The pilot corrected but the plane was sluggish. Smoke coursed out of the engine, the rightside prop locked up and stopped, looking very wrong this high in the sky. He smelled flame engulfing the ruined engine, he saw smoke streaming in through punctures in the fuselage. He noted that the turret above the cockpit had gone silent. The bomber's other guns continued to rail, but the raw numbers and facts of Breit's predicament asserted themselves through his shock and fear. It was inevitable that the bomber and everyone inside were going to be cut to pieces by these flashing Soviet planes.

In that moment, he had his proof. One of the crew

careened down the aisle to his seat, hauling two parachute packs. Panic warped the young man's face. Blood spattered his cheeks and neck. The airman slung a chute into Breit's lap. Breit had to pry his hands from the seat arms to catch it.

The crewman shouted, 'Put it on! We're getting out! Now!'

Breit hesitated. How do you do this? he wondered, too frightened to even open his mouth to ask. He'd never had any jump training, why would he?

The crewman hauled the second knapsack over his own shoulders, jamming his arms through two straps. He reached down between his legs for two dangling belts, grabbed them, and clicked one each into the shoulder straps to form a harness.

'Get up!' the man yelled.

Breit undid his seat belt. He stood, unsure if his legs would hold him on the listing floor. He slid the pack over his own shoulders and aped what the airman had done, clicking his arms and waist into the straps. A scarlet light blinked over his empty seat. The whole crew, those still alive, were bailing out.

The crewman staggered to the door in the plane's midsection. With a strong twirl of a fat handle, he yanked the portal open. He stepped to the threshold. Breit moved close behind him, crowding. He was stricken with fear, his movements were automatic. He had no idea what to do except whatever this crewman did. Wind whipped past in a deafening rush. The engine, seen now not through a window but dead ahead in the same windy, horrifying world as Breit, trailed a seam of smoke for kilometers behind them.

The crewman laid both hands under Breit's straps and with urgent tugs tightened everything on the parachute around Breit's shoulders and hips. He pounded a fist, on a handle attached over Breit's heart.

He took Breit in both fists and jerked him closer, almost as though to begin a fight, and bellowed. 'Pull *this* when you get clear of the plane!'

With that, he spun Breit around and flung him out the door. The wind swept everything away – the plane, smoke, noise – and Breit tumbled head over heels.

In the first second of the fall he lost the plane, then he lost the ground, somersaulting through the rasping air. He shut his eyes against the sting. With crazed hands he clawed for the ripcord handle, then remembered the crewman's thump over his heart. He fumbled at a metal clasp and yanked on it hard, once, twice, nothing happened, no parachute sprang to his rescue, he was tugging on something that wasn't the ripcord! Wind roared in his ears, blood surged in his temples from his spinning and hysteria. He slapped all over his chest for the ripcord. He found nothing but straps and buckles. He forced open his eyes and the whirling world dizzied him almost to blackness. Then he caught sight of the handle flapping on the left strap. He plunged his right hand for it, snared it, and pulled, accepting that this was his last chance.

A pop and a flutter went off at his back. A solid grip snared him in the air, his shoulders and pelvis were wrenched. His legs flew out and almost out of joint, but now he was not wheeling over and over, he'd been yanked out of his fall. A white canopy unfurled overhead. Breit's stomach had endured enough, he vomited into the open air, so hard all of it missed his uniform and boots. He watched the stream break into brown drops and fall. Breit was stricken by how close he was to the ground, the vast, twilit steppe.

Falling slowly now, Breit hung limp, exhausted. He looked up for the parachutes of the rest of the crew, hoping to see five. Only one white bloom trailed after him.

The He-111 smoked from both engines. Breit watched

the Yak fighters ravening after it. He could count them easily now, there were four. He was still in the air with them, and their sounds hounding the dying bomber wracked his ears. Their guns chattered. Breit believed he could make out the sizzle of the rounds and the metal patter of their strikes. The smoking track of the bomber's flight bent downward. The plane was riddled and killed. It whined, remorseful and beaten, then crashed into a proud fireball.

Breit tore his gaze from the crewman floating far above him. The young airman was the most helpless creature Breit had ever seen. The Red fighters came at him in a line, firing in sport at the dangling German. Breit listened to the machine-guns and yowling engines. He saw the airman wriggle to make himself hard to hit – how funny that must have seemed to the Soviet pilots – then churn as the huge rounds slammed into him. Breit looked away.

The fighters came around in a tight bank, propellers and tails almost grinding each other up. They came for him. Breit looked to the rising ground and pleaded with it to hurry. Break my legs, he thought, but hurry! He shot his eyes down to the earth, then back to the planes, measuring seconds and distance.

The first fighter leveled out. The other three zoomed behind it. Breit braced for the sparks of their guns. He looked below his boots, ten more seconds until he was down. The fighters traced the steppe, blowing back the grasses with the wash of their passing. The lead plane took a blast at Breit. Zings whipped by him, terrifying and invisible. He did the same dance as the dead crewman still drifting above, wiggling in the air to make himself a harder target.

Another burst from the first plane seared to his left, then the Yak roared by so close, his parachute swung in the roiled air. The second fighter closed fast and drew a bead. Breit nailed his eyes on the plane's cowling, the muzzle for the cannon. The gun flashed.

Breit's body jerked. He screamed, sure he'd been hit. His ankles and knees buckled with unexpected force and he crumpled forward. He landed on his right shoulder, stopping his screaming. He was down. He pitched to his back, looking up into the rippling, folding chute. The remaining fighters tore past so low the parachute caught their wind and tried to haul him back into the sky. He struggled with the pack and scrambled away.

Breit ran through a flat expanse of grass. The Yaks rolled again in formation, were they coming back for him? His breathing filled his ears, he didn't know how to escape, he was no combat soldier. He dove into the thin reeds and lay still, panting. After seconds he peeked above the heads of the stalks. The fighters had cut short their circle and flew off to the north. Breit saw only the descent of the dead airman, who returned to earth without a whisper. The sky was clear and tinting red, stained.

July 9
0005 hours
somewhere west of Slatino

Past nightfall, a pillar of smoke spiraled from the downed bomber three kilometers away. Breit watched the black column rise and bend to the breezes that cooled the steppe and tossed the heads of the grasses where he sat. Night closed in and he did not think once to head away from the smoldering wreck or move off from the markers of the dead man's parachute and his own. He waited where he believed German rear troops would come to investigate the crash and look for survivors. He had no idea what else to do, he wasn't sure how this part of war worked. He was in German-held territory, but he was still in Russia. So he stayed in place and sat quiet under the most stars and the farthest-flung sky he'd ever seen.

Breit had been saved from the bomber by a miracle. The odds greatly favored his dying with the five crewmen, of Abram Breit becoming one of the fuels making that shaft of smoke still rising out there in the dark, or lying under his own silk chute, cut in half. Instead he was whole and alive and he had to get back to Berlin and to Lucy. Breit was not much of a believer in God, but he could not ignore evidence. Even if God had nothing to do with his narrow escape, Breit did believe in purpose. He'd been spared and that was enough to affirm his suspicion that he was on a great mission. The Soviets needed to know what he had to tell them, his facts and numbers, his insight about the Tiger tanks, the need to single them out everywhere they showed up. Abram Breit had been selected and protected for this very task. He didn't ask by whom under the stars, but in his whole life he'd never been the one picked. He'd been on no adventures ever, until he became a spy. He'd not had that kind of youth, the campfire and skinned-knee boyhood of others, as a young man the sports teams and beering of men around him. Breit had studied, then taught, then as a soldier he'd catalogued stolen property. That was all changed now. Today's exploit with the downed plane and the murdering Russian fighters and this black empty steppe was terrifying and had cost lives. This was war, and he was in it. Tonight he was special, a survivor. He carried the keys to history in his head. He felt alert and exhilarated.

Twice in the late dusk he saw locals moving across the grassland before the nightfall curfew. One group led a mule back from the plow somewhere. The old men and women stopped and gawked at the German plane burning at the far end of the field in the last red glow of day. A half hour after that, Breit lay on his stomach, pressed to the ground, as two peasants came near to harvest the silk of the collapsed chutes. He worried that the two old men might see the track of crushed stalks where he'd run from his chute, ending where he now lay. They would find him and do what? He was a German officer. They wouldn't dare touch him. The reprisals on their village would be fierce. He hid anyway, not certain. The men cut the white chutes from the cords and lapped them around their shoulders. They left the airman's grisly body alone and continued across the field chattering over their good fortune.

Breit waited for rescue. It was past midnight now. He listened intently, standing full in the darkness to cast his senses out in the field. Where was the German patrol investigating the crash? Isn't that sort of thing done? he wondered. Of course it is. Perhaps with the battle going so hot, all the troops were committed to the north, pressing the attack. Yes, that's it. Someone would come, certainly, but not tonight.

Breit had to reach a German outpost. He needed another plane to Berlin, soon. Maybe the radio in the bomber was still intact. He could call for help. What else could he do? Sit here and wait the rest of the night, all day tomorrow, silent again when he should be heard? No. No more of that.

Breit trod across the grass. Tassels brushed the backs of his swinging hands. Boots and trousers swished through the tall blades. His shoulder ached from the rough landing. Breit walked toward the bomber, imagining what cooked things he was going to have to see to get to the radio. He set his jaw against the images. He looked instead into the trillion stars spiked into the Russian night, parsed only by a small fire still flicking in the wreckage.

He stepped into what felt like a hole, his boot did not find the ground. He collapsed toward it. In an exploding moment, the stars burst. They were fleeting and canceled by the ground striking his bad shoulder, then cuffing his face. Light flared in his eyes. Breit knew light though he could never paint it, and he knew this light was false, rupturing only inside him. Before he shut his eyes from the glare, he caught the ovals of boots, the cylinders of pants legs.

The last to succumb was his skin. A dab of spit landed on Breit's neck.

CHAPTER 16

July 9
0310 hours
moving north with the 3rd Mechanized Brigade along the Oboyan road

Dimitri could not even muster a spit. His mouth was a pit coated with diesel soot and dust. He rode on top of the *General*, clinging to a handle behind the turret, sitting on the deck above the hot engine. Sasha had asked to drive tonight for a portion of the retreat, to let Dimitri rest and get some air. The skinny boy, even with a chunk torn out of his biceps from a German bullet, had an adequate touch with the T-34, there was more strength in him than you could read by looking at him.

The air had cooled since midnight. Dank sheets of mist filled the hollows and dips of the fields under a waxing moon. On all sides of the *General,* the remnants of 3rd Mechanized Corps beat across the steppe, fleeing north to find another place to defend the Oboyan road now that it had lost Syrtsev, Alekseyevka, and the Luchanino River. Dimitri was thirsty. Every crevice from his crotch to his eyelids was caked with a paste of sweat, dust, and exhaust fumes. Overhead the stars glittered and the night was calm, but Dimitri did not see the black curtain; instead he projected on it the fighting, the flames and blasts that had claimed sixty T-34s and their crews, two out of three in his battalion. Their hulks and bodies rested tonight on ground ceded back to the Germans. That was the worst taste on his tongue, the retreat.

Valentin's head bobbed in his hatch. Dimitri was disconnected from the intercom, and there was too much engine noise and squealing of treads all around for the two to speak. Just as well, thought Dimitri. With every round fired in the past two days, every order tapped on his shoulders or shouted in his headgear, he'd felt the distance magnifying between him and Valya as father and son, splitting them and changing them into what they had to become to survive, private and sergeant. He'd followed every one of Valya's orders without debate. In the thick of the combat, he found himself responding to his son's instincts, trusting him the way a horse comes to trust its rider. Left! Right! Speed! Stop! Go! Back, back! All without thought, just action. The upshot was they were still alive and had left a half dozen German tanks burning in trade for the land they'd yielded. But the payment inside Dimitri was that he did not want to clap a hand on his son's shoulder tonight, to tell him he'd done well. He sat outside the tank and looked to the stars, seeing flashes that were not there, smelling fire that was not on the breeze. He lowered his gaze to the back of Valentin's head, to a son who was no longer near.

In the withdrawing convoy with them tonight were tanks, self-propelled artillery, tractors towing big fieldpieces, armored personnel carriers, and trucks with riflemen crammed in the beds. The cacophony of a thousand wheels, treads, and engines sounded mighty, the ground shook under their collective power, but the direction was wrong, and the gray faces told the real tale. Every man was grimy and sotted with exhaustion, none of them more than Dimitri. He looked around at what the sliver of moon could show him through the roiling dust. He didn't know where the *General* was in any formation, there were no tanks in the front or rear of him that he recognized from his company. The retreat was just a hodgepodge of scurrying Red machines and men, beaten in one spot and hoping in the short night to find some rest and the resolve to not be driven away from the next place they would stand.

Dimitri sat numb.

He jolted awake, his eyes snapped open. The *General* had stopped in the night. Other machines by the dozens trundled by, continuing the retreat. The moon showed them rising across a broad sloping face; they'd come to the foot of a slow rise. The Oboyan road ran straight up its middle. This would be the next line of defense. On the steppe, any high ground was worth dying for.

Pasha and Sasha clambered out of the *General*'s hatches. They stood on the dark ground which shuddered under so much passing steel, and stretched their backs. They looked around, not recognizing where they were and not caring, either; wherever they were was where they would fight, they knew this on just their fourth day of battle. These two boys were changed, too, in those four flaming days. Dimitri watched them splay on the raw ground beside the treads. In moments they were asleep.

He kept his perch on the tank, watching columns stagger alongside the rising road. Mechanics came and added oil to the *General*'s motor. An armaments wagon stopped and off-loaded stacks of shells. A barrel of diesel was dumped into the fuel tank. None of this clatter awoke Pasha or Sasha. Valentin was gone into the gloom to meet with platoon leaders from whichever armored companies had made this backward trip with them. Dimitri slumped against the turret. His tank squad was all dead. His company had been decimated and dispersed. His crew had gone silent, his son was severed from him, his pilot daughter off somewhere facing who knew what, his army was in retreat.

July 9
0520 hours
at the foot of Hill 260.8
third Soviet defense belt
the Oboyan road

Dimitri cracked his lids. The color he saw in the sky made him shut them again. The dawn had come bluish pink, it looked like meat, the insides of a man. Because he could not close his ears he heard noises: shovels, and he thought of graves. A vivid, foul mood had taken him in his sleep. He lay curled on his side, arms crossed, the ground crawled with vibrations. He wanted peace and comfort, his family and his village around him, a drink, a woman, and a horse, he wanted labor where no one was killed, food from a stove served on a table. Everything he desired had been ripped from him by three years of fighting, and he was at last like the Red Army stretched across the Oboyan road, down to his last defenses. He screwed down his lids, tightened his arms, and refused to wake up.

When finally a tap came at the sole of his boots, he ignored it. I've done enough, he thought. I've given enough. I'm down to me. Leave me alone.

Someone kicked a bit harder at his feet. Dimitri sprang from his curl like a sprung trap. He felt no pain or night stiffness, nothing but the lunge and it felt good, violent, released. Blindly, he gripped a tunic with both hands, he drove the body he clutched against the side of the tank. He screamed into the flesh in front of his nose and did not know what he screamed.

He heard his name, 'Dima, Dima ...' His breathing came hard, steaming with anger, filling his ears. 'Dima, let me go... .'

Other hands took him by the shoulders. They did not tug to peel him away but were gentler hands that told him they were there, careful and frightened. He pushed himself back from his clutch. The face above the throat he gripped was round and red and stupid. Pasha. Pasha had come to wake him. The other boy, Sasha, stood behind Dimitri, speaking. 'It's alright, Dima. Dima, calm down, it's us.'

Dimitri let Pasha's tunic loose. The boy looked scared and indignant all at once. He rubbed the back of his crewcut where Dimitri had rammed him into the *General*. 'What was that about?' he muttered. Dimitri gave no answer or apology. He slumped away to the back of the tank with the two boys staring after him. He walked a few steps and undid his fly to take a leak. He was dehydrated and could barely piss.

When he was finished, Dimitri gazed up the hill in front of him. He knew this hill, had driven past it a dozen times in the month of war games before the battle. He'd never imagined things would go so badly in the battle that he'd actually have it at his back. This was Hill 260.8, named like every other piece of high ground on the military maps for its metric height above sea level. Hill 260.8 had a commanding view of the approaching steppe. It was the final natural defense before Oboyan. To make sure the Germans and Russians met right here, the Oboyan road cut the hill in half. Six kilometers to the north was the village of Novoselovka. Twenty kilometers beyond that was Oboyan and a straight course into Kursk. Hill 260.8 was in the center of the Red Army's third and final major defensive belt on the southern front. It was their last stand.

Dimitri kept himself apart from Pasha and Sasha. He bummed a cigarette and a light from a passing soldier, noting the man was with the 309th Rifle Division. So it was their positions that his torn-up battalion had escaped to in the night. Five thousand foot soldiers dug more holes for themselves a kilometer in each direction across the road, like prairie creatures. The young soldier struck a match for Dimitri and cupped the flame. Dimitri leaned his mouth into the man's hands. His fingers and nails were clean, his hands did not tremble. He was fresh, still unbludgeoned by the Germans. The man stood while Dimitri inhaled the tobacco, waiting for some word, something brotherly between fighting men. But he was not dirty enough. Dimitri turned his gaze south, across the plain where the Germans would follow in a few more hours, and could not describe for this clean soldier what was going to happen. You're going to die, Dimitri thought, sucking the cigarette, and walked away as if the man were already a corpse and beyond thanking.

Dimitri smoked while Pasha and Sasha hefted shells into the *General*'s bins. He let the rising sun warm his face and unbuttoned his coveralls at the chest. He smoked the cigarette down to where he kissed his fingertips to get the last of it. On every side, men labored, vehicles churned, weapons were loaded, but he did not lift a hand. He stood tilting his face into the light. It calmed him to do nothing while many thousands around him worked, it felt like power.

A commissar bustled down the line of tanks, handing out paper sheets. He thrust one at Dimitri with a scowl, then moved on. The paper bore a one-sentence message: 'The Germans must not break through to Oboyan, at all costs.' It was sent by General Vatutin, commander of the Voronezh Front, and Nikita Khrushchev, political chief. Dimitri let the page flutter to the ground. He closed his eyes and returned his face to the warm and waiting sky. Yes, he thought. At all costs, of course. We wouldn't have it any other way.

'Pick that up.'

Dimitri opened his eyes into his own youthful face glaring at him.

Valentin said again, 'Pick that up.'

In Valya's hand, Dimitri saw the same page sent from

the general and the *apparatchik*. He bent and plucked his own sheet from the dirt, as ordered. Valentin stared at him. The boy creased his own page neatly and slipped it into his breast pocket over his heart. Dimitri crinkled the paper in his fist and crammed it in his pocket.

'Do you have any work to do?'

The boy's skin was smirched below a white mask around the eyes where his goggles had been. Valya was a better fighter than most, and for that Dimitri was proud of him. But Dimitri was so tired, standing in front of his Communist son, he was frazzled by his black mood and the prospect of another day's battle. The boy had walked over just to take what small shred of power Dimitri was gleaning from this morning, pretending to be a *hetman* while others did their chores and he merely watched, an elder, a personage. This is what the Communists do, he thought. They make everyone equal by seeing that everyone obeys. That's not freedom. Sometimes freedom is to throw the fucking paper on the ground and leave it there. Valya was waiting for an answer. Dimitri looked at his boy and felt himself sinking into Valentin's equality, where he had no more temper, no miserable mood to call his own, no warm sky to pause under, he was not a *hetman*. It seemed he'd been fighting everything and everyone, across every tick of the damn clock for years. The tank, the Germans, his fear, his exhaustion – and the one fight he wanted, the one for his son's soul, he could not take the battlefield, because his son would not call him Papa.

He was so tired.

Dimitri swayed on his feet. What was this? The rider in his heart had gone shaky in the stirrups. The Cossack was about to tumble from the saddle.

Dimitri raised a hand to find steadiness. Valya did not move. So Dimitri caught himself.

And he laughed, a reflex that welled out of him.

'You're right,' he said to his son, chuckling and free again. 'I have plenty to do.'

Dimitri turned his back on Valya. He went to his toolbox and selected a wrench. He opened the *General*'s transmission compartment and leaned in to lay his palms on the cool machinery. He tapped the wrench against metal, imitating the sounds of working. After he'd gotten enough grease on his hands to appear that he'd been busy, he lowered the door and tightened it again. He looked around for Valentin and did not find him. He smeared a little oil on his face to add to the film that had grown on him in the past several days. Another soldier hurried by smoking; Dimitri hooked a cigarette from him. He sucked a deep breath, the smoke flooded his blood with a lie of well-being. The soldier jogged off. Dimitri stood in the vast morning, 0700 hours on his watch. He gazed up Hill 260.8, this day the most strategic spot in all of Russia, to be defended at all costs. Dimitri was ready for that, to lay down his life on this road to help trip the Germans walking over it. On every side of him were trenches and earthworks teeming with armed men and boys, manning guns large and small, guns rooted and guns on the move. Around them was the coming battle; on all sides of the battle was the war; and beyond the war was the world and the shape it would take, on and on it spun, into history and eternity and oblivion. It all pivoted around him, Dimitri and his cigarette. This was what Valentin couldn't take from him, what the Communists could not dominate. This. His spirit. He took one more draft of the cigarette, raised both hands above his shoulders in welcome, and blew a cloud of smoke at the German Stuka fighters droning in high over the steppe from the south. Here they come, he thought. He made a fist and thumped his chest. Sirens sounded. Men ran to their stations, tanks cranked their engines, anti-aircraft batteries pounded from the hill behind him. Dimitri stood alone in the swirl of it all. He thought, before joining the battle, that he had never been lonelier, or sadder, than this.

One by one the gull-wing Stukas broke formation and dove. Their engines railed at the speed they gathered, their wings whistled, and they re-formed into a black knife's edge in the sky, a scythe sweeping down at Dimitri. Sasha and Pasha ran past. Pasha vaulted onto the *General* and disappeared into his hatch like a rabbit into its hutch. Sasha stopped in front of Dimitri, the whine of the fighter bombers climbing. Dimitri did not bring his face down from the sky or lower his arms until Sasha kicked him in the shin.

'Dima!' the boy shouted. His face glowed red under the grime. 'Drive!'

Dima watched the world turning and not the event in front of him. He lowered his hands. He took the cigarette off his lips and tossed it aside. The diving German planes screeched from a long way off. They were coming, but there was time. Where was Valya? Ah, there, running up, so young and beautiful, he comes fast, too, like the Germans. Dimitri licked the tobacco taste on his lips. Drive? Alright.

Sasha leaped onto the tank and slipped down the hatch. Dimitri found himself sliding into his seat and firing up the engine before Valentin had tumbled in and began shouting orders, even before all their headsets were tugged on. The *General* shot forward. Dimitri's hands took the steering levers in a strong grip. Oddly, his weakness and exhaustion had vanished. Sasha tilted his machine-gun up toward the onrushing Stukas and let loose an entire belt of ammunition. Dimitri drove straight at the diving planes. He knew their tactic: Make the Russian tanks veer away, then fire their 30 mm cannons into the thinly armored rear engine compartments. Valya's boots on his shoulders did nothing to pull him away from his headlong charge into the German guns. Dimitri watched them come through his open hatch door. Their shrieking dives were lost under the clank of his tank. The planes split out of their tight black blade, choosing targets. One pilot singled Dimitri out. Twin flashes stuttered under the Junker's wings. Sasha answered the blast with his own, punier machine-gun. Good for you, Dimitri thought. Talk back to him, Sasha. Black flak bursts spat in the air around the German. Dimitri eyed the ground for the fountains of dirt plowed up by the Stuka's glittering guns. There, to the right, like a seam bursting in the earth. Valya's boot almost kicked Dimitri down out of his seat, shoving him left, left! Dimitri threw the right lever, hauled back on the left and in an instant shifted into the next gear, the *General* tipped up onto the port tread but crashed back down and dashed out of the row of the bullets. The Stuka pulled up from his dive and Dimitri heard it, an angry bitch of a wail, he thought, and suddenly, under the black bent wings of the fighter-bomber streaking past, he awoke from his slow-motion world to the sweat-dripping fearful peril that he and his son and his crew were in.

Dimitri kept the *General* lunging in crazy patterns. Valya did not guide him; how could he? There was no path to follow from the diving rampage of the Stukas. Everywhere Dimitri turned, another T-34 erupted in flames, flinging pieces from the bombs and guns at them out of the morning. The Stukas dove and pecked at the scattering tanks like gulls on the beach, high-pitched voices squalling, and Dimitri could do nothing but run circles, squiggles, any maneuver to thwart the onslaught. The tanks were the targets for the Stukas, they ignored for now the dug-in Red infantry and the massed artillery on Hill 260.8. This told Dimitri that German tanks were headed their way in the next wave.

The *General*'s intercom was silent. No one uttered anything for the minutes Dimitri skirted the cratering ground, no one of them cheered him on, racing out of the Stukas' guns. Dimitri had the only upward view through his raised hatch; the sky was a rumpled quilt of smoke and darting wings. The rattling bang of the Stukas' machine-guns melded with the roar of their engines and the noises Dimitri wrung from the *General*'s motor. The battlefield was insane. A row of bullets marched right up the glacis plate and across the turret, like a dozen hammers and chisels, bits of the *General* were chewed off but the armor held. Beside Dimitri, Sasha swiveled his machine-gun with a fury, looking for something to shoot at. Dimitri guessed there were sixty Stukas in the air. The Germans wanted Hill 260.8 bad, they wanted to bust open the Oboyan road, some urgency drove them this morning even harder than in the past four days of combat. These planes were but the leading edge of a battering ram. Dimitri sensed it, the desperation of the Germans. They're running out of time. We need to live a little longer, he thought to his son and his crew, his tank and his army under the onslaught around him.

Dimitri swerved right. He took his hands from the levers and pushed up his sleeves. He'd drenched himself with sweat, his goggles ran with dribbles and he tore them off. There was no fatigue or pain, they would have been luxuries. A roar filled the swaying compartment. Everyone heard it, Sasha looked up from his machine-gun into the low green roof of his metal place. A Stuka had angled in right above them, diving fast, shrieking in its speed, plummeting at them from behind. Dimitri flung the levers to pivot. He did not pray; that, too, would have been a luxury. The *General* was going as fast as it could, faster than anyone in the company could drive over this terrain. The screaming engine peaked, the bullets and bombs would come now. A blast hit the ground ten meters to Dimitri's right, the *General* shook with the impact. Dimitri tensed, knowing the bomb blast was close enough to kill him. But the thing that hit the ground was not a bomb but the Stuka itself, shot out of the sky and pranged into the earth right beside the *General*. The *whomp* of the plane rattled through Dimitri's spinning treads. He cracked the silence in the intercom, he shouted or laughed, he didn't know which but he had gone a bit crazy himself fleeing from the Stukas, wondering where the Red fighter planes were in their defense. He mashed the accelerator and flew past the splintered and smoking fuselage. Another set of wings soared over his head, red stars emblazoned on their bottoms. A silver Sturmovik did a barrel roll twenty meters off the ground, leaving a twist of smoke in his wake. Valentin ballyhooed, too, into the ears of the crew, everyone in the tank balled a fist and rattled it. Dimitri glanced over to Sasha, the machine-gunner smiled hugely. He'd been crying. Dimitri punched the boy in the shoulder.

'Not dead yet!' he shouted. 'Eh, Sasha, my boy?'

Sasha wiped a hand over his dirty scarlet cheeks.

What Dimitri saw across the plain below Hill 260.8 throttled his heart. Tanks. A hundred of them, in a line as far east and west as he could see to the limits of his open hatch, tanks like a poisoned vein, venom in the earth. They had to stretch from Verkhopenye to Sokho-Solotino, a ten-kilometer swath on either side of the Oboyan road, with Dimitri smack in the middle. The Stukas overhead now had the Sturmoviks to contend with. The ground attack was the real hammer blow of the German battering ram to snatch the road. This was tank against tank.

Valya's boot touched his neck. *Stop*. Dimitri down-shifted and dug the tank in. Without the clatter of the treads to obscure it he heard the deepness of the day's battle, the booms and lashes of artillery and cannons, the pops of small-arms fire, the rip of airplane engines and guns overhead, and tanks dashing past, forming up into their units to confront the German battle group rumbling and smoking, kicking dust and closing across the grassland from the south. Dimitri waited while Valya waved flags to his ragtag platoon. Another plane crashed down, evicted out of the melee in the air. Beside Dimitri, Sasha fingered his trigger. On the cusp of standing on the fuel pedal and plunging ahead, Dimitri rummaged inside himself, for sorrow, or humility, or regret at how he'd handled his life, something benevolent to please God with what might turn out to be his last worldly thoughts, but he found none of it, nothing good to drape about him before facing today's certain death. He stared straight ahead into the plain and turned up nothing but the exhilaration of war. I tried, he told himself, and told God, too, should God be listening, and took the levers.

Valya clanged shut his hatch. The *General* idled on the steppe, other tanks moved beside it. The Germans weren't near enough yet to trade shots. Dimitri thought, Why wait? Valentin read his mind and toed the top of Dimitri's head.

Go.

July 9
at the foot of Hill 260.8
0750 hours
the Oboyan road

Dimitri descended into the battle. It took its shape around him, like a current flowing past a prow. The immense noise and shuddering vibrations faded to a fizz in his ears. His feet on the pedals and his fists on the levers ruddered the tank through the flow of fires and howl. Pasha and Sasha faded, too, they moved like dipping oars, propelling the General into the waves of combat. Dimitri did not notice the ruin and din the way a sailor does not focus on the water, his eye is to the wind that drives him. Valya was that wind. The boy issued orders with voice and tapping feet, he lit up the morning with bonfires that were enemies, he started and halted the tank, rocked it with the cannon and recoil, every move was commanded by him. Valentin fought the battle, and Dimitri fought only the tank. There was peace in this, peace in the midst of horror. Dimitri left his hatch door open, to see as much of the field as he could. He exposed himself to exploding shrapnel, to a million zinging bullets, but there was nothing left to him in the world, he had no clan, he was no one's *hetman*. The day was enormous, bigger and more tumultuous than anything he'd ever experienced.

The German tanks rolled over the advance trenches of the third and final defense belt etched across the Oboyan road. The Red soldiers of the 309th Rifle Division held their ground against the charge of metal but by 1000 hours the tanks sliced through them and the German grenadiers followed, falling into the defense works, cauterizing them in close-quarters fighting. Dimitri saw the blasts of grenades, bodies flung on the black concussions; arms rose and fell with bayonets and trenching tools. German bravery poured itself over Russian bravery and together they boiled in the pits dug by Just Sonya and her thousand civilians. The unsheathed men of both armies mangled one another. The German tanks rumbled past their skirmish, spraying defenders with machine-gun fire and point-blank cannon until they had punched through the defense line. In a clanking, jagged line, buttoned tight and spewing shells and smoke, they treaded up the elevated ground that lay before Hill 260.8 and the Oboyan road and Dimitri.

The field that separated the T-34s from the German tanks was five kilometers deep and fifteen kilometers wide. The land was even and colored by smashed grasses, with no trees or streams to break the table. The slope up to Dimitri's position was gentle and his view of the enemy tanks was unhindered, despite the battle haze, the fumes and spittle of fighting and dying machines. A medley of German tanks clattered forward. Dimitri spotted mostly boxy Mark IVs coming in wedge formations. A handful of feeble Mark IIIs bounced over the ruts like runt schoolkids desperate to keep up. He swept his gaze over the German advance, no fewer than fifty tanks spread before him. He wondered how many he did not see. The leviathans in their pack could not be hidden. Tigers.

'AP!' hollered Valya. Pasha slammed a shell into the breech. The *General*'s interior stank with sulphur backwash. A boot on Dimitri's cap brought the tank to a halt. The turret whined to the right. Dimitri sat on the shuddering idle, downshifting to first, keeping the clutch depressed, his hands on the levers to leap ahead the instant the shell was gone. Valentin toed the firing pedal and the *General* shook. Without an order, Dimitri bolted ahead, going nowhere, but moving: A still tank on a battlefield is a fatal thing. The roiled ground fountained in the cannon blast, Valentin did not ask Dimitri to wait until he could confirm a hit through the dust and grass, they just kept moving.

The Germans stayed back, they came no closer than a thousand meters. Some tank from either side would bolt ahead into the seven-, even six-hundred-meter range, not careful where his comrades were. He'd get off a shot or two and more often than not die right there, becoming a sort of fiery pylon demarking the ravaged boundaries between the forces. Valentin lost control of his tank squadron early, this was a free-for-all. He picked solitary targets across the distance of the field, using the small advantage of the elevation provided by the landscape, and was in turn picked by enemies. He shouted every order to Pasha, and only spoke to Dimitri when he had the turret rotated far enough to pull his feet from his father's shoulders. Sasha fired at streaking Stukas when he could, but as yet there were no German infantry in range. The duels were impromptu across the field, gunner against gunner. This was tank battle in open land.

Dimitri ran wicked patterns across the field. He ducked in and out of the other T-34s, getting Valya the best flank shots he could while making himself hard to hit. He even went so far as to speed behind other idling Red tanks who were sitting still for moments to finalize their own targets, to scrape off the attention of any German commander who might be following the *General* in his periscope. Twice the *General* was struck, both glancing shots off the sloped armor that did not explode but struck like a bell clapper, dulling every ear inside for a minute. The crew stayed alive because Valentin was remarkably fast with his marksmanship, Pasha showed the determination of a machine, and Dimitri flogged the tank in and out of gears with the hands of a tillerman and a hard rider, lurching and careering, reversing just to be random and maddening.

He spun through a field increasingly clotted with burning T-34s. Twenty or more tanks smoldered in varying stages of destruction, some wrecked and dismembered, some aflame and whole, some silent and still. The toll of the battle was swinging away from him. Red soldiers trotted past, retreating north up the road and Hill 260.8, some without weapons, running from the beating they'd taken in their forward trenches. Two thousand black jots appeared around the arrays of German tanks, their panzergrenadiers advancing alongside their armor, the classic *Blitzkrieg* tactic, unbeatable. The first tier of the final Soviet defense line before Oboyan had been breached. German tanks began to roll in front of their smoking dead comrades, the battlefield gobbled a hundred, two hundred meters more of the Oboyan road. Now the distance between the two tank armies was lessened. Valentin's shots came faster, the enemy was larger in his sights. Dimitri rambled through a thinning Russian force, the Germans came up the long grade like a tide, sweeping into the trenches, bubbling over the sandcastle redoubts of Russia that would not hold them back.

Dimitri parked between two immobile T-34s, one raging on fire, the other mute and whole. Sasha and Pasha went out the hatches at Valentin's command to scavenge ammunition from the quiet tank. Sasha slithered out his escape hatch below his feet with a red stouthearted face, eager to do something besides shoot at airplanes he could never hit. Valentin heaved empty shell casings out his open hatch. Dimitri eased his hands, hoping the shroud of greasy vapor from the burning tank would hide the *General*'s life from the closing Germans. He lowered his goggles over his eyes against the smoke wafting in his hatch, and breathed into his sleeve to filter the smoke. Pasha and Sasha ferried shells in to Valentin, who shoved them into the racks. The flames from the tank beside Dimitri murmured and lapped. He looked out his hatch at the Germans teeming around the Oboyan road. The ranks of the Mark IVs and Mark IIIs crept closer, they were within five hundred meters now. Infantry ran hunched behind and beside them. A company of sappers crept ahead, watching for mines, dangerous work. He stared into the gaps in the swirling pall and knew the Oboyan road was about to be lost. The German formations came like spears. Then, while he watched, the tips of the wedges seemed to open, the lead tanks pulled aside. Out from their shield, moving to the point of the advance, rolled six Tigers. All six of the giants fired at once. The boom pushed aside every other noise of the battle, six smoke rings stupefied Dimitri in the split second before the rounds landed.

The barrage struck other targets, the ruse of the smoke had worked. The .88s of the Tigers raised plumes in the dirt that sent Sasha and Pasha tumbling and squirming back into the *General,* hatch doors were screwed shut fast. Valentin's voice cut through the scrambling in a bellow. 'Go, go, *go*!'

Dimitri reacted by instinct, cutting loose the tank, shifting gears, pistoning his feet. But he did not pivot back up the hill to join the retreat. Instead, he wheeled the *General* at the Germans.

For a moment Valya gave no reaction. Dimitri gunned into second gear and did not veer. Valentin's boot tapped on Dimitri's right shoulder. *Turn,* the boot asked. Dimitri did not yield, driving at the heart of an enemy wedge, into the smoking center where a Tiger towered. The boot nudged again, like a kind angel on his shoulder beseeching him to come around and flee, to live and bear these others in the tank with him away to live. Why? he asked, and in answer the center of the wedge four hundred meters away smoked again, a shell on a flat trajectory shrieked past and exploded somewhere behind. Sasha beside him leaned into his machine-gun and his vision block, firing and spinning the barrel at targets, they were close enough now to the German sappers for the boy to pitch in, and Dimitri thought, Good for you, Sasha. He was sorry to carry the two youngsters with him into the blackness he foresaw in his and his son's futures, where there was no clan, where the Germans took the road today and Russia lost the battle for Kursk maybe tomorrow and finally the war, so there would be no more freedom. That would be a dead life, a conquered life. Sasha and Pasha won't want that life, either. The battle mists sucked him forward, Dimitri shifted gears again. He didn't decide this, to die today. But the leaflet had said 'at all costs.' What was he, Dimitri Berko, to not be spent on the Oboyan road? He knew he was nothing worth preserving.

The *General* bounded over the field past charring hulks, into a range where there were no other living Red tanks but his. He waited for his son's boots on his shoulders, for his earphones to split with a screamed command to turn and join the retreat. But behind him Pasha rammed one more of the rescued rounds into the breech. Sasha sprayed the machine-gun, and Valentin acquired a target.

Alright, Dimitri thought. He was so tired, and this felt good, to be almost finished.

He reached up and lowered his armored hatch door, cutting down his vision of the battlefield to nothing but the rectangular slice glowing inside his vision block. He gave the T-34 over to Valentin this way, completely, and gave himself away, too.

Now the tank was enclosed around the four of them. The close green walls shook, the treads ground and squeaked, the diesel engine blared. Sasha exhausted one ammo belt and plucked another off the wall, slapping it into his breech. He laid on the trigger, *brrrap, brrrap!* Dimitri felt virtuous that he'd brought the red quiet child to this place where he was a man and hero. Pasha behind him, too, with a shell in his lap, sleeves rolled up, dirty and streaked, a warrior. Valentin's boots on his shoulders were gentle, patting pressure left and right instead of pounding with insistence or panic or anger.

Both boot soles pressed beside Dimitri's neck. At the signal he skidded to a halt. Sasha swayed at the failing momentum but kept firing his machine-gun, baring his teeth at what he watched himself do through his periscope. One of Valya's feet left Dimitri's shoulder for the firing pedal. There were plenty of targets, tanks everywhere three hundred meters away. Valentin wasted no time picking an enemy and letting fly. Within seconds the inside of the *General* was packed with the chattering machine-gun and the cannon, the reek of sulphur, the recoil and hot spitting of the spent casing, then the winding engine and Dimitri's flailing arms weaving the *General* back and forth, wending snake-patterns into the path of the German advance. They were hectic moving toward their finish, all four doing their jobs, focused on their purposes, to finish well. How many shells did they have left? Dimitri wondered. They'd picked up an extra dozen, maybe they had twenty on board, five more machine-gun belts – it didn't matter, there wasn't enough, whatever the number. Dimitri drew the *General* closer to the advancing Germans.

He drove the tank into a crater, he hadn't seen it coming. The chassis dipped. Dimitri's head snapped forward. He downshifted to power out of the hole.

The intercom crackled.

'Stay here.'

Dimitri halted the tank.

'Back up.'

Dimitri reversed into the crater and eased the *General*'s hull below ground level. Only the turret was exposed now to the sights of the German armor.

'HEAT,' Valya called to Pasha. The boy laid aside the AP shell he'd cradled and dug up another. Valya lowered the long main gun. At this distance a high-explosive shell would penetrate a Mark IV's frontal armor and turn it into an oven.

Dimitri saw nothing but the scorched dirt wall of the crater in front of him. Valentin goosed the turret left and fired. The scalding casing flopped on the rubber mat, hissing. Pasha fed the breech and swept the casing aside. Dimitri turned in his seat to watch his son. The boy's face was smashed against his range finder, his hands played the traverse and elevation controls. The tank seemed to bend itself around him, gauges and handles, switches and eyepieces. He was a Communist, a drone, and this Soviet tank was made for him, for the peasants and the fighting believers. Dimitri had done his son a huge kindness bringing him here to the brink, where he could lay down his life for Lenin and Stalin, those purgatives of the human spirit. No one would forget Valentin Berko after today, the

Cossack sergeant who charged straight into the German maw while the rest of the Red force withdrew up the hill. Pasha and Sasha, they didn't know they were going to die. They would be forgotten.

The cannon fired again. The *General* shied from the crater wall, then settled again.

Dimitri looked at Sasha. The boy had no one to shoot at, Dimitri nowhere to drive.

'You know, it's a beautiful morning out there.'

The boy blinked, confused. He'd been ejected from the battle with his finger still on the trigger, he licked his lips for more blood to spill.

Dimitri reached for the lever to his hatch cover and gave it a twist.

'Let's go have a look.'

He shoved open the hatch and stood. The blue sky was immense and patient. With sore hands Dimitri boosted himself onto the glacis plate, then walked along the *General*'s fender to squat on his haunches behind the turret. Sasha appeared at the rear of the idling tank. Dimitri lent a hand to lift him onto the engine deck, and together they peered at the battleground.

Valentin and Pasha fired. The long cannon swiveled, paused, and fired again. The tank jumped with the reports, but no more than a horse over a hedge and Dimitri sat on his heels, balanced, while Sasha held on. The turret rested for long moments, listless smoke trailed out of the big gun. Then the fat round turret whirred and rotated far to the right, away from the dozen or so enemy tanks and thousand grenadiers bearing straight down on the *General*'s crater. This close to the leading edge of the German advance, Valentin chose for his last precious rounds to target a Tiger four hundred meters to the left. The giant was at the head of a wedge, broadside. It rumbled slowly across the field, inexorable and unwitting, vulnerable.

Dimitri waited beside Sasha for Valya and Pasha to strike. The seconds of the morning had no ticking clock to pace them; instead there was the whine and rolling creak of steel, the thrum of cannon blasts from the broad German advance in front, and from behind on the Russian-held hill and the Oboyan road. Above, planes slashed in crisscross duels with fantastic, straining motors. Sasha and Dimitri were the only still and silent things of the battlefield, except the dead. The boy's eyes darted, nervous and aroused. He knew now.

Valentin took his time targeting the Tiger. The monster was moving and Valya had to give the proper lead. Dimitri slid across the T-34's deck to sit beside Sasha. He wrapped his arm about the boy's shoulders. Sasha trembled as if he were cold. Dimitri kissed the boy on a fuzzy cheek. He turned his head to the Tiger. Sasha's thin arm nestled around Dimitri's waist, and his head turned, too.

The *General*'s gun crept to the right, stopped, and fired. The roar was splendid. A corona of blasted air and dust swept up from the steppe, then returned to it tumbling. The Tiger smoked. Valya scored a direct hit on the massive tread. The Tiger jerked as though tripped and did not move. Behind it, the wedge of armor slowed and halted, unsure. Valentin fired again, splurging his waning ammunition on the Tiger, to make certain the thing was killed. The big tank disappeared in a ragged globe of fire.

The German wedge was motionless. Valentin and Pasha went into a frenzy. The *General*'s cannon erupted six times in under two minutes, each shell pummeling the weaker side armor of the several Mark IVs accompanying the ignited Tiger. Dimitri and Sasha thrilled and gripped each other with each report. Sasha began to cheer. Valya had torn a hole in the German assault. Dimitri looked across the battlefield and was surprised to see the entire German advance paused to consider this little, lone T-34 dug into a crater smacking them on the nose. Dimitri thought, Keep it up, Valya! Hammer them good!

But the cannon did not fire again. The turret did not pivot for another target. The ammunition was gone.

The air keened in Dimitri's ears. In the fraction of a second left to him, he cut his gaze straight ahead, to a Tiger 250 meters away. He stared straight down the muzzle of the gigantic, smoking barrel.

The lip of the crater erupted. He was blown off the tank, Sasha was ripped from his arm. He landed beside the *General*'s port tread; dirt showered on him. His head pounded and his goggles were gone. All the buttons on his coveralls were missing, the pockets and chest flapped open. He staggered to his knees.

He scrabbled on all fours around the links of the *General*'s tracks. Haze wafted off the glacis plate. The .88 shell had pierced the crater berm and struck the frontal armor of the T-34. Dimitri had no way to know if the plating had held, if Valentin and Pasha were dead.

Sasha lay on his back on the other side of the tank. Dimitri skidded to him. The boy was unconscious, his goggles were cracked. A gash drooled blood down his brow. Dimitri lifted the boy's head into his lap. The sky sizzled, another shell coming in. Dimitri clutched Sasha to his bare chest. He would die after all with a son in his arms.

He looked up. No explosion hit the *General*. The round he'd heard wasn't coming in. It was going out.

Beyond the rim, the sounds of artillery mounted. Shells whooshed over his head, ripping down from Hill 260.8. Thunder in the earth shook under his seat in the crater. Sasha's head wound dribbled into his thigh. His face to the sky, Dimitri tried to catch silver glimpses of the sibilant shells flashing past. The rounds tore in twos and threes, a Russian barrage concentrated to save the brave crew of the *General Platov*.

Three Sturmoviks broke their engagements in the

mansion of sky and streaked down, trailing vapor, wings sparking cannon fire and smoke. They dove in low over the crater – *zoom!* one, two, three – Dimitri listened to them attack and bank out. The Soviet fighters circled to come around again. More artillery poured down from the hill. Sasha stirred. Dimitri pinched shut the gash in Sasha's forehead, the bleeding eased between his grubby fingers. He sat like this, marveling at the furor around him; the clash between armies right now was fought not for control of the Oboyan road, not for anything historic at all, but roared and erupted just for him and these boys he'd brought out here. This was majestic. Sasha needed to wake to see it. Dimitri squeezed the boy's earlobe.

Sasha sputtered and sat up. Dimitri took away his hand from the boy's head, blood seeped from the cut. Sasha drew a sharp breath and set loose wild eyes, he'd awakened expecting to be dead. Dimitri patted the boy's leg.

'Are you alright?'

Sasha blinked. 'What happened?'

'You keep trying to get yourself killed. You're not very good at it.'

The boy touched the blood trail warming his temple. He looked at his fingertips. Dimitri pressed back a black chuckle in his breast, he did not say to the boy that they would probably both get it right before the morning was out.

The commander's hatch lifted open. Valentin stood in the turret. He saw the two of them sitting beside the treads.

Valentin said nothing.

Behind and above Valya, more artillery shells rent invisible stripes through the air. Dimitri heard the rounds whispering over his son's shoulder, a moment later blasting into the German advance. The three Red fighter planes tilted behind him, hung on the blue like ornaments. Valentin was a hero this minute, the hero of the Oboyan road. The exploding tableau around him would be painted as the backdrop to his portrait one day.

Dimitri stood from Sasha, trailing a hand over the boy's shoulder before he stepped away. Sasha sat still. Dimitri swung up onto the T-34's deck. He rose to his full height beside the turret looking over the crater's lip. A wall of eruptions barred the Germans from coming any closer. Round after round detonated in their ranks; the rest of the enemy advance on all sides was being ignored by every gunner on Hill 260.8 and in the remaining defense bunkers along the road and by the three Soviet fighter planes who'd taken up the mission to save the gallant little T-34 that had knocked out six German tanks single-handedly, including a Tiger. The German wedge closest to the crater recoiled under the concerted Russian salvos, their tanks and infantry temporarily stymied.

Everything on the battlefield Dimitri had in his heart. Confusion, reprieve, bedlam. There would be more, Dimitri decided, standing beside his son on the brink. There would be more.

CHAPTER 17

July 9
1005 hours
the village of Kriulkovo

Outside the barn, the day promised to be hot. Thin tiers of light grinned in the space between the weathered wood slats. Inside the barn, the air stayed cool, there was room for the heat in the bare rafters. Daniel and Ivan lay on piles of straw, chewing pieces of it. To Katya they looked like lazy farmhands hiding from work.

The three of them were hiding. Plokhoi's cell had dispersed for the day into this farming village ten kilometers north of Borisovka. The older men of the cell worked in the fields this morning helping villagers with their hoeing. Plokhoi himself dug potatoes and beans. The younger ones, the ones who could be spotted by roving German patrols as not belonging in civilian clothes, stayed out of sight. Plokhoi let Katya rest after her scare beside the railroad tracks. She'd been given a minute in the river, a change of clothes, and another horse.

She leaned over the rail of the stall where her new mount stood. She caressed the ear of the horse. The ear twitched under her fingers. Katya rose on tiptoe and blew into it. She whispered into the pink folds.

'Your name now is Svetlana. That was my mother's name. I will call you Lana.'

The horse shook its head away from her hand. Katya

kept her lips close to the horse's ear, whispering.

'Don't be like that, Lana.'

'Leave the poor animal alone, Witch,' Daniel called from his mound. 'It's understandable if she doesn't like you.'

From his straw pile, Ivan laughed. The sight of Katya covered in Anna's gore had lost its grimness and become something to joke with her about. She had risked the mission, but then saved it. She had earned some ribbing from the partisans, and some respect.

'Ignore them, Lanyushka,' she told the horse. 'Did you know your predecessor was a very brave horse?' Katya recalled drawing her knife under Anna's throat, how terrified Anna had been after the C-3 gutted her, how she'd tried to stand and run. Katya resolved to remember Anna always as brave. That was all she could do, all anyone could do for a comrade's death.

Lana tossed her head out of Katya's hands. Katya reached to pat the receding mane and the horse dodged her.

Ivan laughed. 'You're losing your touch, Cossack.'

'Too many airplanes,' added Daniel.

'Did you see what she did to her plane?' Ivan rolled over on his straw. 'Planes probably don't like her anymore, either.'

The two soldiers guffawed. Katya glared at them without mirth. Left in that airplane was Vera, also brave and sacrificed by Katya. The two men did not catch the look on her face as they chuckled to themselves. Katya stepped toward Ivan, the bigger one, to kick him in the ribs.

The barn door creaked open.

A German soldier stepped inside.

Ivan and Daniel rolled off their backs, scrambling for their rifles and to get to their feet. Katya stood in the middle of the barn floor with nowhere to run, no weapon at hand. She went rigid, afraid and certain that guns were about to blaze.

A partisan stepped out of the sun behind the German.

The enemy soldier stared down the long barrels pointed at him by Daniel and Ivan. The partisan gave the man a shove in the back. The German stumbled into the barn. Katya saw his hands were tied.

'We got this one out of a downed bomber last night,' the partisan announced. 'Plokhoi said to keep him out of sight in here.'

Katya did not know this partisan, bearded and deep-eyed, another product of privation and anger. He was new to Colonel Bad's collection of aging peasant fighters.

Ivan set down his rifle and dug into his pack. Daniel was slower to lower his gun. Ivan took out a coil of rope. The old partisan nodded when he saw big Ivan moving to take control of the prisoner. The old man pocketed the pistol he'd kept in the German's back and slipped out the barn door. He dissolved into the summer light and closed the door behind him.

Ivan approached the prisoner, towering over him. The German was short and lean, with close-cropped hair. He was a high officer, that was clear by his filthy uniform. That was why he was brought in as a prisoner instead of shot on sight. Plokhoi will want this officer interrogated. The German looked up at Ivan. The expression on his face was not fear or disdain. He seemed to want to cooperate. Ivan pointed to the barn floor at the foot of a support column. The prisoner sat. Ivan lapped the rope around the man's chest and waist and knotted him in.

Katya came close. The prisoner watched Ivan tying him down, then gazed up at Katya. He blinked and gave a weary smile. His face was grimy across the brow and cheeks, he'd been wearing goggles. His uniform was dirty, too, and tailored. On his left breast hung a medal, a swastika emblem inside a German cross, resting on two crossed swords. On his right collar tab were twin lightning bolts. The man was SS.

Ivan finished and went back to his pile of straw. Daniel

was already on his back again, chewing another strand. Katya glared at the prisoner. SS, she thought. The worst. The most dangerous. He's small, he doesn't look like much. Neither do snakes.

The prisoner did not pull his eyes from hers. He was captured, he was hated. She thought he should hang his head.

'Bitte,' he said. His voice was low enough for only her to hear.

Katya was dumbfounded, she could not believe he would speak. She felt affronted by his voice. Who, where does he think he is? He's a prisoner. He's going to Siberia or a firing squad when the interrogators are done with him. She wanted to exact a vengeance on this SS officer right now, to kick him and beat him for Vera, Leonid, all her dead pilots and friends, dead Russians, her family at war, burned villages, the entire damned war, beat him for it until she fell.

'Bitte,' he whispered again. He looked down at his ropes, then back up to her and said, *'Du musst mich gehen lassen.'* Katya guessed it was about the fact that he was tied up. She gawped at his face, amazed. The man was certain, quietly, even pleasantly so, that she should take the ropes off him.

She drove forward and sent her boot into his rib cage. The German's filthy face puckered at the blow. She stepped back and watched the pain work in him. She'd kick him again if he opened his mouth.

He nodded at her. Alright, he said with the gesture. He hung his head as she wanted.

July 9
1340 hours

The German officer said nothing for the hours he sat tied to the beam.

Katya had never been this close to a German before. She'd always flown over their heads in the night, catching glimpses only in firelight and bomb flash. The only others had been the two guards next to the rail tracks, but Katya's eyes were shut, playing dead. This German tied to the post was no foot soldier. He was a ranking SS officer, with a silver medal and high boots. She watched him from beside Lana's stall, she was letting her new horse get used to her smell. The prisoner had an unusual quality, how motionless he could sit. He seemed focused on being still; after Katya kicked him he'd taken the message to heart. He didn't shift a finger of his bound hands, never raised his head. She studied him and imagined the worst of what this man likely had done. Executions, atrocities, the number of Russians he'd killed in battle.

Across the barn Daniel yawned, Ivan snored. Katya took a swallow from her canteen. She wanted to see if the German would react, ask for water. To tempt him, she offered water to her horse. Lana dropped her reluctance and Katya poured water over Lana's loud lapping tongue, wasting much of it. She spoke gently to the horse, to show the German she was human and tender, to remind him that he had killed Russian women and men just like her, good people who loved animals, who did not want this war but he had brought it here. She wanted to make the prisoner ashamed.

Katya strode in front of the German. She tilted the canteen's mouth and dribbled water in the dirt beside him. Look up at me, she thought.

He lifted his eyes. His jaw was set, ready for another kick.

Katya moved the falling dribble over his chest, to make him lean forward and lick it out of the air, like her horse, like an animal. He drank with greed and without meeting her eyes.

The barn door creaked open. She stepped away from the German. His tunic was wet. Under her gaze he retreated to his stillness.

Colonel Plokhoi came out of the blinding day. Behind him walked the *starosta* Filip.

Both men were sweaty and soiled. Both wore their wool coats and dark hats. Katya admired the will of these old men, to work in this heat wearing such clothes. She knew it was Plokhoi's command, because they might have to bolt from the fields at a moment's notice.

The two partisans stood in front of the prisoner. They removed their hats and mopped bare foreheads with open palms. The German did not lift his gaze from their boots. Plokhoi dropped a bead of sweat near the prisoner's tethered legs, his black beard and raven eyes hovered like a storm above the prisoner's head. Plokhoi spoke, his voice so restrained she could hear the madness in it.

'What is your name and rank?'

Filip translated in a monotone. For Katya, the German tongue was guttural next to the fluid mouthings of Russian.

The prisoner lifted his chin and gazed up to Plokhoi. He seemed timid, Katya decided, afraid to give offense. Or no, something else. Calculating. He wanted something.

'Standartenführer Abram Breit.'

'What is your unit?'

'Erste SS Leibstandarte Adolf Hitler.'

Plokhoi mulled these words. He hated everything German, this prisoner, the language of the enemy. Hitler's name here in the cool barn under the glare of Colonel Plokhoi was like a match to straw, Katya sensed Plokhoi smoldering.

'Filip.'

'Yes.'

'Tell him everything I say. Word for word.'

'Yes.'

'Listen to me, Nazi.'

Filip translated this.

The prisoner did as he was told, raising his face full to the partisan leader. Filip spoke a quiet stream beside Plokhoi's words.

'It's hard for me to keep from killing you right now. I have you here and no one would miss you. Your army thinks you're dead already in that plane crash. You understand?'

Katya watched the translation strike home. The prisoner's eyes tumbled for a moment, then returned to Plokhoi's, and she saw the man did understand. He was going to be left alive. He was relieved, the lines in his face smoothed, and more. He seemed sorry for Plokhoi's hatred, as though he knew and accepted the reasons for it.

Plokhoi and Filip continued.

'If you do not do exactly what you are told, I will have you shot and nailed to a tree.'

The prisoner nodded, agreeable. This bothered Katya, that an SS officer would behave this way, without defiance, with such cooperation. His name was Breit. He didn't seem frightened. He didn't know Plokhoi, or he would have been.

The prisoner said, '*Ja.*'

'I've been given orders to have you taken back across the lines to be interrogated. My superiors think you know something. Do you know something, *Standartenführer*?'

'*Ja.*'

'Good. Pray you live long enough to tell it.'

The German did not watch Filip speaking. Instead, he searched Plokhoi's face for clues, gathering what he could out of Plokhoi's tone.

'Nazi?'

'*Ja.*'

'I have seen and lost far too much. So have my men. I

am going to trust you to the mercies of the Witch here. She and this old man will deliver you across the lines tomorrow morning.'

Katya did not wait for Filip to make the full translation. She stepped to Plokhoi's side. The partisan leader did not look at her, his eyes were screwed on the German.

'Colonel,' she said. 'Colonel.'

Plokhoi glared down at her, the black furls of his beard wavered over his working jaw. She sensed the malice in him.

'Colonel, a word.'

Plokhoi drew a deep breath. He'd heard her and ascended from whatever pit he'd been in. He turned to her. He bore her a smile, a strange counterpoint to his anger. Plokhoi was mercurial this way, it made him charismatic and dangerous.

'Yes, Witch.'

'I believe I know where Leonid Lumanov is.'

'Your pilot.'

'Yes. I intend to rescue him.'

'You intend.'

Katya did not hesitate. 'Yes. Tomorrow.'

Plokhoi said, 'I don't have orders for that.'

'Yes you do. You had them a week ago. You never said they were rescinded.'

'That's true.' Plokhoi appeared amused at her cleverness.

He said, 'And what if you and Filip are captured? The two of you know a great deal about us by now, Witch. I think it's safer asking you to stay out of sight and get across the lines with this Nazi than to take on a German garrison.'

'My brothers,' Filip piped up, 'they will come, too. Seven of us. We'll go with the Witch to get the pilot.'

'No,' Plokhoi decreed. 'They're not trained for that sort of thing.'

Daniel stood from his straw pile. 'I'll go along, Colonel. I owe her one.'

Big Ivan rose, too, coming alongside Daniel and nodding his great head.

'We were supposed to bring him in, Colonel,' he said. 'I think we still ought to try if we can.'

Katya promised Plokhoi she would deliver the prisoner after retrieving Leonid.

'Where is your pilot?' Plokhoi asked her.

Katya did not look at Daniel and Ivan. She did not know who the traitor was in their cell. It could even be Plokhoi himself. But if they were going to help her retrieve Leonid, she would have to risk trusting them.

'He's close by,' she answered. 'Just fifteen kilometers away, in Kazatskoe. We'll set out at sunrise as soon as curfew ends. After we have him, we can make our way northwest across the lines. I'll hand your German over. But, Colonel, you have to let me do this first.'

Plokhoi scratched in his beard with dirty nails. 'Josef will come with you. You'll need him if there's going to be more of your heroics, Witch.'

She heaved a sigh of gratitude. 'Thank you, Colonel.'

Plokhoi put on his hat, expressionless. Daniel and Ivan went back to lying on their straw beds. Katya reached out to squeeze Filip's arm.

The partisan leader opened the barn door. The day's light blazed behind him. He called out, 'Witch?'

'Yes, Colonel?'

'After you save this pilot of yours and deliver the prisoner, will you be going back to your air unit?'

'I don't know.'

Colonel Bad tipped his cap to her.

'Please consider it.'

July 9
2130 hours

A farmer's wife brought in a pot of stew. Outside the open barn door the first blushes of the long dusk filtered through the fields. Katya watched the villagers and partisans shuffle in together from the furrows, to move inside the huts and houses before the German-imposed curfew took hold here in the occupied land. The old woman shuffled past the enemy prisoner bound against the post, surprised to see him; this made sense, she did not know he was here. She stopped to look him over. The stew pot steamed in her hands, she gripped the kettle through her lifted apron. She nodded looking down at Breit, perhaps imagining some justice she wanted to befall this SS man. She set out four bowls on the straw-strewn floor.

'Five, Mother,' Filip said. He jabbed his long nose at the German. 'He has to go a long way tomorrow.'

The woman tossed another bowl to the ground. She did not pour the stew into them but set the pot down and smoothed her apron. She stared down at Breit. The German looked only at her dusty shoes. Katya knew this woman did not see one German tied up for her but all of them. Her old head sagged and she began to whimper. Filip rose and stood beside her, he put his arm gently around her shoulders and turned her away.

'If he's too much trouble,' the woman said, walking for the door, her voice trembling, 'you can leave him here.'

Filip closed the barn door behind her. Ivan poured the stew into the bowls. Daniel handed them out. It was left to Filip to give food to the German.

'Danke,' Breit said.

Filip spoke with the German. They kept their voices low in the fading light of the barn. Katya listened from where she sat. The language the two men spoke was harsh, it sounded like a sweeping broom. She thought about how little she knew of Germans and Germany. There had never been a need to be familiar with them, they were targets, invaders of Russia. Nothing ever written or spoken about them by the Soviets had given the impression that these were men at all. Just cruel creatures to be stamped out by any means possible, no sacrifice was too great to kill a German. She watched this one sip stew out of the bowl with his tied hands, the way any man would. Filip squatted on his haunches at the prisoner's feet. The two chatted. Filip nodded many times to things the German had to say.

Katya finished her bowl and set it down. Lana licked at it through the stall gate. Katya walked over to Filip and Breit.

'The two of you be quiet,' she said. 'Filip, feed him and leave him alone.'

'Witch,' said Filip, looking up at her with a crinkled face, a serious mien. 'Wait. This is an educated man.'

'Educated in what?' Katya wanted to kick the German's ribs again. 'Murder? Rape?'

Filip shushed her. He motioned Katya to come lower and to ease her voice.

Whatever he had to say on behalf of this German was not for Daniel and Ivan to hear.

Katya sighed with impatience. She took a knee beside Filip. The old *starosta* leaned close.

'This is Colonel Abram Breit. He's an intelligence officer. He says he's not a combat soldier.'

'Look at him, Filip. He's covered in dirt. Look at his face, he was wearing damn goggles. He's a tanker, an artillery man. He's been fighting on the front lines. He's even got a medal for it.'

While Katya growled, pointing at Breit's uniform, medallion, and gritty face, Filip turned her words into quiet German so Breit could follow and reply. The

German waited until Katya paused. He spoke to Filip, still avoiding Katya's eyes.

The elder translated while the German talked.

'I'm not dirty from fighting. I rode a motorcycle from Belgorod to the airfield. I wore goggles then, the road was crowded with trucks. Look, I carried no gun on me, not even a holster or a knife. The medal is for administrative work. I was an art historian. I am not a fighter. I have never shot anyone.'

Filip whispered all this to Katya. She listened, watching Breit's lips while the elder spoke for him.

'I don't believe you. You were shot down in a bomber.'

'I was heading back to Berlin. A bomber was the plane arranged for me. I had nothing to do with it.'

'Why were you going to Berlin?'

'I'm an intelligence officer. I was going to make a report.'

'An art historian. An intelligence officer. If that's what you say, good. Now you're a prisoner. That's all you are anymore.'

'No. I'm something else.'

The German looked squarely at Katya. He studied her face. He pivoted his eyes to Filip and whispered a question.

Filip turned to Katya.

'He wants to know if he can trust you.'

Katya almost laughed when Filip gave these words to the German. She laid a finger to her own breast.

'Me? Trust me? I'm not the one he has to worry about. If he tries anything, Ivan over there will break his neck. Or Josef will cut it.'

The German shook his head even before Filip had translated any of this.

Filip said to Katya, 'No, Witch. I don't think that's what he means.'

The *starosta* sat on crossed legs in front of the prisoner.

The elder liked the mystery of this tied-up German, he was intrigued with the secrets that came in the barn with him. Filip was a Russian peasant, the ancient kind who had always loved his betters, a slave for the Tsars and now the Soviets. It was plain this prisoner had been schooled, he had bearing even tied to a post, he might even be a gentleman in Berlin. He worked some thrall over simple Filip.

'Why are you here?' Katya asked Breit. She wanted the German to say it, to admit in front of Filip that he beheld himself the master race, a destiny in his bloodline, to rule. She would kick him again for it and go back to her horse.

'I was hit on the head.'

'No ...' He tested Katya's patience. 'No, why is *Germany* here? In Russia. Making war.'

Breit composed his answer. He said only 'Conquest.'

'There,' she said, slapping Filip's arm when he translated the word. The *starosta* nodded that she was right.

The prisoner continued. Filip perked up and listened, then sweetened more harsh German into Russian.

'Conquest is merely a shorthand to greatness. It's a sickness that every nation endures at some point when its pride has grown too fast. The urge to take overwhelms the will to create. It's a malady of power. It's something your country will go through, young lady. If you win this war, you watch. Keep an eye on what Russia does, then judge Germany.'

These words spilled from Filip, making the old man more eloquent than he likely had ever been. Filip had a German speaking for him now. A shiver crept through Katya. Filip talking this way seemed very wrong, a little invasion and occupation here in the barn.

She meant to put a stop to the conversation. She didn't want to know any more about this SS officer. She was going to deliver him across the lines or see him killed in the process. She would send him back into his prisoner's silence and give Filip back his *volnitsa* from this German's tongue.

'We will win,' she said. 'We are winning.'

'Are you? What do you know?'

Breit cocked his head at her. Katya took in the gesture, then glanced over at Filip. The *starosta* was dumb, waiting for the German's next utterance.

'Do you know,' Breit said through the elder, 'that in the south the SS has penetrated to your last defense belt? That the fighting has moved within sight of the towers of Oboyan? Your Soviet army is losing three men for every German soldier. Three tanks for every German tank. Planes. Artillery. Everything. Do you know how long you can stand this kind of carnage until the weight of the battle shifts away from you? Do you? I don't. And I know a great deal more than you can imagine.'

Katya reeled at this. She had no idea, just as the prisoner implied. What foot soldier or running partisan could ever know beyond what they saw? She had been shot down behind the lines just as the battle started. This was the first news, not even Plokhoi told their cell how things were going. The battle for Kursk was surely huge, ranging over so much steppe, far beyond the struggles of one, beyond the rivers and bends in the earth, even past what she had glimpsed from her cockpit. But was this German telling the truth? Probably not. Why would he? He's spouting propaganda. Perhaps he believes what he says because it's what he's been told. Even so, she recalled the hundred-plus night bombing missions she'd been on. The Germans always had more supplies to be blown up. Always another train puffing in. Germany was an industrial giant next to Russia. They'd declared war on England and America, too. What kind of people can do that? Could they still win in Russia?

Breit leaned forward against his ropes. 'You do not know how important it is that Russia wins this battle. The world will turn on what happens here. You have no idea.'

Katya made no reply. Why would an SS officer say that? The look on her face must have told the prisoner to keep talking.

'I have in my head every fact. Every detail and number about the German assault on Kursk. I must get this information to the Soviets.'

Katya was befuddled. Of course that's what he was going to do. Tomorrow, after she'd gotten Leonid back. This Abram Breit was going to be handed over. He will tell whatever he has in that head to whoever puts a gun to it and asks. What was he talking about?

Breit said something to Filip. The old man gasped and rattled his gray head in wonderment.

Katya prodded. 'What?'

'He says,' Filip whispered, 'he is a spy. For Russia.'

Katya rubbed a hand across her forehead. She could not restrain a little chuckle. 'So this is why he wants to know if he can trust me?'

'Yes,' Filip answered without speaking for the German, knowing what Breit would say. 'He wants you to let him go.'

Katya nodded into the German's eyes. She grinned mockingly.

'Please,' Breit said through Filip, 'tell no one else. If either of you tells your commander, he will radio that he has captured a spy and ask for orders. There are many German spies in Moscow, in your army and your government. One of them will find out who I am. I'll be intercepted and killed, either in Moscow or back in Berlin. You have to let me slip away. I am helping Russia. You must believe me.'

Katya puzzled at the tale. It was fantastic, that anyone would say these things after being captured. This German was inventive, and plausible in his performance, quietly frantic. This was a plot out of an adventure book, a fiction about a swashbuckling spy. She gazed at the thin, dirty German wrapped in ropes on this plank floor. This was no hero.

'I will turn you over to a commissar tomorrow evening, Colonel. That's when I will let you go. You can tell him all your numbers then. You'll be a great help. Russia will thank you appropriately, I'm sure.'

Filip translated this without the sarcasm from her tone. Breit grew urgent.

'You can't! I must get back to Berlin!'

Katya stood, feeling the whiplash of anger. This was enough of Breit; he was something she'd been curious about – an enemy brought close for a little while, for an afternoon and night in a remote village barn – but like a cave she'd wandered into, now she was far enough from the light at the opening to turn around and go back. She lacked the desire to delve farther. Tomorrow she would try to rescue Leonid, she may die in the attempt along with this German and the old *starosta*. She worried every day for Papa and Valentin, she grieved for Vera and too many others already. Where was the room in her for Breit's pleading? If by any chance he was a spy, then he was a traitor to his own country, and the Cossack in her found that sour and wormy. If not, then he was just a liar and a coward. In either case, his story was not worth reporting to Colonel Bad. She would keep the prisoner's secret, not because he asked her but because she would look foolish repeating it.

She was done with Breit. Time for him to become what he was, all he was, spy or no. A prisoner.

She walked away. She was not going to let him go. No one was going to do that.

CHAPTER 18

July 9
2250 hours
Hill 260.8

Luis dropped a knee to the ground. He laid his palm on the earth. There was not a blade of grass under his fingers, or anywhere on the crest of the hill, just scorched flat ash. The dirt glowed pregnant with heat, not from the slanting sun but explosions. And it trembled.

His crew tottered around the Tiger. The men were the incarnations of exhaustion. Sooted faces gazed at shaking hands. The tank itself, as stern and hard a thing as it was, seemed to rest, steaming from the engine compartment, sighing gases out of the cabin through open hatches. In a hundred places on its skin, the *zimmerit* paste was cracked and dented from bullets and shells. Luis scooped a handful of dirt from this defended hill and let the grains dribble through his fingers, like a farmer with his black soil. He loved this ground because it was conquered.

The wreckage of the Russian resistance on this crest was everywhere. Abandoned American trucks tilted on blown tires bearing empty Katyusha missile racks in the beds. Artillery pieces with spiked barrels were left aimed at level trajectories, the fighting had been so close. Only a few Red tanks remained behind when they retreated off Hill 260.8, just the ones blown to hell beyond repair. The battle for Kursk had become a tank battle, the Reds and

Germans alike knew that, and the Soviets were uncanny at getting their smoking T-34s off the battlefield and ready for combat the next day. This was their genius, Luis thought, numbers. Men and machines and the dead. Around him lay more bodies than he'd ever seen on one field; the Russians got their tanks off this hill but there were too many dead to cart away.

Balthasar the gunner came to stand beside him, binoculars around his neck. The man smelled the worst of anyone in the crew. In days of intense fighting, Balthasar had worked the hardest, spinning the handwheel to elevate the giant gun, pressing his eyes to the padded browpieces to take aim, firing and finding another target. The others did their jobs, hoisting shells, working the radio and machine-gun, driving. But this one was the reaper. There is a God, Luis thought, and to undo His work there is a toll. Balthasar showed that cost in his stink and in eyes that were barely able to focus after staring so long through magnifying optics, past cross-hatches and range numerals.

The young sergeant's eyes blinked south over the reddening plain below the hill, where they had fought all that day. To the right, the battered Wehrmacht divisions of *Grossdeutschland* and 11th Panzer battled northward. Their infantry and armor swarmed along the Oboyan road to hold the gains of the day. Theirs was the heavy quiver in the earth because they were the only German forces moving up. Leftward spread the rest of *Leibstandarte,* holding its position, stretching five kilometers to the east and Sukho-Solotino.

Balthasar wanted something from the panorama below, he squinted to see deep into the ranks of *Leibstandarte*. Smoke filtered into the air from a dozen smoldering hulks, ruined and juxtaposed against the fifty tanks and twenty assault guns surviving in the division. A handful of shot-down airplanes littered the grassland too, bent propellers like dried daisies. Luis studied the young gunner beside him and for the first time wondered about him. So cool and competent, such a chill in his fighting, angular and Germanic in profile in the waning day. No wonder Hitler had been so confident to make his war, with a nation of these boys to do it. Their uniforms were designed dark for a reason, to show off how white his soldiers were against them, how pure and potent they were. Not like the Soviets, in their yellow-brown khakis, earthen creatures, muddy. Balthasar stirred. He pointed.

'There,' the gunner said. 'There they are.'

Luis followed the direction of the gunner's dirty finger. Hunkering among the tanks and milling battalions of panzergrenadiers were three more Tigers, repaired at Luchki and put back into the field this evening. Even at a distance, their great bulk was discernible among the Mark IIIs and IVs. Now *Leibstandarte* had four Tigers.

'Just in time,' Luis said.

Balthasar nodded. He turned away from the southern field and the long slope of Hill 260.8 they had taken. Six kilometers north lay the town of Novoselovka. Beyond the town, the river valley of the Psel ran wide and smooth. Luis could see deep into the plain, even through a gray haze of dusk and engine fumes. The Russians had retreated off this hill, into the town and that valley, girding their last hard defenses along the Oboyan road. Behind them, the Psel River was the final natural barrier to Oboyan, then on to Kursk. *Grossdeutschland* moved down the hill to form skirmish lines against the Reds in Novoselovka. The Soviet defenses could be cracked here, tonight, or tomorrow. Balthasar lifted his binoculars and spied across the steppe. Luis watched him, fascinated with the soldier's blue eyes, opaline like Thoma's. It takes a thousand years of solitude to make a blue-eyed people, Luis thought.

Luis put out his hand for the binoculars. Balthasar

turned them over. Through the glasses, beyond the Soviets' spiny bunkers and trenches, rose the towers of Oboyan. The city was in sight, in reach.

'In time for what?' Balthasar asked.

Luis lowered the field glasses. In his breast pocket were four folded sheets, handed to him five minutes ago as company commander. The papers were Division Order No. 17, for II SS Panzer Corps.

Balthasar prodded. 'We're going to Oboyan, aren't we?'

Luis turned west, away from the objective city and the precious road leading to it twenty kilometers over the steppe. Hill 260.8 stood as the deepest incursion into the Russian lines on the southern front. With one more strong heave, with *Leibstandarte* alongside 11th Panzer and *Grossdeutschland*, the Oboyan road would fall. But the forces guarding their right and left flanks were taking terrible hits from the Reds every day, and their northward pace continued to slog. Hill 260.8 was too far out in front and exposed to Red flank attacks. The drive on Oboyan was being thwarted not from the extended center but from the sides. So tonight, under the order in Luis's pocket issued from General Hoth, the spear thrust of the German strike at Kursk was to be blunted and split into a trident. Eleventh Panzer had been ordered to pivot to the west, away from the Oboyan road, to clean up Soviet flank assaults north of Verkhopenye. *Grossdeutschland* would regroup here astride the road and relieve elements of *Leibstandarte*. The three divisions of II SS Panzer Corps were directed to shift their advance away from Oboyan, to the northeast. The hope was that they would crush Soviet resistance there and unlock the gates for Kempf's overdue army. The still-powerful SS divisions would encounter strong Russian reserves after wheeling to the east, but with enough Luftwaffe support, and the return of more repaired Tigers, *Totenkopf*, *Leibstandarte*, and *Das Reich* ought to smash open a new – though longer – route to Kursk.

'No,' said Luis, returning the field glasses to Balthasar, 'we're not going to Oboyan.'

He recalled the situation room in Belgorod. He envisioned the long paddles pushing the blocks of the II SS Panzer Corps off to the east, crawling past blue lines of steppe and forest and villages tonight and tomorrow, reforming again into a lance. He thought of Breit and Grimm, smoking and sweating, the two of them, watching the grand collision take its shape, knowing that Luis Ruiz de Vega rode the first of the black blocks into the fight. He imagined the battle taking place just like that, a game of skittles, his lone block bowling the many red ones out of the way. He had no reason to believe it would happen any other way. He commanded the blue eyes of Balthasar, the blood of Thoma still riding on the Tiger, he had this hungry but tireless body, and a tank the Russians could do nothing to but pock and jostle. And now there were other Tigers returning to the fold, tomorrow and the next day would bring more. This change in direction to the east was fine with him. He didn't care one way or another for the city of Oboyan or the road going to it. The Soviet forces in front of him had been sacrificed, they played their role and stopped the German advance on Oboyan. Good for them, they'd paid for it. But the II SS Panzer Corps remained unmauled and cohesive. It had been given a pivotal command by Hoth. The three divisions were going into battle alone this time, with no one to guard their flanks but each other. The fate of Citadel hung on him and the SS, like a medal, and this would showcase them as what Luis knew them to be: the finest fighting men and machines the world had ever witnessed.

There was still time. The Americans were not in Europe yet. He had in his grasp exactly what he wanted: The battle for Kursk had come down to him.

He laid his hand to Balthasar's back. He did not feel spindly at all touching the broad muscles of the young soldier. Because he controlled them, they were his muscles, as well.

Luis faced east. The land there darkened first.

'We're going to Prokhorovka.'

CHAPTER 19

July 10
0415 hours
Orlovka

Dimitri was glad to be soaked. He felt washed in the light rain, sweat and grease dribbled off him, some blood, too. Throughout the slight hours of the steppe night, the sky flared with the fighting that had stopped the Germans north of Novoselovka. The Oboyan road was denied to the enemy by 10th Tank Corps, 31st Tank Corps, by 3rd Mechanized Corps, and by the infantry of 6th Guards Army. Every one of these units was bled white over the last four days, only scraps were left of them. This was a shame, the way they had fought, what Dimitri had seen them do with fire and smoke, the tools of gods, it was a damn shame for Russia and mankind to have those men dead in such numbers. But the Germans would have to go around now, through somewhere else, not Oboyan, and fuck them, Dimitri thought. He sat against the *General* facing south, waiting for enough dusk light, his eyes on the flashes like crashing stars. After midnight the rain began and the vaulting glimmers were smothered, the night was being washed, too. Dimitri finally slept.

Awake now, he licked fresh rain from his lips. He was wet and suffering, starving and bone weary at war. Good, he thought. This is when a man rises. He needed his physical pangs, he could grapple with them and win, something he did not hope to do with the pain in his heart.

He walked to the front of the *General*. Mud sucked at his boots, a tasting, chewy sound, and he thought of food, the hot breakfast he would not have today. A deep gouge marred the sloped glacis plate below his driver's hatch. This was where the Tiger's shell struck and deflected after burrowing through the dirt berm of the crater. He balled his fist and laid all of it inside the scoop, this was how deep the shell had penetrated the armor. There wasn't much metal left, less than the thickness of a finger.

Something happened in that crater, something was left behind in its bowl. When Dimitri lifted groggy Sasha up on the tank deck, Valya came out of the hatch to help. Pasha followed. The son and the boy both glared down at Sasha, disapproving, as if Sasha were indulgent to be bleeding again. The look on Pasha's platter face was the same as that on Valya's, a sort of scowl from on high, that Communist disdain for the individual. And it is always individuals who bleed. Sides had been chosen, Dimitri could tell. Pasha the loader joined with Sergeant Berko the commander, versus the two in the lower half of the tank, skinny quiet Sasha with his little machine-gun and penchant for being shot and old stubborn Dima. Sasha held on to the turret handles outside for the second time in three days while Dimitri jumped back into his driver's seat and roared the T-34 out of the hole. The Soviet counter-assault from the hill shielded their retreat, and they got away. Valya sat on his rattling throne with Pasha beside him, the silent hot cannon between them, the wheels and dials of the tank all around him – Valentin, the gunner hero – the ammo racks were all empty, the floor bins were rifled and depleted – Pasha the loader of every round – and no one spoke while old Cossack Dima scrambled them up the hill and back inside the withdrawing Red lines.

When he finally stopped, they were behind the defensive positions of the 309th Rifle Division east of Novoselovka. Soldiers manned the hundred artillery pieces that had saved the *General,* they kept blasting away at the resumed German advance creeping up the Oboyan road. These men shouted *Urrah!* and raised their helmets to the little T-34 in their midst, the brave tank they'd rescued. Dimitri shut the engine down and clambered out. Sasha had climbed down under his own steam, and a field medic was already there reaching for stitches and a bandage. Valentin lifted his hatch cover and exited the turret. The artillerymen gave him a cheer. Valentin smiled uncomfortably from the deck of the tank. Then he did something Dimitri had never seen him do. He lifted his arm and acknowledged the salvos of applause from the artillery. Dimitri detached himself from any emotion about the scene. He squeezed Sasha's hand and left it for later to wonder about.

That was what he did now, in the drizzle, walking to the repair tent in the blue-gray morning. It was a terrible thing, he thought, that wave of Valentin's. It was a wave of goodbye. Goodbye. I no longer belong to you. I am swept up in this applause. I have found a new home away from the village and the clan. I am a Communist and see how they welcome me back from the brink where you took us. I walk off on to my future unfolding, Father, away from the village, away from you, to Stalin the greater Father, Russia the only mother. I am not your son anymore. I am reborn. Hold the hand of your new son, Sasha the stripling. Save Sasha instead.

A metallic knock from under the repair tent reared him out of his reverie, and sadness ran down him with the droplets off his ears and nose. He was drenched with a bowed head. Soldiers splashed past him on their way in their own lives. Dimitri felt nothing of the warmth of these men around him, they might have been made of iron.

He stepped under the tent, through a little cascade of runoff that spilled down his back in a cool rivulet. He lifted his head and shivered, putting on a carefree face, just a dirty tanker taking a morning shower in his dirty buttonless coveralls. A comic man, he was a bold one in a hard graying body, everyone's father.

'Hey,' he shouted, 'I need a welder.'

'What for?' came an answer from a big fellow behind a truck wheel.

'I've got a fucking hole in my tank. I want to cover it up.'

'Alright.' The large man let the tire fall over and roll at his feet. His gesture said, A truck can wait for a tank.

Together with the mechanic, Dimitri gathered up the man's welding tools, plus a tarpaulin and two metal rods. The mechanic had an angular face, he was bald, and powerfully built. He led the way out of the tent – he had to duck, he was so tall – to a quarter-ton truck parked with a large electric welding generator hitched to it. The rumbles of fighting eight kilometers to the south muttered under the rainfall and their sloshing boots. The Germans would not get the Oboyan road; even so, they were keeping up the pressure to stop the Reds from going over to the offensive. The Germans weren't quitting. They'd come close, maybe closer than they knew, to breaking through to Oboyan. The mechanic climbed into the truck, filling the seat with his midriff, the steering wheel almost touched his belly. Cursing the nasty weather under his breath, he wheeled the truck and trailer through the mud, dodging the human traffic growing with the lifting light. He did not smile at Dimitri.

When they reached the *General,* Dimitri saw that Valentin and Pasha had not yet risen. Their boots lay side by side between the treads, pointing up, and the T-34 seemed to be some grand headstone for the two of them, a green sarcophagus carved in the shape of a tank to mark the heroes' last place. The mechanic pulled up close to the *General* and got out, slamming the truck door, thoughtless of the late snoozers under the tank. He walked up to the glacis plate and ran his fingertips into the bottom of the scoop below the driver's hatch. The big man whistled.

'This was a Tiger.' The mechanic looked up at the turret, at the name of the tank painted there by Dimitri only two weeks ago.

'You're the tank that was out front. The one in the crater.'

Dimitri nodded.

The mechanic wagged his head to say: *You all ought to be dead.* Dimitri thought, Yes, we tried.

The man went back to the truck for the tarpaulin, then clambered up on the tank to hang the oiled sheet across the main gun barrel. Dimitri spread the tarp and secured it to make a tent, to keep the spot dry where the mechanic would work. The big man jumped down, mud sprayed. Dimitri stepped back. The rain tapped on his hair and shoulders, he was lost again, dissolved into the dank. He stared beneath the tank at the bottom of Valentin's boots, the boots that rode like angels or devils on his shoulders in the tank.

The mechanic cranked up the generator. The pistons made a diesel racket, the generator coughed as though it had a cold in this dreary weather. But the engine sounded alright to the mechanic. He took his dark welding goggles from a hook on the trailer and slipped them over his cloth hat. He moved under the spread-out tarp and dried the glacis plate with his sleeve. He laid the first of the metal bars horizontally across the bottom of the sloped plating and lit his welding rod. The generator jerked into some higher mode and a blue flaming dot popped at the end of the wand in the mechanic's mitt. Dimitri had to turn away, the electric dot was blinding. The mechanic set to work under the tarpaulin, glittering like lightning with the welding. Dimitri grabbed the tank fender and sprang onto the *General*'s treads and up on the deck. Yes, we tried, he thought, of the time in the crater. Maybe we succeeded.

Inside the turret, he unhooked from the wall the first of the three spare tread links the mechanic would wedge over the glacis plate between the two welded bars. Each link weighed almost half of what Dimitri weighed, but he hefted them one at a time out of the hatch and tossed them to the soft ground. They landed with splashing thuds. He left the hatch open when he was done, to let the rain fall in and wet Valya's seat. He'd say he was sorry, he was busy.

Dimitri stacked the three links beside the flashing mechanic. His biceps and back muscles thickened with the strain of lifting and carrying the things, he sweat under the coating of drizzle. He stood back and watched the sparks fall and bounce around Valentin's and Pasha's boots.

The mechanic was almost finished securing the second bar when Valya and Pasha slumped around from the rear of the *General*, puffy-faced and aggrieved at being wakened to rain and welding. Valentin came over to inspect the work. The mechanic in his goggles and scorching noise did not know Valya was there behind him. Valentin waited to be acknowledged, then touched the mechanic's shoulder. The man shut down his wand and turned, raising his goggles.

'Let me take a look,' Valya said to him. The mechanic shrugged, then backed from under the cover. He stood beside Dimitri and cut his eyes to the back of the lean sergeant bending over the still-smoking metal. He glanced at Dimitri. That your boy? the look asked. Dimitri nodded.

Valentin stayed under the tarpaulin longer than someone should who knew nothing about welding. The mechanic cast his eyes over at Pasha. Dark specks of rain spattered on the boy's dry coveralls.

Pasha asked the big man, 'Did you hear about us?'

The mechanic's chest jiggled. He laughs to himself, Dimitri thought, just like I do. He laughs at Pasha's brand of heroism, at a boy stupid and ungrateful to be alive. How many other, quieter heroes has this mechanic scraped out of tanks into buckets to get the machines ready for another crew?

'Yeah,' he answered Pasha, indulgent. 'I heard of you.'

'We took out four tanks. And a Tiger. We ran out of ammunition.'

Valentin was done looking at the welded bars. 'Very good,' he said, backing out from under cover.

'I've got a little left to do,' the mechanic said. He towered over Valentin, over all of them. 'We've got to secure the links.'

Valya seemed uncomfortable. 'Alright. Get to it then.'

Dimitri winced. This was how Valentin evened the score, always. He'd taught the young boy the sword, Valya had excelled with it in the *sietch*. Now in life, Valentin the man knows nothing else.

The mechanic nodded his great bald head. 'Yes, Lieutenant.'

Valentin wore the mustard and red badges of promotion. Dimitri had not noticed. It must have happened yesterday, while he was off finding new orders.

'You should both know,' Valentin said, taking in Pasha and Dimitri with a regal turn of his head. 'We've been transferred. The three SS divisions are regrouping and moving east, around Oboyan. Some units from 3rd Mechanized and 10th Tank are being sent to reinforce 5th Guards Tank Army at Prokhorovka. I volunteered the *General*. We'll leave as soon as we take on more ammunition. Where's the machine-gunner?'

Dimitri said, 'Sasha will be back from the infirmary this morning.'

Valentin turned away, certain of his victory over the mechanic, that seemed to be what he wanted, as though the mechanic had not come in the rain to help but to bring some encounter. Valentin was on a winning streak, he wanted to stay on it. He walked off to show there was some very dutiful chore on his mind. Pasha stayed behind, a stunned look on his face. He hadn't known about Prokhorovka, either.

The mechanic was a kind man. 'Four tanks. And a Tiger. Well done, loader.' Pasha seemed ready to cry, not so heroic. Then he, too, turned away, to follow Valentin and fetch more ammunition, to return to the battle.

The mechanic smiled now.

'Yes,' he said with a different inflection than when he'd spoken these words to Pasha, 'I've heard of you.'

He drew from his pocket a small jackknife. He opened the blade. With quick snips, he cut from his own coveralls all the buttons holding the fabric together over his chest.

'Prokhorovka,' the mechanic mumbled while he cut.

With the black buttons heaped in his large palm, he poured them into Dimitri's accepting hands.

'Here, Papa.'

CHAPTER 20

July 10
0640 hours
beside the Vorskla River
5 kilometers southwest of the village of Vorskla

The big one called Ivan woke him with a boot. Old man Filip brought him a canteen for a swallow, and that was all. He was untied from the barn post where he dozed the short night sitting up, drooling on his Merit Cross with swords. He was helped off the ground onto vague legs and tossed a wool jacket and a cap. He stripped off his SS coat and left it on the Russian ground bearing his lone medal. Abram Breit was put on a horse.

Now Breit wiped sweat from his brow with a freed hand. He held out his arm to examine the rope burn on his wrist.

Such heat, he thought, so early in the morning. What kind of people are made by this sort of land? The steppe was featureless, the little river dallied through it, only a bland green seam across a limitless fabric of yellows and greens, a bleak sky that seemed not lofty at all but oddly, oppressively low, heavy like water. The land makes the people. Are they harsh, too? Are they as dull as this? Certainly, they were as vast, from what Breit knew of the way the Russians fought and perished in their astonishing numbers. He studied the five partisans riding on all sides of him. They fit here. The land and they bore each other in their countenances, determined, endless, and yes, dull. Germans do not belong here, he realized. This is Asia. We are socialized. We were not left to grow so wild by such immense stretches without people. These Russians. These peasants, burdened and ignorant. They will be set loose on Germany if they win the war, on Europe. Breit considered what he had done so far to help bring Hitler down, what he needed to continue doing, and was fearful for what might arise from his brave deeds and good intentions.

They rode in the open. The land was so flat that no German patrol could come within kilometers of them without being seen. The six were just a handful of Russians going between towns after daybreak, nothing suspicious about that in a landscape of farmers. Breit was no horseman. His mount's head bobbed walking along the river, balking and wanting to turn always out of the group, down to the water.

Filip rode alongside.

'Tighten your reins, Colonel. The horse will go more smoothly.'

Breit took in slack from the leather straps. His horse nickered and shook his mane, objecting.

Breit was given his hands and feet. The ropes were looped and stored in the big one's knapsack. His name was Ivan, a funny name for a Russian, it was the nickname the Germans used for all Russians, they were 'the Ivans.' A skinny one with slits for eyes was Daniel, who carried knives and guns bulging on him like pine cones. The woman was Katya. She was a pretty girl, almond-eyed and lean. The old man Filip called her *'Hexe,'* a witch, and did not explain why. Riding behind her, Breit made up his own reasons. She was a witch because she seemed as mean as anything out of a fairy tale. She rode her horse like a broom. She did not hate, though. Not like the old hard one named Josef. That one was a crow. He was black, silent, surely an evil portent when he appeared on any doorstep.

'Filip,' Breit whispered to the elder riding close to him. If he had any hope of getting away from these partisans – a slim hope, a dangerous thing even to consider – if he was even to survive the day, it would be this German-speaking old man who must help him. 'May I have some water?'

The old one lifted the canteen from around his saddle pommel. Breit took it and swallowed as much as he could. He did not know when he would be allowed to drink again. He was proven right when the big one barked something and Filip reached up for the canteen, splashing water over Breit's chin in mid-gulp.

Breit did not know if the witch girl had done as he'd begged and not told anyone he'd said he was a spy. The leader of this partisan cell did not return to the barn and ask more questions; Breit figured he would have if the girl had mentioned anything to him. She'd probably tell the Reds when she handed him over, if he was alive for that. Thc Reds would interrogate him. The inquisitors wouldn't have to lift a finger, he'd spill everything he knew about the German dispositions in the field. His wellspring of facts and figures could help the Soviets, of course, and might still tilt the battle their way if they acted fast enough on what he told them. But if he managed somehow to slip these partisans and reach Berlin, his information would come through Lucy. The Soviets would jump on Lucy intelligence within the hour of receiving it instead of reading a report several days from now penned by some obscure commissar. He needed to speak to the Soviets from Berlin.

The *Hexe* had made it clear, he was not going to be released, it was an absurd thing to ask. He knew it when he asked, but what else could he do? Filip whispered to him this morning not to try anything, they would hurt him for it, perhaps kill him. Breit knew, if the witch turned him over to the Red Army, that would likely be the end of him. At worst, he'd be shot after his interrogation, tossed into an unmarked grave in empty Russia. At best, the long miseries of Siberia.

He had no plan to escape. If he bolted, he'd be ridden down and brought back, or shot. There were no German patrols out this morning, every available soldier was either at the front or walking the train tracks to protect them from these same partisans. No, there would be no rescue. All of them except Filip – and this included the witch – looked like they'd just as soon slit his throat as have him along. The black partisan Josef seemed to be restraining himself from doing that anyway. How could he escape? He could not calculate his chances, he lacked enough facts. He supposed his odds were poor. Where were they right now, what river was that? Where were they going? He knew only that he was surrounded and abhorred. He could not out-fight or out-ride them. He was certainly no braver than them, these men and a girl who lived in shadows under the noses of an entire German army. He would have to out-think them. They were Russians, he could do it. But when would there be an opportunity for that, when being smarter might overcome being faster, harder, nastier?

Swaying in his saddle, his rear and crotch chafed. He was perspiring under the wool jacket and hat. He conjured images of his death, from a hole in the head, or freezing in Siberia, torture in Moscow. He missed his old life, the safe one spent in classrooms, in quiet galleries and Jew basements, even two days ago beside a map table, a spy. He invented artistic ways how Picasso might treat each of his deaths. A comical birdhouse inside the hole in his head. Five bodies attached to one strange head to depict his wintry shivering. Torture, Picasso would have a Cubist's field day with that, suns and stars bursting inside a body broken into geometric bits.

Am I brave enough, Breit wondered inside the morbid gallery of his imagination, to make a break for it? I have a very valuable skin to save. I have a cause, a war to alter. I am historic. Will I try? Or will I shuffle out of the history books off to Siberia, quiet again, quiet forever? I don't know. When I became a spy, I didn't prepare myself for dying, not the way a soldier does. I am so scared.

Breit decided to gather more facts, to watch for the elements of his day, the basics of his fate. Then he would see if he owned the courage to act.

He tried to prod his horse closer to Filip's. With a few soft kicks, the animal broke into a little trot, then slowed and stumbled sideways.

'Filip,' he muttered, 'where are we going?'

A rustle of hooves rose behind Breit. He turned his head in time to see dark Josef's raised and swinging elbow. The blow caught him in the temple.

Breit would have collapsed out of the saddle but his boots snagged in the stirrups and did not let him go over. Through sizzles of pain in his skull, his senses took hold enough to tell him he was dangling, wincing into the ribs of his horse. He cowered behind a raised arm and clung to the saddle pommel with the other. He feared to sit upright into another shot from Josef. He gulped air to quell the pounding in his head. He straightened before he tumbled to the ground. The reins had slipped through his hands, hanging loose around the horse's neck. The stubborn animal began to angle down to the river. Breit blinked, doing his best to gather the reins in.

No one spoke. No one struck him again. Filip nudged his horse away to put distance between them.

CHAPTER 21

July 10
0715
outside the village of Vorskla

Katya reined in her horse. The carbine strapped across her back jangled, the pistol in her belt poked at her abdomen. Filip stopped his mount beside her. Daniel, Ivan, and Josef hung back with the German prisoner behind the crest overlooking the village, out of sight in their saddles.

The Vorskla River ran glinting behind the rows of small houses. The village was partitioned by pickets and dirt alleys. Women milled in the spaces between structures with aprons empty of bread, no chickens to feed, and no seed to toss them if there were. A few men bent in the broken fields, scavenging for unripe vegetables to eat. Filip shook his head. He was still the *starosta* of this village, and it was dying. He tugged the brim of his felt hat and rode forward without Katya. She prodded Lana and moved behind him down the long incline to the sad streets.

Approaching the village, a clutch of women looked up at the clopping horses. The women moved closer together the way penned animals do, until their hips touched, their aprons made a white barrier to the two riders. Filip was their elder. This made no difference to the old women barring his way. Filip rode into the village with a partisan.

One of the women spoke up to Filip. The elder man

had drawn himself very erect, his hands were crossed on the saddle pommel. He donned the cold posture of the brigand, of Colonel Plokhoi.

'You're back,' the woman said.

Filip nodded. His wide brim bobbed, shading his face.

'Leave him alone, Filip Filipovich,' the woman said. 'He's your brother.'

The *starosta* made no notice of her words.

'He's frightened, Filip Filipovich,' she said.

The elder lifted his eyes from the woman. He goaded his horse toward her and the three women beside her, women Katya decided were her sisters. The aprons parted and Filip rode past without another glance downward. Katya followed.

The morning street raised dust under their hooves. The northern horizon was quiet now, the sounds of the battle raging did not reach the village. Vorskla was no longer just ten kilometers from the front, the Germans had pushed the Soviet lines far back. How far, Katya did not know. But it was a bad thing that she did not hear the fighting.

Every movement in the village stopped when they rode past. The few men straightened in the fields to look over the tops of stalks and grasses, they looked like scarecrows in white billowy blouses. Women continued to gravitate toward each other, pressing shoulders and hips, whispers to ears. Filip rode to a small blue house. Its eaves were festooned with white gingerbread and shutters. Filip stopped in front of the porch. Neighbor women came on their stoops to watch and cluck. Katya saw her first child in this village. A boy, very dirty, gripped a woman's skirt and pulled it in front of him, a naive shield. Filip did not dismount. He waited, his horse shifted, the rifle on Filip's back creaked, the leather and harness rattled.

The door to the house stood open, the day was going to grow hot. Inside, the house was full of shadows. Filip stared straight ahead, some duel of wills going on with the brother inside. The man's a coward, Katya thought. He's a collaborator. Enough.

She slid off her horse and hit the ground walking. Before she'd taken two steps, the pistol was in her hand and cocked.

'Nikolai!' the *starosta* called to his brother. Katya halted.

Inside the house, footsteps dragged on the boards. A man emerged from the shadowed rooms. Katya stood in the full steppe sun and it took a moment for her to realize what she saw standing on the rickety porch.

Filip's twin.

The two old men shared the same nose, lean stature, gray grimness, everything that brothers born seconds apart can share. But in a moment Katya saw what they did not have in common. This brother was weak. Filip would truly kill him one day.

Filip spoke. 'You're coming with us.'

The twin eyed his brother with a wary grimace. 'I'm no fighter. You're the fighter.'

Katya kept herself in check. She almost spoke for Filip Filipovich, she almost said to this brother, 'And you're the traitor. Now get on a fucking horse.'

'Katya. Get the others.'

Filip did not look away from Nikolai. The eyes of the two were ensnared, the brothers' glares tangled like snakes across the dusty road. Katya tucked the pistol into her belt. She swung to her saddle and turned for the hill where the others waited with the prisoner and an extra mount. Riding away, she saw over her shoulder Nikolai turn and go back inside his house. Filip stayed in his saddle, staring after his brother, his face obscured under the big felt hat.

July 10
0800 hours
three kilometers west of Kazatskoe

The partisans, Breit the prisoner, and Nikolai the traitor rode through an eerie peace. They took their horses and the empty mount into the open, across fallow fields and wide vales of grass. The sun stood at its highest and the horses walked on their own shadows. Nothing impeded the riders' vision for many kilometers, the land sprawled even and untended. The riders were far from the fighting here and the day appeared normal, sunny and quiet. Katya was lulled for a little while by the sounds of hooves in dirt, men in saddles, and the gold of warmth on her skin.

None of the men spoke. Filip rode in front, leading his twin brother to Kazatskoe. Daniel and Ivan came next, riding on either side of the German. Breit kept his mouth shut since Josef had clouted him, and he rode better, too, wanting no more attention for himself. Good, Katya thought, she had enough to worry about. Josef came at the rear. She turned to look at him from time to time to be sure the man was still there, separate and grim.

She cued her horse ahead of Daniel, Breit, and Ivan. She passed Nikolai. The brother's head was down, as though riding to his gallows. She sidled up next to Filip. The *starosta* did not turn his head.

'Are you angry with me, Filip?'

'Yes. I don't want to do this.'

Katya leaned from her saddle to touch the old man's forearm. 'I know.'

'He's my brother.'

Now Filip swiveled his face to her. His eyes glistened.

'It's easy, Witch, when he's not right here behind me. It's easy to talk about how I'll do this and that. But I understand him. Better than anybody.'

His long nose was sharper than any feature of the landscape. His eyes were fixed on nothing Katya could see with him.

'I'm sorry, Filip Filipovich.'

The *starosta* nodded, his big brim dipped.

'We were all so hungry, Witch. I'm sure you don't understand that kind of hunger. The Germans gave us food because Nikolai helped them. They stopped punishing our village, stopped taking our men. Nikolai saved us. I ate the food. I lived in my house. I'm as bad as him. I won't judge him.'

Katya looked into the sky, her former battlefield, and thought of the danger she'd met up there in the past year. She and all the warriors, on air and ground and sea, they forgot. They were young and they bled, they gathered the war to themselves like their own hell and they did not see this old man and his old twin brother, how war does not always come in a different uniform or bursts of flame but may come as your brother, your village, your own soul. What can war not break? Nothing, if it can break a family. She blinked at a sudden tear. She turned her cheek away from Filip, to let it dry in the breeze before she spoke.

'Is he there, do you think? The pilot?' She kept to herself that his name was Leonid, she hid in her breast who the pilot was to her.

Filip sighed and considered. 'Yes. Nikolai said he was there three days ago. With so much going on at the front, I doubt there's been time to take him anywhere else.'

'Did you ask him if he knew the pilot's name?'

'He doesn't. Nikolai asked ... other questions for the Germans.'

'What did he look like?'

'Average. Brown hair. Slender.'

'What color eyes? Does your brother remember?'

'His eyes were too swollen to see their color, Witch.'

She envisioned this. Leonid, she thought. God, Leonid. She asked, 'What will happen if we don't get to him?'

'He'll be taken back to Germany as a slave. Or shot.'

The *starosta* said all this without emotion. He almost relished making these dire descriptions and the prediction, dispensing for Katya some pain to counterweight his own agony. He'd guessed the rescue of the pilot meant more to the Witch than freeing a downed Soviet flyer. Katya said nothing more. Filip was entitled. She'd brought him out here, to face his twin and save Leonid, for her own purposes. She pulled in her reins and let Filip ride past, then came Nikolai, the same man made twice, their hurt borne on two horses. Daniel and Ivan with the prisoner caught up to her.

'Collaborator,' Ivan sneered loud enough for Nikolai to hear. Daniel added nothing. Ivan jerked his head at Breit. 'At least this son of a bitch wears a uniform. He won a medal.'

They rode for another hour, skirting Tomarovka on their right. They cloaked themselves in the safety of the open, riding as innocuous peasants. From a distance they'd look smudged and humble, posing no danger. Besides, the Germans were not on the lookout for partisans during the daylight hours. The night was when the partisans struck.

At 0915 hours the village of Kazatskoe appeared, an oasis of farm buildings in an expanse of greens and brown. From her saddle five kilometers away, the village appeared to Katya something dreamy and liquid, standing in a pool of shimmering heat mirage against the earth. Three silos rose as centurions, the rest of the village hunkered around them, homes and outbuildings. Five days ago when the battle started, this place was only four kilometers from the front lines. Now it was a drained place, intact but emptied. The Germans had billeted here, fortified the little town, then moved north with their attack.

They left silence, like a spoiled well. There should be tractors, she thought, there should be a blacksmith's anvil clanging through this heat, laundry snapping on lines. The war was here in the ghosts of sound.

Josef trotted forward.

'You all stay here,' he ordered with his sunken-eyed intensity. The riders stopped.

Nikolai did not turn his horse, he fixed his eyes on Kazatskoe and his back on Filip.

'Hiwi.' Josef snarled the curse name for collaborators at the rear of Nikolai's head. 'Turn around, *hiwi*.'

Nikolai made no move to comply. Big Ivan grunted. He wheeled his mount beside the twin and snatched the reins to bring Nikolai around to face Josef. The prisoner Breit gritted his teeth, he knew already that Josef was no one to ignore. Filip could not watch. He hung his head and the brim of his hat again covered his eyes.

'The *hiwi* will take me into the town,' Josef said. 'We'll find the house where the pilot is. Then we'll come back and decide what to do. *Hiwi*.'

'Yes.' Nikolai answered with a quaver in his chin, like a man answering a judge, or the Reaper.

'Know now I will kill you the instant you do anything other than what I tell you.'

'I know.'

'If you take me to any house but the one the pilot is in, you won't come back from that village.'

Nikolai rested his eyes on black Josef. Seconds passed in the crackling quiet field. The twin seemed to soothe, a man finally at his destined place, at his gallows.

'Yes,' answered Nikolai.

Josef swung in his saddle to face Breit.

'Nazi. If you twitch the wrong way, Daniel will shoot you out of the saddle. Tell him, Filip Filipovich.'

Josef swung his horse now to Katya.

'Witch,' he said, 'I'll find your pilot for you.'

Katya was stunned. Josef tipped his hat brim to her and turned. Nikolai fell in and the two rode toward Kazatskoe.

She watched them go, amazed at the turn in Josef. She trusted what he'd said.

Ivan nestled his horse beside Katya, gazing off at Kazatskoe with her. Daniel was restive. He dropped from his saddle to grab a stem of grass, then climbed back up to chew on the blade. He settled behind the German, as though measuring Breit for a bullet. Filip sat his horse alone, head slumped away from the hot world. The four of them waited like this under the sun, sweating and without shade.

'I hope we find him,' Ivan said. 'Is this pilot your lover?'

Katya was uneasy with the question. 'Lover.' It was a term from peacetime, when girls and boys paired off like that, not when they were forced to spend years away from home – changing and hardening years – not when they died by the hundreds and thousands every day. And there was Filip, lonely and hating being here, a man who'd claimed he would murder his brother. Could Katya have a boyfriend in front of poor Filip?

'Yes,' she said without intending. 'Yes,' she said, needing it to be so.

'Good for you,' said Daniel from behind the German. He spit out the weed and climbed down to pluck a new one. He looked up at Katya. He seemed wounded somehow by her smile.

Josef and Nikolai were gone no more than thirty minutes. They returned across the long field; at a distance they rode on shimmers from the heat. Katya wanted to ride to them but Ivan stopped her. 'We wait,' he said, 'like we were told.'

The two came slowly, no need for haste and attention. Josef rode behind Nikolai, who kept his head down, the match to his brother Filip. When they were close, the twins did not look at each other.

'There's a house on the western edge of the village,' Josef said. 'I couldn't get a look inside the windows. But there are two guards. The *hiwi* says the guards were there a couple of days ago when he was taken to that house.'

'He's in there,' Nikolai said.

Katya's heart gripped. There was a pilot in that house. Was it Leonid?

'What are we going to do?' Daniel asked, standing beside his saddle. 'Wait until dark?'

'No,' Josef decided, scratching deep into his beard. 'The village is mostly deserted. There's maybe two dozen Germans spread out, staying out of the sun. If we go in after curfew and we're spotted, we're definitely partisans. I say now, while there's only the two guards.'

'How do we get inside?' Ivan asked.

Josef shook his head. 'I don't know yet.'

The sun beat on them pondering this question. Katya waited for Josef to concoct a plan. The horses shifted hoof to hoof. Filip never raised his gaze from beneath his brim.

Katya spoke.

'Nikolai?'

'What?' the twin answered. He'd become more lively than his brother. Perhaps he hoped to wipe away his stain by helping free the downed pilot.

'The two guards. Were they the same ones who were there three days ago?'

'I don't … let me see. Yes, I think yes. I'm sure at least one of them was.'

'Alright. Ivan, how much food do we have with us?'

Ivan swung his backpack around and dug into it. He pulled from it a canteen and a broad, hard loaf.

'Bread and water,' Katya said. 'Perfect.'

Josef asked, 'You have an idea, Witch?' The dark man

looked at her with new eyes today. Katya worried all the time who in the partisan cell might be the spy, who had betrayed the Night Witches and the partisans beside the railroad. She'd been troubled that it might have been Josef, he seemed so distant and embittered. She began to believe it would not prove to be him.

She pointed at the twin. 'At least one of the guards has seen Nikolai before, right? He knows Nikolai is an interpreter.'

She swung the finger to the *starosta,* stricken in his saddle. Filip seemed to have swapped roles with his traitor twin, he bore the millstone of guilt now.

'Filip will go instead. The guard won't know the difference. I'll pose as a nurse and go with him carrying the food. We'll tell the guards we're waiting for the Gestapo, they're going to interrogate the prisoner again. We're there to feed the pilot and get him ready. We'll get one of the guards to come inside. Then Josef, you take care of the one outside.'

'And the guard inside, Witch?'

She thought of Leonid's face, too bashed to tell the color of his eyes. His eyes were blue. Sky blue. She fingered the knife at her hip, the pistol in her belt.

'I'll do what I have to.' She looked over to the *starosta*. The old man still eyed the warm ground.

Josef turned in his saddle to the soldiers Daniel and Ivan, bookends around the German prisoner. Breit did not understand anything being said, his eyes darted to every speaker.

'Alright,' Josef said. 'When both guards are down, you two come with the Nazi and the extra horse for the pilot. Witch, you and Filip ...'

'I'll go.'

Nikolai sat straight in his saddle. The twin spoke with his chin high; his brother peered out from under his brim to listen.

'Filip can stay here where it's safe. I'll go. They know me.'

Katya cut her eyes to Josef. Even under such a sun, his gaze was hooded.

'I'll go,' Nikolai said again. 'I've done enough to my brother.'

Josef growled, 'Shut up, *hiwi*.' He faced Filip. 'Old man? Go or stay?'

Filip raised his head to his twin. Katya watched them stare at each other, the two faces so identical, and so different.

'No,' the *starosta* said. 'Nikolai will tell the guards. He'll get the Witch killed and he'll make a run for it. You can't trust him. I'll go.'

Filip pivoted to Katya. The elder nodded at her. The resolve she'd seen earlier on Nikolai's face was now on Filip's, the gallows. 'I'll do what I have to.'

Josef wasted no time for the tempest on Nikolai's face; the twin wanted to object but everyone had turned their backs to him. Daniel swung up in his stirrups, a fresh weed clamped in his teeth. Ivan handed the bread and canteen to Katya.

'I'll be one minute behind you, Witch,' Josef said. 'Count to sixty before you make a move. Start counting when you get inside. I'll be watching. If you hear gunshots, you've got to act quick. The rest of the garrison will come running, we'll only have a few seconds. Daniel, you and Ivan stay a hundred meters back. When you see us come out with the pilot, bring the horses fast. Bring the German, and the *hiwi,* too. If either one of them flinches the wrong way, kill him. Filip, give me your rifle. Witch, the pistol.'

The *starosta* unstrapped his carbine from his back and handed it over. The German guards would not let any Russian come near them with guns, not even a turncoat interpreter and a peasant woman in men's clothing. Josef reached for the loaf of bread in Katya's hands. He ripped it open at one end, the stiff crust snapped and flaked. He scooped out a plug of soft bread.

'Give me your knife.'

Katya pulled the blade from her belt. Josef unsheathed it and slid the knife inside the crust, then packed the white pulp on top of the grip to hide it. He handed the loaf back to Katya. The bread had an odd and deadly weight.

Josef nodded to Katya.

'The blue house on the far western street. There's a broken shutter on the front. Look for the guards. You'll see them.'

'Blue house. Shutter,' she repeated.

'One minute.'

'Once we're inside. I understand.'

'Good. Go get your pilot, Witch.'

Katya moved out, Filip at her side. She remembered the last words of Vera. *Go get him.*

July 10
1030 hours
one kilometer west of Kazatskoe

Without hurry, Filip and Katya rode toward the western rim of the village. The sun seemed not to have moved from its noon-high perch. It glowered on the two riders, hot and intent, in audience to the rescue they would attempt. Katya sweated in her loose wool coat. She wanted shade and rest. She wanted not to be afraid. A few times during the ride to the village, she glanced behind her to spot Josef. The man rode far to their left, then was nowhere to be seen.

Filip dug out a kerchief and handed it to Katya.

'Put this around your hair, Witch. You need to look more like a peasant.'

She mopped her brow with the red rag, then quickly tied back her hair with it.

Filip asked, 'Have you ever killed a man?'

Katya thought of her missions, hundreds of raids. 'I've dropped bombs.'

'I mean ever killed a man looking into his face.'

'No.'

'I haven't, either,' the *starosta* said.

The elder raised his eyes and looked around him, at the nearing village, dark soil hot as tar under the horses' hooves. He gazed into a blazing sky. He grimaced under his hat.

Katya cradled the loaf in her arm, sensing the knife stashed inside it. It was strange to be in this world, to have a reason to kill. A need to kill. She thought of the weight of a life, how heavy would it be in your hand if the years could be stacked? Would it weigh less than the knife? Yes. A knife, a bullet, a shard of shrapnel, they all outweigh any life. She was sure men had died under her Night Witch wings, and she never once felt the weight of their deaths. It was insanity for it to be so. She rode toward this madness with a life tucked inside the bread, held easily in one hand. It was strange because this was not the real world, girls and old men going off to kill; this was a war world, temporary, a nightmare where the only way to wake up was to stay asleep and kill enough. And it was strange, too, because now she was not afraid, the twisting in her stomach was gone. She said Leonid's name out loud, to announce the release of her fear.

'Is that your pilot?' Filip asked.

'Leonid Lumanov. Yes. My pilot.'

Less than fifty dwellings made up the hamlet, with a half dozen large barns clustered near the silos. Nothing moved in the streets or alleys, the barns were empty and cool, a handful of scattered military vehicles baked in the open. A wind vane creaked somewhere. Their horses made the only living sounds.

The blue house with a busted shutter stood near the end of its dirt street. She cued her horse toward it.

She opened the canteen, her mouth was parched. She swallowed and offered the water to the elder. He declined. The look on Filip's face was kindly, his many wrinkles arranged themselves into a melancholy welcome of what awaited them. It was a brave face. Impulsively, Katya reached to touch the old man's arm.

'You're the interpreter. You were here three days ago. I'm a nurse. We'll get inside and I'll start counting. Even if it's not Leonid in there, we're going to get the pilot out. Just move when I move.'

'Yes, Witch. I hope it's your pilot.'

Katya felt the twinge of both sides of this coin, that it would not be Leonid lying beaten in that blue house, scared that it would be.

'We can do this,' Filip said, squeezing her hand before letting go.

They rode up the last of the street. A curl of smoke issued from the porch of the house, a guard sat there on the steps smoking, his machine pistol lay across his lap. He peered at them across the sunny day. They did not dismount, staying in their saddles until the guard rose and donned his helmet. He took a few steps into the lane. He did not toss away the cigarette but kept it between the fingers he slipped around his weapon.

'Ja? Was ist los?'

Filip answered in German. He indicated himself, then Katya. She held up the loaf of bread, feeling the heft of this guard's life inside it. Another guard appeared around the corner of the house. He called to the one in the street. They waved to each other with lackluster motions, dulled by the heat and boring duty. The second guard eyed the two riders and went back to his station at the rear of the little house. The soldier in the street barked at them to come down and tie up their horses. He returned the cigarette to his lips and waited.

Filip and Katya dismounted. Katya felt as though the point of the knife inside the bread were held to her own innards. Filip was intent and silent. They tied the horses to the porch railing. Katya stroked Lana before moving away, to compose herself.

The guard climbed the steps. Filip went second, Katya, with the loaf tucked under her arm, came last. She walked across the threshold and began the count. *One.* The reek that assaulted her inside was unmistakably human.

The room was bare, stripped down to the wood floors and plaster walls. A single chair, stiff-backed and old, stood in the center. Katya knew the chair in an instant for what it was, like this house, it was an innocent thing become wicked. *Two,* she thought.

Leonid lay curled in the far right corner.

Katya heard herself gasp. She flicked her eyes to the guard, but Filip covered the sound with conversation and the guard made no reaction to her. *Three.*

She reined herself in tight, she knew she would dash across the room to him if she did not. *Four.* Leonid did not open his eyes, he lay motionless with his wrists between his knees. She approached him, holding the bread out now like a gift, to keep both her hands full so she would not cradle him. She knelt beside him. She set the loaf on the floor. *Nine.* Leonid's face was bruised and swollen, dark and straining the skin, the brutal fruit of his interrogations. Had Nikolai stood here asking the questions in Russian while this was done? She glanced back to Filip and saw him staring down at Leonid, wondering the same. The guard asked Filip a question. Even in a foreign tongue Katya could tell Filip's reply was terse. *Eighteen.*

She stroked Leonid's hair, to gentle him awake. His hair was matted, filthy. His ear was crusted brown from blood, probably a burst eardrum. His body stank with the biting tart of urine. Katya pressed her hand harder to his forehead. His eyelids flickered. *Twenty-seven.*

She did not say his name, the guard would catch that. She murmured, 'Lie still. It's me, we're here for you. Pretend to be unconscious. Can you walk?'

Leonid's head bobbed one tremor under her hand.

'Be ready,' she said.

Thirty-five.

Katya's heart beat like an engine when she took up the bread and rose from the floor. She turned to Filip and the guard. The soldier smiled at her. She resisted any urge to determine anything about this German, his age, skin tone, his own smells of cigarette and summer wool. She returned his smile and looked only at his hands on his machine pistol. She counted *Forty.* Filip faded behind the guard.

She walked forward. The chair in the middle of the room stood in her path to the guard. She envisioned Leonid in it, tied to it. She held out the loaf, hiding the opened end behind her palm.

'Would you like a piece of bread?'

Forty-five.

The guard slung both his elbows over his machine pistol hanging across his waist. He nodded at the bread, yes, he would like some. And you shall have it, thought Katya.

Fifty-two.

She tore away a portion of the bread, keeping the opened end facing her breast. The guard reached for the offered chunk. The black metal haft of the knife was there, ready for her fingers. She dug her hand into the crust, as though to pull for the soldier another hunk. Filip slipped closer behind him. She did not look into the guard's face as the man brought the bread up to his mouth.

Sixty.

She closed her hand around the knife's haft, buried in

the cool spongy bread. She took a step toward the guard, to have her momentum driving forward. She let her mind flee for one beat to Leonid in the corner behind her, to the purple of his lips and sockets, his stench, mentally touching him like she had touched the horse outside, for calm and power. The gray of a German uniform was one stride away, crumbs tumbled down the buttons. The knife was held tight in her hand. She kept her eyes fixed to the guard's chest, to the spot above the dangling gun, beneath the crumbs, at the heart.

Katya plunged the dagger deep above a pocket on the tunic. The German's hands tried to rise but Filip pinned his arms at the elbows. The haft of the knife shook with the violence of the guard's reaction, the man's throat was plugged by a swallow of bread, he choked out a cry, the knife handle jerked loose from her grip. She was shocked by this because she thought she'd held it with all her might, believed she'd stabbed the blade into the man's working heart as hard as she could, but the German still stood, wrestling in Filip's old grasp, he did not go down, the knife stuck in his chest, not dead. He made another strangled cry, bucking in Filip's arms, twisting back and forth, left and right. Filip strained to hold him. Katya followed the handle with seeking and urgent hands, to catch it and draw it out to shove it in again, to cut the man's throat if she had to, but Filip could not hold him still and the haft evaded her, she struggled at the guard's chest to grab the knife and could not.

The guard coughed out the gob of bread, the wad hit Katya. He screamed. One of his hands broke from Filip's clench. He fumbled to lift the machine pistol. The knife handle, slick with blood, slipped through her fingers again. Where was Josef? Where were the others?

Panic jettisoned into her blood. Filip lost his grasp, the guard reeled back a step from her, knocking over the chair. Filip tried again to control the frenzied guard but was thrown off. The soldier had both hands on his gun now. The knife protruded from his chest like the key to a mad wind-up doll.

The soldier twisted away from her, badly out of balance but keeping his feet. He juggled the barrel of the gun to raise it at Filip. The old man jumped sideways and the quick burst from the machine pistol hit him in the hip. Filip went down yelling. Staggering, the guard turned his head for Katya. He licked blood off his lips. The machine pistol wavered to find her.

She would not die motionless. She hurled herself at the guard.

A strong hand snared her from behind. She was stopped and flung aside.

Leonid flashed past her, another mad doll, this one broken and filthy but infuriated. He was on the guard in a single long step, shoving the machine pistol down with one hand. He grabbed the haft of the knife with his other fist and plucked the blade from the guard's chest with a strength born out of fury, then hacked it into the German two, three, four more times, in and out, dicing the man's heart until the guard's knees were on the floor, and again Leonid drove in the knife.

Leonid breathed hard. He left the dagger in the guard and stood, teetering, emptied of rage and strength. Katya caught him before he sank beside the corpse. There were only seconds left until the rest of the German garrison hurried to this little blue house on the edge of the village to investigate the gunshots.

The door burst open.

Josef filled the opening. His pistol was leveled. The old partisan stepped into the bare room. His mitts were bloody. He took in the dead German with one glance, saw the rips in the soldier's chest and the spreading pool beneath him, and raised an eyebrow at Katya. Without a word, he moved to Filip on the floor. He gathered the old man to his feet.

'Can you ride, old man?'

Filip made no reply. Supported by Josef, he scowled and tested his wounded hip with a few struggling steps.

Katya led Leonid toward the open door. The clatter of saddles and horseshoes swirled in the street outside. He hesitated in Katya's grasp.

'Leonya, we've got to hurry.'

'The rest of the garrison is coming,' Josef added with urgency. 'We have to get out now.'

'No,' Leonid said, resisting Katya's tugs. He twisted in her arms, pointing behind him into the house, at a closed door. 'A woman. In that room. Another ... prisoner.'

Josef left Filip. The *starosta* hobbled standing alone, favoring his right side. His trousers were torn below the belt where the bullet caught him. Josef sprang to the closed door.

'Get them outside,' he ordered Katya. 'The horses are there.'

In that instant, gunfire spat from the rear of the building. The shots were answered by others, farther away, burps of bullets from German weapons. Ivan's voice drilled through the walls and the rifle reports, 'Dammit, Witch, get out of the house!'

Ivan was holding off the approaching German troops. Daniel must be outside with the horses and the German prisoner and Nikolai. Josef crashed into the back room. Katya impelled Leonid forward.

Daniel appeared on the porch, his pistol raised. In that moment, Josef emerged from the room with a woman clinging to his arm. She was starved and frail, her skirt and blouse stained; she'd been a beautiful girl before the abuse she suffered in this house. Now she was a dirty wraith.

The gun battle at the rear of the house surged. Ivan

shouted again to Katya, firing his carbine.

In the bright doorway, Daniel did not lower his pistol. He looked across the room, past the corpse on the floor and the spilled chair and blood at the girl wavering on Josef's arm. She said something, too weak for Katya to hear over the gunshots outside.

Daniel aimed the pistol at Josef.

'Let her go,' he said.

Josef stepped forward, drawing the feeble girl close. Filip gimped backward from Daniel's raised gun until he stood beside Josef and the girl.

'This is your wife,' Josef said.

Daniel answered, 'We're taking two horses. Let her go.'

Katya tensed. Outside the horses nickered, frightened by the gunfire coming quicker and closer. Leonid swayed on her arm, bewildered. The girl looked at Daniel with frenzied eyes, confused. Why was her husband aiming a gun at the people who'd come with him to rescue her and the poor Soviet pilot?

She got her answer when Katya spoke.

'You're the spy in the cell,' she said.

'Shut up, Witch.'

The girl's face twitched. She tried to move to her husband but Josef would not release her. Daniel took a step closer, sighting down his pistol at Josef's head.

'Let us go, Josef. Please.'

Katya thought of all the dead betrayed for this man's wife. Their deaths choked the room, partisans and Witches. Leonid, nearly beaten to death. And herself, almost killed beside the tracks when Daniel told Ivan to blow the charge. She had no weapon, the knife was plunged in the German.

'Please, Josef,' Daniel said again, cocking his head, and Katya knew these would be his last words before shooting.

Filip hobbled, the only motion in the room. He slipped

himself sideways in front of the girl.

'You asked me if I can ride,' he said over his shoulder to Josef, staring at the little mouth of Daniel's gun.

'No,' the *starosta* said.

With that, Filip dragged himself in front of Josef. Behind him the old partisan flashed his pistol up. The girl screamed and Daniel fired. Josef's gun roared, and for an exploding moment the two fired at each other across the barren room. Then Daniel crashed down, his chest dotted with three punctures. Filip fell next.

The gunfight outside the house broke off. Heavy steps pounded onto the porch. Big Ivan bolted into the room, his rifle ready. He stood dumb at what he found.

The girl had thrown up her hands in terror, still screaming. Josef let her loose. He knelt beside Filip. The elder croaked something with lifted head and fists balled in Josef's coat. The girl stifled. Katya heard the *starosta* mutter, she caught only his brother's name. Filip released Josef. The old man sighed and sagged to the floor.

Josef did not pause. He leaped and came to Katya to take Leonid from her, hurrying the pilot out the door, past thunderstruck Ivan. Katya followed. The girl was left behind, rigid in her horror pose, staring without believing at Daniel, the dead traitor, her hero.

Katya shoved Ivan out the door. Leonid was already in a saddle. Josef moved fast to get onto his own horse. Ivan lumbered to his mount. Katya stared across the wide steppe, at the two dust clouds roiling behind the *hiwi* Nikolai and the escaping prisoner Breit, galloping away.

Katya flew into her saddle. Down the street a rifle snapped, a bullet whizzed past. All the riders kicked their horses and bolted. Katya saw how Leonid rode, not well and barely steady. Ivan stayed close beside him. The four riders lit out into the fields, the thud of rifles bit beneath their hoofbeats. The *hiwi* and the German absconded in different directions, both away from Kazatskoe. Nikolai scurried back to his home village. Breit ran anywhere, away from the partisans, away from the village where the guards, his countrymen, were shooting at everything on horseback.

The guards fired after the partisans for seconds but hit none of them through the dust billows rising behind the horses. Katya kept her eyes on fading Nikolai and, farther to the north, Breit, doing his best to stay in the saddle.

She pulled alongside Josef.

'Give me my pistol!' she shouted.

Josef glanced past his bouncing shoulder at the receding village, at Filip. He reached into his waistband and took out her gun. He handed it over across the bounding neck of his own horse.

'Go get the prisoner!'

Katya cut her eyes to Nikolai, then to Breit. She could catch either of them easily.

Josef shouted again, reading her expression.

'We have orders, Witch! The German!'

'No!'

Old dark Josef took one more look over his shoulder, to the little house where the brave *starosta* clutched him and spoke his last wish. He'd heard Filip's last bloody whisper, the traitorous twin Nikolai's name, and what else?

Katya turned to wheel her horse away. Nikolai and Breit grew more distant by the second.

Josef looked out to Nikolai. There was no more time to choose between vendetta and his orders.

'Go!' Josef shouted. 'I'll deal with fucking Plokhoi. Go!'

'Take care of Leonid! I'll catch you!'

With that, Katya yanked Lana's head around. The horse responded like a *dzhigitka* mount, digging in her hooves and whirling quick and nimble. Katya clamped tight with her thighs and struck a furious pace straight at

Nikolai. She tucked herself low over Lana's lathering neck, clicking and urging the horse, *'Tick, tick, hiya!'* absorbing the pumping and pounding of the animal, swelling with it to do the murder that grew closer with every reach of Lana's long strides.

Katya snared one last glimpse of the prisoner Breit off to her right. The man was a terrible rider, he bounced like he was on a camel. She could have run circles around him. But as clumsy a horseman as the German was, he'd put enough distance between him and Katya speeding the other direction to disappear over a low rise in the steppe, and he was gone.

I hope you are a spy, Katya thought, matching her hips and arms to the rhythm of her sprinting horse. I hope you are and you go to Berlin and you help us. Or I hope your horse steps in a hole and you break your neck. Go, Colonel Breit. Count your blessings.

Katya laid her eyes to the *hiwi* and galloped.

Nikolai saw her coming. He did his best to outrace her but he stood no chance with a Cossack in the coming saddle. Katya closed the distance and there was nothing the *hiwi* could do.

Filip is clan, Katya thought. He took me to Leonid, then he died to save us.

He is clan. This was his wish.

Nikolai, as though hearing her thoughts broadcast over the steppe, reined in his horse. The last hundred meters of grassland rushed beneath her. The pistol in her hand weighed nothing, it was the weight of the life she rode up to, the traitor. Nikolai lifted his hands, surrendering.

'Witch,' he pleaded.

Katya gave him no chance to say more. She stopped two meters away and raised the gun. She aimed it into his forehead, into the hawk-nosed face that was Filip's. This angered her more, that Nikolai should have such a hero's face. This *hiwi* would not profane that face any longer, and he would not take it with him to Hell. She pulled the trigger.

She circled the fallen body. She looked down, there was no question he was dead. She stuck the warm pistol in her waist and took the reins of Nikolai's emptied horse, the partisans always needed extra mounts.

She sped off, eager to catch up to Leonid. Nikolai's horse loped beside her. She bent low over Lana's mane and let the blowing strands graze her cheeks. The reins felt good in her hands.

She'd killed a man today, a traitor, and attacked another, a German, trying to kill him, too. She spurred the horses away from the twin and the soldier, leaving their corpses well behind. She rode hard for several kilometers until she saw Josef, Ivan, and Leonid in the distance. They'd slowed. None of the enemy garrison from the village pursued them, the German war vehicles could not travel as fast over the roadless Russian steppe as horsemen. Leonid was too beaten to be taken anywhere but back to the partisan cell to rest and heal. Josef would tell Colonel Bad the prisoner Breit had been killed in the action, the German had tried to escape and paid for it. But she had come through. She'd saved Leonid. The spy in their cell, bastard Daniel, was exposed and handed the bill for his treachery, in front of his wife. Filip was old, and he died a memorable way, strong and selfless. A tear cooled in the wind against her cheek. Katya wanted to whoop out loud, a cry for Vera, for Filip.

Instead, she pulled the bandanna out of her hair and threw it away. She tugged the reins of Nikolai's mount to bring the horse closer alongside Lana. When the two horses were shoulder to shoulder, she pulled her boots from her stirrups, coiled her knees, and leaped to stand, one foot each on the two rocking saddles.

Like this Katya rode past Ivan, Josef, and Leonid. She rode with her bloody arms widespread into the vast and open day.

DEATH RIDE

The armored clashes around Prokhorovka have attained almost legendary status as the greatest armored combat of World War II, and perhaps the greatest of all time.

David M. Glantz and Jonathan M. House
The Battle of Kursk

The 5th Guards Tank Army delivered a frontal attack against crack German panzer divisions which, without an essential superiority in forces, could at best result in driving the enemy back. Since the Germans in turn were also assembling forces and were preparing to continue their ongoing offensive, a large tank battle was in prospect, which indeed, broke out during the day on 12 July.

Soviet General Staff Study
The Battle of Kursk, 1943

... Citadel was to be a veritable death ride.

Major General F. W. von Mellenthin
Panzer Battles

CHAPTER 22

July 10
1030 hours
Hill 256.6
near Teterevino,
alongside the Prokhorovka road

Luis drummed his fingers on the warm metal of the turret. His tapping made no sound he could hear above the thrum of the Tiger's idling engine.

For minutes he'd been watching the motorcycle courier course from the west across the steppe. On the western approaches to Prokhorovka, *Leibstandarte*'s tanks and grenadiers were finally outside the deep defense works of the Soviets. These fields were untrammeled, a fresh, undulating table without the gargantuan grazes of tank ditches, bunkers, and trenches that marred the lanes to Oboyan.

Luis watched the motorcycle. He grew bored waiting. From his vantage on this hill, he noted how the land fell away to the north, sloping into shallow valleys that shaped the basin of the Psel River. In the eastern distance, close to Prokhorovka, he glimpsed patches of yellow, swaths of sunflowers, vibrant and misfit on this cloudy day.

The motorcycle skidded closer. Luis climbed out of the turret to receive the message standing high on the Tiger. He would not hop down into the mud. He looked at his watch. Damn *Totenkopf*, he thought. They should have taken their objective hours ago. He turned away from the sputtering motorcycle to face north, where *Totenkopf* struggled to cross a bend in the Psel River and overrun a key hill. The Reds were putting up a tough defense in the many small settlements along the riverbank. The sounds of the fighting crackled up from the river basin under a smoky shroud in the hazy late morning. *Totenkopf* was held up on the left flank: This delayed the start of the assault by the other two divisions south of the river, *Das Reich* and *Leibstandarte*. Luis again traveled in his mind back to the dark map room, imagining the long poles waiting to push the three SS blocks eastward. He stood on his tank, idling with the Tiger under his boots and the long poles in his head. The motorcycle rider slid closer in the muck until he rode beneath the fat barrel of the main gun.

Luis leaned down for the message, a yellow sheet folded and taped over. The courier was spattered with mud. The soldier did not wait for Luis to read the note but gunned his throttle and puttered off, spraying the Tiger.

Luis read the two lines of the message. The attack was to resume at 1045 hours. The objectives for his division were to clean out Komsomolets state farm on the Prokhorovka road, then capture Hill 241.6, just east of the town. *Totenkopf* couldn't be waited on any longer.

He stayed on the shuddering deck alone for another minute, surveying the battlefield. Far to his left flowed the Psel. On the right ran the Prokhorovka road and a parallel railway mound. In between was this long stretch of steppe, an alley about five kilometers wide.

This attack had three prongs: *Totenkopf* to the north across the river, *Das Reich* in the south below the road and rail tracks, and *Leibstandarte* in the middle. The other two divisions had more tanks: *Das Reich* possessed almost seventy tanks, *Totenkopf* over eighty. But theirs were mostly the impotent Mark IIIs. *Das Reich* was left with a dozen and a half Mark IVs and only one Tiger; *Totenkopf* had two dozen Mark IVs and just two Tigers. *Leibstandarte* operated sixty-seven tanks, forty-one of them Mark IVs, and four Tigers. Even though *Leibstandarte* had not fully regrouped after its pivot away from Oboyan, it was still the most potent of the three SS divisions. So it was the force chosen to go up the gut in the onslaught on Prokhorovka.

The mission for *Leibstandarte* was a simple one: Lead the charge to Prokhorovka, and crush everything in the way. *Totenkopf* was already encountering running battles in and out of the small farm villages and river lowlands. In another fifteen minutes when the full attack started, *Das Reich* would have to charge ahead on the other side of the road and rail line, through scattered forests and rolling knolls where the Reds could duck and counter-punch. *Leibstandarte* in the middle stared across a mostly level plain where visibility would be exceptional, where enemies would face little but each other. Luis thought of a bullring, where nothing separated the combatants but their wills to kill and survive. He fingered the hilt of the SS knife at his belt. He searched again for the partisan's pulse in his hand and found it. He turned to the turret, to the raised hatch cover for the mark of Erich Thoma and found it, too, brown and flaking, no longer blood but like the partisan, a memory of blood.

The fourteen tanks of his company began to jerk forward, firming into their wedges and positions around him, dustless over the damp earth. His own driver waited for his command. The long poles in the faraway map room waited, too. The sunflowers in the gray distance beyond Komsomolets farm called to him. Luis had always liked sunflowers, a very Spanish bloom, evoking long hot days and idleness.

'He llegado,' he spoke to the Red fighters, the angry

host standing hard between him and the sunflowers' gold. *I have come.* I have come for the honor of the Blue Division. I have come for my father and for Spain. I have come for the lost parts of me. *Soy la Daga.*

July 10
1125 hours

The first seconds of the assault stunned him. Cropland and grasses as far as Luis could see, which had been swaying in the dreary wind moments before, now rose together and advanced. Twenty thousand men and weapons, three hundred revving tanks and assault guns, all stirred at once, as though the plates of the earth had shifted; the ground itself seemed to slide forward. The gray-clad grenadier regiments of the three SS divisions put their guns in their hands and their boots into the soil and river and stomped east, over the tracks, across the florid flat steppe. Then came the first flights of air cover. The Luftwaffe's Henschel 129s droned in slow and wicked, searching for targets in the fields and villages ahead, and above them the sirens of the diving Stukas began to whine in powered dives. There was inconceivable German power concentrated here. The world tilted east at the Russians and Luis urged his Tiger to join the rolling crest. He wondered what the Reds could do to stop them. He unwrapped a packet of crackers and chewed, almost too excited to swallow; he had to guzzle from his canteen to get the crackers down.

The first answering cannonade whistled in from across the Psel. Damn *Totenkopf,* Luis thought again, they can't even keep the Reds busy enough in their own sector to stop them from firing at us south of the river. The rounds landed wildly among his panzers, striking nothing but damp ground and flinging muddy clumps. Luis did not batten down his hatch. He kept his eyes on the dark ten thousands walking and riding around him into the Russian defenders of Komsomolets. He was not impatient or jealous that these others came along, too. He was not afraid he would die today. He laid his hands on the quivering, creeping Tiger. Men and machines kept pace around the tank, believing in this machine as a salvation. Balthasar and the hidden crew waited for his order, and then whoever he chose would die instead of him.

In the next second a hundred reasons for doubting the magic of his life tore through the sky from the north. Like locusts came a screeching mass of rockets, Katyushas, the feared Stalin organs. The missiles rode on comet tails against the charcoal daylight and ripped into the *Leibstandarte* lines. The explosions pounded on the earth in fantastic rhythm, one boom scarcely separated from the next. The rockets pelted with the speed of a wild heartbeat, and the panzergrenadiers could leap neither left nor right under them but only fall to their bellies where they were and cover their ears. Luis ordered the driver to stop under the hail, soldiers were sprawled in the Tiger's path. He ducked in the hatch, listening to the Valkyrie screams of the rockets. A few eruptions came close to his Tiger. The Katyushas were not precision weapons. They were designed to sow havoc and fear, but they could kill what they hit. He stayed low in the fuselage until the last rocket fell. His loader cast him a bemused grin across the giant breech.

'Raining, Captain?'

Luis felt no friendship for these men in his crew. They were his tools. But he'd never been one to let his *banderillas* grow dull or rusty, the spikes were sharpened before every *corrida*. He smiled for the loader although he did not try to remember the boy's name.

'I don't think they make umbrellas for this kind of rain.'

The loader chuckled, making a show of approval for the remark. That was witty, Luis thought, I made a funny comment. He was pleased with his show of humor, something he used to have in his command of men when he was the Spaniard.

He stood. The Soviet rockets had shot their bolt and the grenadiers were on their feet and moving again. Luis ordered the driver forward. The plain was not cratered much by the Katyushas, the missiles were more frightening than effective. Only one soldier did not rise to join the advance. Luis rode past the body and felt nothing. This wasn't the time to take stock of his remaining humanity. The Tiger lumbered forward, men walking beside him and standing in other turrets looked up at him; the last thing they wanted from this Tiger tank's commander right now was introspection.

A Henschel ground-attack plane drove low across his regiment's line. The pilot tossed out a purple smoke grenade. The canister hit the ground and raised an oily, pastel stink. Luis curled his nostrils and focused on where he was. The signal meant one thing. Tanks.

He hoisted his field glasses toward Komsomolets, five kilometers ahead now. The clot of structures was a state farm; several grain silos and claret-painted outbuildings were clustered beside the Prokhorovka road and rail mound. A swarm of T-34s raced out from behind cover. He estimated a hundred Soviet tanks burst across the fields, fanning to the left in a flanking action. Sturmovik fighters scorched out behind them. The Luftwaffe planes powered into this Red air cover and they struck up their customary tangled dances overhead. The SS tanks halted. Luis picked his first dashing targets through the binoculars while the Russians were still at the disadvantage of distance. By the time the Reds came close enough to become worrisome, he was certain Balthasar would have a half dozen of them in bits.

Balthasar spoke in the intercom, he had a target. Luis gave him permission to fire. The tank bucked around Luis when the cannon let go. The other three Tigers in the panzer regiment bayed at almost the same moment. In the following seconds, two dozen assault guns and self-propelled tank destroyers joined in. Two kilometers away, the first towers of smoke and steppe drifted into the air among the charging Red tanks. Luis stood in the turret, bracing himself against every blast from Balthasar's long barrel, wiping his goggles after each of the gunner's shots. Balthasar and his loader worked as fast as Luis could give them instructions. Their readiness with another shell and firing solution flowed in tempo with the battle beginning to swirl in the fields. Luis held on tight and between rounds ordered the Tiger forward in careful steps, to keep up with the running grenadiers but not to shorten the distance to the rushing T-34s any quicker than he had to. When Balthasar had a target acquired, Luis stopped to let him fire, put his hands over his helmeted ears, then crept ahead in pace with the infantry. The radio operator transmitted Luis's commands to the rest of the company, for his platoon to stay in wedge formation around his Tiger, and for the other three platoons of Mark IVs to swing into an echelon left position to protect the flank from T-34s coming in wide from the north. More artillery cascaded in from across the Psel, and another barrage of Katyushas stymied the advance for a minute, driving Luis back inside the Tiger, drawing more mirth from his sweaty crew.

Nothing about the Soviet counterstroke impressed Luis, not even their numbers and the will to squander them. Without their network of trenches and solid defenseworks, the Red infantry were routed swiftly out of foxholes. Anti-tank guns were abandoned, damaged T-34s were left with their motors running, prisoners came out of the haze with empty hands high. *Leibstandarte* was outnumbered and outgunned in the grainfields in front of

Komsomolets, as they had been on every battlefield since Citadel began. Even so, the Soviet resistance moved aside from Luis's tanks like geese in the road. By noon, the first grenadiers had entered Komsomolets. Twenty T-34s stood ruined on the steppe behind them, most killed by German tanks, a few blown up by grenadiers in close fighting. The rest of the Soviet force retreated east of the state farm to regroup behind Hill 241.6, to come in another wave later. *Leibstandarte* captured the farm and spent none of its own precious tanks, perhaps fifteen soldiers dead and fifty wounded. In the lull before grinding up Hill 241.6, while the grenadiers consolidated their hold on the farm buildings, Luis slipped his panzer company into the small forest next to the riddled silos. He crashed his Tiger and his Mark IVs into tree trunks, knocking them down with a careless pride, to make a place for his men and weapons to rest a little while. The green calm of the trees belied the havoc beside the Prokhorovka road. He ordered up ammunition and fuel, food and cigarettes for his tankers. He accepted a mound of mashed potatoes on a plate topped with a warm brown gruel and ate only a quarter of it. Strolling to the edge of the copse, he looked two kilometers east, up the gradual incline of Hill 241.6, the next objective on the road to Prokhorovka.

This is the soldier's discipline, he thought. Do the job at hand, nothing more, then wait for orders to do another. But he believed he was here in this battle for a reason beyond the others, the grimy tankers and dirty plodding infantrymen, half-deaf artillerymen, crazy pilots, even the fat generals and their pretty staffs. Luis, alone of them all across every horizon today, knew there was no battle for Kursk, there was no Citadel. Those were only labels that would live in history books. No man lives on a page, he lives in his minutes and his skin. Whatever kingdom Germany or Russia carved out of this bloodied land would not survive, none ever has and none ever will, power is transitory, dominion becomes printer's ink and dust. Nothing outlives a man, not a crown, not a conquest, nothing but a name and honor. It is better to be honored than to be a king. Luis crossed himself there on the edge of the woods, it felt like he was praying, and he thought of Jesus, who was not a king, he thought of his own father, who had outlived many bulls and recalled all the best of them. He thought of Thoma who'd died so stupidly, all his honor trickled out. He smiled at the Russians on Hill 241.6, because he was sent here out of the many thousands to become great.

He turned and looked down the line of his fourteen tanks, at all the pushed-down trees and bared roots. Men sat on the prone trunks eating rations, fuel trucks delivered drums of gasoline, more shells were loaded by bare-chested soldiers. He stood before them and they were oblivious to his gaze, as they should be. They were invisible to history. Anything these men and tanks did belonged to him, their names would make a stack to lift his own.

Luis was in a fine mood. He chuckled at the sight and sound of the little motorcycle coming again to bring him a message. The bike with its toy spitting engine seemed funny beside Luis's goliaths, the motorcycle dodged the trees his company had knocked over. The courier again found Luis and *pip-pip*-ed to him, holding out a yellow note. Luis gazed after the rider sliding away, and wondered if that rider would tell his grandchildren one day that at Kursk he was a delivery boy to *la Daga*.

Luis read the note. The attack on Hill 241.6 was to start at 1300 hours. *Totenkopf* had not yet crossed the Psel. South of the rail mound, *Das Reich* was barely keeping up with *Leibstandarte*'s forward units. Nonetheless, *Leibstandarte* was ordered to plunge ahead and take the hill. Again, Luis thought, I am at the knife's point of the battle. He folded the note into his pocket and walked to stand near his massive Tiger, to be seen with it, linked to it always by those who would tell later of these fiery days.

At the assigned moment, his company roared out of the forest beside Komsomolets farm. Luis ordered all tank commanders to exit the copse with hatches down and secured. Within seconds of leaving cover, the Soviet artillery opened up on them. He shouted a command into the radio for his company to scatter by platoon and provide support for the advancing grenadiers. 'Come left!' he called to his driver. There was no way to motor straight up the slope, the defense was too withering. He stared into his optics, straining to find a target but so much earth was suspended in the air from the artillery lavished down on them he couldn't pick out anything that resembled a Russian tank. Balthasar had his hand poised on his flywheel to respond the moment Luis called him into a shot. The loader squatted on his stool with a shell across his lap, ever faithful to the always-hungry breech.

For thirty minutes Luis yanked his Tiger and his Mark IVs back and forth along the base of the long hill. The Russians on the high ground did not spare their ammunition, and he kept his tanks running and difficult to hit. Balthasar did not fire a round, but the Tiger crept among the grenadiers, waiting, prowling for a prey. None presented itself, and Luis would not fire blindly at the crest of the hill, that was the job for his own artillery. He was a tank hunter. The Reds would oblige him if he was patient.

By 1400 hours the grenadiers had slogged only a hundred meters up the grade of Hill 241.6. His company skulked alongside them, still without the Soviet armor offering itself for an open fight. Gazing out his periscope, Luis saw the first globs of rain splash on the deck. Thunder added its voice to the growl of his Tiger's massive engine and the cracking rumble of cannon fire.

This weather takes care of the air cover, Luis thought. A slow approach had just become slower.

The Tiger jolted. Luis snapped back from the brow pad of his optics, Balthasar below him recoiled as if hit in the jaw. Luis's ears rang even under his padded helmet and headphones. He darted his eyes about the tank compartment; everything was intact. Balthasar shook his head and rammed his eyes back into his range finder. Luis did the same. His vision was blocked by a lick of flame and billowing smoke. A Red shell had smacked his Tiger on the nose. Luis ordered the driver to stop. As long as the Reds were coming straight for him, the Tiger's armor could stand up to anything they threw. He wanted a clear, still look at what had shot him.

The smoke wafted away. Under a beaded curtain of rain, he spotted ranks of Soviet tanks in two, three, four rows powering down the hill. The Russians always attacked in waves. The T-34s rolled down in another hundred, as though that were their smallest integer. They were speedy, better in the mud than the heavy Tiger, even quicker than the Mark IVs. The panzer grenadiers greeted the Red tanks with anti-tank fire that knocked out a quarter of the first echelon in the initial minute of the charge. Balthasar, unleashed, stomped on the firing pedal again and again. Luis gave orders with his eyes glued to his commander's optics.

The Russians stayed at a distance and Luis's company parried, toiling forward only slightly, trading shots. Luis held his panzers back; why charge into a charge and lose every advantage? The Reds had superior numbers, and after another hour of tumult, when the first tank assault was beaten back, a second torrent came down the hill. Luis had days ago stopped being dumbfounded at the multitudes the Soviets tossed into battle, but he shook his head at this. He followed his grenadiers through the clinging mud, keeping his fourteen tanks at a snail's pace alongside them, answering the Red tanks, keeping them at bay. It would do no good for his company to mount the hill alone, they would not hold it against Red infantry; this was always the perversion of mobile armor, a machine was at its most vulnerable against a man.

The fighting on the incline of the hill dragged on through lightning and deepening muck. Twice more Luis's Tiger took blows, all of them glancing and disconcerting but without damage. Three of his Mark IVs were knocked out. In the middle afternoon he ordered his company by platoon back to Komsomolets to refuel and rearm. Though he was famished and out of crackers he was also without fatigue. His little body could stay in this fray for hours more, his focus through the scope and his strength to command were untarnished by the intensity of the last five hours of battle. Balthasar wanted to stay when Luis gave the order to retreat to the trees, he had a T-34 in his sights. Luis let his gunner fire one more round. Balthasar missed.

The Tiger was the last to withdraw the two kilometers to cover. Field kitchens, fuel trucks, and a medic station waited under the dripping trees. The thunderstorm had moved on, leaving dusk in its wake like a bruise. Hill 241.6 fell into German hands while Luis sat on a tree chewing bread. The sounds of fighting from the Psel finally began to rise from a point north of the river, where *Totenkopf* had at last established a bridgehead. *Das Reich* made progress south of the road in the forests and villages there. *Leibstandarte*'s grenadiers dug into positions on top of the hill and between the slope and the rail tracks. All three SS divisions were inching forward to Prokhorovka.

Luis kept his company under the trees until 2200 hours. He mounted his Tiger and rode out into a quiet field under a tufted, starless sky. His eleven remaining tanks moved abreast. They found no standing grass or grain to trample, every blade was flattened and scored by the day's fighting or blown to bits in the bottom of craters. There were no German tanks or bodies. Salvage and burial: These were extra benefits of winning the ground. Luis did not bother to count the number of Red T-34s and lighter T-70s left in hulks in a variety of reposes. A graveyard eeriness swept past his lurching turret as though, in moving across today's battlefield, he were motoring through some gray vision of his own future, one of wreckage.

At midnight Luis was on top of Hill 241.6. An intense humidity seeped out of the ground. His crew had stripped to their skivvies to try and sleep on a spread tarpaulin. Luis was finished conferring with the other company commanders over a lantern. The casualty report was light for *Leibstandarte,* only twenty-six killed, one hundred and sixty-eight wounded, and three missing. Estimates indicated the division had smashed over fifty Red tanks. The company commanders were informed that the two other SS divisions were both shy of their objectives on the left and right flanks. None of *Totenkopf*'s armor had crossed the Psel yet, and *Das Reich* had not fought any farther than Yasnaya Poliyana, five kilometers behind *Leibstandarte,* which remained at the leading edge of the assault. During this night, the rest of *Leibstandarte*'s force would complete its turn away from Oboyan and catch up, bringing the division to full strength. Hopefully the trailing regiments would be accompanied by more repaired tanks. This would allow the division to send a panzergrenadier regiment across the road and rail mound in the morning to assist *Das Reich* with its progress through the defended forests and villages there.

Luis stood over his snoring crew, white-skinned in their underwear in the clouded half-moon light. The four were curled like giant grubs brought out of the ground by the moisture, heaped at the feet of the Tiger. He had no urge to lie down among his men and rest. He would stay erect and private to ensure that any word spoken about him now or later would be spoken with awe.

Luis had no duty for several more hours. He was not sleepy, he snapped his fingers walking around his tank to burn off energy. The Tiger was armed and fueled, it, too, needed nothing. He climbed up on the deck and stood over the engine in the filtered moonlight, looking east from the hill's summit. The next day's objective was to advance another five kilometers up the Prokhorovka road, that black ribbon below dissolving into the night. The Reds out there were keeping their lights off, shifting their thousands in the dark. The first morning target will be another strategic high ground beside the road, Hill 252.2. Once that fell, his panzers would swing northwest and attack another state farm, Oktyabrski. It would be the following day, the twelfth of July, that would send *Leibstandarte* into Prokhorovka itself. That will be the day, Luis thought. He could not foretell what would happen, he did not have that power. But standing on his Tiger looking into the murky east, he felt certain of when.

He turned to look back at the alley between the Psel and the rail mound. A line of vehicle headlamps snaked his direction along the battered road. The late-arriving regiments of his division wouldn't run with their lights on like that; if they did, there would be a hundred trucks and armored carriers and tanks, they'd light up the whole river valley. No, these were other vehicles, ones not accustomed to battlefields and the need to travel below notice.

Staff cars.

Luis watched them wend closer, he heard the fine engines of Mercedes sedans and the tinny pops of several motorcycles in retinue. This was someone important coming.

The cars stopped and dodged potholes in the road. Luis folded his arms and stared. The sky was too low for there to be any risk to this little convoy of enemy bombers. The night brooded, a boxer awaiting the next bout. The column of cars and motorbikes slipped past Komsomolets state farm, heading straight for the base of Hill 241.6. There the column stopped.

A motorcycle split off from the convoy and came across the field. In a broken path – the rider may have seen Red bodies on the ground in his headlamps – it came up the hill. This motorcycle had a sidecar attached to it. Without concern for the noise he made or the sleeping soldiers sitting up from their ground cloths, the rider stopped at one of the Mark IVs in Luis's company. He paused, then revved his little motor down the line to the rear of the Tiger.

'Captain de Vega, sir?'

Luis stayed high on the Tiger. The light from the motorcycle spilled over him, he was spotlit.

'What is it?'

'Major Grimm would like a word with you, sir.'

Luis glanced down at his crew. Balthasar sat upright in his underclothes. The gunner elbowed the radioman, who elbowed the loader and the driver. All watched.

Luis jumped off the Tiger and landed like a cat. He strode to the sidecar without a word and climbed in. The courier whisked him away in a sharp turn, the headlamp swept in a circle across many white faces turned his way.

The motorcycle caromed down the hillside, avoiding lifeless Soviet tanks, craters, and gloomy lumps that had been men. At the bottom of the hill, the row of vehicles had shut down to wait inside the night. Major Grimm had come all the way up from Belgorod to see Luis, over thirty miles of battered road and ground, with six vehicles attending him, twenty armed men. Why?

The courier halted next to a long black Mercedes. Luis rose out of the sidecar. A Wehrmacht private opened the rear door of the Mercedes. The courier pulled the motorcycle a few meters away and cut his engine. Luis folded and got into the car.

He chose the open seat, the bench facing the rear. On the opposite long seat was a heavy man mopping his brow.

Luis inclined his head. 'Major.'

'Captain de Vega.' Grimm spoke, lowering his kerchief for a moment. He looked out the car window at the dim silhouettes of Soviet tanks across the slope.

The major said, 'You've been doing well, Captain. We've pushed your block quite a ways in the past five days. Now you're on your way to Prokhorovka. Then Kursk, we hope.'

'Yes, sir.' Luis was not glad to see Grimm, even with his constant affability. What did the major want? Grimm knitted flabby fingers in his lap to keep himself from tapping on his knees.

The major said, 'I thought I owed you a visit.'

'Thank you, Major.'

Grimm swiped his kerchief under his bullfrog neck. 'Captain.'

'Yes, Major.'

'You have performed well. First you defended the Tigers against the partisans. Then you served Colonel Breit and myself capably in the situation room. And you have done splendidly in the field. You know this.'

'Thank you, sir.'

'You have been put up for several medals.'

Luis said nothing. It was good to hear but this was not the point of the midnight visit.

Grimm's eyes flagged. Some new defeat was in them, something not on the map table.

'I understand, son.' Grimm aimed a finger at Luis's chest. 'I know how important it is to you. And you've done well.'

Luis was impatient. He cocked his head and prodded. 'But?'

Grimm did not hesitate anymore.

'But the Americans invaded Sicily this morning.'

Luis was rocked more by this statement than by any shell that had hit his Tiger. The news pierced him, his chances for redemption.

Grimm continued. 'Over three thousand ships. The American landing force consisted of eight divisions. Reports say that some of Mussolini's troops helped the Americans unload their transports.'

'And what about Citadel?' Luis forced himself to keep his voice even. 'Is the battle called off?'

'Not yet. Hitler's waiting to see the progress at Prokhorovka. There's no more movement in the north. Model's been completely stopped there. The same on the Oboyan road, Hoth is at a standstill dealing with attacks on his left flank. The only chance to reach Kursk is here. With you and the SS through Prokhorovka. I came to see your positions for myself. And to tell you. Privately. This is not information for anyone else. You're the only one, Captain, who I am certain will fight harder because of it. The rest of the men will find out when they have to. You understand.'

'Yes, sir. Of course.'

Grimm ran a hand across his pate, the bristles of his cropped rim of hair sizzled under his palm. He looked again out at the dim battlefield. There were plenty of knocked-out Soviet tanks there. If Hitler could come and see for himself, Luis thought, he would never stop Citadel. We're still strong, we'll beat them. Let us fight. Let me fight.

'Two or three days, Captain,' Grimm said. 'That's all the *Führer* is going to wait. If there's no breakthrough at Prokhorovka, he'll put a stop to this. So.'

'I will do my duty, Major.'

Grimm smiled again, insipid and still eager to please. 'I'll keep an eye on your block, Captain *la Daga*.'

Luis wanted to lean forward from his seat and snarl at the tip of Grimm's fat nose. Climb into my Tiger with me, you tubby slab of shit, keep an eye on me there! Tell Hitler to let me fight!

Luis took one breath to calm himself, he drew in the safe stink from this officer, his sweat and resignation, the cleanliness of his game board in Belgorod. Luis knew his lips were tight, clamped against his anger at the news and the man who'd brought it, even his kindness in doing so. You've done well, Captain. But not well enough. I thought you'd like to know. You've got two days to take Prokhorovka. The Americans, you understand. Out of my hands.

The staff car started and flung on its lights. Luis watched it pull off the road and circle to return west, followed by its entourage, except for the sidecar motorcycle. He waved the rider off. The courier nodded, then followed Grimm.

Luis had hours left to him before morning. He'd walk up the long hill and count the dead Russian tanks.

CHAPTER 23

July 11
0540 hours
the Karteshevka-Prokhorovka road

Dimitri had never seen this much traffic. He moved the General at a slow walk, the pace of the thousands of men and trucks ambling east with him over the road and in the fields on all sides this morning. He hadn't shifted past second gear in more than four hours, most of that spent jerking along in first. He'd grown impatient with the bumpy ride and the grinding transmission. He wanted to stand up and yell at the shuffling soldiers and spewing trucks, You're in the way of a tank! A tank! With a shell or two in their tails they'd clear the road fast enough and let the *General* speed through.

Dimitri was simmering, warming and angry since sunup inside the empty tank. The rest of the crew rode outside on the deck in the fresh air, Valentin with his new lieutenant's stars, admired by Pasha, and poor Sasha, a cliché of the wounded patriot soldier with white gauze lapped around his head. Dimitri felt used. Last night rolling, crawling, with the metal tide along the road, Valentin's boots propped out of habit on his shoulders, he felt like a horse, blinkered and reined and ridden. For the first several hours he'd muttered to himself that he was a Cossack and a *hetman* and many things that were not a horse, but his mumblings had been shaken out of him by the long ride in first gear and by no one to listen; now he stared out his open hatch, out of grim eyes at the exhaust smoke pouring from beneath the truck bumper directly in front of him.

A major reshuffling of forces was taking place. It seemed every able-bodied man, truck, and tank was being crammed into the area around Prokhorovka. The *General* had picked up a dozen hitchers since sunrise. Valentin had told the crew they were headed southeast to join the defense of Prokhorovka. They were going to hook up with the 32nd Tank Brigade of the 29th Tank Corps. Dimitri had heard nothing about this unit. What had they done in the battle of Kursk? They were Steppe Front units, reserves. He had been running under enemy gun sights for a week now, he'd carted Valentin and his cannon in front of a hundred German tanks, Sasha had depleted fifty ammo belts, Pasha had re-loaded his bins a dozen times. He'd got them all out safe every time. Now they were going to join a brigade of sixty tanks that didn't even have a scuff on the paint yet. Valentin told them the 32nd Tank Brigade was arrayed directly beside the Prokhorovka road, right in the Germans' route. Valya was proud, calling it the place of honor. Pasha nearly shit himself hearing this. Another road to defend, Dimitri thought, as if this were some specialty they'd developed. More like a curse, he thought. He swished his tongue but found no moisture, just road dust and ire.

He pulled the *General* out of line, off the road. He shut down the engine and stood in his hatch, pushing past a thicket of strange legs and muddy boots to shove himself out of the opening and drop to the ground. He looked up at his tank, it was scabbed with soldiers clinging to every open spot. He stomped into the field away from the road and the endless line of creeping vehicles, all of them going too slow. Behind him men called Hey and What's he doing? Dimitri walked far enough into the field to not hear them, he stood looking north into open land where a horseman could clip along nicely. Out of the south the booms of combat lobbed over his head.

He expected his son, waiting with his back turned. If he sends Sasha he's a coward, Dimitri thought. Come yourself.

Finally boots kicked through the crop rows, coming to him. He had swearing ready and his tired hands were balled.

'Papa.'

Dimitri turned. Pasha and Sasha watched from the deck of the tank. Valentin was bareheaded. Dimitri pulled his own padded helmet off and dropped it on the ground. He ran both hands through his damp hair, grimacing beneath his mitts.

'Papa, I've got to ask you to stop this.'

So easy a trap I could lay for him, Dimitri thought. I could demand, Stop what? Make him say it. Stop being insubordinate, Papa. Stop being a danger. Stop being unpredictable. Then I can yell back.

'Why am I so mad at you all the time, Valya?'

Valentin knew the answer, and he said it.

'We've traded places, Papa. You weren't ready for it. That's all.'

Dimitri had seen a wife die. Comrades skewered or shot. A powerful father wasted to illness and gone too young. He'd seen a man's life and knew he should not have this as his saddest moment. But there it was, and it seemed so wrong to be this crushed at something a boy said.

Is this what happens to every father, at war or not? Does this moment hurt all fathers this much? When did I do this to mine? Did I stare him down like a dog that got too old to hunt?

Dimitri gazed at the ground and waited for it, the notion to slap his son. Then he lifted his eyes to his son's face.

Valentin had not moved or flinched. His son stood with the backdrop of a mural behind him, men and machines rushing to the defense of Russia, to bar the road to Prokhorovka; this Lieutenant Berko and his crew had fought in the worst of the battles for Kursk and now hurried to fight in another. Dimitri's hands relaxed. He chuckled at himself. No matter how little else was left to him, either pride or time, he was the father of a Soviet hero. In a Soviet country, this was not so bad a thing.

When will he know me, Dimitri wondered? Never. The roads separated too soon, my son's and mine, there was not enough time, the war and the Communists came too swiftly. This boy learned the sword and now the tank. But Valya does not know his father, as I did not know mine until now. Perhaps that's just how it works. We do not know, that's why wars are fought, great wars like the one in the river valley at the end of this road, infinitesimal wars like the one in the space between the locked eyes of father and son. And perhaps we will not know God the Father until too late also. Dimitri sighed for all this stumbling around blind. What a design, to make things this way, pieces that will never fit, what sort of machine is life to be like that? That's why it runs so rough. Before his sigh was done it became a good laugh. This was Dimitri's gift, the true Cossack's gift, to switch sides nimbly, to pick the winner and go with him.

He eased beside Valentin, and laid his arm across the boy's shoulders. He gave Valya's frame a squeeze, pleased to feel muscle and grit there.

'Have you heard from your sister?'

'No. She hasn't written in weeks.'

'I'm sure she's alright.' Dimitri turned his son away from the free northern fields, back to the waiting tank and the clustered, diesel-choked road to Prokhorovka. 'She doesn't have me to deal with. Come on, Lieutenant. Put your arm around me. I'm just your father.'

Valentin's hand did not go around Dimitri. The boy said, 'Papa, let me go.'

Dimitri took down his arm, as ordered.

July 11
0900 hours
Voroshilov

After the Psel river bridge at Voroshilov, the traffic thinned. They were all now within the lines of 5th Guards Tank Army. Vehicles and infantry scattered south into the fields to reinforce their assigned units. The sounds of combat batted in the air, rising on smoke. The Germans were trying hard to move up north of the Psel, to keep abreast of their advance on Prokhorovka south of the river. More soldiers Valentin had picked up jumped off the *General* after crossing the bridge. Open-bedded trucks waited for them. The soldiers packed themselves in and were jolted across the valley grasses to be set like pikes in the Germans' way. Sasha, Pasha, and Valentin dropped back into their seats. Valentin stood in his turret. Dimitri kept the *General* stroking ahead southeast on the road, pushing them through a ground-hugging haze of artillery smoke. The guns were firing from a nearby hill into the alley of land west of Prokhorovka, where the battle with the SS waged.

Last night's rains and high winds had given way to a morning of rising heat and humidity. Cloud cover clamped them down to the earth like a hen's feathered rear. Dimitri's goggles fogged on him but he couldn't pull them down because of the dust he drove into. He refused to lower his hatch, that would make him too dependent on Valya's directions or the boy lieutenant's damned boots. Dimitri had accepted his place in the confusing schemes of life and war, but this did not mean he relished it.

At mid-morning Valya ordered him off the road. Ahead, a handful of T-34s did the same and led the way south. Dimitri got in behind them and finally let the *General* bolt. He shook Valya out of his turret hatch and made the boy settle his rear into the safety of his seat. Five tanks, all scarred T-34s, raced over the fields. Dimitri pulled even with them and they ran side by side, no one eating dust this way. They passed an immense concentration of weapons and men, all of them on the move or digging in. Trucks towed artillery pieces into long lines and tiers by caliber, tankers hollowed out trenches for hull-down firing positions, pyramids of artillery rounds waited to be stashed, soldiers shoveled out foxholes to stand their ground. Dimitri kept the throttle open. The five T-34s shot past rifle brigades, tank brigades, a regiment of airborne looking sharp and determined marching forward, every one of them fresh and unblooded. Every man they passed turned their way, to watch the five veteran tanks fly forward, trailing dust plumes like wild stallions.

One by one the tanks peeled away, finding their units, until only the *General Platov* was left. Valentin's boot low on his neck told Dimitri to slow down. He shifted back reluctantly, clinging to the thrill of rushing over flat ground and rippling stalks of grass, carefree and racing alongside steely comrades. It felt good to fly.

The *General* passed a crossroads town. This was Prokhorovka. The place wasn't much more than a collection of shanties and outbuildings, a handful of barns, a granary, a meeting hall. A railroad track ran atop an embankment into the center. The town, like every civilian area in the battle zone, was overtaken by guns. On all sides Prokhorovka was bracketed by armor and artillery facing west, a hundred tanks, twice that number in field pieces, a hundred times that in men and rifles. Dimitri couldn't help but think if these machines of war had been tractors, if the host of soldiers digging the black steppe had been plowing, if this need to fight were instead a will to harvest, Prokhorovka would be a kingdom of plenty. Breaking things was always fun, but when the battles were over Dimitri rode away from the pieces and forgot them. What made him wistful now looking at Prokhorovka sliding behind him was the waste, for this town, for himself, for all these young men, because what will count in the end for them will be not what they destroyed but what they planted. Crops. Children. The things a man doesn't ride away from.

When he was called to a halt, he shut the *General* down. The other three climbed out of the tank. Sasha leaned his head into the driver's hatch and said, 'Come on, Dima, let's get some air,' but Dimitri kept his seat. Freshly painted tanks moved on all sides, skidding to take up positions. The air Sasha wanted to breathe was clogged with metallic noise. This place was so far from where Dimitri wanted to be. He wanted nothing of these new comrades or this task.

Five kilometers ahead, an awful battle roiled, kicking up roars and billows of smoke, the smell on the breeze was explosives. The battle raged around a spot of high ground beside the Prokhorovka road, and for a small state farm below it. From the looks of things at this short distance, ample Soviet forces were keeping the Germans at bay for the morning. But this was the SS out there. Dimitri knew his time would be tomorrow, with the 32nd Tank Brigade around him and the four, five, six hundred other Russian tanks in more waiting units, when the SS broke through and came for Prokhorovka.

He stood out of his hatch into the buzzing day. He scanned the land corridor before him, five kilometers wide between the Psel and the rail mound, searching for the place where he would fight. If he had a horse he would ride the terrain, know the land before you trust it to be your ally. But there was only a slowly undulating steppe expanse here, wide and shallow *balka* valleys without features of advantage for either army, the earth would not choose sides here. Straight to the west rose the curtain of smoke and clamor, the opening fight for the hill and state farm. Opposite, in the east, looking on from the outskirts of Prokhorovka, Dimitri stood in his driver's place.

In the middle, on the floor of a broad and shallow valley, set like a golden stamp in a great brown sheet, spread a field of sunflowers. These blooms turned their heads with the shifting light. Today they gaped right, then left, at warring nations. Tomorrow, Dimitri knew, there would be none of them standing at all.

CHAPTER 24

July 11
1840 hours
Oktyabrski state farm

'Walk with me, Balthasar.'

The gunner rose from the ground on rubbery feet. No one but Luis in the Tiger crew had straightened his legs in over six hours. Luis stood aside until the gunner took his hands from the tank and was steady. The other three crewmen had sat up when Luis approached. They laid themselves out flat when Balthasar and Luis walked away.

Luis and the gunner strode off from the rest of the tanks in the company. Again Luis had brought them through another day of hard fighting without losing a tank. In fact, when the trailing elements of *Leibstandarte* caught up to the rest of the division in the early morning, they brought with them six more Mark IVs, two had been assigned to Luis. Now, at the end of his fourth day commanding the company in combat, they numbered sixteen tanks.

Luis and Balthasar walked through the remains of Oktyabrski. A gray snow of ash filtered down from the smoldering timbers of barns and silos. A dead Russian lay face up with his hands and legs spread wide, blown there to the ground, a teenager, and he looked to Luis like a boy making a snow angel in the spilling ashes. This was a cold image, Luis did not like it. It reminded him of Leningrad, where he took his wound.

He opened his mouth to speak to Balthasar, then thought better of it. He would have to shout to be heard in this dirt lane, crowded with grenadiers flooding in to take positions in the rubble. Tanks and armored troop carriers careered around the debris piles, and medical wagons collected SS dead and wounded. All the Red corpses were hoisted onto trucks and dumped out on the steppe to be burned. The snow-angel boy was so stiff he was lifted and swung up to the truck like a hammock.

Luis walked Balthasar toward the western edge of the state farm. He smelled himself and the gunner. Their odors were identical, acidy from the backwash of daylong cannon fire, a sort of spoiled citrus tang of sweat and chemical stained their skin and uniforms. The smell of mechanized combat was on them. Luis wanted a postcard of this, to send to his father, and one to Hitler.

The two stood where it was quieter now. They gazed over the terrain they'd seized today. *Leibstandarte* had clawed another five kilometers closer to Prokhorovka, lunging at first light northeast out of Komsomolets state farm. The division attacked across a wide front, spanning all across the land corridor, from the edge of the Psel to south of the rail mound. The Russians fought hardest on this ground, defending the state farm in the middle. When his panzer company rolled up to attack, they came up short in front of the biggest anti-tank ditch he could imagine, the proportions were remarkable, the thing was as wide and deep as a river. This underscored Luis's loathing for the Soviet peoples, revived his thinking of them as drones, to dig such a thing was primitive. His armored attack was thwarted for the morning. This angered him more for the hissing in his head, the sound of the *Führer*'s draining patience for this misadventure in Russia. The assault was redirected until bridging equipment could be brought up to cross the giant ditch. An hour later, after regrouping, Luis's company came at

Oktyabrski from the northwest, where the Reds were expecting them. A barrage of machine-gun fire sprang out of the farm buildings, catching the accompanying grenadiers by surprise; even behind tanks they couldn't advance. Luis would not move ahead into the sting of the dug-in Red infantry without ground troops – this was how Thoma had lost so many tanks – and the attack stalled again. Luis grew grimmer in his commander's seat, counting minutes, knowing that Hitler in Berlin counted minutes and the swelling number of Americans on the beaches in Sicily. Stukas were called in to cover the pioneers bridging the tank moat in front of the state farm. Finally, at 1400 hours, the ditch was spanned. Every tank of *Leibstandarte* attacked at once. Ground was gained a meter at a time. Armored transports hauled a full regiment of panzergrenadiers to the leading edge of the battle, Luis's tanks provided cover and firepower, and together they plowed into the defenders of Oktyabrski. The Reds sent out a paltry rank of T-34s to deflect the assault; a dozen were shot out of their number in the first ten minutes. Balthasar got three of them. The Tiger gunner showed an uncanny hand now with the speed and agility of the Soviet tanks, they didn't dodge him so well anymore. The state farm fell twenty minutes ago, and with it the last high ground before Prokhorovka, Hill 252.2. *Leibstandarte* claimed twenty-one Soviet tanks destroyed.

The division was called to a final halt for the day. Again the flanking forces had lagged, leaving *Leibstandarte* exposed in the middle. The attack on Prokhorovka was forced to wait until morning, to allow *Das Reich* and *Totenkopf* to pull alongside. Luis looked backward, at the seven more kilometers they'd captured, up from Komsomolets state farm. The land was darkened and shredded by fighting. Rear elements of the division crept over the plain in the late-afternoon light, bringing food and ammunition and bandages to the warriors walking under the drifting ash of the state farm. It seemed a mighty thing to have done, to have taken this ground back from the Russians. Luis wanted Hitler to stand here with him and see it, he would present Hitler with this present of a swath of Russia, and promise him more.

But the Americans. How can Hitler ignore them? They're an unknown quantity, an industrial behemoth let loose now in the war in Europe. What kind of fighters will the Americans be? Luis knew the Yanks were in the Pacific tangling with the Japanese, but nothing else. He stared over the churned patch of Russia he'd conquered that day. Japan, America, Italy – those nations were far away and without weight, they were not here in the smoke of killed tanks out on that plain and the burned state farm behind him. He could not conceive that what Grimm had told him would come true, that Hitler would lose his nerve and take this away from him. He did not believe that tomorrow the SS would fail to ram forward another seven kilometers and take Prokhorovka. What could the Reds throw at him tomorrow that they had not thrown today?

Luis raised a palm over the captured plain. His hand floated in the air above the crushed grasses and turned soil, some black smoke plumes. This hand, frail and pale as chalk, did this to the land.

'It seems like a lot, doesn't it?' he asked Balthasar.

'Yes, sir. It does.'

Luis lowered his hand.

'It's not enough.'

Balthasar made no answer. Luis was not curious for what the gunner's silence said about the man's reasons for fighting. Probably he's like the rest, Luis thought. He's here because he believes in Germany more than he believes in himself. Luis couldn't be more different. He didn't want to stop the advance because Germany might get a bloody nose. He'd cover Germany in blood if he could. Russia, too. And Italy and America. Luis alone would know when there had been enough.

'We can take Prokhorovka,' he said. 'Did you know I used to be a bullfighter?'

Balthasar showed nothing of the disdain the Nordic peoples held for the barbarism of bullfighting. The gunner was still a very young man, he'd likely never been far from his own town in Germany before the war swept him up, never known a Spaniard. Balthasar probably thought all Spaniards were bullfighters.

'No, sir.'

'I can read what a bull is thinking. I can tell which way he's going to jump. My father taught me this. Having my life depend on it taught me, too. And I can tell you, Balthasar, about the Russians. I can read them. We can beat them. They know it. All their attacks are from the flanks. They're afraid to come right at us. They nibble at our sides. Every one of their direct assaults has been weak. They're defensive. We've bled them, Balthasar, we've bled them almost to where they'll fall. We've got to go forward. We've got to push the blade in deeper.'

Luis and Balthasar looked west, at the depth the blade was already into the Russian heart. It was not enough.

'Tomorrow,' Luis promised.

This sun over the conquered western corridor went down in the time of Luis's mind and came back up tomorrow, glowing red in the east, chasing stars, beginning the end. And there it was again, the partisan's heart beating in his hand. And there were bulls' hearts throbbing there, too. But the sensation was different, not only the pump of one man's stolen heart and the ended lives of animals but the pulse of all Russia, right in Luis's fist. He held his hand up, cupped as though holding a real heart, and looked into his curled palm.

'Tomorrow,' he said again, 'we'll take Prokhorovka.'

CHAPTER 25

July 12
0410 hours
with the 32nd Tank Brigade
2 kilometers west of Prokhorovka

The commissars surfaced at first light. They came with bottles of vodka.

The cartons in their grips rang with knocking glass. The boxes sounded to Dimitri like the bells of fishermen on the Black Sea, when the boats came home from a day's haul and called all to the docks who wanted to buy fresh catch. The commissars spread out among the tank brigade, ringing the men awake in the charcoal morning. They wore the same mustard uniforms as infantrymen, but with many medals and ribbons pinned to their tunics, and with only a sidearm slapped on their belts. The *politrooks* set the cardboard cartons down at their feet. They began their own calls, fishermen themselves, baiting with the vodka.

Dimitri had been awake for hours, watching lightning ripple over the steppe. He'd listened to the night workers out on the battlefield, to the thumps of explosives as engineers blew up disabled T-34s too damaged to be towed away and repaired. Sappers crawled to the front to lay mines where German tanks were certain to come today. From the other direction came the logistics corps bringing up food and ammo, lubricants and diesel. Dimitri eyed the laden commissars, he was the first to traipse to the nearest one. He leaned down to take a bottle by the neck out of the box. The bottle was corked by a bit of rag.

'Courage!' the commissar bellowed at Dimitri, as though the two were on opposite sides of a field. Dimitri held the bottle up by the neck like a chicken for dinner.

'Courage,' he echoed and walked off.

Sasha appeared from somewhere in the night – Dimitri stayed close only to his tank, casting his senses out to the battlefield, to the dark sunflower field on the valley floor – and slid down beside him. The boy was freckled and orange-cast and wrapped white, grinning bravely through his pain. Dimitri handed the warm glass over. The two sat listening to the keening commissar.

A crowd of the tankers gathered around the man, perhaps a hundred. They came for the bottles and stayed in the commissar's net. None of these boys had been in the fight for Kursk yet, Dimitri could see it on them. They were frightened and needy of the commissar's calls for bravado, they did not know yet what they would do today. Great things, the commissar told them, great things, and Dimitri knew this to be true, because living through today or dying in these flowers and grainfields would be remembered as great.

Dimitri and Sasha shared the bottle, neither speaking when the commissar called into the center of his gathered ring the young lieutenant from 3rd Mechanized Corps and the battle for the Oboyan road, the commander of the tank *General Platov*. The Germans were stopped on the road to Oboyan and they would not pass to Prokhorovka, the Lieutenant told them. He was cheered with *Urrahs*, clapping, and lifted bottles. Thick Pasha was one of the applauders, his coveralls dirtier than any of the others standing around him.

Valentin reached into his breast pocket for a folded sheet of paper. This was something official, a communiqué from headquarters. A new duty, Dimitri thought. Splendid. We don't have enough to do today.

'We will face a powerful German force today,' Valya announced, rattling the page as if the paper meant something that could equal a man's life. 'We have orders not to budge away from the Prokhorovka road. There will be no retreat today. There will be only victory.'

The men cheered again. They don't know, Dimitri thought, and turned to see the same high spirits on Sasha's tired face. The cheers put a mad taste in his mouth and he sipped more vodka to wash it away. Valentin let the tankers roar their approval that they should die today. Dimitri paid little attention, hearing nothing new from the mouth of a Soviet.

Valya told them what was on the sheet, what they would be facing today: three highly trained and veteran SS divisions. These were men and weapons diverted from the assault on the Oboyan road where they could not break through. Now they would try the way through Prokhorovka. They will have with them fifty-seven assault guns and two hundred and thirty-six tanks. Ninety-one of the tanks will be Mark IVs, and fifteen will be Mark VI Tigers.

Where did the Red Army get these facts and figures, Dimitri marveled, how could they be this exact? He hoisted his bottle and tapped the lip of it to an invisible drinking partner, toasting whoever was responsible for this kind of precision. That's why we're here, he thought, the Soviets have lined up every tank and gun they could scrounge in front of the damn SS. That kind of information was worth its weight in gold. Not that it will save any lives, but it was damn impressive.

Valya described the size and power of the Tiger tank. Red Army Headquarters had determined that a priority target for the battle of Prokhorovka was the Mark VI Tigers. Every Soviet tank was to find and wipe out every

Tiger they could. Valentin reminded the men of their training, to approach the Mark VI from the sides, to attack it with numbers in your favor, to aim for the treads first to disable the mammoth, then move in for the kill.

Valentin pocketed the paper. This brought the commissar back to his side. Another, final round of *urrahs* rang from the crowd for the young hero of Oboyan, and soon, of Prokhorovka.

July 12
0630 hours

He was in his driver's seat when the first German fighters swooped past. His head ached a little from the dawn vodka. The day grew fat with humidity and he sat swiping beads from his forehead, slinging them off his fingers out his open hatch. When he saw the first black blurs his hand froze, as though waving hello to them.

One flight of three fighters roared by wing-to-wing without firing a round, then were followed by another flight. The planes dove in low formation, then carved away into sharp banks. They were remarkably swift, beautiful even. Dimitri shook his headache at war in the sky; when he was a boy the skies were blue and black and gray, they were birds and constellations and mansions of cloud and the place where God lived. But never again would children know that kind of sky, war was in it now, and war was out on the ocean, too, and under the water, and one day it will be in the stars, he knew. Wherever men go, we'll take death with us. Dimitri thought of Katya and imagined her a star pilot flying a machine he could not envision. A rocket, perhaps, free and fast like she always was.

Sasha burrowed up from his escape hatch between the treads. Behind, Pasha tumbled in the commander's hatch, cursing the planes. Valentin, his other child, did not follow. He's probably getting one last round of inspiration from the commissars, Dimitri decided. He ogled another line of streaking black Messerschmitts and was glad to be a throwback warrior, even riding a steel horse. This was his place; it was enough to know that these things in the sky and sea and one day the stars belonged to others. He was a Cossack plainsman and had lived all his days true to that.

The countermove arrived inside of a minute. Soviet Yak-9s and Lavochkin-5s swept in lower than the German fighters, not afraid of ground fire over their own troops, and climbed up into the Messerschmitts' bellies. Like twists of smoke from two different fires they twined and rose off the ground, twirling around each other in a cyclone of wings, chattering machine-guns, and yawping cannons. Dimitri watched them rise, taking their swiping engine noises with them into a backdrop of din and plummeting pieces of themselves he figured would last all day. He scraped another film of sweat off his brow.

For the next hour he told Sasha what he saw in the sky. The boy sat with his chin to his thin chest. Pasha stood in Valentin's commander's hatch and watched the action high above for himself, unplugged from the intracom. Pasha did everything now with a stupid and sober eagerness, he'd become a hunting dog. Dimitri talked to Sasha because it kept the two of them from growing frightened. This morning they hadn't re-filled their resolve from the well of the commissar's entreaties for courage. They'd filled themselves with vodka instead and were left now with only what they'd started their day with, each other and the remnants of the drink.

Stukas blared their banshee sirens in dives over the villages, copses, and orchards where much of the Soviet armor was lagered. Dimitri didn't have to count the planes to know there were more than a hundred. This was a major commitment of air power to Prokhorovka, a bad, bad sign of how badly the Germans wanted it today.

'The Stukas look like buzzards. Big slow buzzards. The trees are burning around Storozhevoe. And some of the wheat fields along the river are on fire.'

Sasha nodded once in a while, or his head lolled, Dimitri could not be certain. Either way, Dimitri kept up his narrative for the both of them. Behind his head, Pasha's boots stamped whenever a German or Red plane plummeted out of the air battle. Waves of German bombers swept out of the western horizon, matched soon by a greater number of Soviet bombers from the east. Dimitri told this to Sasha. The boy rubbed his closed eyes.

The twin flying armadas rained explosions and shards of themselves across the Prokhorovka corridor on both land armies. The planes scored the morning sky with fireballs that looked small from so far below but must have been fearsome and sudden at their altitude. On the ground, flames and haze from their bombardments began to obscure the sunlight that was already dimming to encroaching clouds. Dimitri looked down from the fury overhead to the sunflower field, two kilometers from where he sat. The giant yellow swath scared him. He did not know what he would find this day in those tall, searching flowers. He did not know his place in there.

At 0815 hours, Soviet artillery opened up. For fifteen minutes thousands of field guns pounded pre-selected positions where enemy armor was believed to be gathered. Dimitri knew the preparation barrage would have only a limited effect on the Germans; likewise the fleet of planes high above, bombarding selected areas. This battle in the Prokhorovka corridor was not a set piece, not a chessboard collision, it had become a living, flexing clash between mobile forces. These were cavalries on the move against each other. They would not be fought and defeated from the air, only by foes on the same level, tank to tank. Dimitri started his engine. The *General* cranked quickly and sounded eager this morning, a tad jealous to have been left to sleep through so much clamor of guns and bombs until now. He checked his gauges, everything ran a little elevated. Sasha lifted his head to the revving motor. The look on his face held the same momentum as the *General*'s excited humming, Let's go.

The artillery fusillade lasted fifteen minutes. The last voice was not the deep boom of cannons but screeching Katyusha rockets, sheets of them flashing overhead and screaming, scythes of fire ripping the air. In seconds they were gone. The last of the explosions rumbled out of the haze that obscured the western fields and began to dim the sunflowers.

Dimitri turned to see Valentin's legs drop through the hatch. The boy arrived cat-nimble and coiled, looking ready to spring right back out the hole over his head. There was no fear in him, no hesitation, he was as impatient as the *General* to light out into the fight and the unblemished sunflower field. He nodded to his father. He clearly meant the gaze to mean so much; Be strong, Papa. Believe, Papa. Be your best today, Papa.

Outside Dimitri's open hatch, the 32nd Tank Brigade surged forward. Engines roared, fumes spat, treads spun, but this was different, Dimitri knew in a flash. This wasn't a move to counter the Germans coming for Prokhorovka, this was not another reaction in defense of the road or the rail or the corridor.

This was a Russian attack.

He shifted the *General* into gear to join the speeding sweep of machinery into the fields. The tank rattled in his hands. Over the intracom, Valya's voice rose. The lieutenant shouted to his crew the signal phrase he and the other tank commanders must have been given from their leaders, to set loose their armor and the day's fate.

'Stal,' the boy shouted, with one boot tapping the syllable into Dimitri's neck.

'Stal! Stal!'

Steel! Steel! Steel!

CHAPTER 26

July 12
0840 hours
one kilometer northwest of Oktyabrski

Sixty-seven tanks of the panzer regiment crept forward, smashing aside skinny scrub trees, branding their treads into the grassy plain. From his cupola, Luis eyed the sixteen tanks of his company, moving in the heart of the assault. He intended to keep his tanks tightly formed, not only to concentrate his firepower but to display his command. Today, everything would be watched and recalled. The four platoons of his company held their wedges well, they did not fray even dodging the smoking craters from the Soviet bombardment. The tank drivers didn't mind plowing over every Russian thing in their way.

All the tanks of *Leibstandarte* were massed and surging toward Prokhorovka in an armored thrust three kilometers wide. *Totenkopf* and *Das Reich,* in their sectors north and south, were doing the same right now, all of them plunging at Prokhorovka in one concerted, lethal strike. The metallic clatter of so much rolling armor thrilled Luis. He stared down the long barrel of his cannon, watching the steppe slip toward him, then beneath and behind him. The tanks on all sides were devouring land without resistance, knocking down grain stalks, gaining momentum and daring. Luis felt none of his usual hunger right now, his gut seemed satisfied by the powerful SS pack on every side of him. He took a moment to believe in the healing power of conquest, that he might never be hungry again if he could just gobble enough of Russia today. He might sit in Spain this year and chew on these days, wash them down with wine under a warm mist from the fountains.

He thought of the Americans in Sicily this morning. Were they moving faster than he was? He saw Italian fountains, with Americans toasting themselves in the warm spray.

'Radio. Stay tight. Keep alert.'

'Ja.' Luis listened in while the radioman repeated his command to the company.

'Balthasar.'

'Fertig.' Ready.

Two hundred meters ahead, the grainfields wrinkled into a lip, disguising a gradual downward slant. Luis stood in his Tiger's cupola and surveyed the coming terrain. An hour ago a regiment of fifteen hundred grenadiers had begun their assault over this rise and into the valley below. Right away, they'd encountered strong Soviet infantry defending the ridgeline. After thirty minutes of fierce exchange, the Reds were shoved back. Luis's panzer regiment was called in to support the grenadiers' advance through the basin. If this valley could be taken, it would open a western attack lane directly to Prokhorovka, only two kilometers away. *Leibstandarte* threw all its tanks into this thrust.

The sounds of small-arms fire sprouted from the hidden valley. Luis and the panzer regiment came carefully up to the ridgeline, sixty-seven cannons pointing and trigger ready. The strength of the Russian defenders beyond the slope was unknown. Every tank slowed, every driver stole up to the rim to peer into the bowl.

The first Mark IVs reached the ridge, climbed, then

slipped over the edge. Luis watched them cleave paths into shrubs and twisty branches, then sink slowly away down the slope. The first tanks of his own platoon passed the ledge, rose as though coasting over the swell of a wave, then tilted downward. His Tiger was next. The whine of his cannon elevating caught his attention, he watched the long barrel lift. Balthasar was clever; the gunner was not going to head down a slope with his weapon depressed. He wanted the gun up where he could defend the rest of the ridgeline above their heads.

The Tiger came to the ledge. The valley below was squarish, not deeply carved but broad. It opened west, draining down to the Psel. Two villages lined the riverbank there, Prelestnoe and Petrovka – the map room was always in Luis's head. The slopes to the north and east leading into the valley were just like the one he was about to descend, all three were weedy and untended. But sprawling over the valley floor, filling it from the river villages to the foot of the bordering slopes, was an immense sea of bright, blossomed sunflowers. The valley walls cupped the gold like hands cradling a gigantic, shining medallion.

Luis gazed in wonder at the vast field of yellow. He did not forget this would be a battleground. But the omen was clear to him, the metaphor of the golden badge too plain to be ignored. His knife hand throbbed, he extended it behind the long, reaching cannon, as if to seize the prize.

The roar of a plane engine split the mists overhead. Luis dropped his hand and his imaginings and ducked into the cupola. He'd forgotten about the air battle raging on the other side of the smoke from artillery and the burning fields, the sounds of the dogfights were smothered on the ground by the rattle of moving armor.

Wings sliced out of the haze. The plane was a German scout flying parallel to the *Leibstandarte* line advancing into the valley. Small canisters tumbled out of an open window in the cockpit. The cans hit the ground and a great froth of purple smoke spewed from each all along the ridgeline.

This was the warning signal for tanks.

Luis looked left across the valley, to the river. He snatched his head around to the right, toward the railroad mound and road. Walls of violet smoke wafted everywhere.

The Reds. Remarkably, the Russians had chosen this moment to start a massive armored offensive. They'd picked the same time to attack, and the same ground, as the SS.

Luis stared into the purple cloak floating on the slope before him. He could not see through it into his yellow valley. The blowing, reddish billows made him angry. Had they taught the Russians nothing, were the Soviets this stupid to come in their Asiatic numbers again and again to be cuffed and killed every time? Luis hadn't noticed but his Tiger had come to a stop. The rest of the panzer regiment was halted, as well. The scout plane powered away to the east, all his canisters puffing on the ground. The plane's engine faded and was replaced by the *zings* and *pops* of small-arms fire in the valley.

Luis chafed in his hatch, waiting for the order to proceed down the slope. The purple smoke did not seem to thin, it waved in their faces and stymied them. The volleys of gunfire thickened in the valley behind the curtain.

'Driver,' he said.

'Ja.'

'Forward.'

The Tiger was the first to move into the vapor. In seconds the other tanks in Luis's company were no longer mesmerized, they lurched, keeping formation. Behind his company the rest of the regiment shivered alive to creak down the incline. Luis had moved on, piercing the color and stink of the canisters ahead of the others.

'Balthasar.'

'Fertig.'

The purple fumes parted, whipped by a breeze flitting off the river. Through fissures in the smoke, Luis caught strains of gold. His Tiger pushed on and downward. Then, with a suddenness that surprised him, the smoke was whipped away.

On all sides, his company rolled out of the shroud, emerging onto the slope above the immense sunflower field. The tall flowers seemed to reflect their blazing color onto the battle mists and the smoke drifting overhead. Luis recalled the childhood game of holding buttercups under his friends' chins, to see if they liked butter. Luis cast his eyes to the right, at the easternmost slope where the sounds of small-arms fire erupted. The Red infantry regiment and the grenadiers were locked in their own battle there. The sunflower field beckoned, as it had done since he arrived in Russia.

He shook his head.

'Trap,' he muttered.

He raised his right arm high, and at the same time gave the order to the driver, then the radio, to halt. The command went out to the rest of the company, then was taken up by the other tanks of the regiment. The grating of treads ceased all along the slope. The flowers stood two hundred meters away, their heads turned east to the sun and the carnage.

Luis looked to the west, to the flatland stemming from the river.

It took him a moment to find them across the bright corner of the sunflowers, the petals so infected the light, but there they were: the first stab from the Soviet offensive into this nodding yellow valley. Three dozen T-34s, maybe more, flowed out of cover from the two villages on the riverbank. They'd been lagered among the buildings, out of sight, planning to hit the Germans in the flank the moment the panzers crossed into the field. Luis's regiment would never have been able to turn fast enough into the assault. The T-34s were intended to hit hard and fast at the vulnerable sides of the Tigers and Mark IVs. There would have been chaos and destruction in the sunflowers, if Luis had not stopped on the slope.

His tanks retained enough of the high ground to have an advantage over the rushing Reds. Had the Russians timed their move better, had they held off another minute until Luis became lulled or impatient enough to enter the valley, their strategy would have worked, the wound would have been deep. But now Luis brought Balthasar to bear. Along the slope, the other gunners turned also to meet the attack.

'Range.'

'Eighteen hundred fifty meters. Closing.'

'At will, gunner.'

Luis no longer specified which shells or targets to choose. The gunner and his loader knew when to use AP or high-explosive rounds. And Balthasar had an uncanny knack for identifying which of the Soviet tanks was the boldest.

Balthasar fired; the fifteen Mark IVs in his company followed. The rest of the regiment opened up. The collective roar was enormous! In one heartbeat the first rank of T-34s took the hits. A dozen of the sixty-seven rounds fired in the opening salvo found their marks. The field geysered on all sides of the rushing Reds. More than a kilometer away, Luis saw two Soviet turrets catapult into the air on jets of steam, going off like teakettles, their ammo lit up from the intense heat of the shells piercing their compartments. The Russians did not veer from the battering but pressed through the edge of the sunflowers, wheeling into the killing range of the handful of Tigers on the slope and inevitably into the reach of the Mark IVs' smaller cannons. Inside a minute every *Leibstandarte* tank was blasting away at the T-34s. So much smoke issued from the barrage it became hard to pick the T-34s out of the sunflowers up to their fenders. The Red armor was swift, cutting through the flowers like razors shaving the long stalks down. They did not stop, rolling inside a thousand meters, then eight hundred meters, close-quarters fighting for tanks. The Russians charged to get inside their own killing distance, no matter the cost they paid to the SS guns raging away above their heads. The corner of the golden field they stormed across was marred again and again under raining shells and the cremation of metal and man. Luis stood in his hatch and marveled at the Russians, not for the first time, but he felt, finally, watching this unreasoning rush into his blazing cannons, that he fully understood them. They were unfeeling to fear, remorseless to loss. They were brutes, truly. Do they feel nothing of their own danger? How can they run at my cannons? Don't they know what I will do to them the closer they come?

Ruin, Luis thought. I will ruin them with blood. I'll gut them.

What will it take to make them give way?

Luis wanted, needed, what existed on the other side of them. The Russians stood in the path of his freedom from this wretched body, they kept him from Spain and the misting Ramblas fountains, away from hands that were not afraid to touch him. Luis wanted to scream the things that welled inside him, make them a cannon shot.

Give me Prokhorovka!

The pulse in Luis's right hand urged at him. All his anger at the Russians and their refusal to stand aside was there in the fist. He slammed it onto the turret. The hand landed hard, not enough meat on it anymore to cushion the blow. The partisan in the hand would not stop wailing, the hundred dead bulls bellowed warnings to him. He narrowed his eyes at the nearest T-34, just six hundred meters away. The first ring of smoke puffed from the barrel of this hard-charging Russian tank, though Luis knew in another moment it was a dead tank, it ran straight into the sight of his own massive gun. Balthasar had the bastard Russian in his sights so close, the gunner was aiming straight down the barrel. Luis could not believe it when the Red shell hit his Tiger.

His feet were knocked out from under him with a tremendous clang. He slipped and fell into the hatch, slamming his chin against the cupola. He saw splinters of light and crumpled across the arm of his commander's seat. He was aware of the main gun breech below his legs heaving back and spitting a smoky casing. No one turned to deal with him, his crew continued to load and move the main gun, idle the Tiger's engine, wait for orders from him.

Yes, he thought, orders. He rubbed blood from under his split chin. He rolled the crimson slick between the fingers and thumb of the right hand, his knife hand. He stood in the cupola. The Russian tank that fired at him was dead. Its crew leaped out. Luis's hull gunner fired the Tiger's machine-gun at them and missed.

Luis pressed a hand under his bleeding chin. The wound hurt. A new throb began in his jaw. He was puzzled, confused: Were the dead partisan and the bulls moving out of his hand and into his head, flowing upstream through the gash? Fucking Russians, he thought. He shook his head, dazed. A loose tooth rattled in his jaw. He flipped blood onto the hatch cover, on top of Thoma.

'Captain.'

Balthasar's voice was tinny over the intracom, another spike in Luis's head. He blinked at the golden expanse below.

'What? Yes.'

'Across the valley, sir.'

The sunflowers seemed to be turning their million eyes to him now. Luis winced to blot out their color and focus over their heads.

Pouring down the far slope, in a cataract of armor into the valley, came an entire army of Red tanks. Luis wondered if his vision was still blurred, there were so many.

CHAPTER 27

July 12
0900 hours
two kilometers west of Prokhorovka

Dimitri propelled the *General* into a brown, swirling silt of soil and crushed weeds, flung into the air, then flung again like balls swatted by children. With his driver's hatch secured, his eyes were reduced to the pinched rectangle of world visible through the vision block. Left, right, and straight ahead – all he could find through the dust were flashes of leaden treads spinning the steppe into the air, and bright slivers of gold.

He barreled down into the valley he'd watched for a night and a long morning. He had no idea how many tanks were rolling with him down the long slope. He didn't even know which units were alongside his brigade. It didn't matter, the number of tanks was astounding. He kept his forehead rammed against the padded periscope browpiece and shifted into third gear. The *General* leaped. Valentin had ordered speed.

No one said anything. Dimitri could only snare a fast glance at Sasha, the downhill driving was too demanding right now. The boy bounced in his seat and tried to hold on tight, he looked like he was on a runaway horse. Valentin's boots danced on Dimitri's shoulders but that was from the rough ride. There was nowhere to turn. Charging T-34s were on all sides, at this pace a swerve would cause an accident in such a density of running tanks. The blind, vaulting charge into the valley chased Dimitri's hangover. He kept his eyes nailed to the padded vision block.

The dust lessened. The sunflower field filled the panorama of his sight. Dimitri watched a dozen T-34s dive into the yellow sea. Long green stalks whiplashed and golden heads snapped under the collision. The tanks chopped out paths crashing through the wall of plants, the flowers fell aside like the wake of horses flailing into a river. He gunned the *General* forward. He closed on the great flowers, two hundred, one hundred, then fifty meters. The slope eased, the *General* leveled out and Dimitri smashed into the field.

In his vision block, sunflowers went down under his treads, clipped by his racing glacis plate. The flowers looked shocked to be hit like this, they flung out their leaves, turned their heads at the last moment, and fell, looking right into his eyes. We're innocent, why do you do this? Crushed, we are crushed. Dimitri could make them no answer why. I have no answer for anything, he realized.

Valentin pressed his boot to the top of his soft helmet, a demand for more speed. Yes, alright, I have an answer for that. He mashed the clutch and shifted into fourth gear.

CHAPTER 28

July 12
0905 hours
sunflower field
3 kilometers west of Prokhorovka

Luis watched blood drip into his palm. The dot pooled in his hand. He waited, and another drop landed inside it, deepening it.

Luis wiped the blood on his trousers. He brought the hand back to his waist, cupped the fingers, and waited again, a little gutter for his blood. Balthasar announced another round was in the breech. Luis aligned his eyes with the long barrel, trying to guess which target the gunner had picked, an absentminded game. That Soviet assault had been cut down by a third but still they pushed through the corner of the field. Luis took only a small interest. Sixty-seven SS tanks stood on the high ground; only a few Mark IVs had even been nicked. The Reds shot on the move, sacrificing accuracy for speed. Luis did not duck inside the hatch before Balthasar's next shell but kept his eyes down at his bloodstained palm. The cannon fired. Luis weathered the backwash of dirt and gases. The long gun whined to fix on another target among the closing Red tanks. Luis caught another drop in his palm.

He lifted his gaze to the far side of the valley, three kilometers away. The first line of T-34s dove into the sunflowers, leaving a black wake for the next wave, and the next. Luis paid no attention to the number of enemy tanks. They were sufficient, whatever their number, for a grand battle in these sunflowers this morning, minutes from now. The ticking of those eclipsing minutes seemed to come in his hand, his knife hand catching his blood. The beat was the patter of his own blood dribbling, tapping.

Russian T-34s closed from the left, maybe twenty of them remained, running hard. The Reds were paying a flaming wage for getting close enough to enter their own effective range, but in moments their shells would start to take the toll on the stationary SS tanks arrayed across the slope. In the valley, what looked like two regiments of Soviet armor coursed through the sunflower field. Their lead formations were probably eighteen hundred meters away and charging at top overland speed.

We don't have time to sit on this slope, he thought. We can't stay still and take potshots, we'll be up to our asses in Red tanks. They'll slam into us, we'll have no room to maneuver, with T-34s on three sides. And we will not go backward.

He watched the Red tanks crush the gold on their side of the valley, pushing into it fast, killing the color. They wore broken yellow petals and severed brown irises across their fenders in ugly spangles. This stoked something in Luis, the last bit of him, bleeding, maddened, hungry all of a sudden, blazing into hatred.

'Radio.'

'Ja.'

'Tell the company to follow. Driver, forward. *Mach schnell.*'

Luis stood in the turret while the Tiger, his company, and then the entire regiment followed his command. Luis felt bold; the wound throbbed in his jaw but it was his throb, there was nothing foreign, no infestation of others in his soul now. He felt the black wooden block of the faraway map room slide forward, slide into this yellow valley that he knew was drawn blue and white on the giant map. He sensed the red blocks sliding to meet him across the table. But there were no long poles pushing them at each other. No, it was Luis making this happen. Let Breit and Grimm and Hitler and the Americans and the world watch Luis Ruiz de Vega go forward, and know that all of them, everything, were impelled by his will alone.

Slowly, then faster, the sixty-seven tanks of *Leibstandarte* gave up the ridge and lowered to the valley floor. The Soviet tanks merged into the field with the Germans. The battleground was level and bright, for these first moments a clean slate of gold.

Luis rode high on the Tiger. He watched the picket of sunflowers approach and succumb beneath his tank. He heard the crunch of snapping stalks and ignored it. He cared nothing for the field. It was land to be taken. They were Russian sunflowers. Not Spanish. Not gold.

CHAPTER 29

July 12
0909 hours
sunflower field
3 kilometers west of Prokhorovka

Dimitri could stand no more blindness, ramming his way through the green and saffron fatness of the sunflowers. He tore forward in the center of a great cavalry charge, into an enemy he had not caught sight of. Only Valentin in his turret could see where this Soviet attack was going, Dimitri could only tell how fast. Beside him, Sasha peered into his own vision block, blotted out by the same crashing field. The full-out sprint inside the *General* had turned claustrophobic, it was down to shuddering metal painted mint green, glass dials, levers, pedals, jiggling ammunition, diesel stink, unseeing men inside speeding steel. Who makes war like this, Dimitri marveled, who in the world? Only us, Russia. Always numbers, blindfolded numbers.

Dimitri had been catapulted into this valley like a lifeless cannonball, not a man entering battle, and he would have no more of it. Without an order from Valya, he angled the *General* to the right, easing sideways until he found the wake of another T-34 racing twenty meters ahead. He laid his own spinning treads into the tracks of that tank and followed, to see better where he was going. Valentin's boots did not prevent him.

Dimitri blinked into his periscope. The tank ahead

boosted flowers and fumes into the air, but for the first time in the attack he could see beyond his own fenders. The opposite slope of the valley dodged in and out of view. His visor shook with the jangling pace. In the glimpses he got of the far side, he noted tread scratches and shell craters in the brush and grasses there. Lots of German tanks had sat on that slope a minute before. How many? Several dozens, fifty at least, their marks covered the whole ridge. There'd been a short firefight. Perhaps the SS had withdrawn in the face of the Red onslaught, maybe they've gone back over the ledge in retreat. That's why we're hauling so fast, he thought. To catch the Germans. Maybe we won't have to fight in this yellow hell.

His answer came in a trumpeting clout against his tank's momentum, the sound like a lightning slash through the *General*'s cabin. His head and shoulders jolted to the impact, back into Valentin's boots, he bit into his lip, his goggles were knocked askew. Both steering rods snapped out of his grip. The *General* careened. Smoke shot in around his hatch.

'Papa!' Valya's scream was small in the turmoil.

Dimitri felt turned upside down, he could not stop blinking and gaping. Sasha was frantically trying to corral the free-flopping levers. Dimitri grabbed the boy by the scruff of his coveralls and flung him back into his own seat. He surrounded the levers with fists and gathered them in, grunting with the dizzy effort.

'What happened?' Pasha had been shouting this the whole time, Dimitri realized. 'Are we hit? What happened?'

'The shell deflected,' Valentin answered. 'It deflected. We're alright. Everyone, lock in. Calm down. Papa?'

The round must have hit the slanted glacis plate right in front of Dimitri's head. The armor held; the tread links the mechanic welded there had probably saved all their lives. Dimitri worked his tongue over his cut lip, the dash of pain yanked him alert. He regained control of the reeling tank.

'Papa.'

'What?'

'They're in the field with us.'

The tank's ventilation system dragged at the strata of smoke between them. Sasha trained bugging eyes on Dimitri, then thrust them into his vision block. He put his hands on his machine-gun. The boy coughed and muttered, 'Son of a bitch.'

Dimitri righted his goggles and muscled the tank forward, straight and fast as before. He waited for Valentin to give the order to stop, to train their big gun on whoever was shooting at them. But Valya kept the *General* charging ahead. Dimitri leaned in to his visor; he'd lost sight of the tanks ahead of him; after the blow the *General* must have spun out of formation. He was blind again, bolting through sunflowers.

Why are the Germans down in the valley with us? he wondered. They never do this, they don't give up the advantage of their cannons. They've got discipline, they sit outside our range and pummel us, make us run under their stronger guns for a thousand meters before we can even squeeze off the first round. By the time we get close enough to hurt them, we're slaughtered. Why are they in these damned flowers with us and not up on that ledge? Something is making them hasty. Something's happened to their timetable.

Christ, Dimitri thought, Christ. This isn't how tanks fight. How close are we going to get?

Again, as it had done moments before, the battle answered his question.

In his visor, the stalks ceased beating themselves against his sprinting tank, just for a second, then returned to their density. Moments later, they ceased again. The

General rolled through gaps in the field.

Dimitri dropped his jaw to this new and worse shock.

No.

Those weren't gaps.

In this instant, Valya's boots struck him hard between the shoulders. *Stop*.

Dimitri's heart clutched. He flung the *General* into lower gears, pressing with every bit of his strength on the brake.

Those were tank tracks, he realized. German tank tracks.

We're side by side in the sunflower field. We've crossed paths. Over two hundred tanks.

My God.

Sasha mumbled, 'Son of a …'

0913 hours

Many of the commanders in his regiment had lowered their hatches and secured themselves in for combat. Luis stood in the astounding morning. This was far too grand a sight to view through an eyepiece, locked inside a great, rumbling can, he thought. No, he'd leave the hatch cover up and let Thoma look with him. He lifted his wounded chin, still cupped in a pressing palm, to take it all in.

'What do you think?' he asked Thoma.

On every side of the great bowl of sunflowers, purple smoke drifted in kilometer-wide sheets. From Petrovka on the river, from Lutovo and Iamki south of the rail mound, the forest around Storozhevoe, across the river at Polezhaev, the air itself seemed to bleed. Russian and German forces vying for this little alleyway to Prokhorovka rammed into each other in unthinkable numbers. If all across the corridor the Russians insisted on the same two-to-one advantage they'd poured into this sunflower field, they'd marshaled five hundred Red tanks against the two hundred and thirty the SS'd brought, and every one of them, Red and German, shoe-horned into such a small arena! The smoke signals were everywhere! So must be the tanks.

Luis wanted to exult at the Russian charge. He wanted to shout, Come on! at the Reds, but he bit the bellow back, it imploded in his chest and fed his temper. The cut in his chin stung from sweat. He switched palms clapped against it, bloodying both hands.

In the valley now, his Tiger had fired no shots into the host of Russian tanks swarming and spreading his way. Luis held Balthasar in check for the first moments when it became plain the Soviets were not going to stop short and duel from their side of the sunflowers. He marveled at the charging Russians, watched the swaying yellow expanse between the Reds and his Tiger grow narrower by the second. Across a broad front, a hundred and more T-34s came nose-to-nose with the first ranks of *Leibstandarte*'s sixty-seven. The Reds ran so much faster than the German tanks, it was awesome to see at point-blank range. Not many rounds were exchanged in these initial seconds when the two forces mingled their armor. There was too much momentum, none dared to stop and take aim. Then the Russians ran right past *Leibstandarte*'s leading tanks, incredible! The two armies were like ghosts, passing into and through each other, a dreadful and unprecedented thing to see. Once contact was made, the ghosts slowed and stared at each other, both furious and invaded. Turrets whined now, treads squeaked to a halt, brakes and gears howled; to Luis the squealing sounds recalled the abattoir, screaming cattle, butchery, also the private whimpers of pain the bull makes, heard only by those close enough in the ring, the ones hurting him.

A hundred tanks of both sides came to a halt and fired

their opening volleys. Many were broadside, aimed at enemies only thirty, forty meters away. The toll in the initial minutes was vicious: cannons rang, gunsmoke spit, tanks erupted into flames. A haze enfolded the valley. A hundred other tanks kept moving, slicing through the flowers, dashing across crushed paths where Red or German tanks had just been a moment before. Luis watched a smoking T-34 tear past him through the flowers. He had no strategy to deal with this. He pressed his driver to continue forward, wading into the valley with his company wavering around him. He ordered them to stay close-knit but instantly saw how impossible that would be in this melee. One by one his Mark IVs peeled out of formation, engaged with one or several Soviet tanks at knife-fighting distance. Luis let them go.

Balthasar asked for firing instructions.

Luis made no response, just rode the Tiger deeper into the clanging flower field. A burning piece of a plane plummeted through the thickening battle fog; the battle for Prokhorovka was a tall thing, too, a giant rearing into the clouds.

He spun his gaze left and right, behind him. The purple smoke was all wafted away, no need for warning anymore, the battle was joined. Russian tanks ran everywhere, on every side. The vast yellow field was fast being crushed, ground down, and erased in curling paths under the two hundred tanks jockeying through the stalks. Dead hulks smoldered at the terminus of many of the routes. Balthasar asked again for instructions, where to shoot, when to begin fighting. The rest of the company was already engaged. Luis opened his mouth. Blood dribbled from his chin, he felt it separate and fall. He could not speak in the face of this titanic morning. He was shocked at himself.

He looked down at his SS uniform, glistening with crimson spots, and wondered: Am I a coward? No, I can't be. He sensed the collision of his long-held anger with an unexpected and primal fear. This battle, he thought, Prokhorovka, it's something I've never seen before. The Reds have carried the fight too far across the sunflower field, too close for strategy, tanks swirling around each other, every distance lethal, in the dust and concussion, it's impossible to tell ally from enemy.

Luis didn't know what to do; the fear drove him backward. This took him home, to Spain. This was where he found his father. He appealed for a lesson from the man. Quick, Father, I have little time here.

Fear. What? Fear, Father.

Yes. An old and worthy theme. I've said many times that I've been afraid in the ring. I've told you, Luis, you remember. Some bulls, they come out snorting snot and clear-eyed and they will knock your knees for you, nothing you can do. The bravest don't show it. But we all feel it. Nothing is harder to do than to match what makes you afraid. Nothing will make you more a man than the moment your knees stop knocking. The roses, hats, the wine sacks flung into the ring, these are for the man who stands his ground, and the *toro* who tries to take it from him. Be afraid, Luis. But stand. I've seen you do this. Do it again.

'Balthasar.'

The intracom crackled. 'Yes, sir.'

'We're close enough.'

Balthasar laughed. Good, Luis thought. The gunner believes this was courage to come so far into the heart of the valley before opening up.

'AP loaded and waiting, sir.'

'Driver, halt.'

The Tiger slowed with a great metal sigh. Luis needed both hands to raise and steady his binoculars. He'd have to let the chin drip awhile.

The Russians knew this was a Tiger. They kept their

distance as best they could, trying first to surround and overwhelm the lesser Mark IVs. Luis peered hard through the haze, smoke growing more impenetrable with every fired round.

From here in the center of the field the Tiger's range extended to every corner of the valley. There was no T-34 he couldn't reach.

0920 hours

'Go, go, Papa, go!'

Dimitri worked the gears. The *General* flattened out and ran like a thoroughbred over the ruts of the sunflower field.

Valentin had gotten them into a race with a Mark IV. Dimitri didn't know how far away the German ran beside them but he guessed it was ridiculously close; everything in this field was.

Valentin's boots were not on Dimitri's shoulders now.

'Ease left!' Valentin ordered. The Mark IV must have tried to shear off, quit the race, but Valya wasn't relenting.

'Straighten out.'

Valentin's voice flipped between steely and excited. He'd already left one Mark IV burning in the first minutes of the battle. Valya had shot him from behind; Dimitri had never in his life been *behind* a German tank! Now this sprinting Mark IV was their second target. Valya was the commander and gunner. He handled both duties – each was enough for one man – with skill and a measure of cool, even in this deadly valley coiled with the SS. Their two forces had rushed into a tank fight no one in either army could have trained for, never imagined would happen. Two hundred tanks inside four square kilometers, it was like a saloon brawl, but not with fists, with cannons! Dimitri wanted to be proud of his son, that would ease his fright at their situation, but he had his hands full flogging the *General* back and forth at Valentin's snap orders, stopping to fire, cranking into gear, and accelerating to keep moving, keep alive. And suddenly this race to the death. For that's what this was: Whoever pulled ahead could hit the brakes first. The other, still moving, would slide by, straight into the sights of the winner. This was an impromptu strategy, made up on the spot. What else could they do? Who knew how to fight like this? Cossacks on horseback, yes, but these weren't horses.

Dimitri eased the *General* in line and felt the speed climb again. The German wasn't getting away so easily.

The yellow field began to scorch and collapse under the great armored fracas. More and more the sunflowers were trampled, or burned by exploding fuel. Dimitri could only see straight ahead, flashing in and out of thinning green and gold patches, through drifts of gray smoke. He dodged other tanks that lurched in his way, tanks locked in their own confrontations; he avoided wrecks. The German was somewhere beside them. Dimitri did everything he could to be faster, to get his son the shot he needed.

He sped over the valley, searching through the whipping flowers for an advantage, anything. The Mark IV was a fleet enough tank to make this race dicey. Fifty meters ahead to the left, a thick column of smoke caught his eye. A T-34 and a Mark IV had rammed each other. The Mark IV had ridden up the Soviet tank's front. They'd both burst into fireballs. Through the smoke Dimitri spotted their criss-crossed turrets.

Valentin thought of the move the same moment Dimitri did.

'Come left.'

The smoking pylon of the two fused tanks was only seconds ahead. Dimitri knew what his son intended:

Valentin was going to shove the racing Mark IV, putting the two dead tanks right in his path. The German will have to swerve left – he won't dodge right, closer to us – or stop. Either way, he'll have to slow down. Valya will guess which way the German's going to jump. We'll stop first and have our cannon waiting.

'Everyone hang on. Papa, full stop!'

Dimitri crammed on the brakes. The *General* skidded, Dimitri corrected to keep the treads sliding straight. He downshifted fast. The *General* tilted forward as though to pour them all out through their hatches but Dimitri had the tank at a dead stop in seconds. Valentin did not fire immediately. The turret whined and rotated degrees right. In his head Dimitri trailed the Mark IV running away, saw it avoid the burning mess in front of it; he imagined the SS commander losing sight of the T-34 that had been broadside for almost a kilometer; the German thought, Oh, no; he screamed at his driver to swerve, evasive turns, now, now!; behind him, not far enough, carefully adjusting, the faster, smarter T-34 commander stayed in his range finder, neither fooled nor hot, following the German with the long eye of his cannon; the German counted seconds, gaining distance; does he shout, Ha ha! that he has got away? Dimitri turned in his seat to watch his son; Valentin toed the firing pedal with an oddly ginger tap for what it set loose; the breech recoiled with a massive shrug; Pasha fed it another round, all one flowing action; Valentin made a small adjustment to his aim and fired again; Pasha never left his knees, never seemed to be without a shell in his arms; Valentin fired again; three smoking casings lay on the matting; did the German commander count the shells coming in when he was done counting seconds?

'Let's get going, Papa.'

For thirty minutes, the *General* wandered over the valley floor, looking for jousts like a medieval knight. The sunflower field lay in total ruin, flattened under so many tracks, so much wrath and murder. Shapes strayed in the smoke. Valentin fired only a dozen more times, reporting no hits. Dimitri had no idea how the battle was going; who was winning? The tally of stilled Soviet tanks was greater than those of the Germans. This was no surprise to him; the Red force in these sunflowers had been held in reserve until Prokhorovka, they'd been untested in Kursk. These Germans were hardened SS. Dimitri felt hunted. He was always lost, reacting to shadows, boots stamped on his shoulders, he ran through stretches of sunflowers left standing that blinded him again, then emerged to no landmarks but more dead hulks. He saw tankers of both armies, out of their machines, scurrying to get away. Sasha took shots at them. He was never certain if the boy shot at SS or Russians, they all ran like any man would. He drove, in circles, straight, he stopped and started, he swerved. He stayed in a clench on the steering levers and waited, moving, never before so scared as he was now.

He drove past a beheaded T-34. The tank's turret lay upside down ten meters from the chassis, pouring fumes. In seconds another ruined Red tank smoldered nearby. Valentin's boot guided the *General* in a wide semicircle to the right, past four more destroyed T-34s, all of them arranged in a singed arc, a clock face of dead tanks.

'Jesus,' Valentin muttered.

'What?' Pasha demanded to know. He did not curb his impatience and Valya didn't reprimand him. 'What?' the boy insisted.

'Tiger,' Valentin told them.

0955 hours

Luis chose the targets.

Balthasar ruined them.

The air hung brackish with haze. After an hour of combat in the sunflower field, fifty tanks burned. Each black spire of smoke fed the haze. Luis stood in his cupola to peer through the mists. High above, rain clouds threatened, dimming the day even more. The optics in the Tiger were excellent, but they could not pierce far enough into the swirling battle. The eyepieces did not draw out Luis's instincts the way his raw eyes could. He remained half outside the tank, turning circles in the cupola, taking in the battle. He could not slake his hunger for the fight, keenly watching tanks of both sides dart through the shifting mists and thinning sunflowers. Packets of crackers stayed in his breast pocket, he let his body hunger like his heart. He followed one Red tank after another, even those thinly visible through the haze. When he knew what that tank would do, where it would turn, or when it would stop, he called Balthasar into the shot. Together, they rarely missed.

The wound in his chin slowed its drip, but not before Luis's breast glistened with blood. He ignored this and stood tall in the cupola, aware of the image he cast, stolid and brave in the Tiger's turret. Other *Leibstandarte* tanks roared past his place in the middle of the field. Luis was careful to show them a smoking barrel, himself in profile, raising a blood-smirched hand to single out another target. The motionless T-34s in a cemetery ring around his Tiger were testimony. This was the makings of legend: Luis, deathly thin and pale, blood-spattered, while his Tiger was the most powerful weapon on the battlefield. There would be talk of *la Daga* after today.

Luis had not moved the Tiger more than two hundred yards in any direction since firing his first shots. The Reds kept their distance, preferring to tangle with the less lethal Mark IVs, dancing in and out of the mists around Luis. Sometimes they darted at him, swooping in closer for a shot and paying for it. For minutes at a time, tanks of his company came to stand by him, idling on his flanks, hoping they were safer in the Tiger's shadow. Luis let them rest to admire his and Balthasar's shooting, then sent them back into the melee, like a father ordering his son outside to face a bully.

He watched one of his Mark IVs leave his side. At three hundred meters, just before disappearing into the mists, the tank was challenged by a T-34. Luis lifted his binoculars and followed the action between the two tanks. They entered into a race, vaulting across the field at top speeds, like two stallions, dashing, almost bumping each other. The Russian was cunning, he steered the Mark IV toward a wreck, making the German commander veer hard, slow down. The Red skidded to a remarkably quick stop, the tank seemed to hop to a standstill. The third shell from the Russian hit the SS tank in the rear; another shaft of smoke added its charcoal tarnish to the sky. Luis did not pull his binoculars from this Russian tank. He watched it circle, careful and nimble all at once. The Russian drove past several of the T-34s he and Balthasar had knocked out. There was an interesting quality to how this one tank moved through the battle and carnage. That race with the Mark IV was phenomenal, but now it seemed to skulk. What did this tank carry inside? It looked like heroism and reluctance married somehow. And something more, something rare. What? Luis considered, calculating.

The Red tank slowed, and Luis knew they had seen each other.

'Balthasar. Sixty degrees right.'

The great turret pivoted around Luis. The gun barrel did not raise at all, every target in the sunflower field was so close there was no need for elevation. Every shot was a flat trajectory.

'Do you see him?'

Balthasar did not answer for a moment. The smoke was thick, tanks ran every direction.

'The one turning toward us?' he said.

'Correct.'

'*Ja.*'

'Range?'

'Six hundred meters.'

'Wait, Balthasar. This one ... wait for him.'

Luis followed the coming Russian. He kept the binoculars up with one hand and patted his tunic pocket with the other. He grabbed a few crackers and slid them over his lips. The chewing made another drop of blood fall from his chin.

1003 hours

Dimitri had crossed boundaries all his life. He was a Cossack, he'd ridden over anyone's land he cared to. He'd played tag with death many times. He'd sneered at any notion that this or that was a place he should not go. Love had corralled him once, inside one woman for their time together. Love bound him again to their children, Katya and Valya. And that was all for the lines drawn across his life. He'd loved his freedom, *Kazak*.

Now, at Valya's command to attack the Tiger, Dimitri felt cold misgiving. He swept past the hulks of slaughtered T-34s. They were disfigured and burned, or simply perforated and still. The Tiger left marks on these T-34s that no other tank could, the destruction was utter. Dimitri skittered past them and it was like entering a boneyard, the scat of killing at the mouth of some monster's cave. The dead Soviet tanks were dark portents, warnings, do not come this way.

Dimitri reached for the handle on his hatch cover. To hell with this, he thought, there's no help from armor so close to a Tiger. One hit, even a glancing shot from that big cannon, and we'll be done. He pushed up the hatch and gazed into the open, seething air. The sunflowers were beaten down in this part of the field, from the Tiger's pacing, from the Russian tanks' bids to engage it, or from their doomed attempts to flee. Even half a kilometer away in the haze, the Tiger loomed a colossus.

Pasha objected to taking on the big tank but no one listened. Sasha stayed affixed to his machine-gun, quiet and uncertain.

Both boots slid off Dimitri's shoulders. He was out of the traces. What was this?

Instead of a heel, a gentle touch of the son's hand tapped beside Dimitri's neck.

'Take us in, Papa.'

Valentin was ceding the tank to Dimitri. That touch said, Ride, old man, old Cossack. Show us and show this German what you've learned, crossing all those times into and out of death. No one else but you can do this. Take us in.

In the last few days Dimitri had made himself want so little from Valentin. The boy had penned himself away from his father. Now the fences of that pen were down. Dimitri was free again, to go where he pleased.

He reined the *General* around at full speed. He crossed into the Tiger's realm of crushed machines and flowers. This was where he wanted to go, because this was where his son needed to go.

The Tiger pivoted its turret to greet them.

1005 hours

Luis had never seen a T-34, or any tank, move like this.

The Russian dashed toward him at top speed; even at four hundred meters off Luis marveled at the rate this tank ran. It came in at a narrow angle, slicing to the left, eating up the smoky distance. Balthasar tracked the sprinting Red with the Tiger's long barrel. The turret inched around Luis standing in his hatch. Luis aimed along with Balthasar, lining up the charging Red tank to the end of the barrel. Just when it seemed the gunner had the T-34 in his sights, the Russian skidded, turned full to the side like a slalom skier kicking up dirt instead of snow, then raced across the center line back to the right in an extraordinary zigzag. Balthasar's hydraulic traverse clunked to a sudden stop. The turret shuddered, then whined – an aggravated sound – to catch up.

Luis dabbed ginger fingers to his chin. Salt from the crackers lingered on his fingertips, making the cut sting when he touched it. He winced and licked the fingertips absently to clean them, licking blood, too.

The Red tank skimmed right, then left again. The driver must be a damned madman, Luis thought, he's scrambling the brains of his entire crew driving like that. For what? To display some panache before dying?

'Balthasar.'

'Sir.'

'Range.'

'Three hundred seventy-five meters.'

'Leave it for a moment. Let them come. They'll be too dizzy to do anything when they get here.'

Chuckles popped in the intracom.

'Driver. Keep us facing him. I want frontal armor on him at all times.'

'Ja.'

The Tiger began to lurch in small, backing steps to stay face-to-face with the jitterbugging Russian. The Tiger's adjustments were staccato, the driver charged one tread, then the other. Every move was jarring and ponderous. For a moment, Luis admired the Russian tank driver. This one had talent, style even, he handled his tank like the best *picadors* on horseback, it was lovely to see. But this Russian driver would die anyway. What could one T-34 do against a Tiger? Show off? Thumb its nose? Luis smiled at the thought of this Soviet horseman in flames in the next several seconds. The gash in his chin stretched, smarting him again, advising him to savor nothing. Prokhorovka would not fall to Luis so long as he was stuck in this field. Without Prokhorovka, he was mired in this body, this narrow ugly life. Every passing second the Americans dug in deeper in Sicily. Luis looked behind the lone charging Russian into the rest of the valley, where the Reds lost tank after tank and still seemed to have more than a hundred careening around, how many hundreds more across the whole corridor today? He swallowed and again tasted his own blood. He was angry in an instant.

'Balthasar.'

'Sir.' The gunner's response was quick, restive. Luis wondered, Is the crew getting nervous over this little pissant Russian?

'Take a shot.'

The T-34 tank was making a long sideways run now to the left, fast and broadside. Balthasar rotated his turret. He drew a perfect bead. Luis braced himself for the blast; the jolt he felt was not the cannon but his driver yanking the Tiger again to keep the Russian to the front, disrupting Balthasar's aim.

'Driver, damn it! Stop!'

The driver shifted to neutral. The tank stilled. The Russian had closed now to within two hundred meters, tightening a loop around the Tiger. The T-34 sped just beyond Balthasar's rate of turret traverse, which was only six degrees per second. With the Russian this close, at that clip, Balthasar could not keep up. Luis locked his eyes on the T-34 knifing through the remaining patches of standing sunflowers and could not believe what he saw. A murky cloud of dirt and the grist of stalks jetted from the Russian's left-hand track. Luis thinned his eyes and leaned forward. Unbelievable. The tread was not moving. The

Red driver had locked his brakes at full speed and somehow – Luis could not imagine it even as he watched it – spun the tank to a full stop. The Russian rocked and stopped two hundred meters away, with its gun facing the Tiger's port side.

'Balthasar!'

'I can't ...'

Luis ducked at the last instant. The woof of the T-34's cannon and the clang of the round striking the side of the Tiger leaped as one, the Russian was so close. Luis brought his hands over his soft helmet, protecting himself without knowing what to expect, no tank had ever fired at him from this distance. His eyes slammed shut, a fleeting death swept over him, but the Tiger shuddered and remained. Luis stood into the turret again. Smoke coursed from the port side. Balthasar never stopped revolving the big gun to the left, to catch the Russian. The cannon almost faced the rear now, but the T-34 was not at the business end of it, the tank had already gone, speeding off in its circle around the Tiger.

'Driver! Move, now! Keep us facing him!'

The Tiger's immense engine revved, the gears slapped into place. The tank seemed to stumble. Something tripped it from the left-hand track.

'What!' Luis shouted into his throat microphone.

'I don't know, sir. We might have taken a hit on a bogey wheel. I don't know.'

The driver's voice was frayed. This worry boded badly, as if it were the machine itself that was afraid.

The T-34 kept racing behind the Tiger. Balthasar traversed the turret as fast as it would go, straining but still lagging badly behind the swift Russian. Luis slid down to the deck. With feline speed Luis clambered over the fender and dropped to the ground beside the port wheels and tread. His cut chin throbbed; it was the least of his problems right now.

He was not surprised by what he saw, the deformed bogey wheel in the center. The Red shell – an armor-piercing round – had struck it near the top, bending the rim back into the two interlocking wheels behind it. The entire left side was sooted from the explosion, but the damage was contained. The Tiger would have to roll with care to avoid throwing the port track. The tank was hobbled, but not beyond repair.

His fury grew in the seconds he stared at the blackened, busted wheel. How was he to ride into Prokhorovka with this? How was he going to lead the assault out of this sunflower valley with a Tiger that couldn't go faster than a walk? Damn it, he thought, damn it! He'd have to deal with this rampaging Russian – there he was, scooting around to the other side with Balthasar chasing him – then limp back up the slope for a field repair. *¡Carajo!*

He leaped free of gravity, shooting off the shivering earth up the side of the Tiger and over the rotating turret. He slid his legs into his hatch and snapped into the intracom. He'd been on the ground for ten seconds, and when he returned to his place he found the T-34 still out-racing the end of Balthasar's cannon. Luis knew: the Russian was going to take a shot at the starboard wheels, to cripple the Tiger entirely. Then he'd circle in for the final blow.

'Driver, it's a port bogey wheel. Reverse starboard track only. Bring us around. Balthasar.'

'*Ja.*'

'He's going to pull the same trick on the other side. I want you to fire at him. Keep him moving. Don't let him stop.'

The Tiger lurched backward, pivoting on the inert left track to turn the Tiger to the right. The driver swung Balthasar's cannon around faster than the traverse could. The tank came to an abrupt halt, swaying Luis in his cupola. He bit back a curse at his driver. There was the T-34. A brown rooster tail spit from his spinning tracks. The Russian ran behind the Tiger's long barrel.

'Range.'

'Three hundred meters.'

'I don't care if you hit him. Let him know you will if he stops again.'

The day was still early. If he shouted enough at the field mechanics, the Tiger could be ready for a charge on Prokhorovka by dusk. He didn't need this lunatic T-34 on his scorecard, not at the risk of returning to his place at the head of the battle by nightfall. Let him go, Luis thought, I'll settle his hash in Prokhorovka if that *pendejo* is still alive tonight.

In the next moment, without warning, Balthasar fired. The report shoved Luis about in the cupola, cudgeling his back into the hard rim. This jarred his temper at the speeding T-34. He said a silent prayer that God would give him the opportunity to kill every man inside that tank.

The round missed, a pillar of steppe dirt rose beyond the Russian. Balthasar gave the T-34 too much range and the shell sailed over his head. But the Russian had to know now he'd pulled the Tiger's whiskers. The loader shoved in another shell. The gunner glued himself to his optics, rotating the turret, talking to the driver to give him another goose around to the left. The starboard tread surged forward and quit. Balthasar's gun came around. The Tiger moved like an old man with a peg leg. Luis lowered himself in the hatch for the blast. Balthasar fired. Luis popped up and peered through the gases and flung soil at the T-34. This shell missed, too, but in front of the Russian. Balthasar was bracketing him.

The T-34 slowed.

'Balthasar, fast! He's coming around for a shot!'

The turret whined, the hydraulic traverse brought the barrel dead on to the Russian tank. Balthasar slipped the tip of the gun just ahead of the T-34. Now, Luis thought, go ahead, *travahata*. Do your dance one more time, under my gun.

The Russian skidded, still the slaloming skier. Balthasar's long lethal eye watched the Red driver's antics, more fabulous moves and jukes. But this time the Red did not spin toward Luis to stop and take a shot at the starboard wheels. He stepped on the gas and headed away from the circle, into the battle mists of the sunflower field. Balthasar had chased him off. Luis was relieved only for a second. No, he thought. This Russian is going away to bring back others, a hunting pack to help him finish off the wounded Tiger before it can drag itself out of the valley.

'Let him go, Captain?'

Luis raised his binoculars. The Russian was hurrying off into the haze, making his little crazed dodges left and right.

'No, gunner. Give him a parting gift. And Balthasar –'

'*Ja.*'

'Hit him this time.'

Luis stared down the long cannon. Balthasar twitched it left, then left a degree more. The T-34 sideslipped, skipping and raising his plume. Balthasar waited. The tip of the barrel elevated a hair. Luis ducked.

The cannon wailed.

The Tiger rocked on its heels, then settled. Luis stood into the miasma of dust and fume. On all sides, the battle in the sunflower field raged on, thunder and flame erupted from every corner of the valley floor. A thin rain began to speckle the deck of the Tiger.

Luis did not need the binoculars to see the Russian smoking and still.

CHAPTER 30

1009 hours

Dimitri groaned. Every joint griped, his neck, hips, and shoulders felt pulled apart and snapped.

His goggles were gone. Smoke raked his eyes, gray billows of oil fumes and steam boiled out his open hatch. He groped through the coils to Sasha. The boy was there, slack and collapsed. Dimitri shook him by the wrist and saw the red face gleam with blood.

'No,' Dimitri muttered.

At that the boy hacked and twisted in his seat, he awoke like a fighting fish. Dimitri took a harder grasp on the boy's arm to tell him he was alive. Dimitri caught a glimpse of the boy's blood splashed on the tank wall where he'd slammed his face when the German shell hit.

Dimitri heard coughing. The intracom was off, the *General* was out cold. The tail of the tank hissed, hot metal sprayed water and diesel.

'Get out,' his son spewed in a huffing voice. 'Everyone out!'

The first thing Dimitri saw in the turret was Pasha's toothless open mouth. The thick boy lay crumpled on the matting, eyes closed and limbs splayed in an awful way to show he was either unconscious or dead. Several teeth lay around his cheek. Dimitri couldn't reach him to check for breathing. Beside Pasha, Valya's boots wobbled but planted him firmly enough to stand and open his hatch to release the smoke.

The Tiger had hit them square in the rear. The engine compartment and radiator were surely torn up and lost, but they'd contained the blast enough to let the crew, or most of them, survive.

'Valya,' Dimitri called. 'Valya.'

His son bent to bring his face down to Dimitri. Smoke poured out above him as though up a chimney.

'Papa.' Valentin grinned. 'Good.' His face was welted and bruised. The bridge of his nose colored, likely broken. He nodded at his father.

Dimitri returned the nod, to tell Valya he was heart-struck the boy was alive.

'Sasha?' Valentin asked.

'He's okay. Cut up a little.'

'Get out, Papa. Get Sasha out.'

Dimitri raised his eyes to the motionless loader. 'Pasha?' he asked.

Valentin shook his head, he didn't know yet. He laid a hand on Pasha's ribs, then nodded. The big loader was breathing. Pasha will have a mouth of gold teeth to show for this day in the sunflowers, Dimitri thought.

'Go, Papa. I'll get Pasha out.'

'We stung him, boy, didn't we?'

'Yes, we damn well did.'

'Someone will finish him off before the day's out.'

'Yes. Someone will. Get going.'

Dimitri started to turn around. He reached a hand out to shake Sasha into action. Valentin stopped him with a hard grip to the shoulder.

'Papa. You were ...'

The look on Valya's face was the awakened gaze of a son at a marvelous father, an indomitable figure.

'I know, boy. Come on. We're not done. Hurry, Valya. See you outside.'

Dimitri got woozy Sasha to open the belly escape hatch between his feet; then helped him slide out of the tank. When Sasha was on the ground, Dimitri tossed a glance over his shoulder to see Valya wrestling with Pasha, who roused like a sleepy child. We're all alive, Dimitri thought, our luck is changing. He rose from his seat through the driver's hatch and stood out into the sunflower field.

Sitting inside the *General,* careening back and forth over the valley floor, he'd had no way of experiencing any part of the battle except his own. Dimitri slid to the ground and felt it tremble.

The noise hit him next. Tank engines howled on every side, an incredible number of them in this valley, more than should fit here, engines crossed paths, pistons decided life and death as much as cannon fire. Tracks squealed over sprockets, more than a hundred guns mauled each other at gladiator distances, and from lifeless tanks strewn all over the field the black pulses of oil flames panted into the morning like the devil's breath. Overhead, unseen behind clouds and haze, more engines struggled to kill one another high in the air. Dimitri felt helpless and out of place, a man on this battlefield racked with motors and clashing steel. He leaped when a hand grabbed at his boot.

'Sasha! Christ, boy, come on, get up.' Dimitri helped the crawling lad from under the *General*'s treads, glad to be startled out of his astonishment. Several dead T-34s and one Mark IV were within a hundred meters. Closer was a deep crater. There was no time to salvage the toolbox he kept kit-strapped to the *General*'s deck. Ah, well, he thought. Better to save boys than wrenches. With Sasha leaning on him, running, Dimitri noticed for the first time a drizzle had begun to fall on the valley.

At the lip of the hole, Dimitri lowered Sasha, then jumped in after him. He clambered up on his elbows to look back at the *General*.

Pasha stumbled over the field behind them, clamping a hand to his bleeding mouth and staggering. Dimitri waved to be sure the loader saw them in the crater. Pasha waved back a crimson palm.

Where was Valya?

Dimitri helped the hurt loader into the crater and lowered him next to Sasha. He did not let go of the boy's arm.

'Where's Valentin? Pasha, listen to me. Where is the lieutenant?'

Pasha shook his head, not wanting to talk through the bloody gaps in his gums. Dimitri shook his arm.

'He'sh in 'e tank,' Pasha burbled. 'He won' come.'

'What ... what do you mean he won't come?'

Pasha pleaded with a puckered face to be left alone, to see if he could live out the rest of the day in this crater. If Lieutenant Berko wanted to stay in the tank, that was fine, because Pasha wanted to stay here and keep his head down. Dimitri stuck a finger at Sasha to instruct him, Pasha was just too stupid.

'Don't move. You're safest here. Wait 'til a T-34 comes by and flag them down and get on. Then get out of here.'

Sasha sat up. 'Where ...?' Dimitri pushed him back down to the warm dirt of the crater. Sasha sank back, unresisting.

'I've got to go, boys.'

Dimitri gripped both lads on their knees and squeezed, to be sure they could feel his parting blessing through their pains. '*Kazak,* Pasha. *Kazak,* Sashinka.'

He scrabbled over the lip of the crater. Every joint ached but he cast his pain off him like cobwebs; this is no time to be an old man, he thought. The two boys he left behind had a chance in the crater if they stayed low, if they had any more luck at all today; they'd used plenty already this morning. But Valentin. What was he doing?

Dimitri ran. His hip stabbed at every step but he would

not let it slow him. He crashed over the few standing sunflowers rather than run around them. He was halfway to the *General* when he stopped.

Forty meters away, the commander's hatch cover to the *General* fell and clinched down. Dimitri's chest seized. Moments later, he watched the driver's door shut, too. He could hear the hard metal clangs, like a closing cell.

Valya had seen him coming. He was not going to leave the tank.

Dimitri screamed across the distance, into the bellow of cannons and screeching shells. He bent double at the waist and balled his fists.

The *General* stood stoic, weeping smoke. The two stood, man and tank, father and son, both exhausted and glaring and absolute.

Then Valentin answered Dimitri. The turret of the dead tank, facing the opposite direction, began to rotate, creaking, turned by the hand crank.

The *General*'s engine and all power were down. But the gun still worked. And Valentin was still the gunner.

'No,' Dimitri protested, knowing the word was useless.

The Tiger.

Dimitri cursed and tore his eyes to the left, across the earsplitting valley. Four hundred meters off, the monstrous German tank was withdrawing, backing away with its frontal armor toward the field. Valentin was going to take another shot.

'At what?' Dimitri raged at his son. 'At what? The fucking thing is leaving, let it go! You can't hurt it, let it go!'

Valentin had no angle if the German retired straight up the slope. Any shell smacking that thick hide would only snag the Tiger's attention and get an answering .88 mm round, aimed at a motionless, defenseless T-34.

Valya said the two of them had traded places. That Dimitri was not ready for it. Dimitri thought now, we have not traded this place, father and son. You will not die first, boy.

'No,' he said again.

This time the word did not feel so without purpose on his lips.

Dimitri whirled from the *General*. Four other T-34s knocked out by the Tiger were within running distance. If he could find one of them that still had a working cannon, he would ...

Before he could take a step, a Mark IV bore down on him out of a patch of sunflowers. He caught the sparking of the machine-gun in the corner of the glacis plate. Bullets ripped up the steppe near his boots, others zinged past like hellion bees. He dove to the dirt. He barely heard the zip of the machine-gun in the loudness of the battle and the crunching of the tracks. The machine-gun looked for him, tossing stalks and dirt into the air, then paused. Dimitri lifted his head out of his hands. The Mark IV still barreled straight for him.

'Damn it,' Dimitri sputtered and jumped off the ground, gritting his teeth against the pain in his leg. He had to lead the Mark IV away from the *General*. He couldn't let the German spot Valya turning the T-34's turret. And he couldn't run back to the crater where Pasha and Sasha lay shaken and bleeding. He sprinted across the field, scrambling over trampled flowers and the dimpled ruts of tank tracks. He headed toward the nearest of the dead T-34s killed by the Tiger. The Red tank was sixty meters off, he needed all his speed. He pumped his arms and the Mark IV turned with him.

Bullets hacked at the ground behind him. He wove his way to the T-34, each shift of direction shot bolts of agony out of his hip. This Red tank was not burned like the others that had died near it. A wide hole had been bored neatly through the middle of the turret. At this range, the Tiger's big cannon had drilled a shell right through one side of the T-34 and out the other! He had only that instant to marvel, the Mark IV's machine-gunner cut loose again. Dimitri threw himself between the T-34's treads just ahead of a sickle of bullets slashing at the soles of his airborne boots. He hit and skidded under the tank, his hip hurt so much, he thought he might have taken a bullet in it. Thirty meters away the Mark IV curled a small semicircle, pondering whether to keep up the chase against this lone tanker, then lost interest and veered away to another of the hundred duels raging in the valley. Dimitri peered out into the rain and watched the tank rumble past the *General*. The German did not see Valya's slowly rotating gun.

Dimitri rolled onto his back. His hip smarted enough to force a tear down his cheek. He heaved for breath.

Just above his nose, the hard belly of the T-34 rattled. Dimitri smelled exhaust.

The tank was running.

Dimitri swept aside his pain again and thrust himself out from between the treads. The hatch was open. The driver was gone, so was the machine-gunner. He spun to look one more time at the *General*. Valya had the turret cranked halfway around to the escaping Tiger. In another fifteen seconds he'd have the gun in position. Dimitri hoisted himself up on the T-34's fender. He stepped down into the driver's hatch. He bent his knees and descended.

Dimitri almost leaped back out. Blood was everywhere. His feet reached for the pedals, skimming through a horrible slick in the bottom of the tank. The driver's gauges and controls were splashed red. Dimitri whirled behind him and recoiled at the bodies of the commander and leader. The German .88 shell had cut through them both; the commander had been standing when the round entered, he was split and folded over at the ribs, his two halves were toppled on their sides, spilling entrails and every fluid the body courses, his shocked face toppled between his own boots. The loader was slumped in his seat, headless. The German shell had cut through his neck, then exited the turret beside him. The neat hole leaving the armor was rimmed with gore where the pressure sucked out, taking the loader's head with it. Shrapnel had whittled both bodies with a thousand crimson pits, their coveralls were shredded. The smell of death cooped in this tank was overpowering: gut, bile, and blood mingled to make the compartment ferocious and sickening. Dimitri gripped the steering levers. The driver and machine-gunner must have leaped out as soon as they discovered they were still alive, no reason to stay in this hellhole.

He shifted into first gear, nailed the accelerator, and took off. The corpses behind him jostled with a damp flop. Dimitri shivered and hit second gear.

'Christ,' he muttered. He had only seconds, so that was all he could say for himself and his dead crew. He sucked his cheeks and found enough moisture in his mouth to spit into the blood at his feet, to clean his tongue of the vomit taste. Go, he thought. Go.

He was not able to see the *General* any longer. He drove hard, shifting again. He said to Valya, 'Wait, boy. Wait for me.'

He slung the T-34 around as fast as he could, the bodies behind him skidded in their butchery but he could pay them no more mind. There was the limping Tiger, retreating into its own exhaust out of the sunflower valley. He sped toward it, skimming the T-34 back and forth as he had done the *General,* but this time not to get a shot, only to draw the Tiger's attention. To make it stop. Make it turn sideways. To make the great son of a bitch aim its cannon at his speeding ghost tank, and not his son.

1012 hours

Luis backed away.

His Tiger could manage no more pace than a brisk walk. An hour ago, he'd rumbled down the slope through the wall of purple smoke, he was the first tank into the valley, blasting Russians and crushing flowers. He'd been a titan, astride a titan's tank. Now he shrank away, stanching his own blood, his Tiger limping on a bad paw, spooling out the land he'd reeled in. Backing away, he was no larger than his little famished body.

Luis contained his anger at the receding battle. He would be back before dusk, mechanics be damned! And then he'd swell with the land again. He surveyed the departing field, the number of hulks he'd left around him. A dozen, more, he imagined their smoke rising into the sky to write his name in dark script. The sunflower field knew he'd been there, and Prokhorovka would know him when he returned tonight.

No other tanks came near. The Russians left him alone. Why would they come after a retreating Tiger; if it's leaving the battlefield, isn't that good enough for today? Why risk taking it on, still dangerous? Balthasar fired no more shots. Luis would not let the driver stop long enough for the gunner to take aim.

He surveyed the valley now that he was leaving it. *Leibstandarte* was stymied down here, but holding its own against vastly superior numbers. The Russians couldn't keep pouring tanks into the fight, their reserves had to have a limit. His division would surely punch through by afternoon. He couldn't tell what was taking place outside the sunflower field, north of the Psel with *Totenkopf* and south of the rail mound for *Das Reich*. The rain added its beaded curtain to the haze, closing down visibility. The valley magnified the wrench of steel and the deep *whumps* of cannons and exploding armor, giving Luis's ears no information from the surrounding frays. He believed they must be as intense as his own, and grimaced that he did not know if the day was being won or lost. But backing away from the battle now, he was amazed at its magnitude. Still almost two hundred tanks clashed at close quarters in the sunflowers. Never before, he thought, and he had to cinch down his rancor at leaving the history that was carving itself out in this field. If Hitler could see this, he would not talk of stopping the assault on Kursk for Italy's sake. He would applaud and come fight alongside us, and be part of this.

Luis had no more to eat. All his crackers and tidbits were gone. His stomach agitated for attention, he had nothing to give it but water. He dipped his head below the hatch to reach for his canteen, then stood in the cupola, unscrewing the canteen cap. He took a swig, eyes open, then lowered the jug too fast in surprise at what he saw. Water drizzled down his chin, cooling his cut; a pink wash slipped down his neck, under his black SS collar.

What was this? He winced into the gunsmoke mist and falling rain, at a Russian tank charging at him, cutting up the ground in that unbelievable lightning zigzag.

The crazy Red driver. It's him again! But Luis killed his tank minutes ago!

He dropped the open canteen, it banged down into the Tiger's well. He raised his binoculars to pierce the haze in the valley.

The T-34 came hard, sideslipping. What was the fool doing? Was this some sort of *loco* Russian cat with nine damned lives?

'Balthasar!'

'I see him, Captain.'

'Range.'

'Three hundred meters. Closing.'

'Stay on him.'

'Jawohl.'

The Tiger's turret jerked awake. The hydraulic traverse began its high-pitched labor to bring the big cannon to bear. Balthasar's voice had betrayed no concern. The gunner was locked in, figuring distance and lead, tracking the target with nothing else to think of. The turret jittered around Luis's chest, left, then right, trying to keep up with the Russian driver all over again. This was the same man, yes? Supposedly a dead man, coming at the Tiger again in another tank. There couldn't be two Red drivers with that ability. The T-34 dodged and weaved, alone in the attack, just like before. Luis recognized every move. He held out no welcome for the return of a worthy foe. He sensed a cold touch of dread. Something was going on that he could not fathom.

The Russian sheered off from his swerving headlong dash. Luis had guessed he would. The T-34 bounded to the left, to advance down the damaged side of the Tiger. Damn it, Luis thought. He's going for the port bogey wheels again! One more hit there and the Tiger will lose a track, we'll only go in circles. Of course!

'Driver! Turn to him. Keep him away from the side. I want frontal armor on him! Move!'

The Tiger jerked to a stop. Gears and driveshaft howled. The Tiger came out of reverse and lurched forward now, spinning only the right tread to push the tank around to the left. Balthasar worked the traverse to catch up with the enemy boring in alongside. Again the swift T-34 managed to stay just ahead of the rotating cannon. But this time the whole crew knew what this Russian had in store. The Tiger's driver did a better job of swinging the chassis around to keep their front trained on the Russian. Balthasar's gun slid ahead of the T-34.

'Got him,' intoned the gunner.

'No. Stay on him. He'll stop in a moment. Then.'

'*Ja.*'

The Red tank kept up its dash along the left side, two

hundred meters off and angling in, narrowing the distance. Balthasar's gun moved with the Russian. Luis stared hard at the T-34. Something was wrong. He raised his binoculars and focused on the neat hole in the center of the Russian's turret. Luis recalled the shot, one of Balthasar's first in the sunflower field. The .88 shell had sliced right through the Russian tank like cheese and left it standing in the field, spookily intact but surely dead. This *loco* Soviet driver and his gunner had somehow survived the hit on their own tank. They'd crept into this one, mice to the cheese, and brought the tank alive for another go at the big cat, Luis's retreating Tiger.

Why, Luis thought? It's insane to come back. I killed you once, I'll do it again! In his mind he hurled this at the Russian tank but felt his warning glance off the slanted green armor. No, they won't heed. The Russians are maniacs, reckless, just like Hitler says, unflinching, witless, subhumans. Do you have to kill them all more than once, is that how this war is going to go? Luis was hungry and had no food. He needed to get his damaged tank repaired, he needed to leave and return to the battle with haste, everything with haste; history and glory look slow in books but these things are only made in flashes of opportunity, by the hand on the trigger. He was incensed that this single T-34 wouldn't let him back away. Luis had already killed this man and this tank! The Russian driver and his gunner were using up more than their allotments of one life each. In Spanish under his breath he cursed them, glaring down the rotating barrel of the Tiger's gun. He would have to stop backing away and fight, though he did not want to, he did not have time for this. The thought of killing something or someone twice did not sit with him, not with what he knew and expected of God and death. This was wrong. This whispered to him with the voice of the T-34's winding diesel – close enough now to breathe in his ear – of *mala suerte,* bad, bad luck.

Just as he predicted, the T-34 stopped, like an arrow finding its mark, sudden but this time unremarkable. The Russian slid to a halt straight at the end of Balthasar's barrel. Its own cannon was off, not fixed on the Tiger.

'Now?' Balthasar asked.

Why stop there, Luis wondered? Why not outrun our turret again? There's nothing the Russian can do, not even this close, a hundred meters away. His round will smack the frontal plating of the Tiger and make no more than a deep dent. One word to Balthasar and I'll blow him backward another hundred meters.

Why isn't his turret moving? He hasn't aimed at us yet. What is he ...?

The T-34 idled.

The Tiger was broadside to the sunflower field, facing the decoy. Luis looked across the short distance into the open driver's hatch. He saw a white face and a bloody palm waving hello. Or goodbye.

'Now?' Balthasar pressed.

Luis turned only his head, knowing he could not turn his tank fast enough.

1014 hours

Valentin's shell hit the Tiger on the starboard bogeys. Dimitri watched the big tank vanish in a maelstrom of smoke and flash. He balled his open hand into a fist and shook it at the instant fireball.

He shouted into the din, 'Good shot, son! Now hit him again!'

The explosion was done in a moment. The Tiger weathered the hit with incredible brawn, it barely shuddered. It was a stupendous sight to see how much damage it could take. When the smoke receded, the German commander was not standing in his cupola. He'd either been blown out or ducked at the last instant.

Valentin was alone in the *General*. The son would have to scoot around the hot extended breech, dig up another AP round from the bins, ram the shell into the breech, and get back to his optics. Any adjustment to his targeting would have to be made with the hand cranks. Valya had a broken nose, and who knew what other injuries, to deal with. Valentin would do what he had to do, no question. Dimitri grinned up into the dark bore of the Tiger's cannon, proud and certain that this best trait of his own, if none of the others, would stay alive in his son.

His hands and feet were ready to shift into gear. The Tiger smoked, brooding. The big tank was bruised, but how badly? Could Valentin fire again and kill it before the Tiger recovered?

The Tiger's enormous engine roared. Its transmission engaged, black exhaust expelled, the tracks of both sides shrieked over damaged wheels.

The tank bucked backward ten meters.

The Tiger could still move!

Dimitri cursed. Now Valya would have to take aim again. Without the *General*'s hydraulics, this would take precious seconds, perhaps more than Valentin had. Damn it!

The Tiger backed and pivoted to the right, racking itself to turn toward the center of the field, a great wounded creature and now certainly angry. Its cannon traversed away from Dimitri, careless for his curses or his life. He was no threat, a T-34 with no gunner, with holes in his turret.

In the Tiger's cupola, the commander reappeared. He waved back at Dimitri, blood on his hand, too. Then he pivoted, with binoculars pressed to his brow, his turret rotating around him. He ignored Dimitri.

The German turned to his right, to Valentin.

Dimitri spit again into the red bog beneath his boots.

Enough, he thought. He shifted the T-34 into gear and mashed the accelerator. Let's shake these bloody hands.

The German commander's face left his binoculars, not ignoring Dimitri now.

1014 hours

Luis believed only for the first second that the loco Russian was leaving. The T-34's treads spun, again with that unlikely acceleration, and the tank with the dead turret turned in to the rain.

Then the Russian swerved back at the Tiger. He angled to the right, racing to stay ahead of the Tiger's turning cannon.

Balthasar's voice bit through the engine clamor.

'What's he doing?'

The gunner had finally gone urgent. Luis fought to keep panic out of his own throat. He needed to give an order, but confusion and dismay delayed him. He was divided in half: one Red tank drew a bead on him from four hundred meters off; another bore in crazily from a hundred meters away. Something wasn't fair here, the *mala suerte*. He felt like he'd stepped in a hornet's nest, why were they coming after him like this? These two madmen working in tandem, why?

Luis found his voice. Only a moment had passed, but all that remained was moments.

'Gunner, stay on target.'

The Tiger's turret continued to rotate clockwise around Luis. The T-34 out there with the live cannon had to be handled first.

'Driver, keep backing, keep turning!'

'*Ja*.'

The damage to the starboard bogeys was bad but no worse than the port wheels. The Tiger could still stumble along slowly, could still get out of this valley. But there was nothing Luis could do to avoid this crazy T-34 closing in. He could have Balthasar try to shoot him down, but that would delay dealing with the other, more dangerous Red tank. The Russian driver continued to skid around to the right, stubbornly staying in front of the pivoting Tiger. With every meter, the Russian tightened his course.

Luis could not use binoculars to check on the shooting T-34 out there in the mist, he had to cut his eyes back and forth between the two attackers. Across the sunflower field, the shooter's power was down; he was aiming at the retreating Tiger manually. Balthasar, with all his hydraulics running, ought to be able to fix on the Russian gunner first, if Luis could keep everyone calm.

What to do with this charging *cabrón*? Kill him, too.

'Bow gunner!'

'Ja!'

'Aim at the driver's hatch!'

The machine-gun in the Tiger's glacis plate added its bursts to the rising din of those desperate seconds. Bullets scorched out of the ball-mounted barrel, tattooing against the wheeling T-34. The rounds ricocheted, striking sparks from the armor. The Russian tank was too much broadside for the bow gunner to have a shot into the open driver's hatch. The Russian bobbed and weaved and drew closer, still running ahead of Balthasar's traversing turret. Luis shook his head at what he saw: this damned driver was only seventy-five meters away now and gaining speed, insanity! What is he doing? I'm simply going to kill the shooter's tank – again! – then I'm going to kill him! What is he doing? Why? Something, something is wrong.

He tore his gaze from the charging tank to glance down the length of the Tiger's cannon. Across the valley the shooter would be in Balthasar's sights in moments. Just fifteen more degrees clockwise. Come on, Luis urged. His thin chest tightened. *Come on!* He couldn't determine through the haze if the Red gunner had them in his own sights yet. But he had no time left to focus on the shooter. Here came the other one.

The speeding Russian tank leveled out, no more dodges marred his approach. He charged straight in, on a diagonal at the Tiger's starboard fender. The angle from the right was too sharp, he was beyond the bow gunner's reach. Luis heard the crazy driver pop his clutch and shift gears, hitting full stride.

'Driver!' Luis hollered, but he had no orders. Someone, several voices, screamed, 'Look out! He's ... !'

He's what? Luis clenched his hands on the cupola rim, bracing for the impact. His mind raced, fast as the charging T-34. He's what? Going to ram us? And seconds after the minor shock of it we're still going to blow up his damned mate across the field; then we're going to pull back from the collision, depress Balthasar's cannon and kill him. What the hell is he ... ?

In the last mote of time, before the final meter between the T-34 and the Tiger slammed shut, Luis understood.

He's not crazy. He knows exactly what he's doing.

The Russian hit hard. He rammed the middle of his glacis plate into the Tiger's right-hand fender. Luis was jolted but his massive tank held its ground, it weighed more than twice the T-34.

Luis roared, 'Back! Keep backing!'

The Tiger tried to pull away from the Russian, the huge Maybach engine strained to revolve the tracks over injured wheels. The screech of metal against metal was excruciating. The T-34 had hit with so much speed and momentum it lodged itself against the Tiger's starboard drive sprocket. The right side of the Tiger was tangled and numbed.

'Driver, port tracks! Full reverse!'

The left-hand treads spun. The Tiger began to peel away from the T-34.

The Russian would not allow this. He hit his gas and the gap closed instantly. The T-34 kept its weight butted against the starboard drive sprocket. With just one working track, the Tiger could only drag itself in a circle.

'He's not letting go!' The driver cried out the obvious.

Balthasar shouted, 'Captain!'

Luis did not need to hear Balthasar's next words. He saw for himself the extent of what the *loco* Russian had done, the method in his madness.

The T-34's cannon had cut in front of the Tiger's long gun, the two long barrels were crossed like fencing swords. Luis's turret was stopped dead, the hydraulic traverse whined in frustration. As long as the tanks stayed jammed together, Balthasar could not rotate clockwise any farther, not the last few crucial degrees toward the shooter across the field.

Luis leaned forward in his cupola to peer down on the smashing T-34. The smaller tank had both tracks stroking wildly, kicking up mud and bits of ruined flowers, as though racing over the valley instead of plunging only torturous centimeters. The two tanks spit billows of exhaust, their squalling engines pushed and pulled but without decision, they were fused as much by force as willpower. Luis leaned out to his right, to look down into the Russian's open hatch. He caught a glimpse of matted gray hair. The face tilted up at him. It was sharp-nosed, grimy and determined. Luis wanted to ask, Is this how you wanted to end up, old man? Here, with me? He yearned to climb down and poke his head into the hatch, to tell the driver – not such a lunatic, now, it seemed – to go away, that Luis didn't want to end up here, either.

The driver bared his teeth up at Luis, either a smile or grim intent. The Tiger kept trying to disengage, bucking and humping backward, both tanks howled. The old man would not let loose. His partner the shooter was still out there, aiming at a Tiger that was being wrestled to a standstill. But the shooter's tank was immobile, and the Tiger still had its thick frontal armor facing him.

Maybe he won't shoot, Luis thought. The one out there. Maybe he's waiting for reinforcements to come teeming after us. Or maybe he won't shoot and risk killing this old man. This what ... beloved commander, friend, uncle? Or father?

'Yes,' Luis said, and the word was buried, even he could not hear it through the clamor of the entangled machines.

Maybe the shooter would wait. But Luis could not.

He tore his cloth helmet from the intracom, leaving the cable looped over the back of his chair. He hoisted his legs out of the cupola and climbed onto the broad turret deck. He drew his Luger sidearm into a blood-crusted hand. The Tiger rollicked from the ramming Russian. Luis knelt to steady himself. He inched forward like a sailor in a tempest. He raised the Luger and snapped off a shot at the T-34's open driver's hatch. The Russian's head ducked, the round glanced off the armor.

Luis crept closer to the rim of the deck for a better look at the Russian. There was the old man's chest, his gray coveralls.

Luis raised the Luger.

'*¡Bastante!*' he yelled down at the Russian. '*¡Bastante, cabrón!*'

The gun wavered with the swaying deck. His bloodied finger tightened on the trigger.

The Tiger's turret moved beneath him.

What? Luis muttered, '*¿Qué pasa?*'

He pulled his eye off the pistol to look down under his boots.

The turret was turning! The long .88 barrel pivoted counterclockwise, freed from the Russian's blocking cannon.

Damn it! Balthasar couldn't wait! Stupid! Without

orders the gunner was traversing the turret the opposite direction, rotating all the way around to the left for a shot at the Red shooter.

Balthasar, the thousand-year Aryan, was turning the Tiger's vulnerable side armor to the sunflower field!

Luis dropped the pistol. He dove backward for the commander's hatch. The turret whined to the left, every second revealing more of its thinner side plating to the Soviet shooter. He rammed his head down into the hatch, past Thoma's blood, and screamed, 'No! Stop! Stop!'

Balthasar had his back turned, his attention was riveted into his optics. Beside the gunner, on the far side of the immense breech, the loader looked up from his seat. Luis screamed at him, gesturing frantically at Balthasar, 'Stop the turret! Stop him!' The loader looked stunned, no idea what was going on. 'Stop him!' Luis screamed.

Beneath Luis the turret kept turning, the huge turret with the undefeatable cannon.

Luis fumbled for the cord to re-connect himself to the intracom. His fingers waggled at it, just out of reach. He'd have to clamber down to his seat to retrieve it, plug in, and scream into the microphone. That would be too late.

The loader got the idea. He set down the shell he cradled. He rose from his seat and leaned far across the breech to tap Balthasar on the back, saying something into the intracom. Balthasar was rapt and did not turn away from his eyepiece. There was a comic aspect to the loader's calm, he was oblivious to their peril. Luis watched the slow drift of events, more seconds gone. The loader was a dead man. So was Balthasar. Luis did not bother to inform them.

By now the turret had spun a quarter way around to the left, exposing its entire side to the field. The waiting, aiming Russian gunner out there in his smoking tank with his live cannon must be amazed at his good fortune. Now he will shoot. He must.

Luis lifted his head out of his hatch, done with frenzy. He lay on his belly, facing the rear of the turret. The Russian driver had not let up for a moment, gnawing and jamming the starboard drive sprocket, holding the Tiger in place. The two tanks seemed to be mating, violent, the cramming of animals. Luis slid forward on his stomach to see better into the Russian hatch. The old man was there, leaning in to his gears and levers; he looked to be gripping the reins of his animal, galloping flat out, going nowhere.

The Russian looked up. His mouth was wide open. He was bellowing.

Luis used the last second to decide, after all, the old man was insane.

1015 hours

Dimitri watched the Tiger's cannon rotate away from his blocking barrel. The Tiger, the tank killer, was laying itself wide open.

With the turret revolving from him, Dimitri could back off. He could fly into reverse, spin around, hit the gas, and get out of there.

But if he freed the Tiger, the big tank would back away, too. Valentin's aim would be thrown off. With just a flywheel, the boy might not be able to adjust his gun fast enough.

The Tiger's turret turned, like a backward second hand, set to go off when it reached Valentin.

Dimitri had to stay, grappling the German to a standstill.

So be it, he thought.

He shouted, 'Yah!' to spur his T-34 faster.

Take the shot, Valya.

Dimitri shoved his T-34 deeper into the Tiger.

He charged one last time into the enemy. He had no

sword to swing and he did not wear the flapping cape of his clan but he spurred his mount and he saw his foe's face. It was a white face, taut and skull-like. It was daubed with blood. It was Death's face, sure enough, looking down on him over the rim of the Tiger's turning turret.

The game T-34 rumbled around him, lunging hard against the Tiger. The two corpses on the tier behind him had settled and gone silent in the last seconds; they were dead and terribly done, and they appreciated his vengeance. But they did not recruit Dimitri, they left all decisions to him.

The Tiger's turret kept turning, ticking more seconds. Dimitri was not alone here. He had his connection to his daughter. He was inside her spirit more than he ever was in Valentin's. He'd lived well in her heart, housed and respected there, he had no worry for Katya the flyer, the rider.

Take the shot, boy. Before the Tiger's turret swivels around the other side. I'll stay here. This is my last saddle, I'll stay in it.

Do it now.

Is there any link left between us, Valya? Hear me. Damn it, hear me, don't let this Tiger leave the valley! Show me you hear me!

The Tiger's turret was full broadside to the sunflower field now. The German commander lay on top of his tank as if to save it, to beg for its life.

Beg all you want, bastard. A Cossack tells you this.

Dimitri closed his eyes. He leaned forward in his seat, pressing his weight, too, into the Tiger, everything he was. Everything.

He drew a deep breath, tasting diesel smoke, metal shavings, blood, the holy steppe, life, and screamed out for victory.

'Take the shot! Take the shot, boy! Yah! Take the shot!'

1015 hours

Luis had time in the air to look but too much pain to make sense of what he saw.

But he knew flame, that was heat. Red below him, black-veined, uncoiling. It reached for him, he sailed ahead of it. There was something else in the air with him, giant, a flipping tiddlywink, a great twisting lollipop.

Sound shut down and then there was no color. He was black but not so black that he was not light, flying in this body, all had slipped him, light and gravity.

He was black but fear welled out of it, congealed, a shadow deeper.

When the ground struck him he'd forgotten about the ground, so intimate was his soaring. He was shocked to stop, and lay aware only that he was still.

His senses stayed away, frightened off by his emptiness the way jackals avoid a fire. He lay with the fear only, because there was nothing else.

This was the hell he'd read about, he'd learned of in church. Fear, alone. It was horrible. Where was the door out, where was his death? He searched in his body for his death but that, too, eluded him. This was the second time looking for death and not finding it. Leningrad was the first, and now. Where? Here. Kursk.

Sound came back, his moan. Then light, fluttering, creeping back to him. He cracked open his eyes.

The blackness began to dispel. His fear did not leave right off but instead ran into his legs and arms, his chest, neck, and head, looking for reasons to stay, places to hide.

The Tiger burned in front of him. The T-34 jammed against it was also swallowed in gouts of fire and smoke; the two machines were catastrophic wrecks, melting together. The Tiger's turret was gone, the hole where it had been was a volcano.

Heat from the blaze lapped at his cheeks. Luis rolled onto his back.

He looked up and did not see vastness, only the low, thick haze from rain and the battle still erupting. He listened and heard the lick of flames even louder than his heart. His body throbbed at him, almost rocking him in a sharpened cradle of pains, but the earth beneath him trembled even more with explosions and the heavy foot of war.

He lay alive, bleeding, broken in places. The battle had been taken from him, and that was all. He tried to be grateful, but that avoided him, as well.

Now that he had failed, everything averted itself from him. Destiny, God, even death.

Luis was again a pariah.

CHAPTER 31

July 12
2110 hours
Monbijou Bridge
Berlin

The air-raid sirens began their city-wide wail.

Abram Breit did not turn around on the bridge across the river Spree to run back to the hospital. He did not run anywhere, his ribs hurt too much and his hips were still sore from his wild gallop on the Russian steppe to escape the crazy partisans. Bruises lined the insides of his thighs and he had a tender spot on his crown from being thumped in the field after the crash. After two days of rest, he'd signed out of the hospital. He intended to make his way to his rooms in his boarding house near the Zoological Gardens in Charlottenburg. The sirens surprised him but would not dissuade him from getting back to his own bed after his Russian adventure. Limping, he ran a hand along the bridge railing, looking up.

He headed south toward the Brandenburg Gate and Unter den Linden. He decided he would not seek shelter during the raid but would walk home through the open spaces of the Tiergarten. He wasn't afraid to do this, and knew in a familiar place inside that he ought to be. Breit considered his new self, and hoped courage would not also make him stupid.

Just over the river Berliners were drawn out of their

buildings by the sirens and into the streets and alleys, then down into the warrens under the city, the shelters and subway tunnels where they were ordered to go when the alarm sounded. Only uniformed soldiers were allowed out during a raid, everyone else was required to be in a shelter or risk arrest. The people, mostly women and elderly, were orderly, even bland, carting babies and food baskets. Hitler and Goebbels bleated constantly about the bravery of the homefront, how Germans would not succumb to these Anglo assaults. Breit noted some weeping among the people flowing by. That's fine, he thought, you can still cry and be brave. I have done it recently.

After ten minutes walking with the howling horns, the first searchlights came on. Nothing showed at the far tips of their pillars. The drone of British Mosquito bombers vibrated over Berlin like metal clouds coming to shower bolts and nuts. It was an eerie noise, rattling out of the night like that, invisible, it struck Breit's memory of the partisans, who, too, worked in the night. There was something unfair about this type of fighting, also something terrifying and effective, coming and going when right people should be finishing dinner, readying for bed. As if war were not terrible enough, Breit thought, it is also the ultimate inconvenience.

He reached the Brandenburg Gate and passed under it. He crossed the wide boulevard and entered the great park in the heart of Berlin. His rib cage and legs complained when he stumbled over a curb, not watching where he walked, his head tilted up to the crossing searchlights. The streets were almost empty now, bearing only the hee-haws of ambulances and fire trucks scrambling into position throughout the city. The Tiergarten was unlit except for the beams. The lights swept to and fro, making the shadows of the trees in the park sway and crawl over the ground, making the whole park teeter. Breit hobbled to a broad plat of grass and sat.

The first bombers buzzed over the city. The evening was clear, searchlights rid the sky of stars. A dozen planes in the first echelon took the stars' places, snared in the beams; the lights stopped their dizzying reel whenever they snared the trophy of a bomber. Breit stared up and saw these planes drop not bombs but flares, green sizzling signals for the ones behind to mark where they should drop their loads. The British did not bomb only factories and military targets. Hitler did not do so when he visited the skies over London, so this was fair, Breit decided, an ugly tit for tat. The flares drifted down on little chutes into the city's center, over the Adlon Hotel, the burned-out Reichstag, Hitler's Chancellery, the dense streets of offices and neighborhoods, and the Tiergarten. It was odd watching their slow fall, the invasion of bad tidings with a touch of sparkles, like holiday lights. Several flares landed in the park around Breit but he did not move to put them out.

Anti-aircraft stations opened up, punching at the Anglo bombers seen and unseen. There were many 88 mm gun emplacements throughout the city. Cannons stood on top of buildings like the IG Farben headquarters in Parisërplatz, there was one at the Red-White Tennis Club. The inner-city's air defense was principally handled by three huge flak towers with eight big guns each. The towers were designed by Albert Speer, built in 1941: at the Zoological Gardens behind the bear cages, in Humbolthain Park, and in Friedrichshain Park. These were massive fortresses, intended by Speer to inspire faith among Berliners. They were gun batteries, as well as bunkers and communications towers, but also castles, almost medieval, meant to be the first of the new buildings for Germania, Hitler's city of the future that would replace Berlin after the war. Breit listened to the three giant bastions open up, heard the woof of smaller guns around the city. Beneath the guns and the sirens was the piping of tumbling British bombs.

The initial barrages landed south of the park, on Wilmersdorf and Shöneberg, residential districts. The first bombs were incendiary, meant to start fires to light the way better for the waves of bombers following, the ones with the big payloads. Berlin was to be handed the butcher's bill tonight for the Reich's failure in Russia. The British wagged a finger in Hitler's face. More fire bombs landed around the city, north and east of Breit, in Mitte over the administrative offices of the Reich, along the river Spree, perhaps on the hospital Breit had just left. The city tried to make itself dark, blast curtains hung over every window, every light was doused, even those of the emergency vehicles running crazy in the erupting streets, but the fire bombs did their work. Berlin burned for them, accommodating the bombers with wooden roofs, kindled ancient spires and domes, blown-open gas lines, flaming cars and trucks, scorching grass. An ignited wind crossed Breit's nostrils, the smells of carbon and fuel. He wrapped his knees in his arms, the instinct was to be small.

Once the city was on fire, the British drone above swelled. Ranks of bombers powered into range, the searchlights went wild with them. The sound was apocalyptic, Breit had never heard anything like this. The sky, as immense as it had been in Russia, seemed even larger this night over Germany, venting the noise of what must have been a thousand bombers. Then came the whistles.

Breit steeled himself, waiting, staring into the trilling night. The searchlights flashed left and right until they caught sight of the falling bombs. The things rushed down through the beams, packed so thick as to be preposterous, they were no more than small gray points in the searchlights but looked like a bed of nails descending on the city. Then the first burst of them landed.

Breit gasped. The explosions raised fireballs in the city.

The flames that had come first danced a sort of glee, like demons welcoming the greater members of their kind to the ground. He watched the entire city under onslaught, a carpet of carnage in every direction. Buildings disappeared in great spouts of blaze and concussion. Places Breit knew, that he could erect in his mind from memory, were scythed to their foundations under the bombs, hammered into shards of stone, broken brick and melted glass, scored timbers. Bombs fell, too, in the Tiergarten. The closest landed a hundred meters from him. Trees became torches, the soil trembled under him. Anti-aircraft batteries emptied themselves straight up at the English, adding their own sharp bits to the night. He made no move to go. He studied the bombardment, every part of it. He listened to the many peals of the attack; soon, the bombs, guns, and sirens blended into one long and unremitting rumble, like a bolt of lightning that would not end.

With every explosion, Breit adjusted his image of Berlin. He blacked out structures and destroyed whole blocks on his mental map table, reshaping the city with the bombs. By dawn Berlin would be changed; how much depended on the firefighters and luck. Breit tried to regard the bombs as allies; wasn't this attack on civilians something for him to cheer for? But just as he was unable to appreciate the Red partisans – they were brutes to him – these English bombs were horrors. That was the lesson tonight. Everything in war, even destruction and killing that serves your own ends, is horrible.

In an hour, the British were spent. They flew away, and the guns firing up at them silenced. Breit could not tell how many planes there had been, or how many of them had been shot down. No matter. The German city they left behind crackled and simmered under a rising, flickering haze. The raid was English vengeance. Breit listened to them fade away west. The British are a cold people when angry, he thought. Not like the Russians, so hot to spill blood. And we Germans, what are we? We're the worst. We believe war is glorious.

Breit rose. His legs and ribs hurt worse now. The adrenaline of the raid had kept him in a clench for an hour. When the tension released he was sore from head to toe. The Tiergarten was not on fire. The park was a dark oasis inside a ring of burning city.

He walked south to Charlottenburg, to see if his boarding house survived. He didn't dwell with worry that it would be standing or not. Abram Breit had been transformed by Citadel. He was a historic figure, he'd effected the result of a massive and pivotal battle. Those pages in history would always bear his imprint, if not his name. Germany would lose this war now. Breit possessed more power than the *Führer* because he had changed the outcome and Hitler no longer could.

Breit ignored the aches in his body. He searched for an avenue where there was fire and smoke, the sounds of Berlin licking its wounds, patching itself up. He wanted to see how bad things were. He wanted to watch Germans put out flames, dig through rubble, save their city and nation, do what he'd been trying to do.

He crossed the Landwehr Canal to Lützow Plaza. A vapor cloud shimmered with firelight. Water cannons hissed and bucket brigades shouted. Bells clanged on the rushing fire trucks. Breit headed toward the ruckus.

He rounded a corner to a street half in conflagration, half threatened. Several hundred Berliners rushed up and down, each with a task, a bucket, a hose, an axe, a child protected in a skirt, a megaphone. Another two fire trucks raced past, furiously tolling their bells. People leaped out of the way to let them through. Breit followed in the wake of the second truck. He was an SS colonel, no one denied him passage right up to the flames.

He walked so close to the worst building that the heat

began to dry the water in his eyeballs. It was a tall stone house, three stories high with an Italian facade. Every window was licked by shoots of flame, this building could not be rescued. Several fire trucks were arrayed along the block, spraying hoses to contain the spread of fire. Breit noted the house next to the doomed one was not yet burning. None of the firefighters paid any attention to it, their water and ladders were aimed at the buildings next to it and across the street. Breit approached a fire brigade officer directing the two trucks that had just arrived. The new men were fast deploying their forces on the opposite side of the street.

The officer saw Breit coming and nodded but kept directing the crews. Breit did not lag back at the man's curt acknowledgment. This was a fire scene, the SS had little jurisdiction here. He drew close to the officer, a fire captain, a red-jowled man Breit's age.

'Captain,' he had to shout over the din, 'Captain!'

The fire officer turned only his head to answer Breit. 'Colonel, I'm quite busy, as you see.'

Breit had to yank to turn him. 'Captain, why are your men not spraying this building?' He pointed at the house next to the one burning faster now. 'It's not on fire yet. You can save it.'

The officer shook his head, his mouth curled in a rebuke.

'This was a Jew house, Colonel. Jews lived there.'

Breit stared. The captain must have figured he did not understand.

'We'll let it burn.'

'Put your hoses on it,' Breit ordered.

'No,' the officer answered. 'Now if you'll excuse me, Colonel.'

With this the captain turned away and trod forward, pointing and bellowing at the firefighters under his command. Breit was left standing behind, gazing up at the face of the Jew house. It was big, all the houses on this block were sizable, these were the homes of the well-to-do. He wondered if the Jews of this home on this street had owned paintings.

He turned from the fire and walked to a policeman.

He held out his hand.

'Officer, give me your sidearm.'

The policeman, seeing Breit's black and silver uniform, did as he was ordered. Breit took the pistol.

He came up behind the fire captain.

He pushed the barrel of the pistol into the shoulder of the Fire Captain's tunic.

Breit repeated his command. 'Put your hoses on that house.'

'Look,' the captain, starting to turn, said, 'I told you ...'

Breit fired.

The man jolted and spun from the gun. The report of the shot was devoured in the roar of flames and water. No one moved toward Breit to disarm him, no one heard or perhaps even saw what he'd done. The captain doubled over. When he came up, his hand was clamped over the hole drilled clean through his shoulder. Breit let the gun hang. The fire captain had a new look on his face.

'Put your hoses on that building, captain. And when you've put out these fires, Berlin will have one more building instead of one less.'

The fire captain glared. He was a tough man, but not so much that he dared another word. He straightened, his eyes fixed on Breit, he did not wince. Breit had no idea what to do with the pistol now, he had no holster for it, and he did not want to tuck it in his belt like a tough guy or the partisans. He walked back to the policeman and returned it. He would not need it again. The fire captain turned his water on the Jew house and soaked it, saving it from the gobbling flames of its burning German neighbor.

Breit stayed for an hour, retiring into the crowd until all the fires on this block were extinguished. He walked fifteen minutes more to his own street, arriving just before midnight. His boarding house was fine, the bombs had missed his neighborhood. No one was outside, no one saw him come home.

CHAPTER 32

July 16
2240 hours
German troop train
five kilometers south of Belgorod

Luis set another cracker on his tongue. He closed his lips around it and sucked, waiting for the wafer to become mush. He gazed out his window at the vast plains and swallowed salty pulp.

With his left hand he raised a glass of water. Even the glass was a misery to lift, the broken ribs on his left side stabbed him. His right arm was no use to him, it was wrapped in a heavy plaster cast, limp in a black sling. He chased the cracker down his throat with little gulps, the five stitches in his chin bleated every time he stretched his jaw to eat or speak. Because of the stitches and the gauze around his head to hold the bandage in place, he ate little. This kept his appetite inflamed. The busted ribs made it hard to drink. Luis stayed hungry and thirsty every waking second now. He made no conversation with the other soldiers in the passenger car who passed his seat, men who saw his wincing efforts to move and offered to help in some way. He grunted in Spanish at the doctor who checked on him and the porter who brought him baskets of bread that went stale waiting for him to eat; the hard mouthings of German made his head hurt, so he stuck to his smoother mother tongue and didn't care if they understood.

The man across from him had sat down only a minute ago and already prattled on. He'd put on such a happy face at seeing Luis on this train leaving Belgorod. Luis answered him with a nod at the padded seat across from him and regretted the offer within seconds. He let the man's words flow past, like the night steppe outside the train, going by and going by, with no more meaning than that, just lost things. He did not turn his head to the fat officer sweating in the seat, the man's knees were too close, they knocked Luis's sore shins whenever the train rattled. Luis laid one more cracker on his tongue and closed his eyes.

'I'll tell you, I'm not sorry to see the last of Belgorod,' Major Grimm said. 'I think I must have smoked two packs a day without ever lighting one cigarette, being cooped up with Colonel Breit like that. Oh! Did you hear about his adventure with the partisans ... ?'

Luis did not need to look at the chatty man, he smelled the perspiration, could hear the officer's hands run over his belly across the stale cloth of his uniform, even through the torrent of talk. In the imposed stillness of his injuries, Luis was turning inward. He found a soothing darkness there, the darkness that first came to him bleeding in the snow at Leningrad and came again beside his burning Tiger at Prokhorovka, and now on his way out of Russia, headed south for Italy, it seemed not to leave.

'... meant to check on you in the hospital at Belgorod when I heard you'd been brought in,' the major rambled, 'but there was so much to do in the last several days, you understand, Captain. Besides, I'm sure you were in a great deal of pain and needed ...'

Luis had made himself stand on the battlefield. He'd been thwarted in Russia but he would not lie like a skewered bull in his own blood. He'd survived the destruction of his tank, a fantastic blast when the Red shooter's shell pierced his Tiger's side armor; a secondary explosion ignited when all the stored rounds went off in the Tiger and the T-34. Everyone died instantly, except Luis. He'd been blown into the air on top of the Tiger's flying turret. When he landed he was somehow alive.

He'd rolled over on his back and raised a hand to God, one last prayer, certain he was about to die. When he did not, there was no more reason to lie there, nothing to wait for. The pain propelled him to his feet. He was in awe again of his flimsy body, what it could endure. Even more than the burning Tiger, it seemed. A Mark IV in his company spotted him and ferried him out of the valley.

'... you were fighting at Prokhorovka, the Americans landed 160,000 men on Sicily, and six hundred tanks. That, of course, changed everything. Hitler's obsessed that Mussolini is going to be overthrown. He summoned von Manstein and Kluge to Rastenburg for a meeting. And on the thirteenth, of course, while you were in the hospital, Hitler called off Citadel.'

Yes, Luis thought, Hitler has taken Russia from me. With it, he's taken Spain. I can't go home.

Tomorrow Hitler will order the rest of *Leibstandarte* out of Russia. So I am to be given Italy next. And the Americans for an enemy. *Bueno*. What do I care? What hasn't been taken from me?

'... Papa Hoth, as you can imagine, was furious and wanted to keep up the attack. Hitler agreed to let the battle in the south go on for a few more days, you know, to try and siphon off the last of the Russians' reserves. But that was destined to be no good at all, you see. And then today, the Russians started their counteroffensive in the north against Orel. Early reports have the Reds already across poor Model's first defense lines... .'

Luis had begun to mutter curt replies, 'Yes,' 'Hmm,' 'Really?' He issued these like boulders or downed trees to try and stem the flow of the major, wanting to dam him up with a blunt, final word.

The porter walked by with a pitcher of water swathed in a white kerchief, the thing looked as bandaged as Luis. He refilled Luis's glass and handed Grimm a full glass. The major downed the water with one swift raise of his arm, the arm that did nothing at Kursk but push toy blocks and lift sheets of paper. Grimm swallowed and said, 'Ahhh,' with satisfaction. Under his tunic Luis's rib cage was wrapped tight. Every breath for him was a task. He glowered at the officer. The fat man would not be plugged.

'... problems began with *Totenkopf* on your left flank. The hope was they would advance far enough to threaten Prokhorovka from the northwest. But the rain made a mess of their river crossings, and resupplying the division across the Psel became impossible. *Totenkopf* couldn't hold their beachhead and had to fall back.'

Luis imagined Grimm in the map room sliding the black blocks backward. He wondered how long until the glass of water Grimm had just gulped ran down his forehead as sweat. The darkness outside his window and inside him was emptiness. Luis looked at this man, his opposite, and considered how full Grimm was, how bursting with noise and memory and need. Look at him, swollen with it all, talking just to keep from popping. The dark required none of this from Luis. The dark was pain, and if you embraced the dark's pain you felt nothing of the world's. That was real power.

'... Kempf, but too little too late. Kempf's linkup with *Das Reich* didn't come until the fifteenth. By then, for all intents and purposes, the battle was over. Oh, you SS chaps might have made a go of it, certainly, but with due respect, Captain, *Leibstandarte*'s inability to take Oktyabrski state farm in the center doomed the attack. Neither *Totenkopf* nor *Das Reich* could defend their flanks after that. By the night of the thirteenth, Prokhorovka was a stalemate. That's when Hitler called it off. And now the damn Ivans are hitting back. Well, it's to be expected. It's what I'd do. It's only a matter of time, I'm afraid....'

Late that afternoon a nurse had come to Luis's bedside. She'd handed him orders to report to this train at the Belgorod station. Apparently Grimm got the same orders. Luis was being sent to defend another yappy fat man, Mussolini. Luis would recuperate in Rome, then take over a panzer company. He would get another Tiger in the sunny south, in a coastal town named Anzio.

'... put you in for a medal, you know. The Iron Cross Second Class. I heard about all the Red tanks you knocked out in that damn sunflower field. Splendid, Captain. You deserve it! And since this is the second time you've been wounded in battle, you'll be getting your silver wound badge....'

Luis heard the talk of medals the way a man listens to the plops of stones landing at the darkness of a well. He dropped the medals into the darkness, *plop, plop*. They were not enough to give him back Barcelona, the Ramblas, his father. He was starting over. In Italy.

He watched Russia recede in his window. *Adios*. The moonlit flats were heaped with Grimm's assessments of failure here, describing the expanse as impregnable, no one had ever conquered it for long. Maybe he's right, Luis thought. Perhaps it was better to get out of here and head south. He thought about Prokhorovka. What had happened? What in hell was that old T-34 driver screaming at the end? What was he saying? What did he want?

Luis licked his dry lips. A dart of pain pricked in his stitched chin. The pain swept the Red driver out of his head, out into the bland deluge of Major Grimm's monologue. Luis didn't care what the crazy old Russian had been yelling. Whatever it was, Death had answered him. The Russian was not going to haunt Luis, there would be no more throbs in his hand like the partisan or the bulls, no. The darkness in Luis left no room for the weakness of curiosity, no dilution of the mind or will, no pride, and certainly no ghosts.

Stay empty, the dark told him. See how powerful you have become. It's simple: first the bullet outside Leningrad, then that crazy old Russian at Prokhorovka. They were sent to you, to change you and make you stronger.

You have nothing.

You are nothing, nothing but *la Daga*.

It will take something stronger than Russia to kill you.

CHAPTER 33

July 16
2350 hours
fifty kilometers north of Khar'kov
Ukraine/Russian border

Colonel Plokhoi was first out of the bushes. A moment after the blast on the rail mound, before the echo was gone from the trees where they hid, he ran from cover with his submachine-gun braced at the hip, chasing his bullets over the open ground. Katya leaped out with the waves of dark partisans, following Colonel Bad, shouting and shooting their weapons into the roofs and sides of the tipping train.

The locomotive careened off the splintered rails and continued on, teetering on its betrayed wheels until it crashed over. Momentum carried it another twenty meters on its side until it plowed to a halt in the scarred earth. The locomotive lay on its side steaming and hot, a ridiculous posture for a great machine. There it lay dying in gushes. It was ignored by Plokhoi and his swarming partisans, who dashed for the five passenger cars. The locomotive had dragged each of the cars off the blown tracks, so that the entire train spilled down the rail mound into a heaped jumble. Smoke roiled from the C-3 explosion and the dirt spewed into the night air, and now the barrels of many weapons added their gunsmoke. Bullets punched holes in the cars' thin frames, paint chipped and bare metal halos showed around every puncture. Partisans ran close and tossed grenades into the shattered windows. The blasts shook the downed cars again, fabric inside began to burn. The partisans stepped back and fired, fired, fired into the cars. Katya lowered her rifle. She hadn't shot it more than twice, she'd seen little need to add her small bark to the furious baying of Plokhoi's men.

Three machine-guns were hustled forward and flung down on tripods. When they opened up the sound was like hail, *ting ting ting ting,* faster than a drum roll. The machine-guns shredded everything in front of them, the shooters swiveled the barrels back and forth without aim, loaders lavished them with belts of ammunition. The partisans emptied their guns into the German train. The night glimmered to the constellation of muzzle flashes, all else was black and grisly. Nothing answered from the cars themselves, not even screams. Where was the time to scream or shout to surrender? The soldiers who'd been asleep awoke to the shock of their world tilting, they tumbled off their seats and benches, dashed against shifting walls and railings, then danced on the strings of these ten thousand bullets fired by a hundred angry fighters who had no interest in taking prisoners.

Katya ran close to Plokhoi. The partisan leader shouted with his trigger pressed, until his magazine was emptied. He dropped the spent gun on the ground and stood spent as well, out of breath and bullets at the same time, a perfection for him.

Plokhoi fired a flare pistol into the air. When the green light struck, everyone quit shooting. Katya gazed into the rent darkness of the besieged cars. Nothing came from them, no light or sound, not even a creak. They were dead, when seconds before they'd been steaming past, headed out of Russia. Now they would stay. The only noise left to the night was the locomotive sighing, sounding sad for this carnage. Katya stepped forward, past

Plokhoi, to do her job. She was joined by Ivan, Josef, and Leonid.

The rest of the partisans receded into the trees without a word. This massacre required nothing more from them. The three machine-guns were lifted off their tripods and hauled back. Plokhoi held his ground, standing over the cooling weapon at his feet.

'You've got five minutes.'

Josef answered, 'Yes, sir,' into the darkness feathering around the partisan leader.

Katya slipped her hand under Leonid's elbow. 'You shouldn't be here, Leonya. It's too soon.'

'Shit,' he grunted, leaning on her arm to keep up. 'So this is what fighting on your feet is like. No wonder we became pilots.' A rifle hung in his free hand. She'd never seen him carry a gun before.

Katya hurried Leonid as much as his healing injuries allowed over the last of the open ground. Ivan and Josef went ahead, reaching the first of the passenger cars. Josef peeked inside through the sieve that was made of the roof, then moved to the second fallen car. When Katya and Leonid caught up at the third car, Ivan had boosted Josef over the perforated roof onto the tilted side. The old man walked along the row of blasted-out windows, peering down into the shambles inside, gripping a ready pistol. Katya gaped at the number of holes in the car, amazed that the remaining metal did not buckle under his weight.

'Alright,' Josef said to the three of them waiting. 'This one will do.'

With that, he disappeared, lowering himself into the bowels of the car. Katya would not let herself imagine what he landed on, what he walked among.

Josef's voice strained through the perforations in the roof.

'Someone get up on top. Let's go!'

Ivan pulled from his ever-present backpack four muslin

sacks. He tossed them to Leonid, then moved close to the car. He linked the fingers of both hands to make a step.

'Up, Witch,' the big soldier said to her.

Katya jerked back at the notion. 'Me? No. Ivan, you go. We'll stay down here. No.'

'And who's going to give me a boost? You? Maybe Lumanov? Come on. Up.'

'He has a point,' Leonid said.

Josef growled inside. 'Now.'

Katya slung her rifle across her back and stepped into Ivan's hands. The big man heaved and she rose easily to land her boots on the side of the car.

Josef's hand speared up through a broken window. He hoisted a machine pistol.

Katya took the German weapon and tossed it down to Leonid. The pilot caught the gun and gave it over to Ivan, who rammed it into a sack.

Josef scavenged among the scattered Germans for their guns, ammunition, and money. She watched from above, aghast at first at the piled corpses. There were seventy men or more, black blooded in the light of a full moon. In the first minute, Josef lifted up a dozen weapons. His hand thrust out of the windows and grew more stained with each rifle or pistol. Katya's hands grew slick with blood. Josef kicked through the bodies like trash, he waded in them and walked on them, tripped and fell among them without a curse or any word, as grim as any of the dead.

By the second minute, the killed mounds at the bottom of the car were nothing to Katya. They were merely arms and legs to be pried out of the way by the dark walker Josef to get at their only worth. She tossed the weapons down to Leonid and watched him stagger to catch them, his legs still bad, his shoulders not recovered. She reveled in Leonid's life, and the fact that she had saved him. The heaps of German dead, by comparison, became just loose figurines. Katya felt this change, a twinge in her gut, something soft stiffened. This is war, she decided, war. She fixed her eyes on Josef. She watched the old man walk through the dead, doing what he had to do. Papa, too, shirked nothing that needed to be done. She wanted to be like that as well, and he could teach her. Katya felt strongly the need to talk with him. She sensed her father was too far away and made herself a promise to write him a letter tomorrow. With that, Papa felt closer.

Ivan called up that their time was running out. Josef heard this and thrashed around the bodies for a last check of weapons. She walked above the old man's head, tracking him while he made his way to the front of the passenger car. There only two bodies lay. By their uniforms and their privacy in the car, these two seemed to be officers. One of the officers was high ranking, a fat man, a big target for the machine-guns and riddled with bullets. The other lay on his back. This one was in a sling with a broken arm, his gaunt face was framed by a gauze wrap. He wore black and silver, an SS officer like Colonel Breit. He was horrid looking, white and gossamer thin, the gauze and cast made him even paler, already a ghost even before he was turned into one by the partisans. She shivered to look at him, that place in her that was hardening somehow did not defend her against this one. He was different, not German, what was he? Barely human, thin like a blade. Josef rifled the body's belt for a holstered Luger pistol. He handed the gun up to Katya. She did not take her eyes off the corpse while Josef clambered on a bench to climb out.

Below, Ivan had divided the weapons among the four satchels. He lapped the fullest one over his back and turned to make for the trees. Leonid struggled with the smallest sack, loaded only with papers and ammo clips.

Josef came up on the deck beside her. Katya held on to the Luger.

Josef slung himself to the ground. He lifted a hand to help her down.

Below, someone moaned. Katya glanced down into the dark recesses, into the piles of upturned and stolen life. One thing moved. The SS man, a gaunt white thing in silver and black, the body of a knife.

Katya lowered the Luger and fired. The thin body settled back. It was wrong to leave anything alive in this train, that was what Plokhoi had come for. To kill all of them, even the ones leaving Russia, to send that message. She fired again, to do what she had to. Josef glared up at her. Ivan and Leonid stopped with the sacks over their backs and turned to look.

The pistol smoked in Katya's hand. A gray spirit trickled from the barrel and drifted past her face – smelling of oiled things, machines, and leather – then moved on.

CHAPTER 34

July 17
1210 hours
Old National Gallery
Berlin

Odd, Breit thought, how suddenly, once again, the numbers don't seem to matter as much.

He rested his eyes on three panels, Gauguin side by side with van Gogh and Degas. The Impressionists again. Humanity. Emotion, randomness, illogic. On the canvas, in the streets, on the battlefield, on the rectangular pages of history, there is in the end nothing but the squiggles of the human hand.

Breit chewed his sandwich. Today he was alone in the gallery except for the museum staff. The air raid over Berlin five days ago was still being dealt with by downtown Berliners, they were not out strolling this afternoon for their luncheon. Hitler himself was not in his Reich capitol to hear the catcalls of sirens and see the trees burst into flame or the giant looping water sprays from fire brigades to put them out. Hitler was in his *Wolfsschanze* castle in East Prussia. It's fine, Breit thought. Hitler doesn't need to see this, the man is miserable enough.

Four days ago in Prussia, Breit had been in Hitler's presence. The morning after the air raid, he was called to Hitler's eastern command lair to report on the battle for Kursk. He was also expected to speak on the Russian partisan movement, since he'd seen them with his own eyes, as if being tied up by one, being kicked by that witch woman, and then escaping them on horseback in a frenzy during a botched raid qualified him to talk about the partisans. He knew nothing about them, except they were determined, they were not ignorant, and they could be vicious. He did not know why the Witch did not come after him, as must surely have been her orders, she could have done it with no trouble. Instead, she'd ridden down the old twin. Breit did not see what happened when she caught him. But she rode like a demon, and a demon, Breit knew, she must have been.

On July thirteenth, the day after the slaughter at Prokhorovka, he was ushered into the large meeting room at the *Wolfsschanze*. He'd heard about the great one-day battle in his sanatorium cafeteria, gathering as much as was known about the aftermath, then he was summoned to Prussia. There'd been no winner at Kursk, he knew only that Germany was badly hurt. Now the Reds would answer, and the end game would begin.

In the meeting, von Manstein urged them to continue Citadel. Victory in the south was still achievable, the Field Marshal argued. He asked Hitler to permit him and von Kluge to relaunch the offensive. The Soviets were pummeled; they would not withstand one more concerted blow. Their reserves were spent defending Prokhorovka, there was nothing left of them. The SS force in the south was paused but not halted. Tiger and Panther tanks were being repaired every minute; if cut loose again, they would retake the battlefield. Kempf was catching up, he would link with II SS Panzer in a day, two at the most. Together they could punch through Prokhorovka, the Reds were reeling there. Von Manstein claimed to have reserves, three panzer divisions, in position. There was nothing the Reds could do to buck up their defenses at Prokhorovka. All their available armor was committed; if they withdrew anywhere along the lines to shore up their positions, their entire defense would collapse.

Hitler listened. Breit watched from the shadows.

Next, von Kluge spoke for himself, instead of letting his rival von Manstein rope him into more offensive operations. The leader of the forces on the northern shoulder advised Hitler that he could not resume any attacks at the moment. He needed all of Model's remaining strength in 9th Army to stem the gathering Soviet counterassault, which was gaining momentum every hour. He beseeched Hitler to allow his force to go on the defensive. His men and resources were exhausted, they would do well to hold their ground, much less take any more.

Von Manstein had come to Hitler prepared with rhetoric, strategies, and pleas. Von Kluge came with numbers. The Reds had suffered terribly in their defense of Kursk, von Kluge began. In two weeks of combat on three defensive fronts, the Soviets had lost one hundred and seventy thousand dead and wounded of the million and a half men they'd begun with. They'd lost a third of their five thousand tanks.

The attacking German force of three-quarters of a million men had been ground down by fifty thousand. Their thirty-three hundred tanks had been depleted by a number von Kluge could only guess at: He predicted a thousand gone, maybe more. And these numbers would grow immensely for both sides now that the Reds had launched their counteroffensive in the north, total losses for the Russians would swell to a million men before the summer ended. As for the German force, the Field Marshal could only shake his aristocratic head. 'It may be catastrophic,' was how he summed up the encroaching costs for the Fatherland. 'We may never recover from Citadel.'

When von Kluge had succumbed to his mournful pause, von Manstein re-took the floor. 'Where is the man?' he asked, peeved, not seeing Breit right away. Breit stood. His uniform coat lacked his medal for administration, and the new jacket fit badly. He stood from his dark chair along the wall and tugged at his hem. What could he say to offset von Kluge's gruesome numbers? Numbers are absolutes, he thought, standing in front of the *Führer*. Plead all you want, imagine all you can, but numbers dictate reality. Numbers are the damning brushstrokes.

Breit waited, unsure.

Hitler erupted.

Hitler did not want to hear any more about Russia. He was sick, near to vomiting, with Russia! His complexion was pasty, his hands flew about and trembled. Breit sat down. He would have left the room, but he stayed to the end, to hear the rest. Hitler calmed, some of his color returned. Without more screaming, he called off the offensive. He reassigned his SS tank corps in Russia; *Leibstandarte* was to head for Italy, effective immediately, *Totenkopf* and *Das Reich* were pulled from the front lines and relocated south, to help fend off the Soviet counterattack directed toward Khar'kov.

Von Manstein objected. Hitler would not yield. The Field Marshal succeeded only in talking Hitler into allowing a few more days for General Hoth to continue southern operations, to inflict a little more damage on the Soviets, but that was all.

Citadel, the last German offensive in Russia, was over. Breit stayed at the *Wolfsschanze* two more days and nights, silent and listening. Then he returned to Berlin.

This afternoon, in the empty museum in the smoldering middle of the capital, Breit finished his sandwich. He thought of the Night Witch, a striking young Russian woman, caught up in war, wearing men's dirty clothes instead of dresses and bows. She so clearly has passion, she ought to be in love. Instead she's in battle, surrounded by killers, she is likely one herself. What has this war done to her, cost her? These thoughts of the grim young Witch led Breit to consider what he had done to Germany, what he had cost it in terms of lives and strength. How many souls were circling him unseen, how many? Far more than the Witch, surely, or even her wild partisans. He looked into the cool air of the gallery and wondered, if he could see them, what would a hundred thousand spirits look like? A million before his work was done? A cyclone of invisible souls would swirl over his head. Still he would add to that number. There was no place he would stop now, no number too horrible, to save Germany from itself.

He crumpled the paper that had wrapped his sandwich, making an echo in the gallery hall, and stuffed the wad into the paper sack. He held up the imperfect circle of his apple. He admired it, red and splotched, uneven, bumpy. Only numbers were perfect, he decided; nothing else of mankind was. But it was their perfection that made numbers cold, made them no longer so important.

Abram Breit left his paper sack on the bench. He set the apple beside it for the lingering guard.

EPILOGUE

April 10, 1946
2:15 p.m.
village of Troickaya
the Kuban

'Katerina Berkovna?'

Katya turned to the voice. Ten meters behind her, an ancient man loomed on the lawn. The sea breeze freshened in his moustaches and crackled in his red *burka* cloak. He was far too broad and erect to be as aged as he was. This, thought Katya, is the Kuban. These are the Cossacks.

'Lumanova,' she said to the cemetery keeper.

She sent a quick glance to Leonid. Her husband stayed to the side in his major's uniform, quiet, folded against the chill swirling off the Black Sea. Leonid nodded to her. I'll be here, his gesture said. Go on.

The elderly giant strode to her. He opened his arms. His breast was mottled with medals.

'Katerina Lumanova,' he said. 'Hero of the Soviet Union. Welcome home.'

Katya held her place while the great arms wrapped her, the dark cloak eased over her. The old man smelled of oils and wax, loam, wind, years.

'Come,' he said.

The old man led Katya into the crowded cemetery. She did not look at any of the crosses and tablets, chiseled and weathered by centuries of this wind. She strode behind the flowing cape, ahead of her quiet husband, through the long path of graves. In a minute, they left the cloture of the cemetery and entered open, rising ground.

The old man led them up a slope, then halted. He stepped aside and Katya lifted her gaze.

There were only two graves on this hillcrest. The earth here was bare but green. The hill presided over the village below and the patchwork fields of spring plantings, all yellow boxes and emerald squares. The Kuban River sallied west to the Azov Sea, cows walked in the shallows. In the southern distance, the Caucasus Mountains serrated the mist, guarding the coastline.

Both graves lay at the foot of marble Orthodox crosses. One grave had grown over nicely, with grass new for the spring. The other was a bald brown rectangle, a hole freshly dug and filled.

Katya sank to her knees. The earth was soft and receiving. She looked to her left, beside her father's bare grave.

'Hello, Valya.' She leaned to run her hand through her brother's grass, like rubbing his head. 'Hello.'

She raised her head to Leonid, standing alone.

'Leonya, come here.'

Her husband padded across the lawn to stand beside her. The cemetery keeper, unbidden, came too. The old man spoke first to Leonid.

'Her father was *hetman* of this village. Did she tell you?'

'Yes.'

'Dimitri Konstantinovich. He was a hellion, he was. His old father was the same. I didn't know the boy here very much. He was always quiet as a youngster. But he was marvelous with a sword. That's all I knew of him. Still, as a man he must have been one hell of a fighter.'

The back of Leonid's hand brushed Katya's hair. 'The three of them,' he said. 'All three Berkos. Heroes of the Soviet Union.'

Hero of the Soviet Union. These were the words etched into the crosses along with the names and dates of death.

'The boy died at Berlin,' the old man told Leonid. 'Right at the end. A shame. Brave, I heard. A tanker, a real German killer. Good for you, lad. You took some hides, didn't you? And Dima here.'

The cemetery keeper pivoted his large, slow hand to point at the bald brown grave. The old man clucked his tongue.

'The damned Communists wanted to keep him in Moscow, you know, put him inside one of their monuments. Hero Dimitri Berko. Cossack. Working for the Reds into eternity. Bah! That would have proven there was no God.'

Katya had petitioned the Soviets to return her father to his village, to lay him next to his son. She, a hero and a hero's daughter and a hero's sister, asked, and the government had finally agreed. They found someone else, someone just as blistered and dead as Dimitri, to ensconce in Moscow. When the government agreed, she came home, too, for the first time since she left ten years past.

'Do you know what happened? How the son here had to fire his cannon to kill a Tiger and so kill his own father?'

Katya stood, to silence the cemetery keeper. She patted his expanse of chest between the wings of cloak.

'Thank you.'

The old man clamped his lips and blinked. He dropped his chin and backed away.

Katya reached for Leonid. He stepped into the vast space left by the old Cossack. Katya linked her arm with Leonid's. She turned him to the graves.

'Papa, Valya. This is my husband, Leonid. We were married right after the war. We live in Kiev now. Leonid still flies fighters. I don't fly anymore.'

Katya eyed Leonid. She squeezed his arm and let go.

Leonid kissed her cheek through her wafting hair. He turned away, taking the cemetery keeper with him back down the hill.

Alone, Katya lifted her face to the sky. She felt lost without Papa and Valya.

She turned to face the wind and the open land below, and began to cry.

This was where Valya and Papa had gone, into the Kuban wind. Into the mountains and seas. Into the earth, not as corpses but wheat and alfalfa, hay and tree, sunflower.

She laid her palm across her stomach. The tears dried on her cheeks.

Papa, Valya, she cast into the wind, knowing this was how they could hear her. I'm going to have a child.

Heroes, she thought. We are heroes, my clan.

The Russians have learned a lot since 1941. They are no longer peasants with simple minds. They have learned the art of war from us.

Colonel General Hermann Hoth,
spoken to Field Marshal Erich von
Manstein after the battle for Kursk

AUTHOR'S HISTORICAL NOTE

For ease of reading, this novel refers to all ranks in the German SS in terms of their American or British equivalents. For historical accuracy, the following table of comparative ranks is included.

SS	BRITISH ARMY	US ARMY
Reichsführer-SS	Field Marshal	General of the Army
SS-Oberstgruppenführer	General	General
SS-Obergruppenführer	Lieutenant-General	Lieutenant-General
SS-Gruppenführer	Major-General	Major-General
SS-Brigadeführer	Brigadier	Brigadier-General
SS-Oberführer	(not applicable)	Senior Colonel
SS Standartenführer	Colonel	Colonel
SS-Obersturmbannführer	Lieutenant-Colonel	Lieutenant-Colonel
SS-Sturmbannführer	Major	Major
SS-Hauptsturmführer	Captain	Captain
SS-Obersturmführer	Lieutenant	1st Lieutenant
SS-Untersturmführer	2nd Lieutenant	2nd Lieutenant
SS-Sturmscharführer	Regimental Sergeant-Major	Sergeant-Major
SS-Hauptscharführer	Sergeant-Major	Master-Sergeant
SS-Oberscharführer	(not applicable)	Technical Sergeant
SS-Scharführer	Staff Sergeant	Staff Sergeant
SS-Unterscharführer	Sergeant	Sergeant
SS-Rottenführer	Corporal	Corporal
SS-Sturmmann	Lance-Corporal	Corporal
SS-Oberschütze	(not applicable)	Private 1st Class
SS-Schütze	Private	Private

BIBLIOGRAPHY

The author would like to acknowledge and recommend each of the following excellent resources for their scholarship and contribution to the novel.

BOOKS:

Beevor, Antony, *The Spanish Civil War,* Orbis Publishing Ltd., London, 1982

Caidin, Martin, *The Tigers Are Burning,* Hawthorn Books, 1974

Cottam, Kazimiera J., ed., *Defending Leningrad: Women Behind Enemy Lines,* New Military Publishing, 1998

Cottam, Kazimiera J., ed., *Women in Air War: The Eastern Front of World War II,* New Military Publishing, 1997

Cottam, Kazimiera J., *Women in War and Resistance,* New Military Publishing, 1998

Cross, Robin, *Citadel: The Battle of Kursk,* Barnes & Noble Books, 1994

Dunn, Walter S., Jr., *Kursk: Hitler's Gamble, 1943,* Praeger, 1997

Feodoroff, Nicholas V., *History of the Cossacks,* Nova Science Publishers, 1999

Folkestad, William B., *The View From the Turret,* Burd Street Press, 2000

Ford, Roger, *The Tiger Tank,* MBI Publishing, 1999

Glantz, David M. and Harold S. Orenstein, eds., *The Battle for Kursk 1943: The Soviet General Staff Study,* Frank Cass & Co., London, 1999

Glantz, David M. and Jonathan M. House, *The Battle of Kursk,* University Press of Kansas, 1999

Grenkevich, Leonid, *The Soviet Partisan Movement: 1941–1945,* Frank Cass & Co., Ltd., London, 1999

Guderian, Heinz, Gen., *Panzer Leader,* Dutton, 1952

Healy, Mark, *Kursk 1943,* Osprey Publishing, 1993

Hindus, Maurice, *The Cossacks: The Story of a Warrior People,* Doubleday, Doran & Co., 1945

Hughes, Matthew, Dr. and Dr. Chris Mann, *The Panther Tank,* MBI Publishing, 2000

Hughes, Matthew, Dr. and Dr. Chris Mann, *The T-34 Battle Tank,* MBI Publishing, 1999

Jukes, Geoffrey, *Kursk, The Clash of Armour,* Ballantine Books, 1969

Luck, Hans von, *Panzer Commander,* Dell Publishing, 1989

Macksey, Kenneth, *Tank Versus Tank,* Grub Street, London, 1999

Mellinthin, F. W. von, Maj. Gen., *Panzer Battles,* University of Oklahoma Press, 1956

Myles, Bruce, *Night Witches,* Presidio Press, 1981

Noggle, Anne, *A Dance with Death: Soviet Airwomen in World War II,* Texas A&M University Press, 1994

Orgill, Douglas, *T-34: Russian Armor,* Ballantine Books, 1971

Piekalkiewicz, Janusz, *The Cavalry of World War II,* Nierhaus, Michaela (trans.), Stein and Day, 1979

Piekalkiewicz, Janusz, *Operation Citadel,* Presidio, 1987

Piekalkiewicz, Janusz, *Tank War: 1939–1945,* van Huerck, Jan (trans.), Blandford Press, 1986

Previtera, Stephen, *The Iron Time, A History of the Iron Cross,* Winadore Press, 1999

Read, Anthony and David Fisher, *The Fall of Berlin,* Da

Capo Press, 1995
Ripley, Tim, *SS Steel Storm: Waffen-SS Panzer Battles on the Eastern Front 1943–1945*, MBI Publishing, 2000
Stein, George H., *The Waffen SS: Hitler's Elite Guard at War,* Cornell University Press, 1966
Time-Life Books, the editors of, *The Armored Fist: The New Face of War,* Time-Life Books, 1998
Williamson, Gordon, *The SS: Hitler's Instrument of Terror,* MBI Publishing, 1998
Zetterling, Niklas and Anders Frankson, *Kursk 1943: A Statistical Analysis,* Frank Cass & Co., London, 2000

WEBSITE:

The Kursk Page, located online at:
http://dspace.dial.pipex.com/town/avenue/vy75/

AUTHOR'S NOTE

The battle for Kursk covered an immense territory. So, too, did the writing of this book. Several people contributed mightily to its creation and guidance.

Vince Moats advised me on partisan tactics, the ways to blow things up and kill people at night behind the lines; Pilot George Delk showed me what a barrel roll feels like (it wasn't good); Evrim Schnayder survived as a young partisan in Russia and told me his story; Jack Atwater, curator of the U.S. Army Ordnance Museum at Aberdeen, M.D., checked my technical details and taught me about tank weaponry; Allan D. Cors let me take a dusty ride in his vintage T-34; Sam Worthington shot the photos while I imagined myself a Soviet tank commander; Jim Redington, M.D., provided his usual advice on all things medical; Rich Teague handled all things veterinary; Danielle Stout did splendid research on Franco's Blue Division; and Mark Lazenby traveled to Russia and Spain with me as a generous and loyal friend.

Once again, I thank my agents, Owen Laster and Tracy Fisher of William Morris, for their faith in me and their ability to wait me out until I calm down.

Kate Miciak, my editor at Bantam, has added me to the long list of admirers of her talent and vision. Both traits grace these pages. Those who know her can see her influence, and those who don't will mistakenly give me all the credit.

available from

THE ORION PUBLISHING GROUP

☐ **War of the Rats** £5.99
DAVID L. ROBBINS
0 75283 403 7

☐ **The End of War** £5.99
DAVID L. ROBBINS
0 75284 402 4

☐ **Scorched Earth** £6.99
DAVID L. ROBBINS
0 75284 260 9

☐ **Last Citadel** £6.99
DAVID L. ROBBINS
0 75285 925 0

All Orion/Phoenix titles are available at your local bookshop or from the following address:

Mail Order Department
Littlehampton Book Services
FREEPOST BR535
Worthing, West Sussex, BN13 3BR
telephone 01903 828503, *facsimile* 01903 828802
e-mail MailOrders@lbsltd.co.uk
(Please ensure that you include full postal address details)

Payment can be made either by credit/debit card (Visa, Mastercard, Access and Switch accepted) or by sending a £ Sterling cheque or postal order made payable to *Littlehampton Book Services*.

DO NOT SEND CASH OR CURRENCY.

Please add the following to cover postage and packing

UK and BFPO:
£1.50 for the first book, and 50p for each additional book to a maximum of £3.50

Overseas and Eire:
£2.50 for the first book plus £1.00 for the second book and 50p for each additional book ordered

BLOCK CAPITALS PLEASE

name of cardholder ....

....

address of cardholder ....

....

....

....

postcode ....

delivery address
(if different from cardholder)

....

....

....

....

postcode ....

☐ I enclose my remittance for £..............................

☐ please debit my Mastercard/Visa/Access/Switch (delete as appropriate)

card number ☐☐☐☐☐☐☐☐☐☐☐☐☐☐☐☐

expiry date ☐☐☐☐ Switch issue no. ☐☐

signature ....

prices and availability are subject to change without notice